Books by Bellora Quinn

AURA

Quinn's Gambit
Flax's Pursuit
Kellen's Awakening

Elemental Evidence

Breathing Betrayal

Books by Sadie Rose Bermingham

Elemental Evidence

Breathing Betrayal

Breathing Betrayal

ISBN # 978-1-78651-348-9

Elemental Evidence

BREATHING BETRAYAL

BELLORA QUINN and
SADIE ROSE
BERMINGHAM

Dedication

This book is dedicated to Steve, for too many nights spent patiently immersed in railway websites, while I swear at the laptop. To my co-writer, Bellora Quinn, without whose constant prodding and enthusiasm I would probably have given up on the written word a long time ago. To my fabulous Mum, for lifelong inspiration and encouragement, even when it looked like I was going nowhere. Last and not least, for Dad, who would have been bemused but proud. "Yes, Dad. More gay goblins."

—Sadie

Prologue

The first thing he noticed was the smell. The rank stench of piss hit him in the back of his throat, unpleasant and out of place, like waking up in a urinal after a night on the lash. Come to think of it, his neck ached and his tongue tasted of old socks, so perhaps there was something in that. He was damned if he could remember going out drinking last night, though. It took three attempts before he got his gummy eyes to open fully, then he wished he'd kept them shut. At first his confused brain refused to register what he was seeing but when it finally kicked in, he jerked back, throwing himself out of bed, his neck creaking a protest at the sudden movement, words falling unchecked from his lips.

"Fuck! Fuck! Oh fuck!"

You would have thought, with all the cop dramas and horror films he'd seen over the years, the sight of a dead man should not have freaked him out so much. And the guy was definitely dead. The smell alone should have told him but the bloated, reddish-purple face, open, glazed and staring eyes and protruding tongue franked it.

Bereft of life…

"Oh my god… Oh god, no…"

At that moment he was too panicked to even feel sick. He knew the face looking blankly back at him, despite the distortion of death. He knew the body that was still hogtied on the bed in bondage gear, the black leather straps stark against pale skin. He knew every square inch of him. The previous evening had been spent learning the feel of him, the taste of him, what made him moan and what made him come.

"Jesus! No…" The words spilling out of him were quieter now as he began to understand that this was no hoax, no drunken party prank.

A length of black nylon rope was twisted around the corpse's neck, pulled tight by his own hands, hands that were bound behind his back. For half a second he felt a flash of relief. Maybe the lad had done it to himself, pulled on the cord until he passed out and…

But it wasn't held by his hands. It was tied around his wrists. He couldn't remember tying the cord like that. Hell, he couldn't remember anything clearly at all. Can I?

Raking his hands through his hair, he tried to think back to the last thing he recalled doing or saying, but nothing was coming. The past, beyond waking up with a dead man in his bed, was a blur of confusion in his panicked mind. His breath started hitching in his chest and the smell of stale urine felt like it was coating his tongue, making him gag. He tore his eyes away from the boy. That sweet body, the warmth of him, gone now, so eager, so uncomplicated.

Yes, he had invited the guy over. They couldn't wait. He'd fucked him, almost fully dressed, pants down, over the kitchen table the minute they'd got into the house, wasting no time. They'd tumbled through to the lounge and shared some whiskey afterward, still breathless and laughing. His enthusiastic guest had started kissing him as they'd sprawled on the sofa. It had been the first time he'd ever kissed a man and it had felt good. At some point it had seemed like a good idea to move to the bedroom and get undressed properly.

The memories were coming in a rush now—stripping him and being stripped in turn, falling onto the bed in a tangle of limbs… He remembered leaning back into the pillows, head swimming, as a soft, warm mouth firmly engulfed his cock. The bluest eyes looked up at him, lips grinned around the dick thrusting between them, then pulled off him, leaving him hanging.

"So you gonna tie me up and spank me good tonight, or what?"

He dredged his memory, but things started getting properly fuzzy around that point. How much had they drunk before coming up to bed? Just a couple of glasses of Glenlivet, surely? He vaguely remembered buckling the straps in place, asking if they were too tight, seeing that eager smile, climbing onto him and fucking his mouth again…then, nothing.

He was breathing too hard and his stomach was doing barrel rolls. If he couldn't calm down, he was going to puke. With rising panic he looked at the clock—half past ten in the morning. Nearly twelve hours since his last coherent memory.

He considered calling for an ambulance and the harsh bark of laughter that burst from his lips was startling in the still of the house. It was way too late for an ambulance, too late for CPR, too late for anything. Even so, he fought to think through the panic and break down the sickly fog still clouding his mind. The paramedics would come and he'd tell them it was an accident, and they would call the police because what else were they going to do when they had a dead man and no rational explanation? The cops would take one look at him, at the situation, and he would be crucified. Accident or not.

No!

Rational thought kicked in, his brain went into survival mode. He would not go down for this. It was a fucking accident, for crying out loud. This wasn't his fault. He could not carry the consequences around for the rest of his natural days. Common sense prevailed. He had to get rid of the body. It was not as if anyone knew he had company here last night. Yes, he would get rid of the mess, then clean up and in real terms this had never happened.

For a moment his gaze lingered on the hard, lean, nude form bound securely to his bed, beautiful even in death, and he felt a sharp, twisting, painful moment of regret before he stumbled to the bathroom to throw up his guts.

Chapter One

Rain *pink-pink-pinked* against the window pane and *drip-drip-dripped* into the pot that Jake had placed under the leak in the hallway. Murky gray morning light greeted him when he opened his eyes. Another drizzly day. He had thought that was just some persistent stereotype, a comic exaggeration—about how rainy it was in London—but so far, this month, it was turning out to be true.

Jake was steadily getting used to the weather. It really wasn't all that different from his native Michigan. He had been told by his colleagues this was an unusually wet November and that when winter finally kicked off, it wouldn't be as severe as he was accustomed to. That was something to be glad about, at least.

The weather was not the only thing he'd had to get used to after moving a little over three and a half thousand miles away from the only place he'd known. London was worlds away from Detroit. It was still alive for one thing, not a dying husk. It was cleaner too, even with more than ten times the population. London had its crime and its dangerous places just like any large city, but even the urban degeneration here had a certain vibrancy to it that was unlike the desperation and decay of Detroit.

Enough of that.

Thinking about home was a guaranteed way to put him in a bad mood. At least he didn't hate his new abode.

The apartment was small and leaky but it was clean and bug free and he didn't have a lot of stuff anyway. Four rooms—kitchen, bathroom, small living room and a closet-sized bedroom that was barely big enough to hold a double bed and the armoire. The kitchen was equally tiny. A small fridge, sink and an ancient two-burner stove. There was just enough counter space to plug in his coffeepot. He was not complaining. The small space made it easy to keep warm and clean and discouraged clutter. It was also paid for, which was another big plus.

He hadn't liked that idea at first. He thought the university should just pay him outright and let him figure out how to deal with the rent and utilities, but he had to admit that having them take care of the bills took some of the worry off his mind. Unfortunately he still had plenty of other things to worry about.

No, he told himself firmly. He was not going to start off the day thinking about home and everything he'd deliberately left behind when he got on the plane. That was over.

Jake dragged himself out of bed and across the living room to the bathroom. After a quick slash, he washed his face, finger-combed his hair with wet hands then threw on some sweats and he was ready for his morning run. There would be time for a shower and food later. Back in Detroit, he would have started his day by driving to the track or the gym to work out before heading to the station house. Here he could walk or use public transportation to get just about anywhere he needed to go. At first the idea of not having a car, of not being able to just hop in and drive wherever he had to go, any time he wanted, had given him more of a panicky, trapped feeling than being an ocean away from everyone he knew and everything familiar. A car was the very first thing he'd asked about, after moving his meager belongings into the apartment. The research assistant who'd been assigned to ensuring he got settled in and had what he needed had told him to give it a week or two and, if he still wanted to purchase a car, the university would arrange it. At the time, Jake had thought there was no possible way he could survive for so long without a vehicle at his disposal, but by the end of his first week he had explored the Tube, the cabs and the buses, got himself an Oyster card and found he could get around remarkably well without having to fight through traffic behind the wheel. He hadn't brought up the need for a car again.

There was a small park only one street over from where he lived, and several right around the university, but they were little more than decorative green space—compact garden squares hemmed in by the tall, dark façades of houses and office buildings—nice for a picnic maybe, but not big enough for a run. Fortunately Regent's Park was fairly close to where he lived and the paths and trails there were perfect. The park was never truly empty but this early in the morning, especially on such a wet, gray day, only the dedicated were out. They all had little earbuds or headphones on and their eyes were fixed forward, everyone in their own private bubbles. No one stopped to say good morning. No one drew him to one side to ask if he could touch their grandmother's wedding ring and tell them if she'd hidden cash somewhere in the attic. It was great. It was almost perfect, except for one thing.

There was one other person from the university that liked to run the same route he did and while Jake didn't see him every morning, it happened often enough that he'd started looking for the guy while he ran. That annoyed him. Running was his time to clear his head. It was meditative. He could tune out and think of nothing. Or at least he could until he started paying more attention to the people he passed than he did the simple rhythm of putting one foot down in front of the other. Now during his morning runs, he was distracted by looking around to see if he'd catch sight of a particular slender figure whose long legs ate up the distance like the wind.

Jake told himself that he was only looking so that he could avoid him, and thereby avoid having to make polite conversation. It definitely wasn't because of the way the ridiculously tight Lycra leggings he wore outlined every muscle in his lean thighs or the way his perfect ass looked so tasty in them. No, not at all.

Jake never had been very good at lying to himself. Even so, admiring that sexy little derrière from a distance was all he would do. He had learned his lesson about getting involved with coworkers. Anyway, it was unlikely he'd see him today, given the dismal weather. He could stop looking around and just concentrate on pushing himself.

* * * *

The park was usually Mari's first call of a morning, though he sometimes gave his running a break when the weather was this grim. Today the rain was that fine, persistent drizzle that evaded umbrellas and invaded just about all items of clothing that weren't a wetsuit. He was used to it, having spent almost the last three of his twenty-seven years here, at UCL, but after the sunshine of his previous job in Barcelona, it was still kind of a comedown to walk out of his front door on a morning like this.

Fortunately the park was just around one corner, and the university campus just around the other, one of the perks of living in town. Papi had wanted to pay for a place out in the countryside, arguing that it would be more peaceful, but his Mama would hear none of it. The London house had been her grandmother's then her father's. He had been renting it out for years while the family lived abroad but now it was finally useful, even if the reason behind its new purpose was a less than happy one. Plus, Mama argued successfully—because no one, not even Papi, would dare to fight with her right now—it was also a short cab ride to the hospital, not an ungodly trek through the suburbs every time she had treatment or saw her oncologist.

He pushed those thoughts away, determined not to dwell on what might be, knowing she would not thank him for it. She had not wanted him to come to London at all, but on that point he had dared to defy her and anyway, he'd already been offered and had accepted the post at University College London. It was a decent job, even if

London was not Barcelona.

There was no one quite like Tomas here, but maybe that was a good thing too.

Mari put his head down and pushed on into the clinging miasma of the chill London rain. Tomas Arregui was something else he would rather not think about right now. With the clarity of hindsight, perhaps it had been for the best that the job had come up with UCL when it did. Given longer to chew over the frustration of his on-again, off-again lover, he might well have been driven to do something he would most certainly regret.

Damn it, though! The memory of Tomas was like a persistent tic that wouldn't let go of his hide once its nasty little fangs had sunk in.

He was glad of the distraction presented in the form of another early-morning loper and his spirits perked up even more when he was able to make out the familiar form and easy gait of the new guy who was working with the Web Security Team. Mari had spotted him striding through the park before, though they had never spoken. Lester in the print room said he was American, though Mari thought there was a slightly Hispanic look to his rough-cut, thick black hair and darkly handsome features. Maybe Romani, even? He couldn't be sure.

He was well built without looking chunky, except when he was bundled up in several layers of damp running gear, and almost as tall as Mari's six-foot-two-inch frame, which was a plus. It got embarrassing trying to flirt with men who were forced to look up at him all the time.

Not that he had any idea if Mr. Tall, Dark and Handsome was even that way inclined. But that never stopped him testing the waters. Alicia in his department said that one day some guy was going to punch his lights out for flirting the way he did, as if every man in the world was automatically gay and, by definition, hot for him.

He'd made her laugh with his mock-horrified response. "You mean they *aren't*?"

* * * *

Jake had just gotten in the zone, hitting his stride in a ground-eating but easy pace when he spotted him. The guy he had seen in the research room at the uni, the same one he'd seen a few times in the park. Fuck. If he stopped, it would screw up his chi, or whatever the buzz from a good run was called. If he just kept going without a word, he'd look like an asshole. Sure, he had seen him running before but it had always been from a distance, or going in opposite directions where a civil conversation wasn't really expected. He was coming down a path that joined up with the one Jake was on and they would probably reach the intersection at just about the same time. Should he stop and say hi? Should he pretend he hadn't recognized him?

Before Jake had fully made up his mind, the other runner came around the corner and raised his hand with a wave and a friendly smile but didn't slow down. He kept right on going. Jake barely had time to lift his own hand in awkward acknowledgment before they were past each other. Well, that was a relief. He hadn't wanted to stop and say good morning and come up with some idle chitchat while he huffed and puffed and tried to catch his breath. That's what he told himself as he craned his neck around to get a glimpse of that perky backside.

His opposite number was turning his head around too, a knowing little grin on his face. Jake flushed and almost tripped over his own feet before he whipped his eyes forward again, glad that the path curved and took him out of sight. Great, just fucking great, now Blondie knew he'd been checking him out.

Mari counted to three after they had passed on the turn back into the Broadwalk and he forced Mr. Dark, Damp and Hunky to acknowledge his wave. Boy, he was shy for a Yank. Mari had always figured most Americans in Britain stood out for being forward but this guy didn't even seem to know how volcanically hot he was. Such a waste.

He turned a fraction from the hips and looked over his shoulder on three. Shy or not, the cutie was already glancing back too and Mari restrained the urge to stop in his tracks and do a little dance. So that answered one question. Hot, cute and most assuredly gay. Or at least bi, which Mari figured he could live with. Scratch that, he *knew* he could.

As he turned back to the path ahead, not wanting to run into a tree and ruin the moment, he debated finding a way to loop back around and cross the new boy's route again but common sense prevailed.

"Patience, Mizz Gale," he told himself. "Go home, get dry, make yourself beautiful. You'll see him at work in less than an hour."

He pushed himself a bit harder on the short run back to the house, but the smile was still on his face when he got there.

* * * *

Jake usually finished his run with a fast walk back to the apartment to cool down but he was in no mood to stroll through the rain now. Besides, he didn't think any amount of walking was going to take the heat out of his cheeks, so he just kept running all the way home. How embarrassing. The cute blond obviously knew he was hot and now that he'd caught Jake staring, he'd probably give him patronizing looks every time they saw each other. Just what he needed.

By the time he got back to the apartment Jake was soaked through from the rain and sweat. Actually he'd been soaking for some time, he just hadn't noticed it as acutely as he did once he stopped moving. One nice thing, even though the shower was as economy-sized as the rest of the apartment, it had good pressure and hot water, lots of it. He blasted some of the chill out of his skin as he soaped up and replayed that brief encounter in the park over and over.

How had the blond known Jake would look? Was he

putting out some kind of vibe? He'd never put much stock in gaydar. He figured if a guy came out and hit on him, that was his clue. It couldn't have been how he was dressed — he was definitely not the trendy type when it came to running gear. He couldn't think of anything he'd said or done that would have tagged him as queer.

Jake got out of the shower and wrapped a towel around his waist. He wiped his hand over the mirror so he could shave but stopped to give his reflection a critical look. Same square-jawed face. Same brown eyes. Same dark, unruly hair that badly needed a cut. Nope, he couldn't see anything that screamed *flaming homo*.

Maybe he would just ask him.

Yeah…how would that go? "*Say, I know you saw me checking out your ass and I was just wondering if you could tell me if I'm giving off some kinda gay vibe that told you I would look?*" No, that wouldn't be weird or insulting at all. Fuck, his head was a mess.

Jake finished shaving and got dressed. He was going to have to grab something to eat on the way if he didn't want to be late.

Chapter Two

Mari got back before Mama was up and about and stripped out of his wet Nikes, shoving them into the machine on his way through to the shower room at the rear of the house, the one that Grandpapi had got installed when the old boy had still been fit enough to tackle the garden here on his own. Mari found it handy for his wet weather running — he could get cleaned up without trailing rain and mud through the house and annoying Izzy, who came in to clean twice a week. Tonka heard him and came snuffling through to say good morning and he scratched the amiable, elderly brindle and white Staffie between his ears for a little while before taking to the shower. The dog sat on guard outside until he was done, waiting patiently for his breakfast.

Mari's thoughts were still focused on the handsome hunk from the park though as he lathered himself up in the small, cream-tiled cubicle, enjoying the warmth that seeped through to his bones as the water zinged off his skin. He had a nice smile, Mr. Dark, Cute and Bi — almost *certainly* bi — yes, a very shy smile, but that wasn't what was uppermost in Mari's thoughts as he showered. He tried to push down on the other horn-inducing images that came to his mind, painfully conscious of the fact that he needed to get ready for work, feed the dog and check on Mama before he left. Even though it would have been delicious to linger in the shower for a few minutes more and enjoy the memory of his strong thighs and firm, high backside in those snug black joggers. The rain had made them cling a little tighter than they might have, perhaps. Or was that also his wishful thinking?

"Uhh...no-no-no!" he told his willful cock, which was begging for attention suddenly, worse than Tonka when he heard the door to the kibble cupboard creak open. "Don't do this to me now!"

As he wrapped his fingers around the straining shaft and began to pump himself rapidly, it was another hand he was imagining there, and another man's breath coming hot and urgent over his skin as he leaned back in that strong embrace. It took less than two minutes for him to come, panting almost silently, wrapped in the sweet fantasy of a stranger's body.

He dried and dressed and decanted dog food in double time, doubly late now and irritated with himself for giving in. Ridiculous of him, fantasizing over a guy that he was only about seventy-five...possibly eighty percent sure was actually gay. Even if he was almost definitely bi. Even so.

But he looked! He so looked, and he took his time turning away when he saw you were looking too! his inner demon chided, whining like a spoiled child.

Shut up!

Mama was on the move before he was ready to leave and came down in her eggshell-blue housecoat to kiss his cheek and wish him a good day. She looked tired, he thought, but still lovely as ever. He ran his fingers over her immaculate blonde hair and told her, as he did every morning, that he loved her and would see her later.

Then he was on his way again, sheltered by his huge umbrella, making the short walk through the streets of Fitzrovia, past the huge stone edifice of Christ the King where his great-great grandmother had fallen under the Presbyterian spell, to the tall, concrete and glass building on Malet Place that had been his workplace for the past few months. He grabbed a coffee and an almond croissant from the café in the Roberts Building on the way in and tapped his ID badge on the scanner at the turnstiles. Then he was in the elevator on his way up to the seventh floor, the same as every other morning.

He dropped into the print room on the way up to see if Lester was there, but he wasn't in yet. In the post room, young Toby was sorting the first mail of the day and his round face lit up with a grin when he spotted Mari.

"Slacking already? It's only half-eight!"

"Cheeky much! I've come for my mail, if that's okay with you."

"I'm spoken for." Toby winked at him and shuffled a half-dozen envelopes of varying colors and sizes across the counter toward him. "Can you take this for Professor Karden as well?"

Mari examined the long cardboard tube curiously and gave it a shake. "New dildo?"

Toby snickered behind his hand. "I can't unthink what that just made me think, Doctor Gale. I'm gonna ban you coming in here."

"Before I walk out of your life forever, Tobias, a favor?" Mari batted his eyelashes like a femme fatale in a 1940s movie.

"I'm going to regret it but..." Toby shrugged, still grinning.

"That new boy in Web Security, the beefcake from... Dakota? Delaware? Somewhere with a D... You know what his name is?" Mari took a bite out of his croissant and pretended disinterest.

"Uh-oh... I thought you were behaving yourself!" Toby wagged a finger at him.

"How is it misbehaving to want to know the name of a *colleague*?" he retorted, dragging out the word deliberately. "I was just wondering if I could take his mail over too. You know, be helpful like."

"You can take the whole trolley if you want." Toby laughed, shaking his head incredulously.

"Forget it. Have a nice life!" Mari finished his snack and washed it down with a couple of mouthfuls of coffee then retrieved the envelopes and the tube and headed for the door with a theatrical sigh.

"Doctor Gale?" Toby was still grinning when he looked back. "His name's Jake, his *first* name. His surname's odd, like Chivers or something, but not that. He's a psychology major, I think."

Mari blew him a kiss and departed, whistling off-key, a little smile twitching at his own lips. There was no fact large or small that eluded the gossip trawler of the post room.

* * * *

When Jake had been working as a detective, he'd had to wear a suit and tie. He hadn't minded. It meant he hadn't had to think too much about what to put on in the morning. He saw no reason to change his habits when he moved to England. Especially since he'd just shelled out a good-sized chunk of change on some suit jackets and trousers after Alex had complained he looked like a slob in the cheapo blazers he got off the rack at Bernie's Discount. A shopping trip to a high-end department store, where sticker shock had just about given him a coronary, had netted him a well-tailored new wardrobe, and a blow job when he'd gotten home. It hadn't stopped Alex from dumping him a month later, but he still had the nice suits, at least.

He wished now he hadn't let his ex talk him into the trim-fit garments that looked 'modern' and 'stylish', as Alex had put it. He might have had the physique to pull them off but he felt like a poser. He should have just stuck with something more classic. Or 'ancient', as Alex had also observed. At least in his roomy old blazers he'd felt like a cop. Maybe it was the new suits that were giving off the gay vibe?

He checked himself irritably. What a stupid thing to think. And why was he so worried about it anyway? It wasn't like it mattered anymore. Working in academia was not like being a cop, where the straight brotherhood would make your life hell if they found out you liked to suck cock. He supposed it was just so ingrained to keep his sexuality a secret that he didn't know how to be any other way. Even if he *was* more…out, he wasn't sure he'd really do anything different. It wasn't like he was going to start marching around waving rainbow flags and all that bullshit. It was just, sometimes he felt like he was acting, playing a role that didn't quite fit, and he wished he could be a little more like…

Jake was so wrapped up in his thoughts he nearly ran right into the guy from the park. They didn't collide but he came close enough to make the man shift around almost gracefully to avoid being mowed down, and he dropped one of the parcels he was carrying.

"Oh shit…sorry!" Jake apologized as he caught the tube before it hit the floor. The bluest eyes he had ever seen in his life virtually smashed the air right out of his lungs as he looked up and held out the package. How had he not noticed in the park? The gray sky must have leached the color away or something. They were so light he could imagine there were actual hints of frost in their depths. He couldn't think of anything more stupid than staring at someone like he'd been poleaxed just because they had amazing eyes. Jesus, he needed to get laid.

"No worries," Mari said quickly, to retrieve the situation, at the same time worrying if his hair was sticking up or he had ground nutmeg on his upper lip. But no, Sexy was looking him directly in the eyes the whole time. He had the most melodious voice, the kind that made Mari's lower body clench in delicious anticipation. He was still silently telling those parts of himself to behave when he realized that Mr. Cute, Dark and Sexy-Voiced was staring at him like he'd turned into a fire breathing dragon or something. "It's only Dr Mengele's new dildo. They're quite resilient, I hear. I'm sure it will survive."

Was that a flush he saw on those sculpted cheekbones? Hard to tell with his skin tone, but Mari thought maybe he detected a hint of a blush there. He put his coffee cup into his left hand and juggled the envelopes and tube under the same arm then held out the other hand when Mr. Sex-on-Legs still just gawped at him.

"Hi. Mari. I mean, that's my name. Not 'do you want to marry me?'"

Idiot! What was that? the rational part of his brain demanded. He struggled to rectify the situation.

"Um... *Dr.* Ilmarinen Gale, that's the official title. My grandfather is a professor of Nordic languages and my grandmother was a Finn. But most people find Mari easier to remember."

His hand was suddenly engulfed in warmth. Not a damp, sweaty grip, but dry, toasty warm and firm without being too aggressive. *Now wouldn't that feel good a little lower down?* he thought, and mentally chastised himself for it at once.

"Jake Chivis." It felt weird to Jake not to add 'detective' to his name. Technically it was still his rank but since he was no longer on active duty and didn't know when or even *if* he would go back to law enforcement, he had decided to leave those details out.

Dr. Ilmarinen Gale certainly didn't look like a doctor. He looked way too young, for one thing. Did doctors make dildo jokes to someone they just met? He supposed he should say something about seeing him in the park, but he really didn't want to talk about getting caught checking him out.

"What kind of doctor are you?" The words tumbled out and he hoped he sounded curious and not skeptical.

Smooth, Jake. Real smooth.

Mari merely grinned at his question. He let his own hand linger in Jake's longer than usual but it was a good, strong grip, nothing pansy about that handshake, and he was the first to disengage.

"Communication Tech, ostensibly," he said, glancing at his feet with a hint of modesty, then returning those brilliant aquamarine eyes to the study of Jake's face. "A step up from media studies but not quite brain surgery. Although I'm working on Artificial Intelligence Systems on the eighth floor at the moment. I wrote my D.Phil. thesis on that. My family thinks it has a bit more gravitas than bog standard programming. So...how are you finding London? You already know the best places to run, I see."

Damn! He wasn't going to just pretend it hadn't happened after all. Jake started to lift his hand to rub the back of his neck but stopped himself. He was trying to get rid of his nervous habits.

"Uh...London is interesting. I'm still getting used to it, I guess. There's a lot more going on here than Detroit, that's for sure."

"Ahh, so that's where that delicious accent hails from. Never been there. My father was at UCLA for a couple of years and I was at Albany for my Masters, so that's east and west coast covered but nowhere in between." He spoke rapidly but quite concisely, with an accent that was not pure English but not New York State either. "Have you found Kalmakis yet? They do the best meze in this part of town."

"Er, no, I haven't," Jake said, not knowing what either of those things were but guessing by the phrasing that it was a restaurant and consequently some kind of food. "I'll, uh, have to look into that."

Oh my god, could I sound any stupider?

How had he transformed into an awkward teenager from just a glance of those pretty eyes? Jake didn't know what else to say though. He figured this gorgeous young man was just being nice after he'd embarrassed himself in the park. There was no way he was actually flirting and, even if he was, he probably didn't mean it seriously. Not that Jake wanted to be flirted with. He needed to get laid, but he was thinking more of a one-night stand, not someone he was bound to run into again and again.

"You really should." Mari looked mildly disappointed that this overture wasn't greeted more enthusiastically. "Of course, if you prefer Italian," he persisted, still in that rapid-fire delivery, clearly fishing for something, "well *then* you are just going to be spoiled for choice. I mean, they say that you don't come to England for the food but *really* some of the eateries here are simply to die for. And you have your pick...solo, couples, family-friendly, anything you could ask for within a mile of here."

Definitely fishing!

Jake was almost positive that was some sort of invitation. How hard would it be to casually ask Dr. Gale if he might like to show him around a bit? Even if Jake *was* attracted to him, that didn't mean he had to act on it. Maybe they could just go out and...and *what*? Sit around in a crowded restaurant while Jake tried not to cringe every time he picked up a glass or had to touch a seat or a tabletop or, god forbid, put a fork that someone else had touched in his mouth. This was undeniably why he had not made a single friend here yet. Come to think of it, that was also why he only had a handful of long-term friends back home.

"I, um, I don't eat out a lot." *Fuckin'-A*, that was about the lamest excuse ever. He had to get out of here before Dr. Gale figured out what a walking freak show he really was. "But thanks for the suggestions, really. I should, uh...go. Um...work, I mean."

Mari juggled the mail back into his free hand and tried not to look as mortified as he clearly felt, letting it go at that. He had the kind of face that didn't hide emotions well.

"Not a problem," he insisted, saluting with the delivery tube and winking at him, determinedly cheerful. "Duty calls, huh? I suppose I ought to get on too... Professor Karden's probably itching to try this long fella out. See you in the park sometime?"

Jake smiled and nodded, because it would be totally rude not to, but he knew his cheeks must be red and he gave a sketchy salute of his own before hurrying off.

Jake headed straight to the research room and tried very hard and entirely unsuccessfully not to replay that scene in the hallway about three hundred times, while berating himself for every stammered word. He had never been the smoothest, suavest, peacock-type of guy but he didn't usually make that big an ass out of himself. He was definitely going to have to avoid bumping into Dr. Ilmarinen Gale again any time soon.

He also told himself sternly that he did not regret the necessity. Sure, the guy was hot as a bonfire on the Fourth of July, but he was not exactly the type of guy that Jake went for. He also ignored the small, internal voice that said that the type of guy he normally went for might just be the problem.

Jake arrived at his desk only a few minutes late, distracted and somewhat irritable. Fortunately he didn't need to speak with anyone right away. He slid behind a computer monitor and logged in, quickly burying himself in the sites he had been working on the day before. It was all really dull stuff, probably not worth his time, but you never knew when you might find a tiny germ of deviance in the reams of tedious typeface. Unfortunately, *Psychometry Through the Ages* was proving to be barren of any such criminal mastery. Jake had heard most of it before. How the frauds had conned their patrons, how supposed psychics used burning herbs or polished stones and crystals to ramp up their 'powers'. He had never put much stock in any of the techniques that were supposed to work. He was of the opinion—a very private opinion—that there wasn't any way to rev up psychic ability. It didn't work like an electrical current where you could turn it on and off, or feed in more juice. It was more like a doorway. Sometimes the door opened and showed him things and sometimes he got nothing but a blank wall.

Most of the time, he was glad when the damned door stayed shut. Of course his current job was more about finding ways that ordinary people could open those portals and methods to stop them doing so and as a consequence, he kept those counterproductive thoughts to himself as well.

As dull as the work was, it still managed to keep his mind busy enough that he stopped thinking about what might have happened had he not just kept on running the other way in the park, or had he asked Mari Gale out for lunch, or maybe dinner. At least it did for a little while. He realized about then that he had just read the same sentence five times.

"Shit!" he muttered under his breath.

"Problem, Detective Chivis?"

Jake looked up from the screen. Professor Newberry was poised at the corner of his desk, watching him intently, her half-frame glasses crooked on her nose. She was a nice enough lady, probably about his mother's age, but Jake hated how she looked at him sometimes, like she was waiting for him to do something interesting. Something *spooky*.

"No, Professor. I think I'm just ready for a break."

"Well, that works out fine then. I actually came over to ask you to take a few minutes." She smiled at him. "I've had a call from Professor Weston and he's asked if you wouldn't mind stopping in to see him this afternoon."

Jake lifted his eyebrows a fraction of an inch. "Did he say what he wanted?"

"He didn't go into details, but he said he'd like to see if you could give him an impression on an item he has."

Jake suppressed a sigh. Technically he could refuse. If it wasn't an official part of the study, he didn't have to do parlor tricks for the staff. However, they hadn't abused his gift so far and he felt kind of shitty turning someone down when it would only take him a minute or two.

"All right, I'll stop by," Jake promised her.

* * * *

Mari slid into the large, open-plan office space on the top floor and tossed his empty coffee cup into the waste bin, having emptied it on the way up the stairs from the floor below. The lift, for some peculiar reason known only to the original team of architects, didn't come all the way up to the eighth floor. Not that he minded the brief climb, unlike some he could think of. He eased the cardboard tube onto the edge of Emmanuel Karden's crowded desk and was making his way back across to his own little booth to fire up his processor when Karden's sharply enunciated tones trickled into his ears.

"Dr. Gale, so *good* of you to join us! We feared we would be *deprived* of your luminous presence this morning."

Mari held up the mail as evidence of his dutiful absence. "Present for you on the desk from the psychometric mapping fairies. They send their regards."

"You amuse me, Gale," the eminent professor chortled, stroking his yard-brush mustache, as he did just about every day.

Mari was unsure what it was about him that the old fraud found so amusing but he just nodded, tapping in his entry code and password, then confirming the password a second time, and murmuring, "We aim to please."

Callum George, thirty-four, though he looked ten years older, jovial, larger than life and solid as a sea defense, occupied the booth adjacent to his. He leaned over as Mari was waiting for the system to creak into life and in a low tone observed, "You've made yourself known to that new chap with the Hacker-Crackers then?"

"Have you been *spying* on me, Professor George?" Mari enquired in a low tone, half turning to let the man see he had a twinkle in his eye. Cal was a forthright Geordie, only six years his senior in reality but older than his father in some ways, emotionally dependable and insatiably curious about everything and everyone.

"I wasn't aware it was a secret assignation, Gale. Spotted you making eyes at him as I was heading for the lift, is all." Callum snared an apple from his desk and took a bite as he jabbed at his keyboard with a chunky finger.

"I was most certainly *not* making eyes at him, though

he couldn't take his eyes off me, I have to say," he replied lightly.

"Well, you certainly don't look most people's idea of an academic, you can't blame him for that. And he's a Yank, so I hear. Pretty conservative, most of them, aren't they? He's probably never come across anything like you before. No pun intended." Callum took another bite and began to open his own mail as Mari worked through the envelopes on his desk methodically.

"I really do think you have no clue what you're talking about," he mused. "Have you even switched on the news in the last ten years? The Americans have Pride Parades and Lady Gaga and everything now."

"So you're not remotely interested then?" Callum laughed huskily and stuffed the new mail, unread, into his already bulging in-tray.

"Did I say that?" Mari asked him without looking up from the single sparsely worded private memo from Weston, in his hand.

Professor Anthony Weston's grandfather had worked during the Second World War with Mari Gale's great-grandmother, Amelia Pallant, and this factor had been instrumental in Mari's return to England from Catalunya. Weston had maneuvered Doctor Pallant's descendant deftly into a post that, to Mari's knowledge, hadn't existed before the professor's intervention, but there were strings attached. When one dealt regularly with people who had half the degree of Elemental blood that Weston did, there were always strings — especially if you had the misfortune to be born into a potent Elemental bloodline, like Ilmarinen Gale.

The memo contained the results from his latest batch of skills tests. Mari hadn't found the tests too onerous, to be honest. Weston had given him unbreakable systems to surf and he'd broken into them. He disliked the feeling that he was only here at UCL as Professor Weston's paranormal guinea pig, though. The idea that his superior, Professor

Karden, knew about this and found it amusing didn't help. Mari was accustomed to doubters, he had been proving himself to his elders and presumed betters since he was old enough to use a keyboard and a monitor, but he always got the impression from Karden that the walrus-faced old bugger thought he was faking it. As if he possibly could!

There were precious few pure human-cyber Interfaces — men and women able to engage their minds directly with telecommunications networks and the worldwide web — working in Europe. As far as he knew there were only two currently here in Britain. He was one of them. The other, it was hinted at, worked in Whitehall.

He snorted softly as he scanned the mostly predictable results of his recent test surfing, annotated in Professor Weston's scratchy hand with little exclamations and observations. The update had not quite failed to distract him from his mental dissection of the meeting with Jake Chivis.

Jake Chivis...even that name sent little shivers through him, it was so deliciously exotic. He shifted in his swivel chair and crossed his long legs in their gunmetal-blue, tailored suit pants as he tried to concentrate on the day ahead, instead of how disastrously he had failed to make an impression on their hottest new import.

* * * *

Professor Weston's office was two floors down and... *somewhere*. How a place with mostly straight hallways managed to seem like such a maze at times was beyond him. Jake had decided to see Weston before lunch. Despite his disdain for most things written about psychic or metaphysical events, there were a few things that actually did hold an element of truth, and one of them was that he could *see* more clearly on an empty stomach. Or maybe that was just a leftover habit from his childhood and it was now deeply embedded in his own psyche, so that was why it seemed to work. Sometimes it was a pain in the ass to be both a psychic and a sceptic.

Okay, he had to be going in circles. Where was the door? Scowling, he swung back around and headed in the direction he had come from. He had to have missed a hallway or something. Either that or he'd been transported magically to Hogwarts, and wouldn't *that* just make for a great research paper?

"Looking for someone?"

The familiar voice made him jump, as did Mari's curious ability to creep up on him without him sensing it. That was rare enough to make him interesting, even if it was something Jake might have been trying to avoid thinking too much about.

The slim, attractive blond was leaning out of a doorway farther along the corridor Jake felt he had walked several times already. He still had that clever, not-quite-grin on his face as if he knew something no one else did. The nicely cut suit pants he wore were not nearly as tight as the spiderweb leggings that he ran in but they were not bags either. And why was he noticing that, for fuck's sake?

Jake tried to smooth the scowl off his face. He knew that his mildly annoyed expression looked to most people like he was primed to explode in a fit of temper, and when he was younger they would have been right, but he'd gotten that under control. Mostly.

"I was looking for Professor Weston's office," Jake said, then hesitated before adding, "And, hello again."

There was no need to be rude, after all.

"Well, hello yourself," Mari said with a chuckle, and if his eyes spent a little too long raking Jake up and down, he did not seem remotely ashamed of that. "You're in the right place. *This* place actually." He inclined his head back toward the room he was in the process of vacating. "Don't be shy, I was just leaving. You two have fun now. Don't wreck the joint."

He didn't seem in too much of a hurry to clear out of the

doorway, though.

Jake was used to people moving out of his way. He was not body builder buff, but he was tall and reasonably broad-shouldered. Mari didn't seem inclined to budge and Jake noticed, as he slid past him, practically eye to eye, that the cute doctor was actually a couple of finger widths taller. He supposed he hadn't noticed it before because Mari wasn't nearly as well-muscled. Nor had he noticed how his butter-pale hair curled a little over the collar of his shirt, not fashionably long enough to tie back in a tail but not utilitarian short either. Jake stepped into the office. Almost unconsciously he turned his head to look over his shoulder, and damn if he didn't get caught again! His face was seriously going to catch fire if he didn't stop making an idiot of himself in front of this gorgeous young man.

Mari winked at him and pursed his lips, although he stopped short of actually blowing him a kiss, which Jake was half expecting in his startled awkwardness. Then he was gone and the door closed behind him with a solid thump.

* * * *

Mari got as far as the gents' toilets on the landing near the elevators before he stopped and caught his breath. *Well, that was interesting!* The way Jake had looked at him, just for a moment. Ilmarinen Gale was not a mind reader, his Elemental gift did not manifest in that way, but he was not immune to body language and if Jake Chivis wasn't attracted to him, he figured he would convert to his great-great-grandmother's peculiar brand of Irvinite Presbyterianism. He pushed through the swing door and splashed his face in the basin because he could actually feel a little rush of heat beneath his skin. As he straightened and mopped his features with a handful of paper towels, the door opened from the corridor and he stroked a hand through his damp and wayward hair to straighten it, half expecting Jake to have followed him.

Mari entertained a brief fantasy where Jake Chivis strode into the conveniences and slammed him up against the wall, melting his lips with a brief, fierce kiss before striding off again to continue with whatever business he had in Professor Weston's office. Then Damien Nolan walked in with a couple of his cronies hot on his heels, snickering at some lame witticism he'd been spouting.

A sneer touched his lips as the young CAD engineer spotted Mari.

"Well, look who it is, fellas, Dr. Gay in the flesh! Wouldn't have thought you'd be hanging around in the *men's* room, Gayboy."

"Well, if I needed an incentive to leave, it just walked in," Mari said, managing some hauteur even if his forelock was still wet from the drenching he'd just given it. At least his cheeks had stopped burning and mercifully he'd managed to keep the blood from rushing off to anywhere more incriminating. "I'll leave you boys to your circle jerk, or whatever it is that you can't manage to do in here on your own."

No one touched him but they didn't exactly make room for him to leave either, so he was forced to push his way out. As the door was swinging shut behind him, he heard the snickering start again and turned it down in his head. Once nonsense like that would have bothered him to extremes, but now he was able to compartmentalize it. In this day and age, people were generally more accepting of him but there were elements within the academic tribe that still had their opinions rooted firmly in the dark ages. Nolan was a troglodyte throwback but, as Mari often reminded himself, there were good reasons why the cavemen died out.

More pressing was the reason why Jake Chivis would be visiting Professor Weston. He could see that he was going to have to do a little bit of detective work.

Chapter Three

Jake maneuvered himself into the small, cluttered office and tried not to trip or knock anything over. He wasn't clumsy but the room was so stuffed that it was difficult to walk without accidentally bumping into teetering towers of books or papers.

He had met Professor Weston twice before. The senior academic was one of the founding members of the Six Elements Worldwide Network universities program that had brought him to London, although Jake hadn't worked with him directly yet. When Jake entered his domain, Weston was waiting behind a large desk, strewn with layer upon layer of periodicals, books, printouts and snippets of ancient, faded articles. The professor was perhaps ten or fifteen years older than him, somewhere in his forties and still physically fit, with just a dusting of gray at the temples of his close-cropped, dark-reddish hair and in the edges of his neatly trimmed, pointed beard. He stood as Jake approached, leaning across the desk and offering his hand. Jake steeled himself and shook it.

Only then did he realize he hadn't done so earlier when he'd accepted Mari's hand. The whole *touching* thing was always worse with strangers. It was as if, once he got used to people, the impressions tuned themselves out, but when he first met a new person it was anyone's guess what he might learn from a simple handshake. He guessed he'd just been too stunned by those gorgeous, frosty blue eyes to be worried about what he might pick up from him in a psychic sense. Thankfully he had not got anything suspicious or disturbing off Mari and he didn't get anything like that from Weston either.

"Detective Chivis. Thank you for coming down. Please, have a seat. Would you like tea? Coffee? Can I get you anything to eat?"

"No, no thanks. I…ah, I work better if I don't have anything in my stomach."

"Oh, is that right? Oh, well, I thank you doubly then for seeing me before lunch."

"It's no trouble. Professor Newberry said that you'd like me to look at an item?" Jake prompted.

"Yes. It's…er, rather personal." Weston opened his top desk drawer and for some ungodly reason Jake thought back to Mari's dildo joke and was convinced he was going to pull out a big fake cock and slap it down in front of him. He closed his eyes, took a deep breath and let it out. When he opened them again he saw a small, black-handled hairbrush sitting in a hastily cleared spot on the desk blotter.

"This is my brother's," Weston explained. "I got it from his flat last night. He hasn't been returning my calls and I finally got worried enough to run by his place. Three days' worth of mail piled up behind the door and no sign of him. It isn't like him to disappear, Detective."

How many times had Jake heard that before? People were generally unpredictable and liable to do just about anything. Most of the time the 'missing person' cases reported turned out to be a spouse that ran off with whoever they were fucking on the side, or a kid who lived with one parent but had run away to throw him or herself on the mercy of the other after a domestic row. Occasionally though, someone went missing then turned up dead.

"Have you told the police?" Jake asked calmly.

Weston waved his hand. "Of course, but he is an adult. The police said they found nothing suspicious and would 'look into it'. Which means they won't."

Jake would have liked to reassure him that the police would do what they could to find his brother but he knew it was unlikely they would investigate very hard unless they identified a crime scene, or he had been gone longer than just a couple of days. He cleared his throat.

"Professor, I'll do my best here, but I have to tell you that my...ah, my ability doesn't always pick up on things and, even when it does, the recalls aren't always useful. I just don't want you to get your hopes up."

"I understand. Still, I'd really appreciate it if you would try."

Jake nodded and suppressed a sigh. He knew that most people expected some kind of theater, like he ought to close his eyes and maybe hold the object in question to his forehead, or some other hokey thing. He didn't need to do any of that. All he needed was to touch an object, and he'd either see something or he wouldn't. He wished the professor had brought him something metal though. Metal held on to impressions better than anything else. The hairbrush was plastic, which was just about the worst.

Jake reached out and touched the handle. He wrapped his fingers around it cautiously and picked it up.

"I don't thi..." The words died on his lips.

A small mirror...rear-view...in a car...blue eyes looking back in reflection...a laugh, pretty, lighthearted, feminine.

"I swear you take longer to get ready than I do, Phil!" the woman scolded and laughed again.

"You want me to look good, don't you? I'll make it up to you, I promise," Blue Eyes said, making the 'promise' a warm purr.

Jake sucked in a breath and set the brush back down. His impressions were not like looking through the lens of a camera, the way the movies made it out to be. When he saw something it was more as if his whole body got sucked into the vision and he was right there. He did not share the memory as an outsider but as the person who had left the impression behind, seeing the scene through their eyes. And when the recall ended, it was disorientating. If the vision lasted long enough, when he came back to the present he sometimes had a hard time telling what was real from what wasn't. This flashback had been very brief, though, and it only took him a moment to readjust.

"Phil, is that your brother?" Jake asked, and tried not to be irritated by the sudden surprise on Weston's face. You would think that people who asked him to use his talent wouldn't be so skeptical, but they always were until you said something to prove yourself.

"Yes, his name is Phil."

"Was he seeing someone?" Jake asked.

"Yes. You saw her?" Weston asked excitedly. "I had a feeling she might be involved. Philip wouldn't say much about her, only that he was busy, and when I pressed him he admitted he was seeing a married woman. When he stopped answering his phone, I just had a bad feeling about the whole thing."

Jake stomped down on the urge to snap that Weston might have told him that to begin with. He hated it when people held back information on purpose, as if they needed to test him to see if he was just fucking around. Weston was part of the Six Elements Worldwide Network, he ought to know better.

"No, I didn't see her. I heard her, though. I heard *someone* anyway. It isn't really very much to go on," he said, still feeling angry.

"Perhaps not," Weston conceded. "But it does tell me that she's real, at least."

Jake said nothing but he looked at Weston closely. Did the man have a reason to mistrust his brother? If he didn't trust Phil, could he really be so certain the man hadn't just disappeared into the sunset with his illicit lover? He didn't know enough about the case to have those answers. Jake stopped that train of thought right there. This was not a case. He was not even licensed to investigate here.

Apparently that was of no concern to Professor Weston. "I know I've already taken up your time, Detective, but I truly am worried that something out of sorts has befallen my brother. I know this is asking a great deal of you but... would you mind perhaps visiting his flat? Seeing if you get any more impressions there? Maybe he left behind some indication as to where he was going."

"Professor, I'm not a P.I., I don't have a license here to do that kind of work..." Jake told him.

The professor waved his hand dismissively again. "I'm not asking you to spy on anyone for me, Detective. I just want you to look around his flat and use your gift. I have a key. I'll pay you for your time."

Jake shook his head. "It's not about money, sir. I'm just concerned. In all likelihood what I tell you will be disappointing." He sighed and clenched his fingers into helpless fists for a moment then let his hands drop tamely by his sides. "Okay. I'll take a look around his place, but please keep in mind that it's not likely I'll find anything to indicate where he went. You might do better to hire a P.I. that could dig up phone and bank records. Those are more likely to tell you what he was doing before he went missing than anything else."

"Thank you, Detective, I will keep that in mind. In fact I know someone already who could assist with that. In the meantime—" He pulled out a key from his breast pocket and pushed it across the desk to Jake, then jotted down his brother's address and passed that over too. "My cell phone number is on there as well. Please call me right away if you find anything, or if you need anything to help the investigation proceed."

Jake took the items and stood, trying not to cringe at the word *investigation*. He really should have corrected Weston about calling him 'detective' too. He was not a cop, not here. Maybe not *anywhere* any more. He tucked the key and the paper into his jacket pocket and shook Weston's hand before he left.

His stomach rumbled angrily once he was in the hall and prompted him to wonder if he would run into Mari again. Maybe if he did, he would ask him if he wanted to go to Kalmakis and he could figure out what the hell a meze was.

* * * *

Mari had been fretting over the curious meeting with the prof this morning ever since he'd seen Jake go into the man's office, hot on his heels. Did that mean Jake Chivis was a part of SEWN-UP as well? Or was he just meeting with Tony Weston as part of his job with the department's Web Security team?

Weston was a serious scientist with a good track record in psychological profiling but he also had a reputation for being a bit of a flake, mostly because of his passion for the extremes of bio and psychological engineering. He collected anyone with the smallest suggestion of paranormal ability and subjected them to his own reams of tests and inquiries.

Naturally, given his ancestry and the gifts passed on to him in the genes he'd got from Great-Grandmama Amelia, Mari had flashed up on Weston's paranormal geek radar as soon as he'd hit college.

Weston had been trying to lure him to London for ten years and Mari had resisted the temptations set in his way for most of that time. When Mama had fallen sick, though, things had changed — his priorities had shifted and suddenly London hadn't seemed such a terrible place to be.

Amelia Pallant had been one of the last true Elementals to work with the University and even she wasn't a pure-blood sylph. Mari disliked Paracelsus' classification. *Sylph* made what he and his kind did sound airy-fairy, like some kind of children's party game and it was certainly not that. Weston had the decency not to label him as such, at least not in his hearing, but he had his doubts about what the man said when he *couldn't* hear it.

He might respect Professor Weston's research but that didn't mean he had to trust the man. One of these days he was going to bug the professor's office and get a bit of gen of his own on the conniving bastard. It wasn't like he didn't have the wherewithal to do it. He might find out what Jake was doing in there while he was at it.

Or you could just ask, his great-grandmother's voice of reason suggested somewhere deep in the back of his skull. Oddly enough, when his conscience communed with him, it tended to be in her very precise, Nordic-accented English.

He considered it, but then he also considered five different reasons not to, foremost being that he didn't want Jake Chivis to think he was some kind of fruitcake.

Why should you care what he thinks? It never made a difference before, did it?

She had him there. He hadn't given a half a hoot what anyone thought since leaving school. So why did this feel different? Why was it suddenly so important to him what Mr. Hot and Tasty Chivis thought of him.

"Shut up!" he told the voice in his head, earning him a curious sidelong look from Professor George, which he ignored with barely a pang.

Mari pretended to work on the detailed coding for Karden's newest, hush-hush government project until a little after three p.m., when his stomach reminded him that it was too long since it had been acquainted with food. The almond croissant, though delicious, had been a long time ago. And maybe Jake would take a coffee break around this time anyway.

He locked down his workstation and killed the screen then slid out from behind his desk and headed for the cafeteria on the fourth floor. One of the perks of this job was that it was deadline rather than timetable driven, so Karden didn't seem to mind so much—in spite of all his poking on the subject of Mari's time keeping—what hours he came and left, so long as the job was completed and signed off when it needed to be.

For a little while, he thought that he might be destined for disappointment. There was barely another soul in the spacious, glass-walled refectory looking out over Malet Place, but just as he was steeling himself to slope back to the office and chain himself to his desk again, he saw a familiar, lofty, nicely muscled figure amble through the door and snag a tray from the counter.

His heart did a little dance in his chest and he cautioned it softly, "Now, now, be still," before raising a hand and wriggling his fingers lightly once Jake's face was pointed roughly in his direction.

"Well, hello. What a lovely surprise!"

Jake cut his eyes to the side to see who might be watching this exchange then immediately felt bad. He hated bigots and he hated bullies, but he did nothing to deter them when he acted like he should be ashamed that someone so…flamboyant said hello to him. It was stupid, and it was exactly why Alex had left him, no matter how much he had tried to tell his ex it was ingrained behavior and didn't mean anything. It had obviously meant something to Alex.

"Hi," Jake said. He tried on a smile and it felt weird on his face. "You following me around?" he joked, and hoped it didn't sound that lame.

By way of an answer, Mari pointed at the pastry crumbs on his plate and his nearly empty cup and chuckled. "Here first! Are *you* following *me* around, Mr. Chivis?"

Jake's first inclination was to duck his head and stammer something diversionary but he was getting sick of acting like an awkward teenager just because Mari Gale was a hot young man. He made himself hold Mari's open, optimistic gaze and tried on a coy smile.

"Maybe."

Whoa! He had not meant the response to sound quite so much like a flirty purr, but it had come out that way and now he couldn't take it back.

Mari's pretty eyes widened and he drew a slow circle around the rim of his coffee mug with one fingertip, still apparently engrossed in whatever was happening on Jake's face.

"Well… I suppose I like the sound of that!" He laughed huskily. His voice was very smooth, an almost accentless tenor, about half an octave lower than Jake would have expected. "I've had far less appealing stalkers. What did the Weston bastard want with you then? Nothing good, I expect."

"Uh...just some research he wanted me to do," Jake said, which was almost the truth. It wasn't that he felt the particular need to conceal what he was doing, but his cop training made him automatically evasive when talking about cases. Plus he wasn't sure Weston wanted the fact that his brother was missing, or screwing someone else's wife, talked about in the halls.

"Mmm-hmm." Mari nodded and swirled the dregs of his coffee in the bottom of the cup before taking a last gulp and licking his lips slowly. "At least he's not sticking probes up your arse and waiting for you to fart him a rainbow. Which is all good."

Jake blinked at him. He could feel the color slowly creeping up his neck. He had no idea how he was supposed to respond to that. Did Mari know something about the 'other' research Professor Weston was conducting here? *Interesting.*

Mari came to his rescue by putting down the cup and pointing at him with a little smile. "Gotcha! You are very easy to tease, did anyone ever tell you that?"

Jake sighed and tried not to roll his eyes. "Yeah. I get the whole 'why so serious' thing a lot. Just the way I am, I guess."

Mari rested his elbow on the table and his chin on his palm, looking up at him more solemnly as Jake loaded his tray and came over to join him. "Nothing wrong with that, Chivis. Some people even find that kind of thing rather sexy, you know. I reckon you could work that in your favor."

Jake looked into those too-blue eyes, pinning him with a stare. "And are you one of those people?" he asked, wondering exactly what he was doing when he'd already told himself he was definitely not getting involved with anyone he knew from work. Especially not with someone like Doctor Ilmarinen Gale.

41

Mari remained silent, just staring back at him for several long seconds. Long enough to making Jake squirm inside, sure he'd said something wrong. He was about to laugh and explain that he was only joking but they were interrupted.

"What have we here?" Nolan drawled, snagging a can of diet soda from one of the coolers and tossing it from hand to hand as he surveyed the scene in the quiet of the refectory. "If it isn't Dr. Gay trying to pull another newbie? You wanna watch your backside round this one, mate," the newcomer said with a crude little snicker, directing his attention to Jake. "Take it from me."

"You'd be hard-pressed to *give* it to anyone, Damien," Mari said darkly. It was as serious as Jake had ever heard him.

Jake very casually set the tray he'd been holding down on the table and turned slightly. He had seen Nolan around the place, usually in company with a gang of youngsters from the Computer Aided Design department on Three. He was probably about Jake's age, late twenties, and a match for him in height, practically, though his build was stockier, already leaning toward a solidity of girth that would transmute itself into fat as he grew older and more sedentary. A lick of mid-brown hair flopped down into his sharp, curious gray eyes.

"Are you for real?" Jake demanded slowly. "Like, are you *seriously* pulling the whole homophobe routine? Dr. Gay? *Really*? What are you, *twelve*? Do you have some disorder where you never grew out of adolescence?"

"He's just an idiot, Jake. Leave it," Mari said very softly. "Damien fancies the pants off me but he hasn't figured that out yet so he feels safer trying to pull my pigtails."

"Bet you'd look cute with pigtails, Marilyn," Nolan flashed back, reaching out to flip Mari's slicked-back, pale blond hair forward over his face.

"Fuck off and play in the sandpit now, Damien," Mari told him more irritably. "The grown-ups are talking." He pushed the silky tumble of his disarrayed fringe back from his face with one hand and eased his chair away from the table, making to rise.

Damien reached toward him again, whether to flip his hair back out of place or something else, but he didn't get that far. Jake grabbed his wrist as he was still reaching out and pulled him forward, off balance, simultaneously pressing his other hand in the center of Nolan's back and twisting his captive arm behind him. He slammed Nolan chest down on the table, making everything on it jump, and those few people standing around them jump too. His free hand twitched toward his waist for half a second before he remembered that he didn't have handcuffs and this wasn't some perp he was arresting. It all happened in the blink of an eye.

"Well, *that* was impressive," Mari stated with a little smirk as he recovered from the shock of seeing a man nearly twice his girth face-planted across the canteen table in front of him. He leaned forward and murmured in his tormentor's ear as he was getting up to go. "Bet that got you hard, Damie, didn't it?"

Then he straightened, ignoring Nolan's impassioned, ranting protest and ran his hand over the tensioned forearm pinning the man down. His voice was little more than a whisper in Jake's ear. "Let him go. He really isn't worth it, you know."

Jake ignored him, one hand on Damien's twisted arm, shoving it between his shoulder blades and the other resting firmly on the back of his neck. He squeezed that hand tighter, knowing if he wanted to he could shift it just a little higher, apply a touch more pressure and it would be lights out. Jake breathed out slowly then. He hadn't been this close to totally losing it in a long time. Coming back to his senses, he eased the pressure off gradually, then let go of Nolan, stepping back as the man flipped himself over at once and recovered his feet, staring at him with wide, disbelieving eyes.

"Consider this a lesson in manners," Jake snapped before

Nolan could yell at him or accuse him of being crazy. "You don't touch him, *or* anyone else that doesn't want to be touched, got it?"

Nolan backed away, eyes narrowed. Jake could see him deliberating, sizing him up, deciding how to retaliate. Nolan was a match for him in height, heavier, and looked like he had a longer reach. Jake tensed, ready for him, but they had already drawn a small, curious audience and Nolan was evidently not prepared to be humiliated a second time.

"Cool it, mate," Nolan said at last, shaking his head and rubbing his upper arm, which still had to be twinging where it had been twisted right around. "You want to sort out those anger issues, you know."

"I'm a cop and I'm from Detroit. This *is* how we work out our anger issues," Jake informed him grimly.

Damien Nolan looked like he might say something more, but in the end he retreated, casting a dark look at Mari as he went. Mari just wiggled his fingers at him casually.

"See ya. Wouldn't wanna be ya!"

Only once Nolan was safely out of sight and the handful of gawkers had begun to disperse did Mari slide around Jake, rubbing up against him like a lithe, blond cat and whispering, "If I wasn't worried that you'd break *my* arm, I'd kiss you for that."

Jake sighed. That was totally not what he had been intending Mari to think — that he was some kind of loose cannon, primed to go off at the slightest provocation.

"I wouldn't break your arm," he said, although he did step back. "That fucker touches you again, report him. Joking or not, if he touches you against your will, it's assault."

"Chivis, it's my word against his and for the sake of a bit of a hair crisis, it really isn't worth the hassle." Mari exhaled. He didn't close the gap Jake had self-consciously put between them, but he did rest one hand lightly on his forearm as he murmured, "Thank you, though. You really didn't have to do that, but it made my day. I owe you dinner at least."

"You don't owe me. I was just..." *Doing my job.* Only it wasn't his job anymore. And he'd wanted to keep that under wraps anyway and instead he'd lost his temper and blurted it out. *Shit.* "Doing what decent people do."

Mari actually looked briefly disappointed, he thought, but the expression was there on his face one second then gone in a flash, carefully hidden behind the smile Jake was learning to recognize—the humorless twitch of his kissable mouth that covered a whole range of suppressed emotions. He removed the warmth of his gentle hand and tucked his long, elegant thumbs into the pockets of his shiny blue suit pants instead.

"Well, I suppose I don't know a whole lot of decent people in that case," he said with an attempt at that perky cheeriness that he'd started out with. "I'd still like to take you out to dinner, though. My treat. Let's call it a...meeting of the decent people!"

Jake could feel the tension tighten in his middle and his mouth started to open to stammer out some lame excuse, but he couldn't shake that small flash of hurt he'd just seen in Mari's face, and he couldn't stand to see it again.

"I...I, um...okay."

Ash-colored eyebrows drew together briefly again and Mari asked, "Are you *embarrassed*? Did I just embarrass you? Because...you know, that wasn't my... Look— Just forget it, okay!" Then, just like that, he was gone, striding back toward the doors and pushing his way through them like they'd insulted him as well. If Jake had not already lost his temper once, he would have picked up a chair and thrown it across the room. He figured he'd better not. It was probably already going to make the rounds that he was nuts.

Great. Just fucking great.

He'd attacked a man for being a jerk, blown his whole 'Jake Chivis, just a regular guy' cover, then pissed off the only person that had shown even a remote interest in being his friend. He was just about out of sighs, so he gave the

45

chair a halfhearted kick and stalked out too, his coffee forgotten. He had tests this afternoon, and none of them involved sticking a probe up his ass.

* * * *

Mari had a sudden overwhelming feeling that his head was going to explode as he plowed out of the cafeteria, shoving his way past startled people, immune to their looks of bewilderment in his all-consuming pall of angst and utter humiliation.

How could he possibly have read that situation so badly? Was he really so desperate that he'd convinced himself Jake Chivis might be interested in him instead of just being a nice, decent human being who hated to see anyone taken advantage of?

And now he'd blown it completely.

There was no way on earth that Jake would even want to be alone in the same room as him now. The look of confusion and mild embarrassment on his kind, beautiful face was like a slap to Mari's own.

He stood up for you. He risked being tarred with the same brush because he's a good person and you rewarded him by showing him up in public. Oh, well done! Well fucking done, Dr. Gale!

He practically threw himself into the toilets, not sure if he wanted to smash things or just throw up. His gut was certainly tight, worse even than when he was toughing out Nolan's bitchy insults. Because at the end of the day, what odious pricks like Nolan thought meant nothing to him.

So you give a damn what someone thinks then... Well, that's a new one! Grandmama Amelia said, her voice in his head tender and bemused.

Mari locked himself in a cubicle and doubled over to puke his guts out. A waste of lunch, he thought grimly, but better down the drain than fighting with his tormented innards. Once there was nothing to eject but bitter bile, he wiped his face and hit the flush then sat on the floor with his head in his hands and tried to stop himself shaking.

Could this possibly get any more humiliating?

The answer was yes but he refused to cry. He had promised Mama when she first got sick that he would not cry and it was easy now to hold back the tears. It hurt like a red hot spike in his chest but he could do it.

Chapter Four

Jake did not go to Professor Weston's brother's place when he left work that evening. His concentration was blown. He doubted they'd gotten anything useful out of him during the testing that afternoon either. He tried to tell himself that it was only because he felt bad about hurting Mari's feelings, but mostly he was beating himself up because he knew he'd been a jerk.

The adult thing to do would be to find Mari and apologize, possibly try to make amends, but he wasn't sure if he should do that right away or let him cool off a bit first. He knew if it were him that was pissed off, it would be better to let the flames die down.

How long, though? Should he try to find his office? Should he wait a couple of days? Or maybe try to talk to him in the park? Would he even see Mari there again? Or would he consciously avoid Jake now?

The questions kept him completely off kilter and as he was passed various objects to hold and asked a bunch of inane questions about each, he just answered that he got nothing, even if there were tiny flashes every now and again. He just didn't care who had last owned the item or what they had been doing.

When he left that evening, instead of going to Phil Weston's apartment to see what he could figure out about the last known movements of the professor's absent brother, he went back to his own flat, took some aspirin and crawled into bed.

* * * *

Next morning it was mercifully dry, but on the chilly side and windy. Jake thought about skipping his run. If Mari never wanted to see his face again, it would be the polite thing to do, to stay out of his way. But, what if he thought Jake was just avoiding him because he was still embarrassed? Wouldn't that make him feel worse? Fuck it. He had never been one not to own up when he was wrong, nor was he the type to hide rather than face something.

All his worrying and questioning was for nothing, it turned out, once he'd dragged himself into his running gear and hauled his ass to Regent's Park, because he didn't catch a glimpse of Mari at all. He felt even more of a jerk then. Should he find the adorable doctor and tell him he didn't have to change his routine — that he would pick somewhere else to run? Would Mari appreciate that, or would he just sound like an arrogant prick? Goddammit, he had no clue what to do.

The uncertainty left him unable to focus and for most of the morning he simply stared at his research notes, not doing a damn thing. He checked his email and poked around online for a while. His phone chirped at him from his pocket and it took him a moment to remember that was the sound it made when he got a text — it had been so long since he'd received one. He checked but it was Weston, asking if they could meet in his office again at noon.

Jake sent him back that it would be better if they could postpone until tomorrow as he hadn't any information for him yet. Not even thirty seconds went by before Weston messaged him again.

I've taken your advice and asked Dr. Gale to work on tracking Phil's whereabouts electronically. Would you mind taking him over to Phil's flat with you this evening so he can collect his laptop?

Jake read the message three times then sent back word that he would. He supposed, if Mari was genuinely avoiding him, then this would be his chance to apologize without making an ass of himself in front of a lot of people.

* * * *

"Is that even legal?" Mari wanted to tell Professor Weston where to go, but at the same time, if he was able to put his less scientific abilities to good use, it might at least help to take his mind off the events of the last twenty-four hours.

Karden had ordered him to go home last night after his inability to concentrate had become obvious even to the normally impervious academic in charge of their small but select bureau. As if that wasn't bad enough, he hadn't been able to keep his mood in check and had wound up snapping at Mama over dinner. He had apologized immediately but by then the damage was done. She'd known something was wrong and hadn't stopped needling him for details. He'd avoided it in the end by taking Tonka for a walk that lasted until they were both cold and weary. But at least on his return, she had gone to bed.

This morning he'd slipped out early, before she was awake, and felt bad for doing it but he could not sleep and, after several hours of lying on his bed staring at the ceiling, he was on the move again as soon as it began to get light. At least the early start put him in Karden's good books and the boss didn't even complain when Mari was summoned by Professor Weston midmorning. Mari was dumbstruck again, his mind trying to process what the man was asking him to do. It was not so much that he doubted his own ability to retrieve the files, but rather that a senior academic was actually asking him to do so in the first place.

"I'm not asking you to hack the White House, Dr. Gale," Weston said gravely. "It's my brother's phone, that's all. I just want to know who he's talking to."

"Can't you ask him?" Mari raised a skeptical eyebrow.

"If I could do that, I wouldn't need to hack his phone, now would I?"

Mari folded his arms, sitting back from the screen where he had been demonstrating, using a set-up account, how easy it was for a trained interface to pull information through from a remote source using a neat combination of clever code and metaphysical manipulation. His gift was almost beautiful in its simplicity really. Dr. Dolittle could talk to the animals. Dr. Ilmarinen Gale could talk to the Internet, and by extension, to the telephone networks and all the ancillary services that relied on one or the other for their communications. He never used the *H* word in relation to his ability. In Mari's opinion, what he could do was a whole world more sophisticated than a basic hack job.

It was a complex and sensitive subject. He knew that Karden was discreetly monitoring his work with Professor Weston. And in turn, what Karden knew, the Security Services also knew. He was treading a very slim line between science and crime and one false step could see him disappear, conveniently, and without a trace.

Right now, with Mama so sick, he could not afford for that to happen.

"I'm not here to spy on your relatives for you, Tony. What's going on here really?"

"Ilmarinen, I wouldn't ask you to do this if I wasn't worried about him," the professor cajoled, changing tack. "I'm working with people that can do things and go places no one else can. And that's why I'm asking you for your help. My brother, Phil, has been missing for four days. No one has heard from him. He's not been back to his flat. And he isn't answering his phone. It's not typical behavior for him. I know there's something wrong."

"I'm not a detective, Professor Weston. Why don't you just call the police?" Mari shook his head stubbornly.

"I've done that, but they won't get involved unless there's some evidence that he's not simply wandered off. I told them it wasn't normal. He's a bit of a lad but he's self-employed. Other people depend on him for their income. He wouldn't just cry off work with no explanation." Weston sighed. "I'm worried. He's my baby brother. Wouldn't you feel the same?"

"I'm an only child," Mari said, tapping his fingertips against his left knee irritably.

"If it was a cousin, or your mother?" the professor persisted, manipulative bastard that he was.

A little huff of impatience was Mari's initial response but at last he relented a little. It was not that he couldn't understand Weston's concern—he was just worried that getting involved in what could well be a simple domestic issue between the professor and his family could easily come back around and bite him in the rear.

"I'll have a look, but that's all," he said finally, with a shake of his head to let the man know he wasn't best pleased about it.

"Thank you, Dr. Gale." Weston looked relieved. "You won't be working on your own. I've asked someone else to give me a hand with the detective work. Have you met Jake Chivis from Web Security yet?"

Mari stared at him for a moment as if he suspected this might be some kind of sick joke. When the professor just seemed to be waiting for a response, he realized that it was far from that. It was his worst nightmare.

"You want me to work with Chivis? Why, exactly?"

"He seems a pleasant enough young man. And he was a police detective in his former life, I thought it might be helpful." Weston smiled encouragingly but the smile faltered as Mari just continued to look at him as if he were out of his mind. "He…he's part of the program, Ilmarinen. He has a gift too. A gift that might help."

"Can't we both just report to you?" Mari pleaded helplessly.

"Do you have some objection to partnering with him?" Weston asked, refusing to give in.

"I… No… I just… I'm not used to working with…"

Hot guys who have a problem with me, his mind supplied, and he shook his head.

"I guess…"

"I just want you to compare notes, that's all. His gift is more for seeing physical things and yours is for communications and remote information. I thought you might be able to combine those skills. It would be an interesting experiment."

Guinea pigs! Mari thought but he said nothing.

"Jake is going to check out Phil's flat tonight. I thought you might want to go along, see if you can get anything from his laptop or his home phone. I gave him the key," Weston said with a relieved smile that did nothing to appease Mari's ill-humor.

* * * *

After the fifth time looking at the clock, Jake turned off his computer and put away the notebook he'd been scribbling in. He felt like a kid waiting for his first date. Which was even more ridiculous considering, if Mari even showed up, he was more likely to give him the cold shoulder than forgive him for being an idiot.

He made a goal with two paper clips and shot little paper balls at it with a rubber band for a while. It had been a whole day since the incident in the cafeteria. Maybe Dr. Gale wouldn't be so mad anymore.

One by one, the team departed. Outside his window the sky was growing darker. Jake was just about to pack up and go on his own when the door opened, so quietly that he almost didn't hear it. His skin prickled a warning though and as he turned around it was to see the pale form of Mari Gale outlined in the half-light from the corridor like a restless ghost, his slim fingers tapping against the doorjamb.

"I didn't set this up, Chivis," Gale said defensively. "I promise I will not flirt, I will not touch you and I won't say a word to mortify you. I just want this over with so I can go home and check on my mother, okay?"

Jake sighed. *So much for him not being mad anymore.* He

stood up and pushed his chair in to give himself a second to think. Which was funny because all he'd been doing all day was thinking, and yet he hadn't been smart enough to plan what he wanted to say.

"You didn't give me a chance to tell you I was sorry yesterday," he began, slowly so he didn't stammer because those beautiful blue eyes were still flashing angrily at him. "You didn't embarrass me. Not in the way you're thinking, anyway. It's not like I wouldn't want to be seen with you or something. If anything, I'd think it might be the other way around, except that you don't seem like you give much of a shit what anyone else thinks. Which is a good thing," he hastily added so he didn't insult him again. He ran a hand over his hair in frustration and let out a short huff. "Jeez, every time I open my mouth around you the wrong thing comes out. Listen, I'm not good with words. I just want you to know, you didn't say or do anything embarrassing and I'm sorry if I insulted you. That was about the last thing I wanted to do."

There! He'd talked enough for a week. Silently he hoped he wasn't about to get the door slammed in his face. Jake was unsure what plan B would entail if his apology wasn't good enough.

Mari was taken aback by Jake's apology—he had not been expecting it. Mostly the guys in his department were too academic to be concerned with such minor concerns as finer feelings or they were blunt and jokey to the point of rudeness, like Nolan. He was not used to frankness or honesty so he was initially cynical, looking for the trap, waiting for Jake to say, *Gotcha!*

When he didn't, Mari was left wrong-footed, not sure what he was supposed to say in response. He didn't consider that Jake had anything to apologize for, not after yesterday, but at the same time he did not want him to think he was ungracious. Jake looked so wary, like a mistreated dog expecting to be chased off with shouts and kicks. Why that should be the case if he wasn't interested, Mari couldn't puzzle out.

At last he drew a shaky breath and exhaled a rapid, tactful, "Apology accepted." Then added, "Now can we do this thing? Isn't that what you cops say?"

Jake's lips twitched into a wry grin at last, which suited him much better than his previous hangdog expression.

"Not any that I know," he said, almost playfully. He shrugged his jacket over his broad shoulders and buttoned it down.

"Is that why you're over here? Investigating us?" Mari eased himself away from the doorframe and fastened his tailored woolen coat as he discreetly watched Jake getting ready, then rebuked himself for checking the guy out when he'd promised him sincerely that he wouldn't.

Jake chuckled softly. "That depends. Who is 'us'?"

"Uh-huh…" Mari tapped his nose lightly with one long finger. "If you don't know, then I'm certainly not going to be the one to tell you. So what's the plan with this missing reprobate brother then? We going to go round there, kick his door down and dust the place?"

He was quietly relieved that Jake was taking this so well, that was something at least. It could have been awful having to work alongside him but it seemed that at least the man was able to smile about what had happened. Mari's insides still felt a little tight when he thought too much about it, but his smile — *All the stars! That smile!* — made him feel a bit better.

Jake looked over at him. His chin was still tucked down slightly, his expression plainly saying he was trying not to grin.

"Well, seeing as how I have the key, I think we can save wasting the door frame." He hesitated a second. "Weston didn't tell you what it is that he asked me to do?"

Mari shook his head as they made their way back to the elevator through the near quiet of the nine-story block. There were still some lights on and he knew that people

55

worked through the night here sometimes but after six p.m. it was a calmer, stiller environment. That too soothed him and he was able to relax.

"No. He said that you were part of the Program but he didn't give me details, just said that my...um...my *specialty* might augment yours. At first I thought it was just because you were a cop before you came here, but it's more than that, isn't it?"

Jake watched him out of the corner of his eye for a moment. Mari recognized that wary glance with a cold water shock. He didn't want people to look at him like he was odd, which was understandable.

"I'm clairvoyant. I can sometimes tell what people were doing if I touch something that belonged to them," Jake said.

Mari looked at him more intently as they waited for the lift to come back up to the seventh floor. He was oddly touched that Jake felt able to tell him that. A lifetime of being considered weird for his abilities gave him at least that much empathy with a fellow oddball.

"For real?"

Jake nodded once.

"I never met a proper clairvoyant before. They said my great-grandmother was one, well, kind of, anyway... Remote Viewing, they called it. She was quite famous for her abilities in her day." He hesitated for a moment. The elevator call button pinged and the doors slid open. Once they were safely inside the little mirrored box, he added, "I never told anyone that before."

"It's something you learn to be secretive about," Jake said. "So people don't get freaked out. So they don't drive you crazy bringing you Great-Grandad's watch and asking if you can 'feel anything'." He met Mari's eyes in the mirror. "I don't tell many people what I can do either. But I guess since I've signed up for being a lab monkey, it comes a little easier."

"So Weston *is* testing you. Is this another part of the

program, do you think, or did you believe his story about his missing brother?" Mari's lips twitched without humor. He had worked with Professor Weston just long enough to know the man was capable of any form of manipulation to get the results he wanted.

Jake considered this for a moment then shook his head. "I don't know, but it would be pretty fucked up to construct a story like that. I can't imagine his brother agreeing to take a vacation and let someone paw through his stuff to see what he's been up to either. Most likely he took off for parts unknown with the woman he was ban—uh, seeing." He grinned sheepishly.

The lift carriage came to a gentle halt on the ground floor and Mari chuckled in recognition of Jake's little slip before they stepped out. He wasn't offended by what Jake had almost said, though apparently his colleague was gentleman enough to worry that he might be. That was quite touching in its way. They exited the lift in a more companionable silence and crossed the foyer toward the turnstiles and the glass doors between them and the cooler night air. He took a moment to appreciate that they looked good together in the reflection from the walls of polished plate glass.

"I bet he's not even got a brother," Mari snickered. "I imagine this is all some cunning ruse to get us into his flat so he can perpetrate evil acts on us. I'm glad I'm not going on my own, is all I can say."

He stretched out his hand to hail a passing Hackney cab as they walked out through the tall black iron gates onto Torrington Place. It pulled in a little farther along the road and they had to run to catch it up in the shadow of the massive church of Christ the King. Once in the warmth of the taxi, Mari gave the driver their destination and they pulled away into the night.

They were both quiet on the cab ride, Jake mostly because he didn't want to talk about their plans with a cabbie listening. He wasn't sure what Mari's reticence was about but he took heart that at least it wasn't an uncomfortable, strained silence. His companion was looking out of the window at the London streets as they hurried by, turning in his seat like a child for a better look whenever something interested him. Once they arrived Mari led the way up to the building and Jake reached out and took his elbow gently before he reached the door.

"Hang back a second, okay. Let me go first," he said. He didn't really expect trouble, but if there was something dangerous on the other side of the door, he'd rather see it before his companion did.

Mari flickered an unreadable look his way. He was definitely biting his tongue about something. Jake knew he was probably overreacting but his companion was no muscle queen — if someone came bowling out to meet them, hell-bent on a fight, Mari would get taken down and he had no intention of letting that happen, whether that dented his ego or not. At last those chilling blue eyes dropped to the hand on his arm and he let go immediately.

"You have the key anyway," Mari demurred finally, giving way, though he stuck close to Jake's side nevertheless.

Jake didn't immediately dip into his pocket. Instead he reached out a hand to the door handle. He turned it so that the backs of his knuckles touched the edge. Doorknobs and the surrounding area were the first place dusted for prints, but they were also the least likely to yield good results. Usually there was too much interference from other users and the movement of the handle often smeared any prints. Still, he didn't intend to contaminate this potential crime scene if he could help it.

Door handles were dicey for him. They were often metal and should hold a good residual, but something about the fact that they were on a threshold messed with the energy. If he got an impression at all, it was usually muddled. This time was no different. He got a flash of random images, carrying in groceries and other mundane activities, most of which were like looking at a flipbook showing an arm reaching for the door handle and turning it before cutting out, over and over. He let out his breath and reached in his pocket for the key, unlocked the door and stepped in, flicking on the light.

The hallway was empty and the silence within spoke of absence more firmly than any conjecture on Professor Weston's part. There was no smell of cooking, no scent of aftershave or cleaning products, not even the usual bodily aromas associated with a smallish space in current occupation. The distant sound of a TV was coming from below, in the flat downstairs.

"Hello?" Mari called out just to be on the safe side. "Anyone home?"

Jake bit his tongue to keep from shushing him. If he had been here officially, he would have called out the same way but since they weren't and there was still the outside chance that someone had made Phil Weston disappear, he didn't want to alert anyone to their presence. Not that it mattered, because he didn't think there was anyone to alert.

He moved farther down the short hall then turned left into the living room. The blinds were down, which was good. He looked left again into the open kitchen and dining nook. So far nothing struck him as out of place. The short hallway continued straight in front of him, ending in a second door. To the right was a third and final point of entry. He was guessing a bedroom hid behind one and a bathroom lay beyond the other.

Magazines were piled up on the coffee table in the lounge, a remote for the TV on top of them. Paper and electronics were not good for holding on to memories. There was a glass ashtray, though, that had a few stubbed out butts in it.

Jake moved into the living room then paused and looked at Mari. "I get kind of…vacant when I slip into a memory. You might not want to watch. I've been told it's creepy."

Mari shrugged. "Vacant men…story of my life!" He rolled his eyes then grinned at Jake and retrieved a pair of latex archival gloves from the pocket of his coat, snapping one of them onto his left hand emphatically. "Don't worry, I won't watch if it gives you performance anxiety. I can check the bedroom. I won't *physically* touch anything. Will that be okay?"

He pulled on the other glove and wriggled his fingers experimentally.

Jake nodded, his eyes on the gloves. He was glad Mari had come prepared. Unfortunately he was going to have to touch things with his bare hands, which might be problematic later if it turned out something sinister had gone down, but until he got a hit on something, they wouldn't know that anyway.

Mari headed off down the hallway and Jake took a breath and let it out. Time to get to work. He touched the edge of the glass ashtray with the back of his hand.

Immediately he was looking out of Phil Weston's eyes. The TV was playing some game show — two competitors and a loquacious host in a loud, yellow suit asking questions with multiple choice answers. Jake thought it seemed vaguely familiar. He memorized the contestants and the questions, planning to look it up later and see what night this was. Phil's arm moved in the periphery of his vision, rising to his mouth, taking a drag on the cigarette. His body was smaller, more compact, and he looked down from the TV to his chest then slipped a hand under the waistband of his boxers. The touch sent a satisfyingly heated rush to his groin.

Jake tried to struggle out of the memory but it was no use. They let him go when they felt like it and not a second before.

His left hand set the cigarette in the ashtray to burn while the other got busy rubbing and tugging. He picked up the remote and the game show was replaced abruptly on the TV by scenes of a naked guy getting fucked by a woman in a tight leather corset, wearing a strap-on dildo.

Jake was suddenly alone in the living room again. He swallowed and wiped his brow on his arm. It was not the first time he'd gotten sexual memories from a contact but this one had been pretty vivid, and Phil had a nice body.

* * * *

The doorway at the end of the hall was for the bathroom and Mari poked his head in there with some trepidation. He had enough experience of the toiletry habits of other single men to be wary but to his surprise, Phil was either a neat freak or he had a housekeeper. The bathroom was not spotless but neither was it the stuff of nightmares. The toilet seat was propped up and there was an ashtray on top of the cistern with a couple of dead fag ends littering it. He wrinkled his nose at the lingering tobacco scent in the air. Another collection of magazines occupied the top of the boxing that enclosed the pipework to one side — a man who liked to take his time in the smallest room, clearly. Mari investigated the magazines and chuckled softly. His expectations said cars or porn and they were a mixture of the two. An interesting selection though, about half and half straight porn and fetish. One had a guy on the cover in bondage, wearing a full gimp mask and shackles, even down to his cock and balls, which were locked in a wicked little cage.

"Naughty boy, Philip!" he murmured with a grin.

A brief check of the windowsill and cupboards revealed that his toothbrush and razor were still in situ. He'd not planned to go on a long trip. There was a back scrubber and flannel in the shower, some cheap brand of shower gel in a lurid plastic container and another bottle which, on closer inspection, turned out to be lubricant.

Mari raised his eyebrows at that and made a mental note of it.

The bedroom was slightly more disheveled, the duvet flung back as if its occupant had merely staggered out to the toilet and would be back at any moment. He shrugged out of his coat and hung it on the hook on the back of the door then began to nose through Phil's wardrobe. He still had his ears pricked for any sound from the other end of the hall that might indicate that Phil had unexpectedly returned from whatever mission it was that had dragged him away. Nothing disturbed him though and Mari could see no obvious signs that Professor Weston's brother had emptied his closet for a long trip.

When he returned to the bed, something else caught his eye — a glint of dull chrome by the headrail. He leaned in to examine it and discovered a set of metal handcuffs like the ones used in seventies TV cop shows, hanging from their connecting chain over the horizontal post.

"You *do* like a bit of kink, don't you?" he whispered, letting them drop back into place.

Mari was not clairvoyant like Jake but he had a vivid imagination and the thought of lying back and letting someone clip those manacles around his wrists as he sprawled on the bed sent a little shiver of pleasure through him, making his cock twitch. He opened the bedside drawer and whistled softly at the collection of sex toys. If Phil was strictly a ladies' man, he liked a serious dominatrix in his bed — there was an assortment of paddles and leather flails in the drawer, together with a black leather blindfold, three anal plugs of varying length and thickness — one glass and two silicone — and a long, black latex dildo.

He shut the drawer again with a little huff, the back of his neck suddenly hot, all too conscious that it had been a long time since anyone had made him feel the way that the sight of all that play equipment did.

"Damn it, Philip! You're a menace," he exhaled huskily, focusing his concentration more squarely on the hunt for Phil's laptop.

* * * *

Phil was not a hoarder, which made Jake's job faster, if not easier. He touched a few more small items in the living room but didn't get much from any of them. He wasn't sure if he was relieved or not. Moving on to the kitchen, he skimmed his fingers over the tabletop, the back of a chair, a ceramic jar. For a moment he heard wispy, feminine laughter, but nothing more. There was a block of kitchen knives and he steeled himself before carefully running his fingertips over each one.

His vision flickered and he caught a brief innocuous memory of chopping carrots. He breathed again once he'd gone through the silverware drawer. As far as he could tell, none of the cutlery had been used to stab anyone to death. It didn't bring him any closer to knowing what had happened to Phil, but he was relieved nonetheless. He had not been able to pick up a blade without tensing since he was thirteen years old and had been sucked into a memory of plunging a steak knife into a woman over and over at a restaurant. Turned out the married chef there had killed a waitress he had been fucking after she'd tried to blackmail him.

Trying to convince the cops of that had been fun.

His fingertips brushed a wooden cutting board and his vision shifted. His hands were planted on the work surface and his face was turned up to the ceiling, his hair caught in an uncomfortable grip. For a second Jake thought this was going to be it, the memory that mattered. Maybe he'd missed a knife in the drawer and someone actually *had* cut Phil's throat.

"Oh god, Phil, yes! Yesss! Like that, baby!"

Jake's body jerked rhythmically, the slap-slap-slap sound of flesh on flesh and the scent of sex rising around him. His breasts bounced and he rocked up onto this toes each time the cock drilled him from behind.

Jake gasped and wiped his hands on his pants back and forth several times, as if he could wipe the memory away. It was bad enough seeing someone get murdered. These private moments he got in the process made him feel like he was totally invading them, which was stupid, because he was the one that had just been invaded.

It was just part of the job. Jake already knew their missing man was seeing a married woman. He had hoped he could slip into one of Phil's memories and get a glimpse of her face. Given what he'd seen so far, he was betting he'd pick up something from Phil's bedroom, but half of him didn't want to go there.

When he pushed open the door with his shoulder he saw Mari was perched on the edge of the bed with Phil's open laptop on one knee. *Metal bed frame,* he thought, instinctively. *Great.*

"Find anything interesting?" he asked. Mari turned the machine to show him the cached log of an extensive chat feed.

"He's a busy boy," Mari told him, his tone somewhere between amused and impressed. "Got a massive online profile. Still downloading but he should keep me awake well past my bedtime. How're you doing?"

"I haven't gotten anything that says he's been murdered or kidnapped, so that's good. I'm willing to bet he ran off with someone's spouse. It's not like it's uncommon," Jake murmured. He noted the rumpled duvet, the handcuff hanging from the bed rail. Sighing, he reached out to touch it.

He should have taken a deeper breath. It felt like all the air was sucked out of his lungs as he was pulled into someone else's body. He was face down on the bed, bony wrists cuffed to the rail.

"Fuck me hard... Ooohh, fuck yeah!" Phil's throaty moans were harsh, panting hard. "Oh god, I'm gonna come." His cock and his prostate were both throbbing. A large palm slapped his ass and that nearly sent him over the edge. "Fuck yes!"

"Oh yeah, that's it, such a dirty boy. Come for me, sweetheart."

That was definitely not a dildo in his ass and that was not a woman's voice and oh, fucking Christ, did it feel good. A furry chest pressed to his back and that big hand gave him the reach around, stroking his aching cock as he pounded his ass. "Fuck,

Phil, you are amazing...so hot...gonna breed your tight little arse."

Jake yanked his hand away from the cuffs and shook it like he was trying to get the feeling back after cutting off his circulation. He sucked in a big gulp of air and stopped just short of groaning aloud. Mari had paused in whatever he was doing and was just looking at him, a little frown of concern between his tawny eyebrows.

"He was seeing a guy too," Jake breathed out. His voice was husky and his dick was half-hard and, stupidly, the only thing he could think was thank god he was only here with Mari and not another cop that would have given him no end of shit.

"Not just one, either," Mari told him, hiding his concern behind a mask of professionalism as he opened another screen on the laptop.

As well as his more arcane talent, Ilmarinen Gale was a self-confessed computer genius. He had been writing code since he was four years old and prided himself on the assertion that there was no system he could not infiltrate. Mind-surfing Phil's online existence would have been quick and easy but if foul play were involved in his disappearance, he figured that the police would want hard evidence, which meant a more conventional hack would be required.

The two flash drive plug-ins he used for this kind of job were write-protected. The first, the tiny one with the grinning pumpkin head sticker, was his backdoor entry key. It could get him into practically any machine, and Phil Weston's security was not as tight as it probably should have been given the nature of some of the sites he visited.

The second drive was his online hack profile and he used it mostly to replicate existing user accounts. That had burned him straight into Phil's business and private life and both were hyperactive.

Phil had a website through which he took bookings for his

decorating business, which tallied with the clean, neutral decor of his unpretentious apartment. He had been working at two addresses the week before he'd vanished and Mari had copied the contact details onto a third memory stick while Jake had been zoned out over the cuffs. Phil's most frequent Internet excursions were to porn sites, which was no great surprise, and webcam chat hosts, which might also offer up some clues as to who he was seeing.

Mari tapped at the keys, keeping half an eye on Jake. He'd never watched a true contact clairvoyant at work and felt a shiver of voyeuristic guilt doing so now but he told himself he was only looking out for his partner. Okay, so Jake wasn't currently a badge-carrying cop and he wasn't technically any sort of investigator at all, but there was no reason why they shouldn't be looking out for each other.

He'd felt his pulse quicken when Jake touched the handcuffs. It happened faster than he had been expecting but he knew at least that Jake was getting something powerful from those cuffs. Something as stimulating as the cam chat links he was already pulling from Phil's well-used laptop as fast as he could.

Jake was not wrong about his gift being freaky. He was leaning forward, gaze unfocused, lips parted, panting. Mari licked his lips because as vacant as his expression had been, there was also something quite hot about sharing a bed with a tasty-looking, breathless man. Whatever Jake had gotten from the cuffs, it seemed to back up some of the web memories Mari was tapping into on the laptop. It was certainly making him hard.

Mari's gift worked differently to Jake's—it was not so much activated by touch as by waves of communication. Brain waves worked in much the same way as radio waves. What mystics had once called 'ether' did not technically exist but what those early boffins—a word Mari loved and had adopted with the zeal of a born-again Brit—had discovered and measured was actually the vast, ceaseless pulsing of brainwaves and other energy fields transmitted by everything from microwave ovens to rocks. They could be harnessed and controlled, just like tuning a radio.

And once a subject grew adept at this tuning process, it was a short step toward using the human brain to tune into other modes of communication. That took time though, so he was copying the web browser history in order to explore it in more detail later. He also used his key program to access Phil's mobile account and copy his call data. That took a little longer because he needed to execute a remote hack into the phone company's database and do a trace back from there to the missing man's equally missing mobile.

While he was roaming Phil Weston's virtual life, he downloaded the man's bank and credit card details too. By the time he had all the data he needed on his memory stick, Jake was coming out of his trance and Mari was enviously trying to ignore the boner it had given him. It was one thing to eavesdrop on a stranger's calls but another thing entirely to hitch a ride in his actual sex life.

So it was that by the time Jake had gasped out his revelation, Mari was already aware that their missing man was not averse to taking it bareback and he didn't seem all that picky about who he took it from either.

He wasn't sure if he ought to be jealous or appalled.

My stars! I want to suck you off! he thought with a little sigh for the unrelieved bulge in his Jake's pants. His private contemplations on the nature of the beast behind Jake's fly buttons were franked by the swollen shape pressing into the straining material of his suit trousers and he had a moment of panic as he wondered if he'd spoken that last thought out loud. Mari snatched his gaze away from the prominence in his partner's pants and concentrated on retrieving his flash drives and shutting down the laptop. He stashed it back under the bed where he had found it and produced a tiny bottle of screen cleaner and a microfiber cloth from his coat pocket. "Show me what you've touched."

Chapter Five

They went through the flat like a pair of professional housebreakers. In the bedroom the only things that Jake had laid a hand on were the cuffs. He didn't want to touch the bedframe. He didn't want to touch *anything* else in Phil Weston's apartment. Every single thing he'd handled so far had thrust him straight into scenes from a porn movie. He tried to ignore the ache in his groin and focus on pointing out to Mari what else he had potentially fingerprinted, hoping he could cool down a bit.

They worked well together, Jake thought. Other than his initial warning call when they'd first entered the apartment, Mari was quiet and efficient. He didn't stare or get in Jake's way either, and he'd probably find more out about Phil than Jake had once he got a close look at his phone records and bank account info.

Jake locked up, Mari wiped the doorknob and by the time they were back on the steps outside, he was in sufficient control of his wayward cock. At least, he was as long as he didn't look at Mari. Every time he glanced at him, his brain insisted on conjuring up the way he looked in his skin-tight running pants, how the curve of that perfect ass made his mouth water. He caught himself looking at Mari's lips and thinking about what they would taste like. The prospect of going back to his apartment alone was not very appealing.

"Would you like to go get something to eat?" Jake asked him. He dreaded the thought of sitting in a restaurant but if he said good night here and now, Mari might consider the job done and that he didn't need to talk to him anymore.

"I…ah… I ought to go home," Mari said ruefully, though his cock was raging at him for the response. His long overcoat concealed the evidence of that well enough, thank goodness. He had been able to hide in it as he'd moved through the apartment, erasing all trace of their presence carefully before they'd left, but it still pulsed eagerly at the memory of how mouth-watering Jake had looked clinging to those cuffs. Whatever he'd seen—and he had not elaborated, nor had Mari pressed him for details—he did not want to talk about how it had made him feel, which was kind of a shame.

Going back to the house, making dinner for Mama and checking over the details he'd pulled from Phil's laptop seemed the sober and sensible option. He still owed his mother a proper apology for his behavior the previous day but at the same time, he was aware that it sounded like he was taking his revenge for Jake's snub in the canteen. Nothing could have been further from his mind.

"Besides, I thought you didn't care for restaurants," he pointed out, just so that this didn't look so one-sided.

I want to eat you, you delicious bastard! his treacherous brain added, and he forced his hands into his pockets, drawing his coat around himself more securely.

"I hate restaurants," Jake admitted. "But I'd put up with being in one if you would keep me company."

Mari looked at him with some surprise. "You're really that desperate not to be alone?"

He bit his tongue right away. That sounded so rude. At once he was shaking his head, apologizing, trying to explain then wondering why he even felt he had to. All he knew was, for whatever reason, he didn't want Jake to think he was a total prick.

Before Mari got more than a handful of stammered words out, Jake turned toward him and Mari put a hand up in defense, not sure if the man was angry, or hurt, or what he was feeling. Then his hand was on Jake's chest in the open neck of his jacket and Jake's mouth was on his and his brain simply stopped working as he reveled in the warmth of the man's lips pressing hungrily against his own. He could feel how fast Jake's heart was beating against the palm of his hand and the impulse that said he shouldn't encourage this lasted no more than seconds. He brought his other hand up and slid it inside Jake's coat, then he was holding him tightly and kissing him back, hard enough that that he thought one of them might suffocate.

They both let go at the same time and Mari took a step back, breathing raggedly, his eyes wide, lips tingling fiercely. When he could breathe normally again, he murmured, "We-ell! That was…unexpected."

"No, it wasn't," Jake contradicted him. "I totally planned to do that." He said it very seriously, then his lips twitched into a grin. A flush of heat and tenderness suffused Mari's pounding heart at the sight. "So, do you *really* need to go home?"

"It's complicated. Damn…that sounds like a lame excuse," Mari said, crestfallen. He stopped and checked his watch. "I guess I don't *have* to go straight back. I need to make a call, though, before we eat. Is that okay?"

Jake caught his hand before he could lower it and brought it up to his lips, brushing a kiss across his knuckles in an oddly chivalrous, old-fashioned gesture. That too did strange things to his insides.

"It's okay. If you have to go, you have to. I don't want you to stress over it, really. As long as you agree to go out with me another night?"

Mari's fingers tightened around his for a moment. He did not want to let go. He wanted to drag Jake Chivis back into the house and… *Stop!* Really, really his thoughts did not need to go there now.

"Jake Chivis, you are…you are an absolute gentleman, and I sincerely, honestly *do* want to go out with you," he said earnestly. "If… Fuck…look, um… Do you want to come back to mine?"

As soon as the words were out of his mouth, he wondered

why he had said them and how he was going to explain the situation to Mama. Not that she would react badly to him having someone over — he knew she was cool with that, so long as he was happy, but this was sudden, even by his standards.

Jake was a little perplexed at Mari's demeanor but he was still thinking that even if they did nothing more than sit in front of the TV together, it was miles better than going home alone. He reminded himself sternly that he hadn't wanted to get involved with a coworker anyway, but he had known when he'd first started watching for Mari Gale in the park that he was just fooling himself. He wanted to know Mari a lot better, in every way.

"Sure," Jake chuckled softly. "I'll try not to touch anything."

"I think that might look a little odd," Mari replied with a husky laugh. "Um…what happens when you touch *people*? I don't think you mentioned that."

He suddenly looked rather startled, as if all manner of ideas were just beginning to occur to him. Jake managed not to sigh. So far Mari had been pretty cool with knowing what he could do, but he was starting to really get it now. He did his best to keep his smile in place but he had a feeling it didn't quite reach his eyes.

"I sometimes get impressions from people, and sometimes not. I *try* not to look. If I do, though, usually it's when I first meet them."

Mari worried his lips for a moment. At last he drew a sharp breath.

"My mother…she is *very* ill. She hides it well, but —" He took another quick breath. "Her doctors don't seem very optimistic. I've tried to spend as much time as I can with her before…"

He closed his mouth and looked away, a small tremor running through him, though his eyes remained clear and bright. There was some tension in the line of his mouth. He

71

turned his head to look back at Jake. "She won't thank you for asking about it, so please don't."

It took Jake a second to figure out why Mari was telling him this now and he put it together that the reason Mari wanted to get home so fast was because he lived with his mother, his very ill mother. And that he'd invited him back to his place, where he would meet her. Not that there was anything wrong with that, but he had still harbored some vague ideas in the back of his head that were decidedly more the type they would need to be alone for.

He cleared his throat softly. "Okay, I won't mention anything about it."

Mari nodded, a look of gratitude in his eyes, and some small measure of relief.

"Will you hold me for a moment? Please?" he asked, very quietly. "It's been so long since I last had a man's arms around me."

Jake blinked slowly, wondering if he would have made a request like that if their situations were reversed and knowing he wouldn't have. Sometimes a person's bravery came through in subtle ways that weren't so easily cataloged or confined by what was considered macho. Without a word he slipped his arms around Mari and pulled him closer. It should have been awkward because Mari was just that little bit taller, but it wasn't at all. He pulled him in and the way Mari folded against him was like the way pieces of a puzzle fitted together, they just clicked right in place.

Mari wrapped his arms around him and rested his cheek against Jake's, nuzzling softly at his ear and the side of his neck. He pressed a little tighter up to the rest of Jake's body and Jake felt the shared warmth spill through him, and Mari's lips moving against his cheek as he whispered, "I think I may need to kiss you again, you are the sweetest soul. I think I could spend all night kissing you, Jake Chivis."

He turned his head before Jake could say anything then their lips were touching again, briefly and tentatively, then more urgently. As Jake's lips parted, Mari's tongue flickered between them and the kiss deepened and grew more heated.

Jake slid his hands around Mari's waist, gliding them down his backside and he wished there weren't quite so many layers between them and Mari's skin. Their tongues found each other again, questing back and forth and Jake caressed lower so he could wriggle his fingers inside Mari's voluminous coat and squeeze the sexy little ass he had been fantasizing about, for weeks, if he was honest. Okay, this was ridiculous, he wanted to strip the clothes right off him and devour him here on the street. He broke the kiss, panting slightly.

"Unless you want me to pull you back into Weston's apartment, I think we have to go."

Mari managed a wicked little chuckle though he was equally breathless.

"Mmmmh...you are very naughty, Mr. Chivis. I rather like that. And you're still very excited too, aren't you?" He slid one hand boldly up Jake's inside leg and gave him a little squeeze that almost had him seeing stars. So much for Mari being flustered. "I'm concerned that we might leave incriminating evidence if we actually screw in his bed though. That would have the forensics boys and girls scratching their heads for days."

Jake gaped at him like he was crazy but his lust-addled wits were not prepared to argue. He pulled the key from his pocket decisively.

"Don't worry, we won't go any farther than the front door."

Mari grinned at him, delight evident on his face, like a child who'd just learned the secret of a magic trick. As the door into the quiet hallway opened, he pushed Jake through and it was clicking shut behind them and he was shoving Jake up against the wall right there, tugging at his jacket and shirt, hungry to get them off him, as if he were ripping the wrapping paper off a special present.

"You are *so* my type," he purred enthusiastically,

admiring the hard lines of Jake's exposed chest and belly through the dusting of dark curls. "I knew it the minute you looked back that day in the park. I was kind of hoping that you'd chase me into the undergrowth that morning, even if it was bloody well tipping down."

Jake grabbed his hands, pulling them out to the sides and dragging him closer at the same time. He fastened his lips back on Mari's, kissing him the way he had wanted to outside, without any restraint. He sucked his bottom lip, then nipped it and kissed him hard, pushing his tongue past his teeth and tasting him deep. Mari made a small yielding sound and Jake swallowed it, pressing their tongues together over and over. When he broke off, it was only to switch their position, turning and pushing Mari up against the wall, letting go of his hands so that he could get his coat and shirt off.

"You are fucking beautiful," he murmured huskily, lips brushing at the side of his throat, pushing the heavy coat down Mari's arms and struggling to shuck his shirt at the same time.

Mari returned the favor by yanking Jake's shirt and jacket sleeves down off his sculpted arms almost violently. Their upper garments dropped to the floor near simultaneously and Mari attacked Jake's belt buckle with a determined smile, tugging it undone, then popping his fly button and yanking down the zipper with a disturbing lack of caution. His hand eased inside and he cupped Jake's jersey-draped cock and balls in those elegant fingers, pale eyes widening in astonishment.

"Mmmhhh...you didn't tell me you were armed and dangerous, Detective!" he crooned, lowering his head to lick and bite Jake's exposed nipples.

Jake tried to laugh but it came out more of a wheeze. It was difficult to appreciate humor when the palm of Mari's hand was pressing his cockhead in a way that sent a surge of lust down to his groin. The graze of Mari's teeth on the stiff bud of his hypersensitive nipple was not helping his concentration any either. He was just as eager to get Mari's pants open but every time he tried, Mari moved fractionally.

"Mmhh...such a hot, ripped bod, you are a fucking wet dream." Mari purred with delight, hooking a finger under the elastic waist of Jake's boxer briefs and pulling the front of the garment down deftly under his balls so his erection was able to stand to attention at last. Mari curled his fingers around the solid shaft of silken muscle and began to work the rippled flesh up and down in firm, steady strokes as he came back up to cover Jake's mouth with his own again, kissing him enthusiastically.

Definitely not shy, then!

Jake settled his hands on Mari's shoulders, sliding them up and down his arms in gentle caresses, almost mimicking the slow glide of Mari's hand on his dick. He pressed in closer, keeping him pinned up against the wall, flexing his hips to push his cock into the curl of Mari's fingers. At last his hands were busy enough that Jake could move his own to Mari's chest, brushing his thumbs over his nipples, pinching them and rolling them between thumb and forefinger, drawing a stifled whine from his lover's mouth as they kissed.

Mari was almost painfully hard, fiercely aroused by the hard, masculine body rubbing up against his. He rolled back the silken-soft folds of Jake's foreskin so that he was able to caress his leaking slit with the pad of his thumb. The wetness made his pumping hand slick and it glided easily up and down from tip to root, over and over. With the other hand, he stroked Jake's naked back and ran his fingertips over what felt like a tracery of scars, fanning out in a roughly circular shape on Jake's warm, smooth, dark-golden skin.

He was so distracted by this mystery that it was a shock when one big, warm hand slid between his legs, cupping his balls gently and palming his cock behind his zipper. Jake's other hand pinched and released his nipple, making him moan at the burn in his chest, then his fingers pushed into Mari's hair at the nape of his neck.

"You have me so turned on I can't think," Jake whispered huskily into his mouth. "I wanna taste you, but I'm aching to have your mouth on me."

His fingers moved over the front of Mari's pants as he spoke, stroking him up and down through the material. Mari grew harder just for his words, the touch was exquisite agony.

"I can try and wait for you...but no promises," Mari growled back hungrily. "Get me free first, though. This... fabulous as it is, it's getting uncomfortable."

His mouth watered at the thought of tasting that beautiful big cock. Ever since the first time he'd checked Jake out, striding through the park in his comfortable sweats, he'd harbored secret fantasies about pulling them down and giving him the blow job of his life. It felt unreal to be standing here, pinned to the wall in the hallway of a stranger's flat by the object of his desires, with that delicious dick in his hand, hearing Jake tell him how eager he was to be sucked and worshiped the way Mari adored him in his dreams.

He shuddered with the wave of pure need it sent through his semi-clad, fully roused body. The frisson he'd experienced checking out Phil's sex toys was nothing compared to this.

Jake popped the tab on Mari's pants and lowered the zipper one-handed, the other still embedded in his hair, gripping firmly and pulling his head back. Jake kissed his neck and pushed his hand inside Mari's underwear, curling his fingers around his shaft. Mari made a breathless sound that was half groan half gasp, his knees turning to water at the way Jake touched him. He swallowed hard and caught his breath when Jake broke the kiss to drop between his feet, dragging his pants and underwear to his thighs as he went. Jake didn't tease him, they were both too hot for that, he went right in for the kill. He nosed into the crease where Mari's hip met his abdomen then brushed over the neat, close-trimmed pubes around his cock. He did not linger over this gentle foreplay. Soon he was licking his way up Mari's length and closing his mouth over the head.

"Ohhh…where *are* you going, Jake Chivis?" Mari chuckled, but the words sounded too sluggish in his mouth. He kept his gaze fixed on the wall behind Jake's head because he felt as if he might just keel over if he looked down at his handsome companion.

This went against everything he had promised himself when he left Barcelona. No, he would not fall straight into bed with the first guy who was nice to him. Certainly he would *never* again date a colleague. Though in his favor, at least Jake wasn't married.

At least, as far as he *knew*, Jake wasn't married.

Oh, Ilmarinen Gale, you idiot! his internal voice whispered wearily.

He pushed his fingers roughly through the dark thatch of Jake's hair and tried to ignore everything else as that hot, wet mouth swallowed him and suddenly *nothing* else mattered to him at all.

Jake caressed Mari's thighs and moaned as he swallowed Mari's cock deeper. His lips were clamped tightly around the shaft and he gulped when the head pushed into his throat, sucking hard as he drew back. Little tremors shook Mari's thighs as Jake nodded low to pull hard on him and moved his hands to cup the curves of Mari's ass cheeks.

A little whine escaped Mari's throat as his hips began to thrust almost of their own volition. His fingers tightened in Jake's thick, dark curls and he twisted and squirmed under the caress of his warm, strong hands, wanting this so much, yet somehow feeling tense and anxious too.

"Mmmnnnnhhh…damn it, Chivis! I'm…ohhhh… Fuck… gonna come. Please!"

Jake's reaction to his plea was to speed up and dig his fingers into Mari's ass, gripping him tight. Mari cried out again as his balls tried to crawl back up into his abdomen at the moment of violent release.

"Ohhhhh!" Mari stuffed one fist into his mouth, remembering too late that they were trying to be quiet. "*Mmmffffffffuuuhhhhhh!*"

Jake swallowed each time a spurt hit his tongue, laving the underside of Mari's pulsing glans. He was breathing hard through his nose, his every exhalation fanning over Mari's groin and belly.

He felt one hand release his hip and as the last little tremors were quaking through him, he looked down to watch Jake stroke his own cock, three or four beats at the most, and his hot cum filled his palm. Jake finally sat back on his haunches, letting Mari's wet cock slip from his lips and looking up at him with eyes half closed and a smile on his face.

Mari slithered to a crouch with his back still pressed against the wall once the quakes began to subside. In this position it was less likely he'd end up sprawled on the floor in an undignified heap and he was also able to look Jake in the eye. He took Jake's sticky hand in one of his own and licked his palm shamelessly.

"You could have left me some," he said mischievously.

"Are you kidding? Like I could wait." Jake chuckled and leaned in to nuzzle behind Mari's ear, breathing him in and watching him lick the cum from his fingers. "Jesus, you are too fucking sexy."

Mari sucked one of his fingers lazily. As the tip of it popped out of his mouth, he murmured, "Too fucking sexy for what?" He craned forward and touched salty lips to Jake's, kissing him softly, tasting his own briny flavor on his sweet, warm mouth.

"I knew you had to have another talent," Mari whispered as their lips parted. He felt a glow of warmth inside that had nothing to do with the fabulous blow job and everything to do with that gorgeous smile on his companion's face.

Jake laughed and shook his head.

"Come on, let's get out of here. For real this time," he said, straightening and pulling Mari back up as well. Mari pouted at him but his lips couldn't check the little smile that wanted out. As Jake turned to pick up his clothes, he could suddenly see that the ridges and lines that he had imagined were scars actually formed an intricate tattoo which covered most of his naked back. It took the form of a rough circle, kind of like a dream catcher, hung with beads and feathers, but minus the spiderweb. The inside of the circle was quartered, each segment infilled with different colors. He blinked at it, half conscious of having seen something like it before, but not sure where. To cover himself, he patted Jake's nicely sculpted backside before the man pulled his pants back up and murmured, "Impressive!"

The grin that snuck across Jake's face this time was cockier than the other sly smirks he'd seen thus far.

"My mouth is talented and my ass is impressive. Keep going like that and you're going to give me a big ego or something."

Mari tugged his suit pants up together with his skimpy briefs, tucking himself in tidily and bending to snare his shirt from the tangle of clothing on the floor.

"Mmmm, *something* anyway." He chuckled, winking at Jake as he wriggled into it. "I'll let you know how big when you let me massage it, perhaps."

Greedy, much! his conscience rebuked him, but he ignored it, too blissed out and content to feel guilty for that.

Jake was busy righting his own clothing and debating if he should wash his hands. Mari had actually cleaned him off pretty well but his palm was still sticky. It had been monumentally stupid to come back in here and leave possible trace evidence behind but he hadn't exactly been thinking with the head on his shoulders at the time. He settled on snagging a few tissues from the box on the hall table and wiping at the stickiness, then shoving them in his pocket. He could wash up better later.

Mari gave everything a last wipe down with his screen cleaner, then they were back out on the street. They had walked a couple of hundred yards before Jake came down enough from the lovely feeling of post-orgasmic bliss to wonder if the invitation to come home with him was still in place now that they had gotten semi-naked together.

Mari flashed him that sidelong smile again and said, "You still hungry? Bet you any money we'll have to walk half a mile before we find a cab round here."

"Tasty as you are, I could use a bite to eat," Jake admitted.

Mari retrieved his phone from inside his many pocketed overcoat. His fingers danced across the touchscreen. "What do you fancy? It might be easier to eat locally if you've worked up an appetite. I'll call home on the way."

He was businesslike again now that they were on the move. Apart from the slight tousle of his normally sleek blond hair and the flush that was still on his smooth, usually pale cheeks, he might have just stepped out of the office.

"Do you like Chinese? Or Thai?" Jake asked, thinking he might get around the problem of touching silverware with chopsticks, or cheap plastic utensils.

"Lived in Hong Kong and Kuala Lumpur for seven years, what do *you* think?" Mari chuckled. "But I'm just as easy with pizza, I'll leave it up to you. There's a Pizza Express less than a mile away and at least three Indians, and ooh... Cantonese, now that's tempting."

He kept the phone in his hand as they walked, his stride long and brisk, using the device to check their route from time to time.

"Sure, Cantonese sounds good." He noticed again that Mari used a lot of words to say what probably could have been said in about half as many, but he was getting used to it. Actually, it was nice that he didn't have to try to keep up. He could just say what was on his mind and Mari sort of filled in the rest.

Mari rang his mother once he was sure where they were going, his voice soft, just on the edge of audible. Jake could hear the reassurance in his tone as he told her he was okay and was going to get dinner in town and did she want him to bring anything. He asked her three times if she was sure and, at least twice, more softly, told her that he loved her. He was quiet once he was off the phone, possibly the quietest he had been since the taxi.

Jake wondered if his thoughts about how chatty Mari was had somehow transmitted into the atmosphere and colluded to shut him up, but he had a feeling it was more to do with the phone call. After half a block or so, Jake slipped his arm around Mari's waist, offering just that bit of comfort. To his relief, the man did not push him away and they remained in that comfortable proximity until they reached the restaurant.

Chapter Six

Mari woke up with a slightly fuzzy head, about an hour later than he would normally rise. For a moment he struggled to reach full awareness but when he did it was with a rush of anxiety. Just as she had promised, Mama had not stayed up, but there had been a little note waiting for him on the shelf in the hall, jotted in her erratic hand on the phone pad, hoping that he'd had a pleasant evening and that the university was not working him too hard. He felt guilty about that too. He hadn't told her he was having dinner with a man, and she hadn't asked, knowing that sometimes when there was a deadline he worked until late and called out for a takeaway. Now it felt as if he had started keeping secrets from her.

He struggled out of bed, completed his ablutions in the compact en-suite and dressed before making his way down to the kitchen in his running gear. He still had a slight headache and was hoping stretching his legs would help, and if he met Jake in the park they could talk about the information he'd extracted from the memory sticks last night once he'd returned home.

Hard work was not entirely to blame for his creeping headache—a bottle of wine and a couple of beers had accompanied dinner, the second to keep Jake talking because Mari hadn't been ready to go home alone and sensed that Jake hadn't wanted to either. Mari suspected that Jake drank out of a need to quell his own social anxiety rather than a liking for beer. Even so, it had not been an uncomfortable meal. The alcohol had loosened Jake's tongue and he'd gradually told Mari a little about his home life and why he'd come to England, which partly revolved around the Program but was mostly to do with wanting a 'new start'.

Even after the wine and the beer, Mari could read between the sparse lines of information Jake had given him. He had worked out that the job Jake had been doing in Detroit—police work that he said he didn't want to bore Mari with but which Mari suspected was not satisfying Jake in some way that he didn't really want to talk about—was not the only reason Jake had wanted that fresh start thousands of miles from his old life. It was all mostly guess work though, and Jake had offered him barely more than isolated fragments.

One of the more interesting things Jake told him was that he was Native American, at least on his father's side. As a child, Mari had absorbed a raft of nineteen-fifties, black and white American TV programs on Hong Kong cable and still thought of the elegant, swarthy, longhaired natives as Red Indians, no matter how un-PC that might be or how dark a look it earned him. It explained his exotic appearance and Mari approved entirely. Much of the conversation had revolved around their ancestors—Jake's paternal Bodewadmi tribal great-grandfather and his own Finnish great-grandmama, Amelia.

He had established, quite firmly, that Jake was not married in any way shape or form, which was one weight off his mind. More than that he'd seemed reluctant to say, beyond the fact that he had been seeing someone in Detroit but it hadn't worked out.

This too, he suspected, if not a lie, was a half-truth at the very least but he had not pushed it. That in turn would have meant having to admit to the embarrassment of his two and a half year affair with Tomas and he did not want to talk about that either.

Mari drank two full tumblers of cold water and felt a little better for that, then he texted Jake and told him he was heading for the park if it wasn't too late to meet him there. A minute later Jake messaged him back to say that he'd been considering not going this morning but since Mari was running, he would give it his best shot.

So, Jake was feeling the worse for wear too, Mari thought. That at least was a small triumph. He wouldn't have to suffer his hangover alone.

When Jake turned up at the park, Mari almost felt sorry for dragging him out of bed. He looked tired and disheveled, though in an entirely sexy way. It took a great strength of will not to dwell on the idea of what it would be like waking up in bed next to him looking like that.

"So, there are no foolproof magical hangover cures in Re — Err...Native American culture either. How disappointing." Mari winked at him to show he was joking. "Are you going to survive this or should we just walk?"

Jake snorted. "Walking is for pussies. C'mon, you'll feel better once we get going."

They got going, taking up a slower pace to start out, which made it easier to talk. "Did you find anything out from the data you took?" Jake asked.

"Like you would not believe," Mari told him with a little chuckle. "The horny bastard kept me awake till about half three. It took over two hours to work my way through his phone and text log alone. Even the way I do it, which is a damned sight quicker than hacking. He lives on his fucking phone, and by that measure I figure he either had it stolen or something happened to his hands around about last Friday night or Saturday morning because his calls stop dead then.

"He wasn't disconnected. His account is still live, he just hasn't used it since Friday afternoon late on. He has most of his billing on direct debits. The last time he withdrew cash was Friday morning when he took out fifty pounds at the Lloyds ATM at Berwick Street just after eight-thirty.

"He has been talking dirty with three different people on the phone in the space of last week alone," Mari told him, pausing for breath.

Jake took advantage of the lull to ask, "Wait...you know the call content? How do you hack that?"

"Professor Weston didn't tell you what my gift is, did he?" Mari looked surprised.

"He just said he knew someone who could look into his online history. He didn't say you could tap the phones and break into his bank account," Jake grumbled. "That's just slightly illegal, you know."

"I didn't tap his phone. That's not how it works, Chivis," Mari huffed impatiently because his flow had been interrupted. "The calls were already made. I just… I suppose I kind of retrieve them…only with my mind, a bit like you see things through touch, right? I can tap into tech. I just need the frequency it went out on. The information stays out there like files on a hard drive. I just have to find them and…play them, I guess."

Jake took two more loping steps then came to a stop, his feet slapping the ground in that jarring way that happened when you didn't slow down first. Mari took a second or two longer to pull himself up and was more graceful about it, turning to look at him questioningly.

"I told you the things I could do yesterday, and you didn't think to tell me you can hack into databases with your mind?"

"Well…no," Mari said, wondering if they were about to have another argument.

Jake didn't look mad, exactly. Incredulous was probably the right word for that expression. Then he shook his head and started running again. Mari paced him, looking at him sidelong. He was just about to ask if he was angry when he saw the hint of a grin curl Jake's lips.

After a little while Jake said, "Let's go talk to Weston first thing. Tell him what we found. See if he can tell us anything else he neglected to mention about his brother."

The run had done its work to invigorate them, and when he and Jake rolled back into the offices at Malet Place an hour or so later, Mari at least was feeling more human and Jake looked his handsome self again. After stopping in at the office, he made his excuses to a mildly incredulous

Professor Karden and promised to make up the time he'd lose before taking the elevator back down to Weston's offices. Jake was already there when he tapped on the door and the professor called him in.

He slid into the seat next to his co-conspirator and leaned back, letting one leg gently brush against Jake's, enjoying the warmth of his powerful thigh. The professor was looking at him curiously, and prompted him as soon as he was in his seat.

"Mr. Chivis tells me that you both found information last night."

"Did he also tell you that it doesn't look good?" Mari responded seriously. He hated to be the bearer of bad tidings but at the same time, the look on Weston's face said he was half expecting something terrible. "You knew he might be in trouble even before you spoke to us, didn't you?"

"Of course I did. Phil might be a bit wild but he's not unreliable. To disappear with no word like this..." He shook his head. "Did you find out who the woman was that he was seeing? I'm convinced she has something to do with it."

Mari looked at Jake quickly, gauging that his reluctant accomplice had not said anything yet about their findings. He drew a short, rapid breath then let it go in a little huff.

"Professor, I think it might be more complicated than that. Yes, he was seeing a woman. His call log has her name down as Amber, nothing more, but I don't think it's her real name. He called her Helen, or Ellen possibly, during their most recent call. She wanted him to come and see her. He told her it was difficult and the inference was that her husband might find out. She wasn't his only assignation, however." He moved his gaze to Jake's quiet, concerned, handsome features as he spoke, wondering just how much they could tell Weston without him freaking out.

"Professor, your brother was seeing several people, not just the woman he told you about," Jake said, not

86

mincing words. "I can confirm what Mari discovered. I got impressions from items in his apartment that told me he was seeing at least one woman *and* a man. Either of them could possibly know where Phil is."

Weston's eyes widened and he shook his head automatically. "There must be some mistake. Phil has been…experimental, in the past but he's never given any recent hint that he might be that way inclined."

Mari chewed on his lips, wary now. Weston knew that he had been in relationships with men and he'd never given Mari any impression that he disapproved, but the professor seemed uncomfortable with the idea of it so close to home.

"Maybe he didn't know how to tell you," he suggested. "It's no mistake, though, I spent a lot of time last night on his Internet history, and trust me, he did not engage in any of the…" Mari glanced down at his phone and checked his notes before proceeding. "*Thirty-four* separate cam chat sessions in the last three weeks, all reluctantly, all of them with men. There was nothing ambiguous about it, Professor Weston. I'm sorry but your brother just can't stop thinking about cock. And when he's not thinking about it, he's checking it out and letting other guys check out his. I don't think that it went further with most of them. They were one-time things, only one guy" — he looked at his notes again — "sorry, no, *two* were repeat performances but I don't have given names for either of them, only chat handles. Is that what they call it, when you pick a ridiculous name to hide behind?"

He lifted his head to look inquiringly at Jake, only to find that both men were staring at him like he'd grown a second nose.

Weston's cheeks had bright high spots of color on them and Mari didn't think it was from embarrassment. He wasn't particularly empathic but he could tell when someone was about to blow up.

"That. Is. Absurd. I'm sure you must have pulled that information from somewhere other than…"

"No, he didn't." Jake cut across the tirade that was gaining steam. "You asked us to look at this, Professor. We only did what you asked of us. Mari didn't make a mistake, and neither did I. I really don't care if you can't handle the idea that your brother's bisexual. You asked us to find out what we could, and we did that. It's your choice if you want us to try and find him."

"I didn't ask you to go trawling for filth like a pair of sleazy tabloid hacks!" Weston raged back, visibly distressed now and angry too. "My brother is a good man. Yes, he has a strong libido, but he is not... The picture you are painting is scandalous and slanderous and simply wrong! That's not the Phil I know. There has to be a mistake, maybe it was someone else..." He trailed off, looking personally wounded.

"Professor Weston, I'm sorry," Mari told him, keeping his voice very calm and sincere, as if he were trying to persuade a jumper down from a ledge. "I know this is probably a shock, but you need to be aware that if we do find him, there is every chance that he won't be alive. His phone has been inactive for nearly five days. The GPS was turned off on Friday afternoon so I don't know where he went after he stopped at the bank that morning. The last appointment in his work calendar was during the week before he went missing. We could maybe go and talk to the client. Or the police could?"

"Haven't you done enough damage to his reputation already?" Weston growled.

"Unfair," Mari challenged, shaking his head at once. His tone was stern when he continued. "We have only spoken to you about what we learned. And, like Jake said, we only went into that place on your request. Strictly speaking, this is an abuse of your authority as a team leader. We could report it, but we're both aware that to do so would only cause problems for all three of us. Please calm down. This is not helping Phil, or you."

Jake refrained from pinching the bridge of his nose like he wanted to. He hated this, hated that it always happened this way. They wanted an answer and so they asked a 'psychic' to find out for them, and when they didn't hear what they wanted, they freaked out and called it all a mistake. There were few things that pissed him off more. Showing how frustrated he was with this whole conversation would not help either.

What he really wished he could do was to take the memories he had gotten from Phil Weston's apartment and download them into his big brother's head so he would know what it was like. How it was to be just minding your own business then suddenly you were someone else for a few seconds, or a few minutes, and you had no control over what you saw or what was done to you. People often thought it would be so great if they could touch something and know who it belonged to and what they had for lunch that day and how they liked to be handcuffed to the bed and fucked hard. They had no idea it was less of a voyeuristic kick and more an invasion of your mind.

Jake took the key to Phil's apartment out of his pocket and placed it on the desk rather than slapping it down as impulse dictated he should.

"If you didn't believe we could do the things you wanted us to do, why did you even persuade us?" Jake asked, far more calmly than he felt. "Why are you even running this Program if you don't think the information we can get, and the means we get it by, are real?"

Weston opened his mouth but he got only as far as snarling, "You arrogant whelp, I *am* the bloody Program!"

Mari interrupted him more evenly. "Strictly speaking, no. You inherited the paperwork, that's all." He turned his head to look at Jake. "He *does* believe we can do it. In his heart he even knows that we're telling him the truth, he just doesn't want to *see* it. You know that too, I can see it in your face." A little sigh escaped him as he swung back around toward the irate professor, whose flushed features were turning paler as the weight of what he had unearthed began to sink in. "Tony, if you really want the proof, you only have to hypnotize me the way you did the last time we tested this. You believed what I told you under hypnosis, didn't you?"

Weston closed his eyes, looking suddenly beaten. He nodded unhappily.

"Do you want us to continue with the investigation or would you like to hire a P.I. now?" Jake asked.

After a long silence Weston said, "No. I want to know what happened to Phil, where he is. I don't think a private investigator would be faster than the two of you. In fact it would probably take considerably more time for them to cover the amount of dust you've already swept from under his carpet. If you can find him, I would be very grateful."

* * * *

Mari was tied up with his actual job for most of the following day. Professor Karden didn't exactly reprimand him about the amount of time he spent sloping off to see Weston but he made a point of stressing their deadline, which was the next best thing, and Mari dutifully knuckled down. He was still replaying in his head much of what they had found at the apartment the other night though, and the emotional confrontation with Professor Weston, even as he tapped away at his keyboard, watching the latest project take shape.

Also in his mind, and no less of a presence, was the memory of what had happened between himself and Jake Chivis at that empty flat. His body still burned with the echoes of their frantic liaison. Too brief to think of even as sex, it had still been a balm to his lonely soul. The speed with which they had slammed into each other was almost frightening though. Mari had promised himself so ardently that he would not fall head over heels for anyone the way that he had fallen for Tomas. The pain of that was fresh in his heart even now. For a little while, he had allowed himself to believe that Tomas Arregui was the love of his life, the one man who would be able to make him happy.

And now, damn it all, he was doing the same thing with Chivis, putting his sexy detective up there on a pedestal to be toppled just as cruelly once Mari discovered his flaw. Because there had to be one, he knew it. He just hadn't been around Jake long enough yet to find out what it was.

A popup box on his monitor warned him that if he continued with the process he had just initiated, his fingers flying, out of sync with his brain, he would delete vital records. Did he want to proceed?

Now there was the question. Did he?

Mari stopped typing and stared at the screen darkly for a moment then he clicked 'Cancel' and put his head in his hands.

Jake texted him at about a quarter to six, asking if he wanted to go for something to eat. Mari desperately did but he messaged back saying that he needed to finish the project he was working on or he would get shit from Karden. It was only half a lie — if the work he'd slacked off yesterday didn't get finished by the end of the week then he *would* get shit from Karden, but it was not like it would be the first time.

It was hard to tell by the medium of SMS whether Jake was disappointed but when he messaged back, it was to ask Mari to send him the details of Phil Weston's last job so that he could check it out over the weekend. He made no allusion to Mari blowing him out, so perhaps it wasn't such a big deal for him after all. Maybe he got to suck off random guys in strangers' flats all the time and it meant nothing more to him than that. Mari swore softly under his breath and Cal looked at him sidelong from the next desk.

"Everything okay?"

"Peachy!" Mari said.

* * * *

Jake stared at the text box with the address Mari had sent him, his thumb absently stroking the side of the phone as he debated sending him another message with something more personal. Something maybe like, 'When can I see you again?' or 'I had a really good time the other night, sucking your cock'. He'd already asked him to dinner though and had been shot down. If he asked again, he wasn't sure if that would seem pushy or just determined.

A small pang reminded him that he hadn't wanted to get involved with anyone anyway, but he'd already obliterated those good intentions when he'd pressed Mari against the wall and blown him until he nearly screamed, so he saw no reason to try to put the genie back in the bottle. But maybe Mari did. Maybe it had been just a spur of the moment thing for him and he'd rather forget about it. Or maybe he'd changed his mind since he'd gotten to know him a little better and had decided that hooking up with a lover who had the potential to pick up his car keys one day and know he'd been fucking some other guy was just too freaky.

Jake put his phone back in his pocket without sending a text. He wasn't quite willing to just give up yet, but if Mari needed some space, he wasn't going to crowd him.

* * * *

Saturday morning was clear and cool but a hint of dampness in the air promised rain later. *More rain. Fantastic!* That matched Jake's mood perfectly. He took the Tube north toward Hampstead Heath, midmorning, not wanting to arrive too early, but wanting to get this over with and determine whether Phil's last clients, the Millers, knew anything about his whereabouts, or could be crossed off the list.

Hampstead was rather more genteel than he was used to in the heart of the city — very leafy and pleasant in the early-winter sunshine. After the last few days of unremitting English drizzle, it was good to be dry and relatively warm

- something he was so grateful for that he walked past his turning in his eagerness to make headway with the case, and had to backtrack from Rosslyn Hill in search of the address. The road was set back from the high street with a row of four-story terraced buildings on one side that would have been called brownstones back home but as he already knew, that raised eyebrows when he used it here. On the other side of the road, the houses were more modest semis and it was one of these that he found himself knocking on the door of, having finally located the number he was searching for.

It took a couple of knocks before he heard the sound of someone rummaging around in the hallway and the front door with its peeling green paint was finally unlocked and yanked open. A disheveled-looking fellow of middling years squinted into the daylight as if it was the first time he had seen it for a while. He looked at Jake like he was an alien.

"You sellin' somethin'? We're not interested." He made to shut the door again.

"I'm not selling anything," Jake said quickly. "I wanted to speak to you about Mr. Phil Weston, I understand he did some work for you?"

The man made a rude noise. "That cunt! He was *supposed* to do some fucking work for us, you mean. Never showed up, did he? Sent some bloke round on his behalf though. The bastard's still here if you want to talk to him. I've never seen anyone make such a cack-handed job of owt. Don't pay them up front if they're working for you, that's my advice."

"You never met with Mr. Weston at all? Or did he just stop showing up?" Jake asked.

"Spoke to him on the phone. Some bloke I do work for gave me his number. Said he'd come round and give me a price to refit my kitchen and decorate in there but he popped in once and spoke to the wife, did some measuring, showed her some pictures on his tablet thing, then the next we know this bloke that's here now is doing the work. I think he's Belgian, doesn't say much. Doesn't *do* much either! He came with a kid last Friday and they ripped the old units out. It still looks like a fucking bomb hit it. Who'd you say you are?"

Jake held out his hand. "Jake Chivis. I'm looking into Mr. Weston's disappearance."

Miller shook his hand briefly and Jake followed the man inside through the lounge and into the kitchen. He wasn't sure if it was normal for Phil to have someone else working for him or not—he'd have to find out.

He had to admit, the kitchen did indeed look like a bomb had hit it recently. This, however, he knew was fairly normal for a remodeling project.

"How did you say you found Mr. Weston?" Jake asked. He'd already said someone at work had recommended Phil, but Jake wanted a name. It could be a dead end but nothing was ruled out until it was ruled out.

"This bloke that my firm does some work for, he's used Weston to do some updating at this house he's selling, up on the other side of the Heath. Said he did an okay job, he's been doing a bit of painting and carpentry and stuff. He didn't seem to have any complaints so I figured it would be okay. Dunno if Weston did the work for him or sent some more of his immigrants round."

"Uh-huh. Do you remember the last time you saw Mr. Weston? He had your name down in his appointment book for last week. Did you hear from him at all then?"

"Hang on..." Mr. Miller stumbled back up the hallway and bellowed up the stairs. "Sylvia? Sylv? You remember when that Weston bloke came round? What day was it? Some bloke down 'ere's askin' about him. I reckon Watchdog are onto him or something?"

A skinny woman in a shabby tracksuit top and ill-fitting jeans came halfway down the stairs and stuck her head over the baluster to get a look at Jake. She scratched her head.

"You from the telly?" she wanted to know.

Jake debated for half a second saying yes, because it might

smooth things over, but he was never good at carrying on with a lie. Instead he gave her his best 'shucks no, ma'am' smile and said, "No, I'm just looking for him. Seems no one has seen him in a few days." That should be mysterious enough to keep her interested and answering his questions, he hoped.

"Bet he's buggered off with the money. Told you that would happen, didn't I?" her husband said darkly.

Mrs. Miller didn't look so sure. She came down to the foot of the stairs and consulted a calendar that was hanging by the phone there. It was covered in scribbled messages over a design of cartoon kittens playing with balls of wool.

"It was Tuesday, the Tuesday before last," she told him wearily. "He said that he could start the work as soon as we were ready. We picked the units out and Van, he's the contractor doing the work, turned up on Friday and him and his lad ripped the old cupboards out, then they took them off in their Transit Saturday night and we didn't see them again till the other day. They've gone out for a lunch break but they're meant to be back soon. We've not seen Philip at all, not since he came round last week. Van reckons he was finishing another job."

"I see," Jake said, still smiling. He wondered if Phil Weston told all his female clients to call him Philip, or if Mrs. Miller just wanted to appear formal, sort of. Mr. Weston would have been more formal. It could be nothing. "Do you mind if I have a look around the work area while I wait for Van to come back?"

"I'll show you," she said, coming back down the hallway and leading him to the kitchen even though her husband had already shown him the way. "*Are* you from the police or something? Is he in trouble?"

"He's not in any trouble that I know of, ma'am," Jake said, answering her second question. He looked around the torn-up kitchen but didn't see anything right off that he thought might give him an impression if Phil had been there recently. "Mr. Miller said that someone he worked with recommended Phil. Do you know if they were happy with his work after it was all done?"

"Well...I suppose so," she told him, given a moment or so to consider this question. "They wouldn't have recommended him otherwise, would they? And he seemed to have a lot of work on. He said we were lucky this week. Someone had postponed because they were going on holiday. The way he was talking, it didn't sound like he was planning to disappear but you never know, do you?"

"Bet he's in Rio de Janeiro by now," Mr. Miller chirped up, shaking his head. "Bastard!"

"Right, well, you never do know, do you?" Jake agreed with Mrs. Miller. "Do you think I could get the number of the person who recommended Phil to you? If you haven't seen him around, maybe they might have."

She looked perturbed. "Ooh... I don't think I've got a number for them, lovey. Brian...?" She looked quizzically at her husband, who shrugged his shoulders.

"Got a business contact address for him, but I've not got his home number. Hang on..." He shambled off again, back into the hall, then returned with a beaten-up iPhone that looked like he'd dropped it a few times. "He's Brendan March — runs a consultancy in the city. His office do some marketing for the firm where I work so he pops by from time to time. Drives one of them Porsche 4x4s with a stupid name. Loaded, I reckon. If that cunt Weston's ripped him off as well, he'll probably not notice for months."

Jake tapped the contact information Miller gave him into his own phone then dropped it back into his pocket. "Thanks, I appreciate it. I won't bother Mr. March with more than a few questions, I promise. I'd just really like to find Mr. Weston." He said that last part very neutrally so Miller could make of it what he would. If he thought Jake was after him to kick his ass, it would probably make him more inclined to help.

"No skin off my nose, mate," Mr. Miller said gruffly. "I figure I owe him one, even if you don't. Wait up, I reckon that's Van pulling up outside. Nothing else makes a racket like that."

He was not wrong. The engine of the Transit could be heard coughing and spluttering from way back in the devastated remains of the Millers' kitchen. When it cut out, a resounding silence filled their ears for a moment then a door slammed and they heard voices.

Jake was glad he'd dressed casually when he saw Van and his assistant come in through the back garden gate and kitchen door. This was definitely a rough-looking character and would probably clam right up at the sight of a suit. As it was, Jake did his best to shed the cop vibe he'd been using to keep the Millers talking.

"Awright?" the older man, easily four inches taller than Jake's six-foot height and nearly twice as broad across the shoulders, greeted his clients and the newcomer warily. His dark-eyed gaze traveled over Jake from head to foot, assimilating him closely. He ran a meaty hand over the close-cropped, dark brown hair on his scalp and flexed one heavily tattooed biceps as he did so. "Don't mind us, mate."

He didn't sound particularly Belgian to Jake's unschooled ear.

"No problem," Jake said. "I was actually waiting for you to get back. I'm looking for Phil Weston, was wondering if you'd seen him lately?"

"Nope. Sorry, mate," the burly builder responded with a little shrug. "Not for a few days. You tried his mobile?"

"Tried it, yeah," Jake said. "He's not answering his calls, which is strange because he's normally attached to his phone." Which Jake only knew because Mari had told him of course, but they didn't need to know *how* he knew. "Do you do work for him regularly?"

"Yeah, on and off," Van conceded almost grudgingly. "He's got a place down on Lowman Road near the Che Guevara. You could try there."

"Thanks, I'll do that," Jake said, not bothering to mention that he'd been there already, or what he'd actually done there. "Well, I guess that's all the questions I have." Jake turned his head to give a last smile to Mrs. Miller and a nod to Mr. Miller. He produced a couple of cards with his name and number on it from his pocket. "Thanks for your time. If you hear anything from Phil, I'd appreciate it if you would call me." He handed one of the cards to Mrs. Miller and the other to Van, who took it reluctantly. "I'll see myself out the back here."

Mrs. Miller murmured something about good luck and Mr. Miller muttered on about Phil being in Tijuana as Jake stepped around the mountain named Van and out into the back garden. He could have stuck around and asked a few more pointed questions but he had a feel for these things and knew he'd tapped that well dry. He could always find Van again if he needed to, especially since he discreetly took a snap of the license plate on the back of the ancient-looking, long wheelbase vehicle as he walked down the path. As he passed the front fender of the beat-up van, he brushed his knuckle along the edge, not expecting to get anything but since he was here, he might as well try. The image that hit him was like jumping off a pier into deep water, a cold slap to the body that drove the air out of his lungs and made him freeze in place.

The smell of urine and shit was strong in his nose and he had tears running down his face. The road in front of him was very dark and he couldn't stop shaking. He turned his head and looked behind into the back of the van, where a bundle of blankets were wrapped around an all-too-familiar shape. A thatch of blond hair stuck out from one end.

Jake staggered as he took another step, and put his hand to his mouth. Phil Weston had been in this van, a very dead Phil Weston. He hadn't gotten a conclusive look at the face, but he'd bet every cent he had on it. The memory still felt very fresh.

"Shit!" He hissed under his breath, still moving, until high shrubs hid him from the Millers' house. He couldn't just keep going. He couldn't leave a murderer behind in the unsuspecting Miller family's torn-up kitchen. Oddly, his first instinct was not to call the police, but to call Mari, and he was pressing send on his phone almost before he knew what he was doing.

Chapter Seven

Mari was lying on the sofa in the bay window that overlooked his mother's garden with the laptop open on his stomach, using it to explore the material he'd pulled from Phil Weston's machine in more detail, when his phone vibrated on the seat cushion beside him. He reached down without even thinking to pick it up, the fingers of his free hand still tapping on the scroll down key. A brief glance at the screen told him who was calling and he experienced a peculiar sense of anxiety that almost saw him put the device back down unanswered before his conscience nagged him that it might be something important.

"Hello, Jake, what gives?" he exhaled as he lifted the slim mobile to his left ear.

"Mari, I...I got something. Got an impression. I'm pretty sure Phil Weston is dead," Jake blurted out in a rush.

Mari put the laptop aside and sat up, that cold sense of shock tightening his gut. Even though he had been expecting this news, it was still hard to hear.

"Where are you?" he wanted to know. "Can you meet me?"

"I'm in Hampstead. About a block from the address of Phil's last job," Jake answered. It was hard to tell over the phone but he thought he heard a tremor in that normally stoic voice.

"Do you want me to come to you? Are you in trouble?" Mari swallowed the lump that this thought put in his throat with some difficulty. "What did you see?"

Jake sigh came through on the other end, a frustrated sound. "I saw a body, *his* body I'm pretty sure, wrapped in a blanket in the back of a work van. The guy that owns the van is someone that Phil worked with." He paused, as if gathering his thoughts. "I don't know what to do. I feel like I can't just walk away and leave those people alone with a potential killer, but what am I supposed to tell the cops if I called them? Hey, I think there might have been a dead guy in this van. No proof of that at all, but check it out. All that will do is...nothing."

"They'll think you're a nutcase," Mari agreed sagely, employing another of his favorite Briticisms. He checked his notes in another window of his laptop. "This is the Kemplay Road job, yes? I can be there in..." He paused and juggled the phone against his ear with his shoulder as he checked the tube map on his laptop. "About twenty minutes, maybe. What's the plan? Are we going to take him down, Detective Chivis?"

He was already putting his laptop to sleep and hunting out his running shoes. The nearest tube station was at Great Portland Street but if he ran up to Mornington Crescent, it would save him having to change lines at King's Cross, and he was pretty sure he could be in Hampstead sooner that way. Mari was not unashamed of his enthusiastic passion for the London Underground system. He figured he was a career geek, it was the way he was wired.

How they were supposed to deal with a suspected murderer he was unsure, but excitement was taking over from the initial trepidation now. Whatever happened, he was determined that he wouldn't let Jake handle it alone.

He could hear Jake's breathing, and heard it start to slow down. Just like that he knew Jake was calming himself, thinking at last, instead of reacting.

"No...no, Mari, don't come out here. There is nothing we can do, for now. Not here and not yet. I have his license plate number. Do you think you can find out a full name, where he lives, any other information on him? We need to start digging and get something more concrete than just my say-so."

Mari was surprised to feel deflated by this outright rejection of his assistance.

"What are *you* going to do?" he asked. "You can't just walk away. What if he's still in the van? Can you tell?"

Jake laughed, one strangled huff of sound that released some of the tension in his voice.

"I didn't look in the back. Some cop, right? Sometimes the visions I get...they're just so real, and the head I was in was so panicked." He took another breath and let it out. "No, I don't think the body is still in there. The guy had an assistant riding with him. Unless he's in on it, I think he'd notice the smell of a nearly week-old corpse in the back." He paused for an even longer moment. "There is nothing to suggest this guy is a spree killer. There aren't bodies piling up, as far as we know. That tells me it was probably a spur of the moment thing, crime of passion maybe. It doesn't mean anyone else around him is in danger. I'm getting back on the train. Until we have something I can take to the cops, there's no point in confronting him. All that would do is give him the idea to destroy evidence, if there's any to be found."

That sounded rational enough, and Mari was reassured by the idea that Jake wasn't going to take on the killer single-handed. He was also, he realized, slightly annoyed that given all the information he already had at his disposal, his colleague had hit the jackpot on his first call. But Jake had given him one thing to mull over—they still didn't know where Phil's corpse had gone. And until they found that, they didn't really have anything concrete to take to the authorities or to share with Professor Weston.

"We need to locate the body," Jake said, as if reading his mind. "And find out all we can about this guy he worked with."

"Send me the plate number," Mari told him, more decisively. "Let's see what we can turn up on the owner."

"Okay, I'll text it to you." He hesitated. "Can I meet with you when I get back?"

Mari was surprised again but obscurely pleased as well. After twenty-four hours spent worrying that Jake was on the outs with him over their last communication, it was like swallowing warm honey to realize that at least his fellow guinea pig still wanted to talk to him. He kicked himself for being needy but didn't have the will to tell him no. "Sure. You want to come over, or meet in a pub or something? That would be more like spies, I think."

Jake laughed, and this time he sounded a little more at ease. "Whatever is better for you, just tell me where."

He deliberated then made a decision. "Come here, it's more private. Mama is having her nap so we can talk without having to worry who hears us. It's Albany Street, do you know where that is?" He gave Jake the number when the man had assured him he would find it.

* * * *

It took Jake more like a half hour to get back to Regent's Park and when he did he checked the address at least four or five times, even though he knew he'd heard it correctly. He found himself in a nice neighborhood close to the college and little more than a couple of streets from Regent's Park. A very, *very* nice neighborhood. London was one of the most expensive cities in the world to live in, even if you couldn't afford luxury. He couldn't begin to imagine what one of these places might cost.

He was not particularly impressed by wealth. Jake had always managed to get by, whether poor or flush with cash. He was fairly certain though that he'd never be able to afford one of these houses, not even when he'd been making his best paycheck as a detective and arson investigator back in Detroit. This was such a far cry from the place he grew up it almost seemed unreal to him. And Mari *lived* here.

He wasn't sure how he felt about that yet so he pushed it aside to turn over in his head later. Right now they had work to do, and that was why he felt nervous and excited to see Mari again. *Right!* He was such a bad liar. He shook his head at his own stupidity and climbed the front steps to ring the bell, wondering as he did so whether a butler named Jeeves would answer the door.

Actually, it was Mari himself who opened up for him. Jake heard a little commotion behind the pristine black-paneled door, which had a heavy, circular chrome knocker as a centerpiece in addition to the bell-push. When it swung inward, he saw a rather frazzled Mari bent forward with his fingers looped in the collar of a small, solid, brindle bull terrier with white paws and a splash of white on its chest. It growled and barked meaningfully when it spotted Jake, until Mari admonished it in a firm voice.

"Tonka, stop being an idiot and say hello to Detective Chivis. He's one of ours, you dumb mutt."

He was dressed about as casually as Jake had ever seen him, outside of park runs, in a pair of loose, brushed cotton, buttermilk-colored sweat pants and a long-sleeved jersey top in pale blue that was almost the same color as his eyes. Those eyes peered up through the tangle of his unbrushed forelock as he grinned up at Jake.

"Come in and shut the door, he's all bark. Just likes people to think he's the boss, that's all."

Jake stepped inside as Mari pulled the dog back. He stood still, and kept his eyes on Mari rather than the dog so that he wouldn't think he was issuing a challenge—the dog, that was.

"Let him come sniff me so he can settle down," Jake suggested.

Mari looked pleased with this. Keeping one finger hooked in the thick band of dark brown leather, he loosened his hold on Tonka's collar so that the ball of bouncy canine muscle at his feet could come over and investigate the new intruder on his patch.

Tonka snuffed his knees and shoes and extended fingers then tried to jump up on him until Mari brought him back down with a little tug and stern, "No."

At last the dog seemed satisfied that Jake was not a major threat to his authority and Mari let him go. Tonka wandered back off along the hallway, nails clicking on the parquetry, tail wagging, pleased with himself.

"I apologize for the boisterous stupidity of my mother's dog," Mari said wearily. "Are you okay?"

"I'm fine, don't worry, I like dogs. Why don't you bring him when you run?" Jake asked.

"Because he's lazy, and he doesn't care for my early-morning starts. I take him out in the evening most days," Mari said with a little smile. "I feel safer running at night with him on my heels."

He looked Jake over as if he was expecting to see signs of violence on him then, satisfied that he hadn't picked a fight with their potential murderer, he turned and led the way back up the hall in the direction taken by the dog.

There was a large, open kitchen and sunroom in the rear with a slope-backed lounger, three-seater sofa and an armchair upholstered in cream velvet situated by the full-length glass doors and windows that took up half of the external wall. They looked out over a little pocket of colorful paving and greenery beyond. A garden was another luxury in London's densely packed urban areas and this one was small, but contained about as much foliage as it was possible to fit into such a cozy space.

"Can I get you some tea, or coffee? Or do you need something stronger?" Mari asked, waving him toward the chair.

"Just water please," Jake said. His gaze slowly roamed over the room and the garden beyond the windows. There was nothing particularly ostentatious about the house, it was a very comfortable space, clean and modern, but it could certainly have graced the glossy pages of a decorating magazine. Not that Jake looked at decorating magazines, but he'd flipped through one once in a doctor's waiting room when there was nothing else to do.

"You sure?" Mari raised a curious eyebrow then returned

to the tall, chrome-fronted refrigerator across the open-plan kitchen space to extract a filter jug. He did add ice cubes and a slice of lime to the concoction without asking, though. Then poured himself a black coffee from the pot on the counter and came back with both drinks to settle on the lounger opposite Jake again, his bare feet drawn up under him neatly.

"So...tell me what you saw. Everything," he insisted solemnly. "And what you felt from the contact, point of view, the whole shebang. Anything could be a clue."

He set his glass coffee mug on a low table beside the lounger and reached for his laptop, flicking the lid back and opening his notes like a psychiatrist, ready to give Jake a grilling. Before he got started, he snared a pair of Perspex-framed reading glasses from the sofa cushion beside him and perched them on the end of his nose.

Jake hid a small grin at Mari's intensity behind a sip of water.

"I've never seen you with glasses. Do you wear contacts?" That might explain why his eyes were the most unusual shade of frost blue he'd ever seen.

"You're avoiding the question," Mari told him seriously, frowning up at him through those narrow, oblong lenses. His gaze still looked intensely blue, even in spectacles. "Yes, I wear contacts at work, okay. It's more practical. But they hurt my eyes, I don't wear them in the house. I only really need them for close work. Now, speaking of work."

"But you're not wearing contacts now. So that really is the color of your eyes?" Jake said.

Mari ignored him and tapped one slim finger on the edge of his screen. In a second window, the laptop was already running a search on the DVLA database, checking out the license number Jake had texted him earlier. It pinged at him and he nodded and typed something into the notebook page that was open beside it.

Jake took another sip of water, watching him work. Watching him pointedly ignore what he'd said about his eyes.

"Are you going to continue avoiding my question?" Mari asked, without lifting his fixed stare from the screen.

Jake stopped fighting the grin. He could have asked him the same thing. The grin faltered though when he thought about how to answer.

"I didn't get a look at who was driving, *I* was driving," he said.

He glanced at Mari, hands poised over the keys, looking back at him with his eyebrows drawn slightly together. Despite the situation and the morbid topic, Jake had to squash the urge to lean in and kiss that furrowed spot between them.

"When I get an impression, it's someone's memory. I see it from their viewpoint, not an outside point of view. Unless they look in a mirror or down at themselves, I don't know who it is or what they look like while I'm seeing out of their eyes," Jake explained. "It's why I say stuff like 'I was driving', it's like I really *was*, for those few seconds, or minutes, or however long."

Mari remained silent as he explained, then in an impatient tone, he said, "I understand that, Jake, I'm not asking you to make me an e-fit. Tell me how you *felt*, how the *driver* felt. What was going through your mind, how was your body reacting? You had a corpse in the back of your van. That must have had some kind of emotional impact, no?"

Jake took another sip of water and set the glass down on a coaster made of small pieces of sanded driftwood that matched the pale aspect of the room. He wasn't sure if he didn't want to revisit this memory himself, or if he just didn't want to tell Mari all the gory details. Which was stupid, because Jake had seen far worse and Mari wasn't some delicate flower he needed to protect.

"It was brief, only a few seconds. I was pulled into the driver's head. It was getting dark out. I could see the road but I don't remember seeing any signs. I don't know where we were headed. I could smell urine and excrement, very strong. Death smells. I looked back, into the van, and there was a blanket, pale colored, I couldn't see the exact shade in the dark. Wrapped around a body. Blond hair sticking out of one end. No visible blood stains on the blanket. Then I was looking at the road again, and that's all."

Jake recited the few seconds of memory in as blank a monotone as he could manage.

Mari's head was bent, his fingers moving rapidly and quietly over the keyboard as Jake talked and when he fell silent, Mari stopped typing but carried on tapping one finger against the side of the machine. "How did it make you feel? Make *him*...or her feel, I mean? The driver? Were you scared? Determined? Angry? When you looked at the body, what emotions did you get?"

"I'm not an empath or a telepath, Mari, I don't read people's minds. It's just memory." Jake said, but he couldn't hold eye contact when Mari stared hard at him. Jake saw him getting ready to ask another question, or probably a half dozen and went on, "The driver was definitely male, not female. Even if they don't look in a mirror, I can usually tell. You can see your own body in your periphery and get a feel for size and shape, usually."

He saw Mari open another window and type something else, a quick side note. When he looked up, his eyes held a brief twinkle of fascination, there then gone. It softened the expression on his face.

"So you don't...*become* them?" he asked carefully. "It's more like a dream?" He paused, not waiting for the answer. "What you said ties up, incidentally. The van is registered to a Mr. Van Michael Guylian, curiously enough. I wonder if he made that first name up as a joke or he was conceived while his parents were listening to Moondance?"

Jake scowled, ignoring the joke and picked up his glass again, taking a longer drink. "No, it's not like a dream at all. It's very real. Very *visceral*. I don't become the person exactly. I mean it's a memory, it's not like I can control movement or say or do anything, I'm just there, along for the ride, watching. If it's the memory of a victim, I can't lift a finger to defend them, I get stabbed or beat up or whatever happened to them…or I do those things to someone else. But I don't *become* them."

Mari looked away for the first time, toying with the keys on his laptop for a moment.

"I'm not trying to tease you, Chivis. Don't sulk at me," he said finally. "I just want to understand, to know what you do and don't perceive when you get these…flashbacks, or whatever they are. If you don't feel their emotions, then… you don't. It would help, maybe, that's all. Don't glare at me like that. I'm not a mind reader either, you know."

His eyes darted back up to Jake's face for a moment then back down to the screen again.

"So…our Mr. Guylian…potentially of Portuguese, Belgian or US origin, but just as likely to be a third- or fourth-generation Eastender." He exhaled. "The vehicle is a white Ford Transit 80 Popular, first registered in 1990 — I am frankly amazed that it still runs. Registration address is Twenty-B Florence Road, Finsbury Park. He and Phil were practically neighbors, how sweet. Do you want to raid *his* flat as well?" He looked up again with a wink and a forced smile.

Jake stared at him so intently he didn't even blink, and he could feel the tightness of the muscles along his jaw. Alex had told him once that that look on his face was like he could burn someone down to their shoes with his eyes alone, and not in a passionate 'let's get naked' kind of way. The thing was, he wasn't angry with Mari. He wasn't even sure it was anger at all. More like dread.

"He was panicked. Utter panic. The kind that makes you sick inside and clammy on the outside," Jake said. "We're not breaking into his flat. Not yet. Keep digging."

Mari blinked at him. He opened his mouth to say something then seemed to think better of it.

"What am I looking for?" he asked rationally, tapping the keyboard and opening yet another window.

"Police record would be the most useful," Jake suggested, easing down the intensity a notch.

Mari shrugged one shoulder and shifted around with his feet on the cushioned seat of the lounger so that the laptop could be balanced against his knees. He called up a page and tapped in his details then navigated deftly through the system to a search page. He rattled in Van Guylian's name and the registration address and hit send. For a few moments, he tapped his fingers restlessly against the edges of the screen again, then as the information scrolled up, he whistled softly through his teeth, eyes widening.

"Jackpot! Oh my!"

Swinging back around, he passed the machine over to Jake and came to perch on the arm of the chair beside him. "Someone has been a very naughty boy. *Now* do you think we have something to go to the police with?"

Jake looked down at the scene and had to scroll. It was quite a rap sheet. Petty larceny, destruction of property, drunk and disorderly, assault. His most recent run-in with the law was four years ago, when he'd gone to prison for rape. Van Guylian was still on parole for that crime. This was good, but the list was generic.

"Can you get into the details of the case? Find out who the victim was that he raped?" Jake asked, handing Mari back his computer.

Mari took the machine back from him and did some more tapping on the keys, this time for several minutes. Jake leaned back and tried to relax while he waited. He was acutely aware of Mari's nearness—he could smell the hint of soap on his skin and feel the warmth of his body all along his arm, even with a few inches separating them. All he would have to do was lean a little and he could put his head on his hip, or slide his hand around his back, pull him down into his lap, nuzzle his hair. *Fuck*. He had to focus and stop thinking with his dick.

"Records of the victims are protected," Mari said absently. "But I ran a cross ref with the BNO and hospital records and found her. The NHS online security is a joke, seriously! She was a minor, fifteen at the time. Name is Samantha Clark. Do you want me to find an address?"

"No, that's okay, that's enough," Jake said. "I just wanted to know male or female and age. See if there was any correlation. Since there isn't, we'll still need to find a motive. Since his previous victim was a young female, it makes it less likely that this was another rape that escalated. It's still possible, but it could just as well have been an argument, something to do with work, jealous rage, who knows." Jake tipped his head against the chair and closed his eyes for a moment. "It's still not a lot to go on, but maybe we can convince his probation office to take a closer look at him. If they find something fishy, we won't have to try and convince the police on our own."

Mari drummed against his front teeth with a fingernail for a moment, then murmured, "This isn't exactly ethical, but I could put a trip on his parole record. He'd get called in and maybe if they question him enough about what he's been up to, he might crack under pressure."

He glanced sidelong at Jake. "You've met him, albeit briefly, you reckon he's the type to babble or clam up?"

Jake shrugged. "Hard to say. I talked to him for less than five minutes. I got the feeling, though, that he's not the chatty type." He opened his eyes and turned his head to look at Mari. "You can put something in his record that specific? To have them question him about Phil? He's not even officially missing. Not according to the police. If we could find his body, that would be different."

Mari laughed softly. "Nothing *so* specific, Jake. But if he's out on probation, it would only take a little bad form to tip the scales for him. If his parole board gets a tip-off that he's violated his conditions, they put a black mark on his file. That's basically what I would be doing. They'd want to talk to him about it. I guess the rest is up to him."

Jake thought about it, turning it over in his head for several moments. Finally he said, "Let's wait a couple days.

Maybe we'll be able to find where Phil was dumped. I still think it would be better to have the body before we point the cops in the right direction. We've got time. It's not going to matter to Phil."

He sighed deeply.

Mari hesitated a moment, then closed his laptop and reached across with one hand to gently stroke Jake's hair. He only let his hand linger there the shortest time then withdrew it.

"You feel for him, don't you? Maybe we should tell Professor Weston that this is as far as we can go with it. That he should call the police. It isn't fair on you to make you see this and not be able to change it," he said quietly.

Jake mulled that over too. He seemed to be channeling a lot of introspection lately. "We should tell Weston, yeah, but let's keep it to ourselves who the suspect is, for now. I don't want to turn him into a vigilante."

"I can't imagine that," Mari chuckled darkly. "But then my track record at reading people is not the best."

He shifted from the arm of the chair and put his laptop down on the side table in order to take a sip from his cooling coffee. As he did so, the door from the hallway opened a crack and Tonka stirred from his doggie bed by the windows and ran toward it, tail wagging.

"Mama," Mari said, looking slightly concerned. "Did we disturb you?"

Even if Jake had not been tipped off, he would not have doubted the familial connection. Mari's mother was tall and willowy like her son but on her face his sharp features were softer, the creamy oval of her cheeks and jawline smoother, though she had the same fine, ash-blond hair, swept up in a messy half knot, and pale, piercing eyes. Her lips twitched around a little smile as she noticed Jake.

"You didn't wake me, I was reading and I wanted a drink, is all. Are you going to introduce your friend?" Even her voice was soft and deeper than expected, like her son's. Except, where he spoke with a carefully enunciated, almost pan-universal English accent tinged slightly with New York state vowels, hers had a hint of something that he couldn't isolate, though it was certainly not American.

Mari waved a hand toward Jake casually. "My work colleague, Jake Chivis. Jake, your fine detective mind will have worked out by now that this is my mother, Doctor Annabel Gale."

Jake had already risen to his feet when she came in, because his maternal grandmother had taught him that was what you did when a woman entered the room. He took a couple of steps so that she didn't have to and extended his hand, clasping hers with just enough of a squeeze when she reached out to take it.

"A pleasure to meet you, Dr. Gale," he said politely. "You have a lovely home."

She raised her eyes to his, not *quite* as tall as Mari when they were standing level, and held on to his hand for a moment more before releasing it. "Well, thank you, Jake. That's kind of you to say. It's a little old-fashioned but then so am I. At the moment it's convenient for my purposes. So, you're a detective? How exciting. I didn't think the university employed detectives. I suppose you teach criminology or something thrilling like that?"

Jake was smiling and he fought down the urge to let his lips twitch. Despite the difference in accent and tonal inflection, she spoke exactly like Mari, with barely a pause between sentences, a fluid stream of thought that said you had better be sharp if you expected to keep up.

"I *was* a detective," Jake clarified. "I'm not currently. Right now I'm working in research."

"Jake's a fellow guinea pig," Mari added from the kitchen where he had the coffee perking again and was adding hot water to a glass pot with a built-in tea strainer, brewing a warm golden beverage that smelled of flowers.

"Ah..." Annabel's tone darkened slightly. "You have a gift then? How interesting. I take it you and my son have been comparing notes. It pays to stay one step in front of

Anthony Weston and his theories."

"Actually, Mama, we were just having a drink," Mari said, firing an apologetic glance at Jake over her shoulder that she must have seen, though she didn't comment on it. He put a glass mug with a banded chrome setting into her hands and she inhaled deeply of the sweet steam rising from it. "Jake dropped by to see if I fancied a run later."

Jake took that to mean Mari hadn't discussed the 'project' that Professor Weston currently had them working on, and keeping it under wraps was fine with Jake.

"Yes, it's nice to run with someone that has long enough legs to keep up," he said.

"I can't argue with that, though I prefer a gentler pace, personally." Mari's mother settled in the chair that he had vacated and looked up at him as she sipped her tea. "Speed is for cars and boats. Although I imagine that you cover some ground." Her gaze wandered up and down him contemplatively. "Not that either of you need so much exercise."

"Mama has never understood the point of running," Mari said tenderly, fingers curled around his newly refilled mug as he watched her from the edge of the kitchen space like she was a rare and precious example of an almost extinct species. "Although at least she doesn't call it *jogging* anymore."

"I run mostly because it clears my head. For exercise I go to the gym." Jake chuckled. Again that earned him a measured perusal.

"It shows," she said.

"Mama!" Mari rebuked her lightly.

"What? It wasn't an insult. He has a very nice body. I'm surprised you haven't noticed already," she demurred.

"Mother." His tone was more serious. "Do you have to flirt with everyone I bring home?"

"It is not as if you bring people home every day of the week," she flipped straight back at him.

"You're embarrassing him," her son pointed out. *And me,*

his expression added.

"I'm your mother, that's my job." Annabel smiled at Jake broadly. "*Am* I embarrassing you, Jake?"

"No, not at all," Jake said, tipping his head toward Mari and lifting his eyebrows a little to point out who was really embarrassed here. He couldn't hold back the grin any longer.

She laughed musically at that and Mari made a ticking noise between his teeth and shook his head at both of them. Annabel tutted at him by way of response.

"My boy is so serious, it's nice that he has a friend that can pull him out of himself sometimes."

"I am not still ten years old, Mama. I do have all kinds of friends," he said a little defensively.

She shook her head more solemnly.

"Nearly three years back in London and I do believe that you are the first boy he has brought home," she told Jake.

That did it, Mari retreated into the kitchen and crumpled there, elbows on the counter and his head in his hands, finally mortified into silence. Jake was biting his lips not to laugh but he took pity on Mari and didn't tease him.

"Well, I hate to cut things short but if we *are* going for a run, I had better get home and changed. It was very nice to meet you, Dr. Gale."

"The pleasure is all mine, former detective Chivis. What an interesting name, by the way. You must come back for dinner one evening and you can tell me all about where that comes from. My grandmother was a professor of linguistics, she left me with a fascination for names." She rose and patted him maternally on the cheek. "And you should call me Anni, too. Doctor Gale sounds so fusty, no?"

Jake nodded agreement and looked over at Mari. "See you in the park in half an hour?"

Mari just waved a hand in his direction, forced into surrender by his mother's tide of amiable charm. He did come to the door to see Jake off, though.

"I apologize for my mother," he whispered. "I adore her,

but she…"

He held out his hands in a helpless shrug.

Jake was still grinning at his discomfort, he couldn't help it. Mari was so fucking adorable, he had to get out of there or risk being indecent.

"There is nothing to apologize for," Jake whispered back, deliberately pitching his voice low, for Mari's ear alone. "She's very sweet. Go get your running pants on and meet me in the park, you're not getting out of it now," he finished, giving Mari's ass a pat and chuckling.

"Oh god, she's rubbing off on you." Mari exhaled, though his lips finally framed a weak smile. "If you promise not to tease me anymore, I will come and run with you."

Jake looked at him, very close, close enough that it wouldn't take much to lean in and steal a kiss.

"No. I can't promise not to tease you, but I will promise that you'll enjoy it if I do." He gave him one last grin and turned on the top step, taking them two at a time, happy he'd gotten the last word for a change.

Chapter Eight

Mari continued to prop up the doorway for a little while after Jake had gone and he had closed the front door. His head was spinning. What, exactly, had just happened there? Jake had most definitely been flirting with him, and in front of his mama too. That was a complete twist on his attitude the other day, when he had seemed almost uncomfortable with the idea that anyone at work might think he was interested in men. This afternoon he had been content to let Mari touch him, quite neutrally, but even so, he knew that some guys didn't like that. Jake on the other hand hadn't pushed him away when Mari had come to sit beside him on the chair arm, even leaning in so that he could feel the warmth of his arm against his thigh as they'd studied the data on his laptop. And the other night as they'd walked to the restaurant, he'd slipped an arm around him as if they were, at least, the best of friends, without an apparent care in the world.

He pushed himself upright and returned to the morning room, still feeling dazed from the encounter. When Jake had called earlier, he had schooled himself to accept that it was just communication in the line of duty, that he wasn't interested in anything more than solving the problem Professor Weston had set them so that he could get on with his own life.

Now...? Now, Mari was not so sure.

"He's sweet," Mama approved when he reappeared. She was sitting back in the comfortable chair that must still be warm from Jake's well-formed backside and muscular thighs, her fingers toying with Tonka's ears while the burly

117

Staffie looked up at her in adoration like a miniature lap dog. "So, are you two...?"

She left the question open but lifted an inquiring eyebrow.

"No, we two are not *anything*," he told her a little more testily than was necessary. "I wish you wouldn't jump to conclusions like that, it's really embarrassing."

"So he doesn't know you like him?" she mused, looking disappointed.

"Who said anything about me liking him?"

"You don't seem to *dislike* him."

Her rational response failed to soothe him and Mari closed his eyes for a moment and banged the heel of his hand against his forehead in frustration.

"It's not that simple, Mother."

She huffed with impatience. "Oh...god forbid that anything you do should be *simple*, Ilmari!"

"*Yes. I like* him. Is *that* what you want to hear?" He slapped his hands against the tops of his thighs, looking down on her in reluctant surrender.

"I *know* that. I'm your mother, as you so tetchily observed. You think I don't know when someone makes my little boy's eyes light up with so much pleasure it does my heart good?" She beckoned him down with a crook of her index finger. "Now give your wise old Mama a kiss and go get ready to chase him around the park like he wants."

Mari shook his head but that last observation forced a reluctant laugh from him and he bent to kiss her on the cheek, then retired to his room to change.

It was getting dark already when he reached Regent's Park and the air was turning colder after a bright day. Mari pushed himself a little harder around the Inner Circle as he waited for Jake to show up, trying not to think too much about what his mother had just put into words. Yes, damn it, he liked Jake — liked him a lot.

Was that the crime of the century?

No. But it wasn't wise. He knew that much. Hiding Tomas from the people they'd both worked with had been difficult enough. Mari didn't think he could go through that again with Jake, but at the same time he didn't think that Jake would want other men knowing that he liked guys, especially not guys with the kind of rep that Mari had quickly obtained. Most of the building knew his proclivities and most were cool with it. Some, like Nolan, and a few of the senior professors, were less cool though. Frigid as icebergs, more like.

That didn't worry him—the censure of his peers was something he could easily live without. He hated the idea that Jake might come to resent him, were they to be associated with each other publicly, though. And given the way he'd shut down on Mari the other day at work, that was highly likely.

Oh, Ilmarinen Gale, what the fuck have you got yourself into? He sighed internally.

"Why the long face?" Jake asked, suddenly appearing beside him. Mari had been so wrapped up in his thoughts he hadn't even seen him coming. "Running is supposed to help you clear your mind. It defeats the purpose to wallow," he told Mari, his tone light, almost teasing.

"Just my bitchy running face," Mari answered him, quickly improvising the lie. "I was mulling over the 'problem', is all."

He crooked his index fingers around the problem word, knowing that Jake would get it.

"What to do about Mr. Guylian, I mean, and wondering if I missed something. I still can't figure out why he'd kill Phil Weston. I can't find any communication between them apart from Phil offering him work. Maybe it was to do with money?"

"Could have been," Jake said simply. They ran together for several more paces before Mari realized that was all he was going to add.

"*What?*" Mari asked him at last, still stealing sideways looks and wondering if Jake was going to speak to him at all or if he'd just asked him out here because he didn't like to run alone, after all. He obviously didn't want to discuss the body in Van's van.

Mari could have slapped himself then because the look on Jake's handsome face told him everything he needed to know. It certainly wasn't Phil Weston's body that he was interested in right now. If he'd been more self-conscious, he might have blushed but instead he bit down on his lips and focused on the path ahead. It would be just the kick in the nuts his ego needed if he went head over heels because he was mooning over his fellow guinea pig.

Mari stole another little look though, just for his own peace of mind. Yes, a very comely guinea pig, he was forced to admit. A dark and sexy guinea pig, with a very naughty twinkle in his eyes. *Seriously?* He almost laughed at the idea.

"You asked me out here to jump my bones?"

"Actually, *you* asked *me* out here," Jake said, that teasing chuckle lurking in his tone. "When you were trying to convince your mother that's the only reason I stopped over. I just went along with it."

Infuriating man. Was he laughing? And he hadn't answered the question. Mari slowed to a stop and put his hands on his hips, giving Jake a scowl that, he hoped, asked 'are you just fucking with my head, or what?'

Jake came to a stop too but when he looked at Mari, those light amber and gold eyes were smoldering with heat, and definitely not the frustrated kind — more like the kind that promised to get him naked.

"You haven't brought anyone home to meet your mother in three years. Is that because you haven't had a relationship in that long, or because you don't date the kind of guys you can bring home?" Jake asked. No accusation, no judgment, just curiosity in his expression.

Mari simmered for a moment or so then, without giving Jake any warning, he clawed one of his hands up the back of his skull, into his hair, and snaked the other one around his back to rest against the wing of Jake's shoulder blade.

He pressed his mouth against Jake's, shutting him up.

Yes, that was what he was doing. Making him be quiet. *Absolutely!*

And if making him be quiet felt so good that he wanted to fly like a rocket over the treetops and burst like a New Year's firework all across the park, then he wasn't complaining about that one bit. The impact of his assault on Jake's mouth carried him backward a couple of steps and suddenly Mari had him pushed up against the trunk of a tree. He invaded Jake's lovely, infuriating head with his tongue and ground his body on him from his lips to his hips, moaning softly at the heat that spread through him from each delicious point of friction.

Up to that point Mari had been prepared to concede that what had happened in Phil's flat was probably, in all eventuality, an aberration—albeit a glorious one. Now he was revising that opinion.

Kissing Jake like this set him on fire from head to toe and he had no intention of this being just a one-time, or even a two-time thing. The sweet warmth and passionate intensity of that powerful body pressing up on his own was all too precious to give up. Until that moment he'd managed to convince himself that he wasn't lonely, that he didn't miss the joy of having another man in his arms, between his legs, in his head. Now he knew that he'd probably been kidding himself all along. There was no pleasure in the world as good as this.

Jake dropped his hands to Mari's hips, pulling him even closer, grinding flush with him in a way that left no doubt he had more on his mind than a run. He pushed a knee between Mari's legs and his fingers curled around the cheeks of his backside, dragging him slowly up his thigh.

"We keep finding the most inappropriate places to make out, you know." Jake chuckled when their lips parted for a moment.

Mari was panting as he freed Jake's mouth, half-amazed that the man was still able to talk. He bucked his hips and rubbed along that hot, muscular thigh, enjoying the feel of it between his own, the brush of light pressure under his balls. His cock swelled greedily in the flexible confines of his leggings and shorts and he drew Jake closer again, nuzzling up against his ear.

"Well, you're the one with an empty apartment but you never invite me back there," he panted, more than a bit astonished at his own forwardness. Somehow it seemed right with Jake though, as if their bodies had been waiting for each other. He certainly hoped so, given the disasters of his previous relationships.

Jake kissed him again, tongue sliding between his lips, pressing and tangling with his own. The hands on his arse squeezed harder, moved him back and forth, pulled him onto his toes again, sliding him up and down on his thigh.

"I believe I can fit two people in the apartment, if we hold our breath." Jake grinned at him. "It would probably be nicer than finding a bush to hide behind and some cold ground to grab anyway."

"When you put it like that, it sounds a whole lot more appealing," Mari told him, only a shade sardonically. He explored Jake's mouth with his tongue again, then leaned back and caught him by the neckline of his jersey top, pulling him forward. "You have the advantage of me. You know where I live but I don't know where to find you when I need you."

Mari pulled him by the collar away from the tree but when they were back on the path Jake caught his wrist and towed Mari back up against his body. Jake's lips hovered just above his own.

"Do you need me, Ilmari?" he breathed into his mouth, easing one hand between them and over the stiff outline of Mari's cock. "Because I *really* need you..."

Mari trembled at the husky tenderness of his voice and he was almost undone when Jake used that childhood diminution of his given name. Usually only family called him Ilmari and it felt odd but not unalluring to have a lover call him that. He whined softly at the touch of Jake's warm hand between his thighs. They dove into another kiss and Jake sucked his gasp into his own mouth, lips moving against his again.

"Ahh... Maybe you *are* in need of *something*, hmm...?" Jake rubbed his palm slowly between his legs, fingers curling sweetly around the swell of him, gently stroking up and down until Mari quivered and a low, frantic moan escaped him. "I better get you back to home sweet hovel then," Jake murmured. "This way."

For once Mari was lost for words, his body answering Jake unquestioningly in the affirmative. He needed this man so much that it frightened him and he let Jake hold him by the wrist like a possession, a trophy, leading him through the park in the opposite direction to the one he normally took.

It was not far, just a few streets from the university campus but on the other side of Great Portland Street, in the shadow of the Telecom Tower. He felt as if he were being led by some mysterious warrior to meet his fate. Outside a bank of shops and a bar, bustling in spite of the early hour, Jake stopped and juggled his key into the lock of a plain, single door between two commercial units.

"I always wondered where odd little doors like these led to," Mari murmured, hoping that his voice didn't tremble too much.

Jake looked over his shoulder at him, the teasing grin he wore earlier back in place. "Usually to trouble. Down rabbit holes and such."

The door opened on a small entry hall. When it closed behind them to the right was an interior door and to the left a stairway, up which Jake led him. At the top they found a landing with cracked linoleum on the floor, windows that faced the street at either end and two doors set into the adjacent walls on either side of the stair. Jake fitted his key in the lock of the right-hand door, pushing it inward, then stood aside to hold it open for him.

Mari hesitated on the threshold into this new world. He

wondered if Jake had a sense of just how anxious he was from holding his wrist, the way that he got flashes of other people's lives from inanimate objects. That thought was so bizarre that he almost backed off but the look in Jake's golden eyes as he turned to welcome him into his domain melted that flight impulse down to a small, soft puddle of no resistance.

"I... I want you to know. I don't make a habit of this. Of casual...stuff. Just so you know."

Jake closed the door behind them but he didn't let go of Mari. Instead he pulled him close, although this time more gently.

"Is that what this is? Casual...stuff?" he asked, his voice a soft purr.

"I've known you, what? All of a week. Nearly." Mari's lips twitched, so close he could feel the warmth of Jake's breath on them. "Hardly an engagement, is it?"

"Hardly," Jake agreed, and it was difficult to tell if there was amusement in his voice or not. He backed off a step and pulled his hooded shirt, and the T-shirt underneath, off in one motion and dropped them onto the floor. "Do you want a drink? Or can I just strip you right now?"

Mari's heart was beating so fast that he thought it might just explode. When Jake peeled the upper garments off that perfectly toned torso and tuned-to-the-minute abs, he felt something inside him turn to molten ice, then burn like a lava spill through his gut. He wanted to feel that perfect body against his own.

"I don't need a drink," he whispered, stretching out his fingers to trace the dark, furred line of Jake's treasure trail slowly down from his navel to the low waistband of his joggers. The outline of his gorgeous cock was pressing its curved prow against the yielding material. He let his hand slide down, caressing the heat and fullness of it in silent wonderment, then laughed nervously as he looked around. "Well, I'm not going to get lost in here, am I?"

"No, no danger of that," Jake said in a softly husky voice.

He pointed at one of two doors. "That's the bathroom." He pointed at the other. "That's the bedroom." Then he settled his hands on Mari's hips. "You don't have to be nervous, Mari. We're not going to do anything you don't want to do. I know that sounds totally cheesy, but I can see the pulse leaping in your throat, so…just relax."

If only! Mari caught his breath, still running restless hands over the beautiful body in front of him. Jake was not a muscle queen like some guys he'd known in America and the Far East but there was a smooth, sculpted beauty to his exposed torso that just cried out to be touched. His nipples were small and dark and very hard. He bent his head and touched his lips to one of them, gently pulling on it then rolling the tip of his tongue around it slowly, enjoying the fact that Jake didn't mind it the way some men did.

"I may be a little bit rusty," he whispered, breaking off to look Jake in the eyes solemnly. Then, when he didn't respond, "I think you said something about stripping me, hmm?"

Jake took both of Mari's hands and walked backward, pulling him toward the bedroom door.

"If you didn't look so serious, I would swear that 'rusty' comment was just an opening to have me offer to oil you up." He winked. The door opened with a nudge of Jake's hip, obviously not having been closed quite all the way. The interior was near claustrophobically small, just enough room for a bed and a dresser in the corner. The bed wasn't made and there was a small pile of clothes on the floor. It didn't look like Jake had been expecting company.

"You mean you *weren't* going to? Hard core!" Mari managed a brittle laugh and moved around him to sit down on the bed. He lifted his hands, letting them glide over the sharp wings of Jake's lean hips and used his thumbs to tow the waistband of Jake's pants down a little farther, admiring the flatness of his stomach and the deep grooves to either side of his abs that were so sleek and sexy that he wanted to press his face into them and lick him all over. He touched his lips to the prominent bulge in Jake's flannels and kissed him through the soft, warm cloth.

Jake's hands hovered over Mari's shoulders for a few moments, obviously just enjoying the feel of him, the softness of his lips grazing over his crotch. Then he leaned in and ran his hands down Mari's back, grabbed the hem of his shirt and pulled it up and off him in a smooth tug that turned it inside out. Grinning, he dropped it on the floor behind him and very deliberately pushed Mari back on the bed. He bent over and popped off his running shoes and each of those were dumped over his shoulder as well, one bouncing clear to land somewhere in the room beyond. Then he hooked his fingers into Mari's shorts and leggings and pulled them off the same way he had his shirt, turning them inside out until he got them all the way down his long legs.

"Not terribly romantic, I know. But efficient," Jake told him.

"Economical," Mari agreed, dizzy with the excitement of being manhandled and unwrapped like an unexpected birthday present in the hands of a deprived child. "That's good. I like efficiency."

He was hard as his cock bounced free of the constraint of his running gear, glad to be liberated from its Lycra prison. Mari felt less nervous, riding on the tide of anticipation, knowing that Jake's strong, manly body would soon be pressing up against his own, nothing between them but the cool, dry air of the apartment's ventilation system.

Jake had kicked his shoes off while Mari spoke and he pushed his pants down with the same efficiency he'd used to strip Mari. The waistband caught on the upright head of his cock for a moment, dragging it down then releasing it to spring back and slap on his stomach. He wasted no time flexing or showing off, somewhat to Mari's disappointment, but slid smoothly on to the bed with him, over him, his hands either side of Mari's shoulders, hovering just above him, one leg pressed between his thighs.

"You are too beautiful for words," Jake murmured along his lips before plunging his tongue between them.

Mari surrendered to the kiss, running his fingers slowly up Jake's naked back, recalling the curve of the curious design tattooed there. He wanted to ask about it but felt that it was hardly the time to start waffling on about ink. As Jake had disrobed, he'd also been reminded of just how big he was, that at least had not been his sex-starved mind playing tricks on him. No man had ever called him beautiful before. He was touched and bemused in equal measure by it.

His brain was telling him that he should return the compliment but all his mouth could manage was, "Let me suck your cock."

He berated himself for the crudeness but he wanted that gorgeous piece in his mouth and he figured that Jake had enough in common with most other men that this would please him, at least. Jake rolled his hips, rubbing his lush, heavy length into the hollow of Mari's hip, his thigh pressing against the underside of Mari's balls.

"It's all yours. You call the shots. You want me on my back, or want me to straddle your face?" Jake said, seemingly not at all afraid of a little crudeness himself.

Mari was intrigued, in spite of his sudden fit of nerves. Jake seemed so...not shy exactly, but definitely reticent when he was at work. It was as if, in private, he became a whole new person, unafraid to articulate his wants and needs. He approved wholeheartedly. For all of his flirtation and frivolity, Mari was a straightforward human being and he appreciated a man who could come straight to the point.

"Turn on your side," he said. "I want to feel you over me but I want to look at you." He took the opportunity to do just that as Jake rolled halfway off him, his knee still between Mari's slim thighs. That cock really was a thing of magnificence. Jake wasn't monstrously hung but his erection was fully worthy of admiration. Mari laid his outstretched fingers against the underside of it, and it was more than the full length of his extended hand span. It felt thick and heavy in his hand as he encircled it with thumb and forefinger, then he worried that he was squeezing too hard but Jake didn't complain.

Mari wriggled down against him, their long legs still entwined as he edged closer to that gorgeous offering. The dusting of mahogany hair across Jake's torso was matched more thickly by the thatch over the base of his cock and Mari indulged his desire to press his face into the deep V of Jake's groin, breathing in the sharp, clean scent of his crotch. His own cock twitched in appreciation as he kissed the swell of Jake's pelvis then began to lip and lick his way up the magnificent shaft in his hand. It felt so silky, so hot under his fingers and lips and he immersed himself in the business of worshiping it, a wondering smile on his face.

All his anxiety melted as he worked up and down that sexy, vein-rippled cock, stroking back the silky-feeling foreskin to run the tip of his tongue over Jake's glans. The first time they'd done this, he had been surprised that Jake wasn't cut. He'd thought most American men were. Mari was glad of it now. That was something else they had in common. And he enjoyed using the play of Jake's foreskin, moving it back and forth between his fingers and thumb, over the protruding, plum-colored head, until Jake was leaking a slippery spill all over Mari's lips and fingers. He swept his tongue over the drooling crown, licking him up, loving the lush, briny taste of his pre-cum. He glanced up at Jake, a proper smile on his face for the first time since his arrival here.

"You like that, big fella?"

Jake's eyes were half-closed, banked embers in their amber depths. He had his head propped on one hand and raked the fingers of the other into Mari's hair.

"Oh yeah, I like that. Can't you see how much I'm leaking for you, how hard I am for you?"

"Just checking." Mari grinned at him delightedly. "You never know. It could just be a Pavlovian response. Eliminate the negatives."

Jake rolled his hips, nudging the crown against Mari's lips. "Suck me, baby, I can't wait to feel your mouth around me."

"Hmm...maybe I should test that hypothesis." Mari pretended to mull it over until the impatient growl rumbling in his chest told him that his lion was waking from slumber and he was a hungry beast for sure.

He bent his head and wrapped moist lips around the swell of Jake's throbbing glans, swallowing it down, running his tongue around the throbbing shaft, then drawing his mouth back along the length of him, taking it slow, until that glossy, wet plum popped back out again. His eyes traveled back up the seductive vista of Jake's mouthwatering, gorgeous body to meet his lover's increasingly frantic gaze.

"Mmhhh...so succulent," he purred in a husky tone. "Is that what you like, Detective? Does that hit the spot for you?"

Jake gave him a hoarse little wheeze of a laugh and his fingers tightened in Mari's hair, pulling him forward more urgently. "I can't tell yet, you're going to have to do it some more."

"So greedy!" Mari chirruped but he dipped his head again, enfolding Jake's lovely penis in his mouth, this time going down deeper on him and sucking harder as he came back up. He had loved giving head ever since he'd learned, at an embarrassingly early age, how easy it was to turn men to putty in his hands by sinking to his knees and using his mouth on them. It could be a transaction, a bribe or an act of the purest love and he adored that curious paradox. Right at that moment, he was unsure what it was that he was offering, only that Jake seemed to need it as much as he did and that was enough for him, for now.

Jake's fingers were still buried in his hair but he didn't push him down, more like he was just resting his hand there, riding along with his movements. His hips flexed but that too was an easy movement, not forcing himself deeper than Mari took him.

"Mmmm yeah, I do believe that is hitting the spot." Jake exhaled. "Ohh, babe, that feels really amazing."

Mari made an affirmative little sound, confirming that he too found the whole experience massively agreeable. He wriggled onto his side so that he was able to reach down and, with the hand that was not gently massaging Jake's groin and working on his lovely, firm balls, he got to work on his own cock, which was pulsing its demands for attention with increasing frequency. A long, low groan of pleasure rose in his chest as he sucked and nodded and stroked for several long minutes, loving the heat that was spilling through him. It had been so long since he'd tumbled into bed with another man and just given himself to the feelings of ecstasy that touching and kissing and sucking could bring. Not for the first time, he wondered why he had left it so long, but that just reminded him of the reasons he had been trying to hide from and his heart quickened again.

Jake was a powerful, masculine lover and he would almost certainly want to go further. And Mari wanted him to, more than he could even bear to say. He was just afraid of what would happen when things moved up a gear.

Bitter, salty drops coated Mari's tongue, and Jake bent the knee of his top leg up, spreading himself open more. He bobbed his head faster and the muscles of Jake's stomach tightened, his chest expanding and contracting with each panting breath.

"Uhh…fuck, you're gonna make me come if you keep it up, Ilmari," Jake whispered.

Mari looked up at him impishly, lips parted around the glossy head of his cock. He wriggled the tip of his tongue against the ridges of sensitive tissue where Jake's hood latched onto the shaft of his long, fat dick. Feeling impish, Mari blew warm, quick breaths over the glistening wetness, making Jake twitch and ooze some more.

"I thought that was kind of the idea, Mr. Detective," he cooed naughtily. "Look at you…so hard and throbbing and wet. I just want to gobble you right up."

Jake tipped his head back and groaned, his cock jumping at every word Mari spoke with his lips pressed against it.

"It is the idea," Jake murmured. "Unless you wanted something else. And if not you're gonna finish me off in another couple of strokes of that sweet mouth."

Mari wrapped his fingers tight around the base of Jake's long shaft and slowly stroked the head back and forth across his lips. From time to time, he stuck out his tongue and rolled it slowly up and down the underside of Jake's cock.

"Look at me," he ordered in a husky whisper. "I want you to look me in the eye while you're coming in my mouth."

He enfolded Jake's swollen glans between his wet lips again, applying firm but gentle suction on just the head of his cock. His thumb moved up and down the spit-drenched line his tongue had just taken and his eyes never left Jake's face the whole time.

Jake's eyes were alight with blazing heat when he looked down at him. His hips jerked harder, pushing his cock into Mari's hand and still deeper into his mouth. His face scrunched when he started to peak but he kept his eyes locked with Mari's as ordered and he drenched his mouth in a salty spill.

Sweet as an angel, Mari handled the explosion without making a sound, keeping Jake in his mouth almost the whole time, swallowing in little gulps as the spurts kept on coming. Only as his lover's climax slowed did he utter a little murmur of satisfaction, before letting Jake slip from his mouth so that he could move further up the mattress, still stroking himself with one hand.

"You are so damned hot, Chivis," he panted. "You have no idea how much I loved watching you come like that."

He leaned forward and tapped the head of his painfully hard cock against Jake's lips, shuddering at the sensations that vibrated back along the shaft and tightened his nuts. Jake reached up and dislodged Mari's hand from his dick, taking over the quick, sure strokes almost without missing a beat. He tilted his head and sucked one of Mari's balls into his mouth then let it pop free while jacking him harder, faster.

"Come on my face, do it," he murmured, his voice gone hoarse.

"Get you, Officer Starsky!" Mari saluted him with a cheeky grin. "I love it when you're forceful." He rolled those lean hips to thrust into Jake's stroking fingers. "And you have a little bit of a kinky streak too. Mmhhh-hmm! That's good."

He was still gazing down barely blinking as he stared into Jake's eyes, watching the man jacking him with a deft hand, and the last couple of words came out in a breathless rush. He edged closer and put his knee against Jake's chest, nudging him onto his back so that he was almost kneeling over him, then leaning forward to rest one hand against the wall behind the head of the bed as his hips and buttocks rose and fell, fucking Jake's pumping hand faster and harder.

"Mmmhhhh…ohhhh…mmm goood!" he mewed as his body began to spasm, responding to the sweet, delicious friction. His insides contracted hard and he stopped bucking moments before the cascade began. A little gasp or two were the only sounds he made though as he came hard, splashing his hot cum all over that handsome face, just as he'd been told to.

Jake aimed the last couple spurts into his mouth and licked his lips and the head of Mari's twitching cock. Pearly ropes of semen gleamed on his cheek and chin. The rumbled sound of contentment in his chest vibrated between Mari's thighs.

"Mmm, just as delicious as you are beautiful," Jake murmured.

Mari quivered while Jake cleaned off his ultrasensitive shaft, then wiggled back down to lie on top of him, pressing up against his firm, hot body. He kissed Jake's semen-streaked face all over, licking him and sliding his tongue into Jake's mouth for a deeper, hotter kiss.

"You are fabulous," he acknowledged as their lips finally

parted and he could catch his breath. "Why does it always feel so much better when someone else does that to you? Thank you."

"It feels better because you don't know what's coming next, how the other person will touch you, stroke you, how hard or fast. Your body has to guess, has to give up a little bit of control. That's my theory, anyway." Jake chuckled. His right hand was cupped to the back of Mari's head and the other was curled just under his ass cheek at the top of his thigh, not embracing him exactly but holding him nonetheless, in an oddly tender way.

Mari curled up on his chest like a kitten, his head on Jake's shoulder, one hand resting on his right biceps, the fingers of the other stroking up and down his left hip. Their cocks were trapped between his belly and Jake's and he could feel the gentle rise and fall of Jake's body as his breathing slowed and steadied, causing a delicate friction that kept him from losing his hard-on completely.

"You are so smart," he mused contentedly. "I like that in a guy. Smart, and fucking hot."

Jake laughed softly. His hand on the back of Mari's head started to stroke, combing gentle fingers through the softness of his hair and massaging his scalp, which felt impossibly good. After a few moments, Jake suggested, "If you're staying for a little while, I could go again."

Mari echoed that husky laugh as they lay there together on the bed, just gazing at one another, unable to stop looking and touching.

"Smart, fucking hot *and* insatiable! Full house!"

He lifted his head and took possession of Jake's mouth once more, indulging him in a long, slow, smoldering kiss. Their lean, nude bodies moved slowly against each other in a sleepy, horizontal dance, legs entwined, arms snaking around bared torsos. It most certainly felt too good to simply stop and dress and go home. He was not ready for the cold night air on his skin just yet.

When Mari paused to catch a breath between kisses, Jake lifted his hand and gave him a smack on the ass, not too hard but enough to make a loud noise.

"No casino jokes," he told him then cracked up at the bewildered look on Mari's face. "Full house? It's a Tribal thing. Sorry. I can never tell when you're serious or you're purposely being un-PC."

He wrapped his arms around Mari before he could retaliate, either with actions or words, and rolled him swiftly over as if he weighed nothing, pressing him down into the mattress and kissing him passionately once more. There was a gleam in those aquamarine eyes when their lips separated and Jake propped himself on his elbows to look down on him. Slim fingers stroked through his hair, tugging him gently, wanting him back down in a closer embrace.

Mari didn't protest the little slap though, and Jake wondered if it hadn't roused some small devilment in him, because the grin on his face was infectious.

Jake answered it with a smirk of his own. He moved his lower half in slow undulations, just rocking and rubbing along that silken body beneath his. His arms were still wrapped around Mari, underneath him, holding him like he was fragile, letting him feel cherished.

"So, you like kinky, huh? How kinky? What flavors of kink do you like?"

"Did I say anything about *that*?" Mari blinked at him then attempted to look innocent. "I said it was tasty that *you* did."

"I saw what a little slap on the ass did to you. Like that, huh?" Jake grinned broader.

"Hmmm...you pay far too much attention to stuff," Mari commented slyly. "You get your dick sucked and you want to slap me about, huh? Bloody He-Man!"

"Not seriously, unless you were into it," Jake said, backtracking, wondering if he'd misread.

"Well, that's a thing." Mari nodded to himself and traced

an invisible swirl on Jake's chest with a fingertip. "Good to know. Did anyone you dated ever ask you to tie them up?"

Jake placed a slow line of kisses along Mari's jaw. "No. But I dated a guy that liked to tie me up."

"Mmhhh…" Mari's eyes glittered again. "Interesting. Did you enjoy it?"

"Some of it," Jake said cryptically. "I got off. What about you? You seem to get hot when I get bossy."

"I like a guy that knows how to take control," Mari admitted, repaying him for that cryptic response. "I never tried it, but my ex once told me that he thought I'd benefit from the experience of being tied to his bed. I think I held out on him just to pay him back for saying it."

"So now that we have each other's bondage history out of the way, what else do you like? Or not like?" Jake asked, still peppering him with kisses.

Mari kept trickling his fingers through his hair and smiled more secretively.

"I like that you do little things like kissing me while you're talking to me," he murmured. "A lot of guys aren't that into kissing and I love it. I love being touched, just about anywhere. I love what you just let me do to you, that was so hot," he added with a grin. "And I could just lick and kiss you all over. You have got the most…*incredible* body, if you don't mind me gushing about it."

Jake didn't mind him gushing at all, and he thought that must be apparent, if the renewing erection pressing into the hollow of Mari's hip was any indication. He reached down between them and stroked his palm over Mari's thickening cock. "So you're only after me for my body, I see how it is," he teased.

"Wellllll…it helps," Mari drawled. He arched his back and bucked his hips, rubbing himself against Jake's hand and uttering little growls of pleasure. "Mmmmhhh…show me what you like then, macho man."

Jake chuckled where his lips pressed to Mari's throat. The vibration must have tickled because his sexy bedmate squirmed and wriggled and groaned very deeply under him. He slid his hands up Mari's sides, over his ribs, and drew his arms up over his head, all very slowly, until he reached Mari's wrists, which he pinned there in the pillows. He traveled downward at the same time, kissing and licking and nipping all along Mari's throat and the edge of his collarbone and down the center of his chest until he found a nipple to tease and play with. The groans became little yelps and whimpers then, but Mari's cock hardened against his belly.

"You make the sexiest sounds when you're turned on," Jake murmured, his breath flowing over the wetness he'd left on Mari's nipple. He ran his tongue over the small nub again, blew on it then sucked it hard into his warm mouth.

Mari moaned helplessly, sprawled beneath him, overcome by his need for Jake's body pressed up tightly against his own. For a little while his private anxieties were simply pushed away. As the fierce spike of desire stabbed upward through his loins in response to that tugging on his sensitive bud, it left him wriggling and sliding his bare feet up and down the backs of Jake's muscular thighs. Mari could almost imagine that this time everything would be fine and he could give himself completely to the gorgeous man on top of him. It wasn't like he hadn't fantasized about it so many times already.

"Uhh...mmmhhh... Damn it, Chivis, I *want* you," he growled, impossibly turned on by the sensation of being pinned and held down. He had never been the fainting flower that most of his straight, or at least *straighter-acting* colleagues, painted him as, but there was something deliciously exciting for him about being with a man who was stronger than him and didn't mind showing it.

Most of his lovers, sadly, had been a bit squeamish about physically forcing him down on the bed and taking what they wanted. Then when he'd found someone who would... Mari pushed that train of thought off the tracks, not wanting to think about Tomas and his handsome, mocking face right now. Not lying here with Jake between his legs, hard and horny for him.

Maybe today would be the day when his ravenous body got what it desired.

Please! Oh please...just let this work! he begged silently.

Jake took his time teasing Mari, his play gradually becoming rougher, his teeth scraping lightly along his skin and when his mouth closed over first one nipple and then the other, he sucked on them hard enough to make it hurt. The whole time Jake was torturing his nipples Mari's lower half lazily bucked, rubbing their erections together side by side.

When he lifted his head, he covered Mari's mouth with his own, plunging his tongue inside and kissing him fiercely, hot and demanding.

"I've got condoms and lube. But you have to say it. Tell me *exactly* what you want, Ilmari," Jake whispered, easing himself up on his forearms to look down on him.

Mari closed his eyes for a moment, lips parted around the gasp of pleasure that fierce tingle in his tortured breast provoked. What to do? He knew what Jake wanted, or thought so anyway. And he wanted it too, more than anything. Why did this always happen? Mari could feel himself tensing up at the thought of letting Jake take things further, though, and try as he might to control it and relax in Jake's strong arms, he just couldn't get there.

He turned his head away, mortified and fighting his emotions. He would not cry in front of the man he wanted so badly that it hurt. He'd made that mistake with Tomas and his ex had never let him forget it. Nor had he been much impressed by it.

"Tears don't turn me on, Ilmarinen."

Mari felt so sick he thought he might retch at the memory and he bit down on his lips until he had enough control for speech.

"Jake...I really want you to," he exhaled. "I do...but I

don't think you will be able to. I'm so sorry."

Chapter Nine

Mari saw the confusion on Jake's face and braced for the inevitable rush of angry questions he knew were coming. Only they didn't.

"Okay," Jake said simply, and kissed his temple, then his cheek and the corner of his mouth tenderly. "Can I kiss you there, touch you there? I know some guys just aren't into rimming. Or would you like to switch places, maybe? Whatever you like, Mari...we can stay just like this too. It feels amazing, just rubbing my dick on you like this," Jake murmured in his ear.

Mari kept his eyes closed a little longer. He could hear the cogs turning in the tone of Jake's gentle voice and couldn't bring himself to look just yet.

Oh hell! Now he thinks you're a freak. Maybe you should have just let him try. He heaved a shaky sigh and forced himself to look up at the man.

"I like that. Yes. Whatever you want to do," he said, the words coming out husky and tentative. "I like being touched there, Jake. It's...kind of complicated. I want to make you feel good but... Shit! This is going to sound so stupid."

Fuck! Don't tell him. He'll think you're retarded or something! He closed his eyes and his mouth and chewed on his lips again, wanting to be honest but afraid of losing his best chance of a lover since splitting with Tomas.

Idiot...you've lost him anyway!

Jake pressed up on his elbows, and his hands framed Mari's face. He waited until Mari opened his eyes and looked at him.

"You think too much," he said simply, and when Mari opened his mouth to say something, Jake continued, "Your ass isn't a set of goalposts, sweetheart. Really. It's not the be all and end all, must-have thing. If you'd just said you didn't want to, or didn't like anal sex, I wouldn't even question it. Some guys aren't into it and there's nothing wrong with that. There's a thousand other ways to have sex that are just as much fun. But, you keep hinting it isn't so much that you're not into it, there's something else, and so I'm going to ask. *Why* do you think it's complicated?"

Mari stared at him. Now that his eyes were locked on to Jake's, he couldn't look away. It wasn't just that he was hot, that he was cute, that every time Mari thought about him, it made him shiver with a sense of wanting that he couldn't fight—Jake looked at him like he was real. And he was the first person, outside a therapist's office, that had ever asked him why he felt that way and what lay beneath his terror. The truly awful thing was that he really didn't know.

Maybe he *was* a freak.

Or maybe Jake had a point and he *did* think too much. That he couldn't help, it was the way he had been raised— to question, to learn, to take things on board, to consider the options, the reasons, the defaults and the logic.

"My shrink says there's a name for it," he said, though it was more that the words were falling out of his head without him being able to censor them. He wanted to shut his eyes but Jake was looking at him so seriously that he wasn't able to tear himself away from that intense gaze. If he opened his heart and Jake laughed, he would die. Simple as that. "It's called anodyspareunia, or just plain old dyspareunia if you prefer. Once upon a time, when women had it, men called them ice queens, or frigid, or worse things." He shook his head. "When I think about sex, I... I just clam up, my whole body goes rigid and I... I just can't. I'm not afraid, I *want* it so much. I masturbate, I think about being fucked and it turns me on, but I just *can't*...my body won't let anyone in. Since the first time, no one has ever fucked me properly again, Jake. Not for the want of trying, either. But most of my adult life, I've never been with a man who was able to get his cock anywhere near enough inside me, without hurting me or hurting himself, to make either of us come. And it drives me crazy."

His voice cracked a little on that last sentence and he turned his head away again, fighting the lump in his throat that wanted to choke him for being such an idiot, for opening his big mouth and letting Jake know how useless he was as a lover.

Jake didn't laugh. He didn't say anything either. He just continued to stroke his fingers gently through Mari's hair with a thoughtful look on his face. Mari closed his eyes and Jake lowered his lips to kiss one fluttering lid.

"I can't imagine how frustrating that must be for you," he whispered nearer to Mari's ear. "You haven't scared me away or freaked me out, if that's what's going through your pretty head. It's not something you can help, Mari. We can still do lots of things together, if you want to."

Mari shook his head, though. His heart felt so heavy that he thought it would just break apart in his chest, even though Jake was doing his best to be kind. He didn't want that kindness, didn't truly deserve it. What he wanted— he tried to turn on his side, to curl up, just to feel some semblance of stillness for a moment— what he wanted more than anything was to mount Jake, to ride his cock, to feel him deep in his body, driving him crazy with ecstasy. And he didn't even know if those feelings were real or something he'd invented on dark, lonely nights, trying to cure himself with just his stroking hand and a stiff, unyielding, probe of lubricated silicone.

"I should go," he said in a dull tone. "I shouldn't have come here. I'm sorry."

Jake pushed himself up on his arms again so that he wasn't quite pinning Mari anymore, but he didn't roll off him entirely.

"I'm going to assume you are so upset that you don't

realize how insulting that is. I can't force you to stay, but I don't *want* you to go. Also, if the men you've been with before made you feel less than the sexy, wonderful and oh-so-satisfying man that you are, that makes *them* assholes, not me."

Mari's head turned sharply. His eyes were a little too bright, his voice brittle.

"You really believe *that's* what I think? You are *not* an asshole, Jake Chivis. If anything, it's me that should feel like that. I didn't mean to insult you. I just— I feel as though I led you on, let you think that this could be something that it can't be, ever." He looked away again, crestfallen and still so frustrated he could have chewed the edge off the mattress. "I let myself hope it could be different this time. I really felt as though…as though… Oh damn, this is stupid, but I felt like we had a connection. I hoped that it would just override my stupid body's stupid fucking idiot reactions, just for once, just long enough that I could… Oh fuck! Fuck!"

He wrenched himself around and buried his face in the pillow, stifling the furious sob that tore itself out of him, hiding the tears that he knew would kill off Jake's last shreds of sympathy. The other night when Jake had just held him tightly in his arms, not questioning his need for that security, he had let his fantasies run away with him. And here he was, almost thirty years old, without the sense most kids were born with, crying his heart out for something that he'd never known it was possible to lose. When Tomas had dumped him in front of everyone, he had not cried. Not even later when he'd been alone in his apartment, ripping holes in everything he could find that belonged to his wretched ex. Why could he not even explain things right now without welling up? What the fuck was wrong with him?

Through the sobs, he heard Jake make a small sound he was sure was a sigh and he got off the bed. Mari really wanted to die then. Wanted the ground to open and swallow him. This was the lowest he'd felt in a long time, and that was saying something considering how down he had been in recent months. He was about to scrape himself together enough to grab his clothes and get out of there when the bed moved again and Jake pulled a blanket over him as he lay down behind him, wrapping one strong arm around him and pulling him back against his chest.

"Shh...shh. It's okay," Jake murmured into the nape of his neck. "There is no reason to be sorry, Ilmari. And there is no reason to think you can change anything all in one night. And if it never changes, you can still be happy with someone. You can still make someone happy."

Mari lay still in his embrace, letting his body go to the quiet place he found in his meditation sessions. When Jake had come back to lie beside him and hold him, he'd calmed down enough to control the vast wave of emotion that had drowned him in a sea of embarrassment. He stared at the wall beyond the edge of the bed, his mind running Jake's words over and over, trying to understand what he was saying.

"Someone," he said at last, in a broken voice, but at least the tears had stopped. He was thankful for that, and for the warmth against his naked back and buttocks. "Not you?"

The hand that Jake was stroking soothingly up and down Mari's chest slowed, but he didn't pull away.

"I didn't want to presume," Jake murmured. "But...yeah. I think you could make me very happy, just the way you are. I'm not so sure I could do the same for you, though. I haven't had much luck keeping anyone happy for long."

Mari shifted in his loose embrace and turned finally, looking up at him. He probably looked awful, he thought. His eyes would be red—some people could cry and still look amazing, but he knew from bitter experience that he wasn't one of them.

What had Tomas called him? An albino Bush Baby, or something?

"I can't imagine that," he said sincerely. "What was

143

wrong with them? Were they not freaks?"

He put a hand over his mouth then lowered it. "I'm sorry, that sounded insulting too. Ignore me, I don't think too well when I get emotional."

Jake brought a hand up to Mari's cheek.

"Close your eyes," he whispered.

Mari thought maybe he just didn't want to look at their bloodshot ugliness but when he closed them, Jake leaned closer and kissed each lid, and just under them, his lips brushing away all the wetness. He kissed the tip of Mari's nose and his tremulous mouth, spreading the salt taste of his tears there.

"There was nothing wrong with them...well, most of them. Not that I've had so many. They had their reasons for leaving, I guess. The last guy I was with thought I wasn't 'gay enough'." He gave a bitter half laugh. "Guess sucking his dick didn't qualify unless I was decked out in rainbows and marching in parades on the weekend. Everyone has their reasons not to be happy, Mari."

"Not gay enough?" Mari echoed his laugh. "What does that even mean? You're either gay or you're not, I mean... weird!" He felt a little better, and something was also tugging at the edges of his consciousness, something else that Jake had said to him while they were just cuddled up under the blanket. "Did you mean that, about me being able to make you happy? Or were you just trying to make me feel better?"

"Both," Jake said.

Mari narrowed his eyes slightly but Jake didn't crack and make a joke. He weighed that up and figured out he couldn't get mad about it either way.

"I'd like to make you happy," he said at last, touching his nose to Jake's and turning his head a little to press his lips to Jake's as well, sowing little kisses along the solemn crease of his mouth.

Jake kissed him back, soft, warm pecks at first, then covering his mouth more firmly, then licking at him. Then they were locked at the lips with their tongues teasing and tasting each other once more until they were both breathless.

"You know what would make me really happy?" Jake asked when they finally stopped for breath. He looked at Mari and lifted both eyebrows, making them wiggle up and down in a comic-book-villain leer.

Mari eyed him with slight trepidation, though finally he succumbed to a little chuckle because Jake's expression was just so comical it made him feel a bit better.

"No-o... What?" he asked warily.

"If you'll stay a little longer, and let me show you some of those ways to get each other off, like I was talking about." Jake's voice dropped back down to a husky purr as he tried to coax him.

Mari felt his tension levels subside slowly as he realized that Jake wasn't taking the piss and he genuinely seemed to want him to stick around.

"Well... I guess it's not so late yet," he murmured, feeling oddly coy in the face of Jake's persuasive tone. "If I'm going to be staying, I ought to just make a call... You don't mind, do you? It won't take me long."

He wasn't used to being overwhelmed with shyness around other men but something in Jake's firm yet gentle manner left him lost for his usual flirtatious composure. He felt like a child again when Jake turned that mild-mannered logic on him. Which in turn was odd because his childhood had been far from conventional. He had never really been treated like a baby by his parents, possibly because he was their only child and possibly because they felt guilty for not being able to stay together.

He had never minded it so much, in truth. Not once in his life had he ever felt unloved by his family. He knew Mama would worry, though, if he was late back and didn't let her know. And he was nothing if not a dutiful son. Thankfully he had lived alone in Barcelona. Tomas would have been merciless in his mockery otherwise.

"Here," Jake said, wrapping the blanket around Mari's

shoulders. "Your phone is still in the living room, I think. It's six steps that way," he joked, nodding toward the door, only he wasn't under-exaggerating.

Mari leaned forward and kissed him on the nose.

"I hope I don't get lost in here," he teased by way of retaliation. "You will come and look for me if I'm not back in an hour?"

Jake swatted his backside and he actually managed to laugh.

He didn't tell Mama where he was or what he was up to, just that he and Jake had stopped for a drink somewhere and got talking. She didn't press him for details but he could hear the smile behind her words as she told him to take care. As usual he told her that he loved her and they hung up. Then he made his precise, six-step return to the cozy bedroom, where he knew Jake must still be, unless he'd decided to climb out of the window.

He was lying on the bed where Mari had left him. Sprawled, actually, would be a better description, on top of the duvet, face down. Jake turned his head when Mari came back in the room, smiling at him lazily.

"Coming back to bed?" he asked.

"Well...given the vista, I might just stand here for a little while," Mari quipped, taking in the delicious curves of Jake's running-toned arse. He slid the blanket off his shoulders and came to sit on the edge of the mattress beside him, running a finger down that gorgeous naked back and fanning his hands across Jake's cheeks to caress him there admiringly. "That really is an amazing derrière, Chivis."

"You like it?" Jake said, wiggling his hips from side to side to show off.

"It has a life all its own," Mari chuckled. His fingers traced the sculpted contours of every visible muscle carefully. "You could give anatomy classes with an arse like that."

"Who says I haven't?" Jake said, looking over his shoulder, a coy little smile on his lips.

"You'd be richer than this." Mari laughed, waving a hand

around at the small square of inhabitable space. He eased his long legs up onto the bed and rolled himself onto Jake, snuggling down with his head resting against the man's shoulder where he could run his fingertips over the slightly raised design on his gloriously nude back. "What exactly *is* this? Some kind of tribal thing?"

"It's a medicine shield," Jake said. "Protection, Strength, Wisdom, Happiness. I had it inked when I joined the force. Figured I better have something to watch my back." He lifted his hips a little, pushing the other object of Mari's admiration into the curve of his pelvis.

"Does it?" Mari asked, slightly amused by this. "Watch over you, I mean?"

He squirmed a little so that his reawakened interest didn't leave him in an uncomfortable situation, trapped hard against Jake's backside. He nudged his overenthusiastic cock into the deep rift between those perfect cheeks and eased his arms around Jake's torso, kissing the back of his neck where his dark hair was soft and downy as it gave way to bare skin.

Jake groaned softly against his arm and Mari heard him swallow before he answered, "So far it has. I was a detective in Detroit, Mari. I've been shot at, had people try and run me over, had junkies try to stab me with needles. Haven't had anything thrown my way hit me yet."

"Or maybe you just left in time." Mari chuckled, still not entirely convinced. His scientific upbringing had left him healthily skeptical about most branches of mysticism. Generally he liked to see proof of a thing's effectiveness before he decided to trust his life to it. He touched his lips to Jake's shoulder and let them roam slowly down his body, following the tracery of his inking in and out of the circle along the quarter lines while he still gently massaged the lightly furred expanse of Jake's chest. "What made you decide to get that particular design? I mean, beyond the esoteric stuff, protection, whatnot?"

"Shields are personal things, usually. Every warrior

makes their own. But they usually share a similarity within tribes. Colors and materials have traditional meanings. Now they are mainly symbolic of course, but we still keep the traditions alive when we can."

"So...you have a totem pole stashed away in here somewhere?" Mari whispered against the soft skin at the small of his back where his lips were still fulfilling their promise to explore every inch of him.

Jake stifled a choked sound.

"That's a different tribe, I'm afraid." He managed to laugh. "I got a different kinda pole for you, though." He wiggled again, shifting slowly from side to side and flexing the muscles of his arse so his cheeks gripped Mari's shaft. "Or you could stash yours someplace," he suggested.

Mari lifted his head for a moment, eyes widening. "Are you suggesting what I think you're suggesting, Mr. Warrior?"

His body was more than up for it, the constriction of Jake's sexy backside only made him harder and he could barely think in a straight line. That was somehow unexpected and even though it wouldn't be the first time he'd fucked a man, it had been a long time since he'd been given that option.

It's like falling off a bike! his inner counsel sniped and he shrugged it off, concentrating on the delicious aspect before him. It had been even longer since he'd ridden a bicycle. He couldn't recall that he'd ever fallen off.

"Is it really that surprising?" Jake asked him. "That is, if you're up for it?" he added quickly, wiggling and clenching his cheeks again in a way that left no doubt Jake thought he was up for it.

"I... Yeah—on both counts." Mari shook his head a little, still dazed by the invitation. "You seemed... I dunno, I guess I thought you seemed more like a top than a bottom. Just goes to show, what they say about books and covers, huh? Um...so where are those rubbers and stuff you were talking about?"

Jake reached over the side of the bed and underneath and

came back up with a box in his hand. When he repeated the exercise he held a small bottle. Mari noted the box was unopened.

"You got these specially then?" he teased, cracking the seal on the cellophane with a thumbnail and breaking open the box to extract the strip of goodies from within. He tore a couple off and dropped them onto the bed beside him, then resumed his stealthy kissing of Jake's body, working his way down to the base of his spine then beginning on those firm, delicious peach halves, touching his lips and nose and tongue to the curves of his arse and the inviting cleft between them. His scent was slightly musky there, like some exotic delicacy and oh-so enticing. Mari wasted no time, licking and kissing him from his tailbone down to his balls and back again. He pressed deliberately with his thumbs on the inner slopes of Jake's sexy crack and spread him wider so that he could get to work on the darker pucker of flesh that guarded his ring. Mari paused once, briefly, in his sensual exploration to murmur, "You like that?"

Jake made a small sound in his throat that sounded like it had to sneak past locked vocal cords then he gave a little gasping chuckle. "Yeah…oh fuck, yeah, I like that, Ilmari."

Mari laughed softly and returned to his industrious laving of Jake's adorable ring. He had almost forgotten how much he enjoyed the business of foreplay. With most of his lovers, that extended licking and kissing and stroking and fingering had been better than the actual sex. The noises Jake made while he was being soaked and probed by Mari's wriggling tongue quivered through flesh and bone and those tremors arrowed straight down to Mari's cock and balls, making him harder than he had been in a long time.

He sucked on his index finger for a moment and pressed it against the well-licked collar of muscle, easing it into the velvet heat of Jake's arse. He did not press too deep, just sliding in as far as the sleek node of his prostate and stroking the lightest touch around it before withdrawing. Mari decided he was not the only one that was tight.

"It's been a while for you too, hasn't it, big fella?" he crooned, blowing on the glistening wetness of his lover's orifice then reaching for the bottle of lube and applying a little trickle to his restlessly wiggling crack.

Jake didn't answer him right off. Instead he bent his knees up, spreading them out to the sides so Mari had more room between his thighs. Bent forward like that, he looked like he was making an offering, or a prayer, or both.

"As much as I love the way that feels, if you don't fuck me soon, it's gonna be all over for me," Jake told him, which counted as a prayer in Mari's book.

"Such an impatient boy!" he purred, using his thumb to slick the lubrication all around Jake's snug entrance then reaching for one of the condoms. He ripped the packet with his teeth and extracted the little cap, deftly slipping it over the head of his straining penis and working it down his shaft with one hand while he used his fingers to ensure that Jake was wet and ready.

"Mmmhh...ribbed too, you like to feel it, don't you?" he crooned, slicking his erection with the silky fluid as well. He was shaking slightly with a mixture of trepidation and eagerness and he knew that he talked too much when he was nervy but he couldn't help it. He wanted his cock inside Jake but he was also a bit worried about hurting him by trying to go too fast, so he forced himself to take it steadily and keep up the gentle stream of inanity, in spite of Jake's frantic plea. Testing the water, he stroked his cock head up and down the cleft of Jake's arse, then pressed the tip harder against the glistening target between his cheeks, applying more pressure with his thumb, just behind the swell of his glans. He moaned too at the squeezing sensation as he nudged inside.

"Oh boy... Ohh...that is so tight, so hot. That feels really incredible, Jake. Are you okay?"

"Rrr-fuuuck..." The words came out soft huffs of breath. "I'm much, much better than just okay." Jake rocked his hips in a short, tight circle, encouraging Mari deeper. "Fuck, baby, that is so good."

His enthusiasm sent little tracers of heat wriggling down through Mari's body to add steel to his erection and he gripped Jake's lean hips, pulling that sexy bottom down harder on his deliciously sensitive phallus. He rolled his hips, burying himself deeper and deeper and uttered a gasp of hungry astonishment at the intense pleasure that tight little bum gave his thrusting cock. Shedding some of his nerves, he gripped Jake almost savagely, pulling him back with rough hands, pressing further with every stroke.

In the end, it was actually *easier* than falling off a bike. Although the thought itself did not come until the deed was done. For the duration he was content to follow the direction of his hard dick and throbbing balls, pumping Jake faster and rougher until said balls were slapping against the man's arse in a satisfying rhythm. It was just so incredible to be inside him, enjoying what was undeniably the best ride of his life. A part of him wanted it to go on forever but the part that was controlled by his genitals was demanding relief all too soon.

Jake had his knees under him, although his legs were still spread so his hips were low, raised just enough to push back to meet Mari but still able to rub the underside of his shaft on the bedding. The little moans and mewls of pleasure Jake made came more regularly the longer Mari pounded him. They fitted together perfectly, and the way Jake arched his back and panted let him know he was hitting the spot just right. When Mari thought he was so close to the edge he didn't know how much longer he could go on, Jake snaked an arm under his body and added a new juddering beat to their pounding rhythm as he stroked his cock.

"Oh god...oh fuck, Mari... Oh, I'm gonna come!" Jake gasped into the bedclothes, clutching his cock with one hand and the sheets with the other as his hole tightened and pulsed around Mari's shaft.

He let his hands glide across Jake's sweat-slick shoulders and around and under him, locking his fingers across his heaving chest and drawing him back, urging him to kneel up so that he could press his body close to Jake's, leaning full against him from his knees to his neck and kissing him breathlessly beneath the curve of his earlobe.

"Come with me, big fella," he whispered hoarsely, hips moving like they were mechanized, slamming him upward into Jake's arse with a single-minded fury as he held on tightly to him. His body was drenched in the sweat of their mutual exertion and the sensation of Jake's naked back and buttocks slithering sensually against his chest, belly and thrusting crotch brought him to a starry-eyed peak. At the same time he felt the muscles of his lover's channel catch him in a shuddering grasp that milked him hard. Even if he hadn't been close, that violent squeezing along the whole length of his throbbing dick would have pulled him over.

If he said anything in the grip of that overpowering orgasm, he could not recall it. He could not recall anything at all but the sensation of pressing his whole body up close against Jake's, inside him, straddled by him, dragging clenching fingers down his heaving chest as he exploded in him — and exploded was the only word for it really, since he didn't think he had ever come so hard or so much in his life.

Afterward he just clung to Jake like a drowning man clinging to a rock in a turbulent sea. His pulse was crashing in his ears and his heart felt as though it were trying to kick-box its way out of his chest. Neither was a contest for his attention compared to the melting sensation in his loins. It seemed as if his balls were throwing a party and they had forgotten to invite him.

He giggled then, giddy at the thought, drunk on the post-orgasmic sensations slamming through his body, a heady cocktail of endorphins that ought to be bottled and sold on Darknet, it was so potent. Jake had flattened to the mattress, his muscles released of all tension and he lay panting with Mari draped over him.

"I don't normally just roll over and fall asleep, honest," Jake murmured drowsily after several long, breathless moments. "But I so could do that right now. I think you melted every bone in my body."

"Mmmmhhh... I feel the same," Mari purred, curling up against his broad back once he had eased off and discarded the spent rubber. He tugged the blanket back around them both then rested his cheek against Jake's shoulder again, his arms writhing around Jake to hold him close once more. "That was s-s-s-s-s-o-o-o-o-o-o good, chief. I am very glad you talked me into sticking around."

Jake sighed and turned his head. He kissed Mari on the nose. "Do me a favor, sweetheart, choose just about anything else to call me, okay?"

Mari looked innocently at him. "Hit a nerve, much?" He pouted. "I didn't mean it in any kind of nasty way."

"I know you didn't, and I'm not mad. But it's still racist." Jake smiled crookedly at him.

"It's a word, Jake." Mari shook his head. "A word for a man I'd really like to let be in charge of me. Yes? I won't make you wear warpaint in bed, if that worries you."

Jake choked back a laugh. "Now you're just trying to distract me. Ilmarinen Gale, I doubt you let *anyone* be in charge of you."

"So you see how special it is, huh?" Mari kissed the tip of his nose. "I really like you, Chivis. I don't want to argue so I won't call you Chief. Don't call me 'sweetheart' though, that's *really* quite patronizing."

He said all of this with a completely straight face, eyes fixed on Jake solemnly.

Jake nodded. "It would be, if I didn't mean it. But okay, deal." He kept Mari's lips busy for a few moments with a kiss and when he leaned back again, he grinned. "How about snookums. Can I call you snookums?"

"Can I stick a broken paddle up your ass and whale you with the floppy end?" Mari said, eyes narrowing slightly. "I have a name, Jake Chivis, you could call me that."

Jake heaved a dramatic sigh. "Yes, dear."

The flat of Mari's hand made ringing contact with his arse.

He liked the sound it made there so he did it again. "You are deliberately being annoying now, aren't you, Chivis? Well, I guess it wouldn't do for you to be *too* perfect." He uttered a little sigh.

"So..." Jake said, nibbling along the side of Mari's throat. "About that paddle..."

The touch of his lips and teeth there melted all of Mari's resolve into a little puddle that pooled in his middle and made him stiffen involuntarily. He slid his arms up around the back of Jake's neck, pulling him closer again, all animosity forgotten in that moment.

"You are so kinky it's fascinating. Did they spank you regularly in detective school or something?"

"The course on BDSM is kinda lacking in detective school," Jake told him. "It's not really that kinky, is it?"

Mari chuckled softly, lips touching his ear. "I just love that you're so hung up on it. Maybe some guys would think it was odd, that you like to get slapped. I just find it quite a turn-on, to be honest."

Jake was quiet for a few moments, then said, "In that case, we'll have to explore it in greater detail when we have more time."

Mari slid around him and beneath him, looking up, searching those warm brown eyes, needing to see the emotions in his face.

"I'm not teasing you, Jake," he whispered. "*Are* you a little bit narked with me?"

Jake's brow scrunched, then smoothed and he wrapped his arms around him. "No, not at all. I was serious. I know you can't stay tonight, as much as I'd like you to. I know you have obligations. I just wanted to...to make sure you were coming back. I was hoping that this wasn't going to just be a one-time thing."

Mari drew him down and kissed his mouth with deliberate tenderness.

"I hope not too," he murmured between Jake's lips. "You try to stop me coming back."

Chapter Ten

Jake woke Sunday morning with the scent of Mari on his sheets, and a massive hard-on. Considering how sex-drugged he'd been the night before, he figured he wouldn't have been so horny so soon, but it was maybe just his body's way of informing him that it was grateful the dry spell was at an end. He stretched and yawned and was thinking about a nice leisurely jerk-off when he remembered that he had made plans to meet with Mari this morning so they could head over to Weston's house to tell him that it was likely Phil was dead. That put a damper on his libido. Working as a detective, he'd occasionally had to deal with victims' families but it had never been something he was good at. He was just a little too blunt to deal with the sorrow and remorse in any way that was better than simply keeping his mouth shut.

He threw back the duvet and got out of bed, noting as he did the way things below the beltline felt different today. His ass wasn't exactly sore but definitely had that 'well-fucked' feeling every time he took a step. He made a cursory clean-up of discarded tissues and condom packaging that he'd been too comfortable to get up and deal with after Mari had left.

Breakfast was a bowl of cereal eaten hastily over the sink before he jumped in the shower. He could probably do with a shave but it was Sunday and he didn't want to bother. Back in the bedroom, he pulled on jeans and a wool-knit sweater that clung to him almost possessively, and told himself he wasn't wearing his favorite shirt just to see if Mari liked it.

Mari... What a strange night it had been. It felt like he'd been up and down on an emotional roller coaster in the space of just a few hours. Jake could understand why he felt the way he did, considering the frustrations he must face, but at the same time, certain little things nagged at him. Mari hadn't brought anyone home to meet his family, but he talked about having past lovers, past relationships. Why hadn't he felt comfortable enough to bring any of them home to meet his momma? And the way he would hesitate before telling Jake things, like he was expecting him to say something awful, expecting to be mocked and laughed at. Then there was his near shock when Jake had suggested they switch things around. Like the thought had never crossed his mind that he could fuck him instead. And given how vigorously in control he'd been, it certainly hadn't been his first time to top.

It all added up in Jake's head to one hell of a toxic relationship that Mari must have been in. He wondered how long it would take to undo some of the damage that had been dealt him. Then he wondered how he could be thinking like that already when he'd been resisting even dating a few days ago. The realist in him said this was happening too fast. He wasn't a kid anymore, to be falling in instant love just because some guy gave him an amazing blow job then fucked him until his legs shook.

So maybe he wasn't ready to admit that he might actually be falling for Ilmarinen Gale just yet, but he saw the potential to fall for him hard.

"Fuck it!" Jake said to himself as he went back into the bathroom and dabbed on a hint of cologne. "You want him. Just give up and go with it," he told his reflection.

Probably terrible advice. Jake didn't care. Humming under his breath, he pulled on a beloved, worn-out leather jacket and locked his apartment behind him.

He met Mari at the Greek café on the corner of his road, where his svelte lover was already waiting, slim fingers cupped around a bowl-sized cup of mocha latte — with extra chocolate sprinkles. He was smart-casual in snug, straight-leg charcoal jeans and a dusky blue fitted jacket with a single button at the waist, worn over a lightweight, jersey roll neck in cream. The tapered toe of one booted foot tapped idly to a tune only he could apparently hear as he studied the broadsheet newspaper unfurled on the table in front of him. With his light-framed reading glasses perched on the end of his nose and his pale blond hair still windblown and unruly from the walk down, he looked like a student in a 1960s French movie.

Mari glanced up with a little twitch of his lips as Jake approached his table. "Well, look at you. That is a very butch look on you, Detective Chivis. Can I get you anything?"

Jake started to say no thanks. He also started to move toward the seat opposite Mari but he stopped short on both counts. He hadn't lied to Mari the night before when he'd said his exes had reasons for leaving him. Some of it had been messy and some of it had been brutal but he wasn't the kind of egoist that couldn't see where some of the fault at least was his. The refusal of any sort of PDA had been a big deal to Alex. He had nagged him about it constantly. About how it made him feel like Jake was ashamed of him. Jake hadn't been ashamed of him, but still he had not been able to bring himself to give Alex what he'd wanted.

He veered toward Mari instead and bent to kiss his cheek before sliding into the other chair. His face felt hot but he was grinning.

"Sure, they got just regular coffee here? Or does it all come with sprinkles?"

Mari chuckled warmly, pushing his spectacles up into his fine, blond hair and lifting his fingers to attract the attention of their barista, a cute little Greek lad with a year-round tan, tight jeans and equally tight buns.

"I'm sure the sprinkles aren't compulsory," he murmured, then as the lad sashayed — actually *sashayed* — over, notepad in hand, "Do you, by any chance, have a robustly masculine coffee for my butch friend?"

The barista's unwavering stare traveled over Jake from head to toe and back up again. His smile suggested he might have more than a coffee in mind but he just said, "I have perfect coffee for you, sir. You will love."

"Isn't that just adorable?" Mari whispered as he swished back to the counter and began banging and clanking around the huge coffee machine behind it. "I could eat him right up."

Jake felt his grin turn to something more sultry, and he gave Mari a smoldering look from under his lashes that said without words that he was thinking of how Mari had eaten him right up last night.

"What's adorable, exactly? The way he walks, how he talks, or just how cute his ass is?" Jake asked.

"Precisely," Mari said with a little grin. "You are *very* observant, Detective." He leaned a little closer, whispering, "How's that sexy derrière this morning?"

"It looked fine to me," Jake said.

"I wasn't talking about *his*."

"I know." Jake couldn't help teasing him a little. He looked so damn cute when he thought Jake was just yanking his chain. After a moment he said, "I'm thinking maybe I'm a little rusty. We'll have to work on that."

"Hmmm…I have just the tool for that job, I think." Mari tucked a strand of pale hair behind his ear. "Don't you worry, once I've got you oiled up and your motor running hot a few times, you'll be just fine." He sipped his coffee to hide the little smirk on his face.

Jake shook his head incredulously, feeling his cheeks go even redder, but there was no one close enough to overhear them really. Maybe their barista, but he was still clanking away with the overly complicated coffee machine and probably hadn't heard. And if he had, so what?

That thought unfolded in Jake's head like a fan of cards. *So fucking what?*

He wasn't under his dad's thumb anymore. He wasn't even on the same continent. He didn't have to see his contemptuous sneer. Didn't have to hear the loathing in his voice as he called him a disgusting faggot. He didn't have to worry about getting hazed daily by his fellow officers if they found out. He didn't have to worry about getting passed over for promotions and given all the shittiest jobs in an attempt to *drive the fag out.* He could just…be himself.

"You are very sexy when you blush like that, you know," his companion observed casually, as if he was pointing out something that Jake was wearing. "How on earth did you survive as a cop?"

Jake was saved from having to come up with an answer right away when their waiter returned with a tall glass mug of something rich and dark that smelled like caffeinated heaven. He set it down in front of Jake with a theatrical smile, then put out cream in a little jug, a tiny silver thimble with a few colored sugar cubes in it and a long-handled spoon.

"You enjoy," he said chirpily. "Is very manly drink. Make you very popular."

And with that he turned away and sauntered back to the bar to watch them from a distance. Jake tried not to roll his eyes. He ignored the sugar cubes but added a good lashing of cream before he took a sip, then a bigger swallow. He did need the caffeine.

"How is your mother?" he asked conversationally.

Mari raised an eyebrow, but if he thought Jake was changing the subject he was polite enough not to mention it.

"Insatiably curious," he answered instead. "She is going to drive me crazy with her questions. I was quite glad to come out this morning, even if the task is a grim one."

Jake grinned into his coffee as he thought about Dr. Gale senior grilling Mari about him. He didn't know why it struck him as funny but he found the picture amusing. He noticed Mari looked at him oddly and tried to wipe the smirk off his face. He must look strange, grinning like a lunatic when they were about to go and deliver such bad news, but refusing to dwell on what had to be done was how Jake had managed to keep his head on his shoulders and not lose it completely when, for example, he'd had to tell a family how their teenage son had been violently killed by a gang, then torched to cover it up.

He drank more coffee and pushed such dark memories away. It was really good stuff. Just bitter enough. He caught Mr. Very Manly Drink watching him from the counter and gave him a wink to let him know he liked the brew.

"I swear, you are in a most peculiar mood this morning," Mari informed him. "Are you high?"

Jake laughed. "Yeah, high on you."

"Well, at least I'm legal, I suppose," the man chuckled wryly. "I hate to be the one to piss metaphorical bromide on your euphoria, but have you figured out what we're going to tell Professor Weston yet?"

"Yes. I'm going to tell him I saw Phil's body and I'm pretty sure he's dead," Jake said flatly.

Mari stared at him like he'd grown an extra head.

"Just like that? You're going to tell him just like that?"

"How else should I tell him?"

"This isn't the result of a scientific trial, Jake." Mari leaned toward him, his expression suddenly serious again. "We're talking about his brother, a little brother that probably stole his toys when they were kids and he taught to ride a bike and chat up girls and stuff. You can't just walk in there and tell him you touched a van and saw his little brother stiff as a board in the back of it. He'll go ballistic. Don't the police get training in how to do stuff like this?"

Jake sighed and took another sip of his coffee. He supposed if he told Mari to calm down, he would really see some fireworks.

"Yes, and they're all pretty shitty at it too. Also, I wasn't going to tell him about the van. Not yet. Not until we have more proof on Guylian. Look, Mari, there is no way, no matter how gently I say it, that Weston isn't going to lose his shit. I can pretty much predict exactly what's going to happen and I don't have a drop of precog ability in me. He's going to flip, he's going to tell us we don't know what we're talking about, and then he's going to throw us out. Nothing about how we break it to him will change that, even a little."

Mari sat back in his chair and looked away for a moment or so, just staring out of the window distractedly, but Jake could tell he was composing his thoughts, tamping down on the urge to argue, to plead for some compassion at least. When he looked back at Jake, his expression was as gloomy as he'd ever seen it.

"I guess we ought to get it over with then." He sighed, stirring a finger around the foam-encrusted innards of his nearly empty cup and sucking the residue off the tip of it delicately.

Jake figured now was not a great time to tell him how he'd like to cover *him* in whipped cream and lick it all off. Instead he reached across the table and tucked his fingers under Mari's chin. "I'll try my best to tell him as gently as I can, okay?"

* * * *

Professor Weston lived in a nice residential neighborhood an inconvenient distance from the college. It took the best part of an hour to get there on foot and public transport. Jake and Mari were currently standing in his living room, in the process of being thrown out. The situation had gone pretty much the way Jake had said it would, with no precognition necessary.

He had told Weston, as gently as he could, what he had seen in his vision, and that he believed Phil had been murdered. Judging by the fact that Mari did not shoot him any eye daggers, he figured he had done fairly well on breaking the news compassionately. It still hadn't stopped Weston from flipping out and accusing him of making it all up, then inviting them in rather less cordial terms to return whence they had come, and posthaste.

They were heading toward the exit, still being shepherded by an irate and agitated academic, when someone rapped firmly on the front door. Jake had a moment of instinctual warning — there was something about the way that authority came knocking that was the same the world over. As he opened the door, his worst-case scenario was franked — two police officers in uniform, one male, one female, stood on the top step, looking solemn and uncomfortable. Once upon a time, it had been a kind of unspoken rule that the force only sent women out on door to door if there was bad news to be broken. Now things were a little more equal and enlightened, and in any case, if the police were at your door, the news was likely to be bad whatever it was they had to say. Still, he tensed, knowing what they had come for, and hoping at least that the professor would accept the truth if it came parceled up in a respectable uniform.

"Professor Anthony Weston?" the male officer asked him as Jake stood staring at them with a mixture of surprise and relief.

Jake shook his head. Mari, at his shoulder stepped aside and gestured back toward their discomfited colleague. "This is Professor Weston, Officer. We were just leaving."

The prof rested a hand on Mari's arm, all the bluster and denial suddenly kicked out of him by the sight of the two constables framed in the doorway. Mari did not move away.

"These are my colleagues, Officer. Is it about Phil?" His voice trembled on his brother's name.

"I'm PC Stanton, this is PC Jackson. May we come in, Professor Weston?" the female officer asked him more gently. "What we have to say might be better received in private."

Weston's nostrils flared and his eyes widened. Jake saw his knuckles go practically white on Mari's arm and Mari murmured, "Do you still want us to go, Professor?"

A shake of the head was his only response. Mari turned back toward him, gently taking his elbow like he was helping a blind man across the road and steering him back inside. He glanced once over his shoulder at Jake, almost helplessly. Jake tried to give him a reassuring smile but there was not much he could do except follow them.

When they were all ensconced in the living room once more, the constable that had identified herself as Stanton got right to the point. "I'm very sorry to inform you, sir, this morning at around six-thirty, we found Philip Weston's body. We have made a positive identification through dental records and fingerprints taken at his apartment."

Weston crumpled onto the sofa like his legs had been kicked out from under him and put his head in his hands. He drew in a long, ragged sob as Mari sat beside him and patted his back comfortingly.

Jake looked at the two police officers.

"Have you found any evidence of how he died?"

"The cause of death is still under investigation," PC Stanton said.

Jake nodded. That was the standard response when the death was obviously not an accident.

Jake held out his hand and waited until Stanton shook it.

"I'm Detective Jake Chivis," he told them. "I was helping Professor Weston look for his brother. Do you have questions for him, or will an investigator be paying him a call?"

Stanton looked surprised. Her colleague narrowed his eyes and asked, "What division are you with, Detective... Chivis?"

"Uh, Detroit PD, actually. I'm not acting in any official capacity." He smiled his most charming smile. The one that said *we're all on the same side here*. He waited a beat then asked quietly, "He was murdered, wasn't he?"

"We are not at liberty to discuss the nature of his death, Detective. You know that," Jackson told him seriously. "Until the pathologist has finished his autopsy report, we don't officially know the cause of death, but it *is* being treated as suspicious."

Stanton added, more for Professor Weston's benefit, "This is difficult, I know, but I can give you the basic details. Philip Weston's body was discovered floating in the Regent's Canal near Victoria Park by a jogger at around six a.m. on Saturday morning. Attempts to resuscitate him were, sadly, academic and he was pronounced dead on arrival at St. Mary's less than an hour later. Initial evidence suggests that he was dead when his body entered the water. Tox reports haven't come back yet."

Jake gave Mari a look that said *and you thought I was blunt.* Mari's lips twitched a tiny, rueful smile that was gone in the same instant it appeared. Jake almost asked if he had also been wrapped in a blanket, or if they had found it nearby, but it would take too much effort to explain why he was asking. Really there was nothing left to do here. If Mari could point Guylian's probation officer in the right direction, they might not have to do anything more at all.

It was the first thing Jake mentioned once they finally left Weston's house and headed back, the professor's sister having arrived to take charge of the situation.

"I hope that they find some evidence on him. Psychic testimony isn't exactly admissible," he added with a huff of irritation.

"At least given the circumstances of his discovery, they aren't going to presume natural causes," Mari exhaled, his gaze fixed ahead as they walked briskly back down toward the tube station. His smile was grim. "Poor Professor Weston, I really feel sorry for him this morning, even though he only brought us in on this as a test. I think he half believed that Phil would show up in a few days like nothing was wrong. What do we do now, Jake? I can work on our suspect's case notes this afternoon but what are you thinking? And don't say nothing, I can tell you have something on your mind."

Jake shrugged. "It's nothing really. I just don't like having to do things covertly like this. I wish we could have just told the cops who they need to take a look at outright." He sighed. "And then once you put the plant in Guylian's case file, we have to just sit around on our hands and hope they aren't so bogged down that, A — they notice it and, B — they actually do something."

"Well, if they get him off the streets, it's a start, I suppose. He can't harm anyone else if he's helping the police with their inquiries." Mari's brow creased in a little frown, though. "I just…something is niggling at me and I'm not sure what I'm missing, but it's bugging me not understanding the reason why Guylian would kill him. As far as I can tell from the phone and chatroom logs, he's not a sex partner — none of the numbers there tie up with the phone he uses to contact Phil about jobs — and from the email cache, he's not even a regular business partner. Phil just hired him on a subcontract basis to do a couple of clearance jobs when he was maxed out. But there was nothing much in Phil's calendar for last week, so why was Guylian working on the Millers' house?"

"We've been over this. It could have been anything. Money, most likely. If there's something to find, the cops should be able to find it, once they know where to look," Jake told him. "I'm not saying you should write anything in his file about a possible homicide, he still has to be tried and everything. I know what I saw, though. Phil Weston's body was in the back of that van. We just need the cops to poke around and figure that out for themselves."

Mari shrugged elegantly and cast him a little smile that didn't quite reach his eyes. "I suppose I had better get back and work some cyber mischief then."

"Uh-huh," Jake said, then stopped, putting his hand on Mari's elbow and pulling him to a stop as well. "You want to tell me what the 'look' is for before you go?"

"Don't get all macho on me, Chivis," Mari said drily. "I was only thinking that if I was going to spend the afternoon getting up to no good, I'd rather be doing it in your bed, that's all."

Jake blinked at him, then a slow smile spread across his face.

"Maybe we should make a detour." He chuckled, then looked at him more seriously. "Mari, if you don't want to put that trip on his file, you don't have to. If you don't feel right about, it's fine. We can think of another way."

Mari tapped him on the nose with the tip of his index finger like he was chastising his mother's dog.

"If we go back to your place I won't do anything about it anyway. And it's not that I'm worried about interfering, I just have an odd feeling about this situation, that's all. Something isn't quite… I don't know. Maybe the police can work it out."

Chapter Eleven

The week was fraught with tension. Professor Weston had taken a leave of absence, which was only to be expected. Even though Jake's assertion that Phil was dead had been proven beyond doubt, it did not make him feel any better. At least Weston was still too grief-stricken to demand that Jake and Mari produce his killer. They were trying to be patient and let the police handle the case but it was slow going and near impossible to extract any information on how the police investigation was proceeding. Mari had been able to sneak into the Met database—after he'd cracked the Probation Service website—and poke around, but he'd come up empty-handed and insisted that the lead investigator must be keeping his notes handwritten. The way he'd said it, as if it was absurd that anyone should resort to actual pen and paper—a personal affront for someone in such a prominent position to stoop to such archaic means—had made Jake secretly chuckle.

Friday rolled around without either fanfare or news and Jake and Mari made plans to meet for lunch on Saturday and maybe go to the Natural History Museum afterward. Jake was pretty sure that, once they had taken a good look at all the old bones on display, they would head back to his apartment for some rather more current boning, seeing as how they'd been spending much of their free time with their hands rammed down each other's pants every chance they got.

He would have to content himself with looking forward to Saturday because Mari had to work late to catch up on a project he was meant to be finishing for Karden, then he was going home to have an evening with his mother because he felt guilty for spending so much time over at Jake's lately. Distracted by his thoughts, Jake almost missed the fact that his door handle turned before he twisted the key in the lock. Had he forgotten to lock the door properly when he left that morning? That seemed really unlikely. As he opened the door, the scent of cigarette smoke tickled his nostrils and made the fine hairs on the back of his neck rise. He stopped before it was fully open and started to yank it shut again but he was too late.

A hand dropped on his wrist and pulled, throwing him off balance and before he got his other arm up to defend himself, a second hand grabbed his shirt and slammed him against the wall just inside his doorway. He heard and felt the bang of the door being kicked shut and then a familiar face was pushed into his own—dark, surly and bearded, his eyes almost black with rage. He slammed both hands into the broad chest of a visibly livid Van Michael Guylian, trying to push him backward into the flat, to give himself some space. Guylian brought his knee up hard and jabbed him in the stomach before the powerful builder spun him and rammed him into the wall again. A kick to the back of his knees dropped Jake to the floor, too stunned to even try to protest.

"You fucking twat! Who the fuck sent you round to check up on me? Are you from the fucking tabloids, you sorry cunt? You're gonna wish you'd learnt to keep your fucking nose out of other people's business by the time I'm done with you. Dickhead!"

Guylian stamped his work boot into the small of Jake's back as he tried to twist out of the way, pushing him back down onto his belly. Then the pressure on his kidneys was gone, moments before the toe of the builder's boot drove into his side and left him gasping for breath as much as words.

Shit! How'd he find out where I live? How come he hasn't been arrested? Thank god Mari didn't come home with me!

All of those thoughts went through Jake's head in an instant but still took precious seconds in which Van pressed his advantage in both surprise and size.

"I don't know what you're talking about!" Jake yelled at him, trying to stall for time. It came out more like an angry wheeze as his lungs struggled to get more air.

"Lying. Fucking. Cunt." Van punctuated the words with the toecap of his boot, practically shunting Jake's prone body into the lounge wall as he raged at him. "I lost my fucking job thanks to you, you nosy slag. Had the cops pokin' around me, the fuckin' probos hauling me in asking stupid fucking questions about Weston. What the fuck 'ave you been telling them, you piece of yank shit?"

He added a period to that inquiry with a kick in the ribs that felt and sounded like it did real damage.

"I didn't tell anyone anything," Jake protested, trying to scrabble backward out of range of those heavy boots. "If they're looking at you, there must be a reason." He was talking fast, trying to keep Van distracted long enough that he could reach some sort of weapon, or at least get to his feet. "He owe you money or something? Did you threaten him? Maybe they know about it, found out you dumped him in the river."

"You told them that? You fucking lying twat! Do you know what you've fucking done? I could go back down for life. I never touched 'im, you interfering tossbag!" Guylian bellowed at him. "You know if I'm gonna go down for something I didn't do anyways, I might as well pay you back, you lying streak of piss!" He aimed a kick for Jake's head that he only managed to avoid by rolling hard. There was hardly any space to maneuver, certainly not enough to get away, but his hand landed right by the leg of one of two kitchen chairs and Jake grabbed it and hefted it in his attacker's general direction. The man swatted it out of his way like it was nothing but it gave Jake the moment he needed to get off the floor. He came up on the balls of his feet lightly and jumped back as Van made another grab for him. His ribs were screaming at him to stop moving but he was pumped so full of adrenaline he could ignore the pain.

"I didn't tell them shit, you fuckwit!" Jake snapped. "You *killed* him and you *know* it." And now the killer was in his apartment and if Jake wasn't fast enough, he might be the next body fished out of the river. His next dodge was unsuccessful, there just wasn't any room to avoid grappling, and Jake already knew that was going to end up very badly for him. The best he could do was try to keep his feet and fight back, which he did by landing two hard jabs to his opponent's abdomen. This earned him a couple of grunts and more cursing but didn't break the man's hold.

Then he was no longer fighting. No longer in his living room. Panic surged into him.

No! No he couldn't afford to get lost in a vision now! He was going to fucking die! If there was a way to stop them though, Jake had never found it. He was pulled right into Van's head.

He saw Phil Weston—*cute, blond twink. Killer smile.* Those were Jake's thoughts. What Van thought of him he hadn't a clue. They were talking about work. About the upcoming job. Joking.

"So I told her we were gonna have to cool it, you know? I mean, she's fuckin' smokin' and she's always up for a shag, right, but the whole married thing…it's just starting to get to me. And I'm more into blokes right now anyway, right."

"Uh-huh. Right."

Jake heard the words coming out of the mouth of the head he was in and they sounded vaguely uncomfortable.

"Plus, she's a top client, which makes things sticky. At least their job's done and dusted now. In more ways than one, eh?" Phil laughed.

"Right. Listen, mate, I got nothing against what you get up to in the bedroom, to each their own. But I don't wanna hear about it, if it's all the same to you."

"Fine, whatever." Phil said it petulantly. He was grinning, though, like he'd been trying to make Van uncomfortable and was

happy with the result. Jake knew that type. Sometimes gay guys poked at straight guys that way to see if maybe they *weren't* so straight.

Phil pulled a wad of cash from his wallet and handed it to Van. "Here's the advance. Let me know if you run into anything unexpected so I can get another draw. You did a great job on the Marches' kitchen. I've got more worked lined up for you too."

"Thanks, mate. That's me gone then."

Jake came back to himself just in time to take a fist to the side of his head that had him seeing stars. He took two steps backward and crashed into the living room wall.

"You stupid fucking dick, what the fuck would I kill him for? Who the fuck else is gonna employ me and ask no questions with my record? Do I look like a guy that can afford to go back to prison for a longer stretch? My life might as well be done and over if that happens, no thanks to you!"

Jake stumbled back and got his hands up to protect his head from another blow. Van was built like an ox and had plenty of reach and power but he was slow.

"You didn't do it, did you?" Jake gasped, dancing back out of his reach and knocking the coffee table out of his way as he did so. He felt sick, and not just from the kicking.

"What the fuck have I been telling you since you come in that door, dickhead?" Van threw another, harder jab at him. At some point he had been trained to fight, that wasn't a random bar brawler's method. Now that the initial rage was wearing off, he was just trying to work out his anger by landing some more bruising on Jake's face by way of a reward for his dropping him in it. "He was my fucking payday. I'll be lucky if I stay on civvie street after this. Only reason I'm still out is that they can't actually find any hard evidence to pin me to the murder. Wonder why that is, huh?"

"Yeah, I fucking wonder," Jake grumbled. The man had stopped swinging for a second but looked about ready to start again so he quickly came to a decision. It didn't matter now if Van thought he was crazy. "I saw Phil Weston's body in the back of your van. Don't ask how. You got any idea who *would* want him dead? And how they used your fucking van to move him?"

Guylian stopped dead, staring at him for a moment as if he'd completely lost his mind.

"You repeat *that* to the cops and I will happily serve time for stringing you up from a fucking lamppost," he growled. "You didn't see shit. He's been nowhere near the back of the Transit, not on my watch. And if you did see something, why didn't you go to the cops with it, then?" His eyes narrowed again and he advanced with murder in his eyes, kicking what remained of the furniture out of his path like Godzilla. "You fuckin' *did*, didn't you? That's why they've been all over me. You little fuck!"

"If I told them that, you'd be behind bars. I'm a cop," Jake growled back. "Besides, I saw it after the fact. I don't have time to explain this shit. If you didn't kill him, I need to figure out how his body got in the back of your van."

As Jake stopped talking, they both heard a siren approaching. It could have been anything but they'd been making enough racket that one of the neighbors might have called the cops. Jake didn't waste any time playing on an ex-con's worst fear.

"That'll be your ride to jail coming. Unless you talk, fast. Tell me what you know and get the fuck out of here and I'll tell 'em it was just some random fuckwit that broke in and got away."

Van hesitated for a couple of heartbeats but in all honesty, Jake had seen some of the fight go out of him the minute he found out that he'd just beaten seven shades of shit out of a cop. It could go either way — Van might try to kill him to keep him quiet, but having been in his head, Jake doubted it. Or he could try to talk his way out of jail time by blaming anyone and everyone else.

He did neither.

"Phil took the van sometimes, when he was on a job a bit

further afield. He had it last weekend when he was working up the other side of the Heath. His fuckin' DNA is gonna be all over it, Jesus F Christ! I reckon he's used it as everything from a B&B to a fuckin' knocking shop. I have to hose the damned thing down inside and out whenever he brings it back, I know that much, the dirty little bastard! I didn't kill him though, honest to fuckin' god. He's a… He was a good bloke, top bloke. He was knocking off some posh bird on one of the last jobs — liked bragging about it, how he'd nailed her against the side of the van and everywhere else. Maybe her old man found out about it and offed him, I dunno."

"Phil had your van the week before last, you're sure?" Jake said, and when Van glared at him he asked, "How'd you get it back? Where was it?"

"He was on a job, said he needed it for the cash and carry. I had all my kit down at the place I was working on so I told him it would be okay. Then I got a phone call… Friday? Yeah, I think Friday morning, that he was going out with her that night and she'd said she'd run him back to his place, so if I needed the Transit over the weekend, I'd have to go and pick it up. I sent Casper up for it on Sunday morning. Didn't think no more about it till the biz…till your lot started sniffing round."

"You got an address?" Jake asked.

Van got an 'aw-fuck' look on his face. He was sweating buckets as the siren got closer.

"Forget it. I'll get it another way. I don't think you killed Phil. No time for explanations. Here is what you are going to do. Go downstairs and walk away casually. Do not fucking clean or do anything else to your van. If there is evidence in there, I'm going to need it in place to clear you. Go home. I'll make sure you get a new probo and there's nothing on your record they'll bother you about. Got it?"

"If you're spinning me a bullshit story so I don't paste you, I will finish you off even if I have to arrange it from inside," Van told him darkly. "Bizzie or not, you clear?"

He turned and headed for the door. For a second, Jake's Detroit roots sizzled and demanded he show this punk-ass motherfucker what happened when you threatened one of the boys in blue, but one thing stopped him. He was not a corrupt cop, not even a *licensed* cop anymore, and he'd already fucked with this guy once.

No, he'd had *Mari* fuck with him, and that was even worse.

Jake let him go without retaliating. He didn't have time to call Mari or work on any better story than 'some junkie broke into his place and he'd surprised him when he got home'. He gave the officers that showed up to the disturbance call as vague a description as he possibly could and they were out of his hair within the hour, after taking his statement. He refused medical attention, though he could tell that the PC who stayed to fill in the incident report wanted to call back in for a paramedic at least.

He wondered if he could ask Mari to just wipe out any record of the incident, but he was also worried about having him do too much poking about in police databases, and he already had to ask him to undo what they had done to Van.

As soon as he heard the heavy footfalls of the cops finally going down his stairs, he was on his phone calling Mari. The door lock was screwed, he thought vaguely as the call picked up. He would need to sort that out.

* * * *

Mari was still at work when his mobile began to chitter at him like an impatient kitten waiting to be fed. He had four screens active on his desk and two cell phones on the go, cross-referencing data from three of the screens as part of the day job and monitoring the situation with Phil Weston's case file on the other. He was conscious of the time, knowing that Mama would be understanding but disappointed if he didn't make it home for dinner. At the same time, he was a little bit anxious and wanting to hear from Jake. The Met Police had just upgraded Phil Weston's death from suspicious to suspected murder and they had also interviewed Van Guylian, and released him pending further inquiries. That had not been part of the plan.

Something else had cropped up as part of his sweep on the younger Weston's phone account, though. Three of his contacts, though using different names, were coming from the same IP address. When he delved deeper, he discovered that Phil had been fucking at least two of them. One of them was Amber, the woman he also referred to as Helen. One, who had called him the day after he was suspected to have been killed, was simply referred to as Cas. The third was in his address book as Mr. B., with an appointment scheduled for Saturday, his last day of life, but only in his 'events' calendar on one of the many social media sites that he used.

Mr. B. aft. Heavy BDwSp. :)'''

"What the living fuck?" Mari tilted his head, trying to figure out this odd little acronym.

As he did so, one of the cross reference screens flickered and died and he cursed a purple streak and was tempted to throw his coffee at it. At that same moment his phone went off and the juddering vibration morphed into the theme from *NYPD Blue,* which was the closest he could get to an American cop show theme when he was looking for an appropriate ringtone.

"Chivis," he declared silkily, picking it up before the second ring. "You can't stay away, can you?"

There was a short pause before Jake's husky voice said, "No, I can't. As much as I would like this to be just a social call, though, I'm afraid I have bad news. Van Guylian didn't kill Phil, Mari. I made a mistake."

"Well, that's a relief, because the Met have just let him go," Mari said, his eyes still watching the remaining screens as he tried to reactivate his primary monitor by repeatedly prodding the power switch on and off. "Are you okay? You sound a little...odd."

"Yeah, I know they let him go. He just left here."

Mari swore heatedly in Suomi, an old habit that harkened back to university where his professor had been vehemently opposed to bad language but conveniently incapable of interpreting the Finnish national tongue. His grandmother's family had their uses.

"What...? *How?* How the fuck did he know where to find you?" Mari stopped poking his screens and sat back with the phone to his ear. His heart was suddenly beating a little too hard and too fast again. "What happened? Did he hurt you?"

"Huh, I didn't think to ask him how he found out where I lived," Jake said. "I did give him my name and number though, in case he heard from Phil. I guess it wouldn't have been too hard for him to find me. I got an impression from him while he was visiting, and it pretty much convinced me he's innocent, or at least that he didn't kill Weston. I have a new lead. Apparently Phil had borrowed Guylian's van the night he was probably murdered. That married woman he was boffing, that the prof was telling us about? She was the job he was working on before the Millers, March is her last name. My guess is her husband came home. I'd need to get over there and poke around to find out for sure, see if I can pick up any memories."

"He let you touch him?" Mari was skeptical suddenly, his mind working overtime. "Did you tell him what you can do?"

He saved the file run on his primary CPU and rebooted, turning the whole setup off and swearing at it silently, though his main focus was suddenly on the man on the other end of the phone line. There was something Jake wasn't telling him but he wasn't sure what it was.

"You could say he didn't give me much choice about touching him. He was pretty determined to reach out and touch me anyway. Not that I can really blame him. He couldn't know for sure that I set his probation bulldog loose on him, but he had a damned good guess."

Mari realized that he was still thinking with his dick when his first emotion was jealousy, then his brain kicked in and he realized what Jake hadn't been telling him.

"Oh…oh, damn it. Jake, did he hurt you? I'm… Let me shut down here, I'm going to come over."

"Bring some ice, would you? My freezer is just a block of frost and the juice I'm holding on my face isn't really cold enough," Jake said plaintively.

"Oh no…no!" Mari hit backup and forced shutdown on all three PCs. He uploaded the files he'd been running from the fourth even as he checked on his second mobile where the nearest pub was and searched through his desk drawers for a carrier or something to put ice cubes in. "Jake…I'm on my way. I'll be there in a few minutes. I've got something to show you when I get there, if you're up to it."

"Okay," Jake said neutrally, *too* neutrally. "And, Mari, don't panic. I'm okay."

"Panic, *moi*? Perish the thought," Mari said, trying to sound cooler than he felt with his heart trying to break out of his chest. Some muscle-bound rapist thug had attacked his gorgeous Jake and just…what exactly? Walked right out like it was fine?

*If I get my hands on that bastard, I'll kill him! I'll rip his fucking liver out and shove it so far down his gullet…*he thought grimly, but all he said was, "Try to rest, Chivis. I'll be there as soon as I can."

Hurling all his mobile tech into a rucksack, Mari shut down his workstation and pulled on his coat then headed for the wine bar on the corner near Waterstones.

Armed with ice and a bottle of brandy from the bar, he ran all the way to Maple Street and when Jake buzzed him in, he raced up the stairs. The damage to the flat was painfully apparent when he let himself in. The lock on the door from the entrance hall was broken and that was nothing compared to the scene of devastation that met his widening eyes. Jake was bruised and bleeding from his nose and one corner of his mouth, dabbing it with a wet towel kind of ineffectually.

"Oh my stars! Did you call the police?" Mari demanded, coming to him at once, the rucksack dropped to the floor, everything forgotten but Jake. With careful fingers he cupped the man's face, tilting it to the light, inspecting the damage, not wanting to cause more.

Jake covered Mari's hands with his own but didn't pull them away, letting him get a look. "No, I didn't call the cops. Neighbors did though, or I assume it was them. He'd gone by the time they showed up anyway. I told them I surprised a burglar."

Mari stared at him incredulously.

"You let him get away with doing this to you? *Why*?"

"Mari, we set the man up. He could have gone to prison for something he didn't do, if the cops had found anything even remotely suspicious, which they didn't. I figured I owed him one." He moved his hands back down as he spoke and winced, although Mari thought he tried hard not to let it show that moving, even just a little, hurt. "Actually I wanted to ask if you could maybe work a little of your magic and give him a clean file again, and a new PO?"

Mari made a disgusted noise at that suggestion.

"I'll put a rocket up his fucking arse if I get close enough. He doesn't deserve it, Jake. Shit…you don't owe him a thing, either. *I* set the dogs on him, if *anyone* deserved it, I did. Damn it! *And* I got you hurt. I'm *so* sorry, Jake. I didn't even stop to think this might happen."

He wanted to kiss Jake but he was worried that it might not be well received right now, or even doable without hurting his gorgeous detective even more. How could it be possible for him to look so sexy when he was so bruised and battered?

What the fuck is wrong with you, Ilmarinen? his conscience chided as he dropped his eyes and looked away. *You can't stop thinking about jumping his bones, even for a minute?*

Jake caught Mari's chin on the side of his fingers and

lifted his head.

"This is *not* your fault. I asked you to do it. And I was wrong on top of it. I refuse to let you take any blame, so stop it." He kissed Mari softly before he could find the words to object. "Is that the ice over there?"

Jake went to pick up the bag but stopped mid-bend and clutched his side before slowly bending his knees to scoop it up. Mari was beside him at once, retrieving the heavy rucksack and pointing toward the bedroom door.

"Let me sort this out. I take it he didn't get as far as demolishing the bed as well? Get in there and take your shirt off. I want to see what that bastard has done to you before I decide to reward him for it."

"It's not that bad," Jake insisted. "He got some punches in and so did I. I'm okay."

Mari didn't believe him for a second.

"Chivalrous Chivis! Why are you holding your side then?"

Jake dropped his hand a beat too quickly.

"Let me see," Mari demanded, and when Jake didn't move to draw up his shirt, he went over to him and pulled the material out of the way himself, which Jake only gave token resistance to. He gasped when he got a look at Jake's torso. Livid bruises covered his ribs and abdomen in black and purple swathes. "Oh my word! His fists did this?"

"Some of it," Jake murmured, obviously not willing to outright lie. "His boots did the rest."

Mari swore and shook his head.

"Go and lie down, Jake. I'll make some ice packs."

"Thank you," Jake said, sounding genuinely grateful, as he shuffled off toward the bedroom.

In the compact kitchenette, Mari decanted handfuls of ice into tea towels then knotted them into little parcels, wrestling two into the frost-packed freezer and pouring a liberal double shot of brandy into a tumbler for Jake as pain relief before returning to the bedroom with the other two ice packs. His hands were shaking but he wasn't sure if that

179

was anger or delayed shock at Jake's bruises, or what.

Jake had dutifully taken his shirt off and lain down on the bed. He looked even more beaten and vulnerable lying down than he had in the living room. Mari handed him the drink, watched him down it in a single gulp then gave him one of the ice packs. Jake applied it to his ribs while Mari gently pressed the other to his cheek. After a moment Jake moved his free hand and placed it over Mari's, looking up at him.

"It looks worse than it is," he soothed. "Don't worry, I'll be fine, just sore for a couple days."

"Keep telling yourself that, He-Man," Mari responded drily. He ran a hand firmly but as gently as he could over Jake's chest where the bruising was beginning to come up a dusky shade of aubergine. When Jake winced in spite of the tough guy performance, he shook his head. "He's sprung a rib for you here, Chivis. No push-ups for you for a few weeks."

"Will you lay down next to me for a minute?" Jake asked.

Mari raised one eyebrow.

"Can you not stop thinking about your dick, even after a kicking?"

"I don't think I could do anything even if I wanted to right now." Jake chuckled, then winced. "I just need to hold you."

Mari was surprised by this admission, but not entirely displeased.

"Let me get my coat off," he said levelly, rising from the bed and easing his overcoat off his shoulders to hang it from the corner of the bedroom door. He returned to Jake's side, sitting down to unzip his boots and wriggle them off too, then lay back and turned to face him on the bed, moving slowly and carefully so as not to hurt him any more than he was already.

"I *knew* there was something wrong, even before you told me. *Well* before I got here and saw you. I could hear it in your voice. What if he comes back? He knows how to get in here," he said, touching Jake's face tenderly with his fingertips. "Do you want me to stay?"

"He won't come back," Jake said. "The cops were already here and he knows it. Also, I think I kinda gave him the impression that I would have to figure out who really killed Phil to clear him. And, I would love you to stay, but your mom needs you."

Mari felt slightly chastened at that pointed reminder of his other responsibility. He leaned in to kiss Jake's battered features, much more softly than he had done the other night.

"I don't think she needs me as much as you do right now, Chivis. And if I told her you'd been beaten up I know she would understand. It isn't like I can't get back home in under half an hour if she *did* want me, is it?"

Jake looked up at him and brought his hand up to touch his face, caressing his cheek.

"Are you sure?"

Mari tilted his head a little, looking around the room as if there might be someone else there that he was talking to, then raised his hand as if to cuff him lightly across the head, pulling it back at the last moment as he remembered how sore Jake was.

"I'm not in the habit of suggesting things I'm not sure about, Kemosabe," he said solemnly. "And you are clearly having a hard time looking after yourself on your own right now. Unless of course, you'd *rather* I left you alone with your ice?"

He stroked a fingertip down Jake's bare chest very slowly, from his collarbone to his navel, his eyes following it all the way then returning to Jake's face inquisitively.

"And you accuse me of always thinking with my dick." Jake tried a grin and it looked a little painful. He caught Mari's hand as he went to pull it away though and brought it up to his lips for a kiss. "I want you to stay."

"All right then, I will stay. I do need to make a call, though, will you be okay with your ice cubes for a few minutes?"

He chuckled softly.

"I dunno, maybe leave the night light on." Jake snickered. "Go on and call. I'll just lie here and try not to move."

"Good idea." Mari rolled over and off the bed as carefully as he had eased himself down on it. "Do you want some more of that brandy?"

"I'm not really a drinker," Jake said, then paused and added, "I suppose I can make an exception tonight."

"That should make it easier for me to get you wasted then." Mari winked at him. "Don't damage anything else while I'm out there."

Mari went and got the brandy, brought it back to the bedroom and poured another stiff measure into Jake's glass, then slipped out into the lounge and fished his phone from his rucksack, hitting the primary contact icon for Mama and still feeling a little bit guilty as he did so. She was a jump ahead of him as usual, though.

"Hello, Ilmari, I was waiting for you to ring. Are you working late?"

"Kind of, Mama," he said wearily.

"I thought so, and is that nice young man Jake working late with you?"

He rolled his eyes.

"Mama, he…he got broken into. The guy beat him up. I said I'd stay here in case he…in case he needed anything. He's hurt pretty badly. I'm so sorry."

"Ilmari, I can count the times you've stood me up on one finger," she said in her warm, unflustered way. "Tonka and I will keep one another company. And I have a new book downloaded that I'm crazy to read. Don't wear him out though, he needs his energy to get better."

"Mama, I know that. And he's too sore for me to wear out in any case. I just want to be here in case he has a concussion or something," Mari protested, almost but not quite convincing himself of that.

"Indeed," she laughed. "Call me in the morning, child. And you take care of that handsome boy. Already he's the best thing that ever happened to you."

"Mother!" he rebuked gently.

"A mother knows these things," she told him. "Go on. I will see you when I see you. Stop worrying, my sweet boy. I will be fine."

"I love you, Mama," he said, a little shamefaced.

"I know, Ilmari. The feeling is mutual. Now go and make him feel better."

He was still a bit red-faced when he came back to the bedroom and settled down on the mattress, trying not to think too hard about what they had been doing the last time he'd lain down on this bed with Jake. He took the empty glass from him and set it aside before he snuggled up and slid an arm around him companionably.

"You are extra adorable when you blush, you know," Jake told him, kissing the top of his head. "Did she not buy the 'just sleeping over at a friend's' story?"

Mari tried to hide his burning face in the cool linen of the pillowcase. In a muffled voice he said, "She's sick, not stupid, Chivis. She knows how I feel about you."

Jake was quiet for the space of a few long heartbeats.

"She does?" he murmured wonderingly. "Maybe I should ask her then."

Mari looked up, a little startled by the seriousness of Jake's words.

"Why would you want to do that?"

Jake smiled crookedly at him.

"Has no one ever told you how hard you are to read? You play your cards awfully close to the chest, Ilmari."

"I always thought I was fairly straightforward, to be honest," he lied, getting a warm feeling in that selfsame chest at the odd little smile on Jake's face. "She told me that I had to take care of you. I think she likes you."

That was only a slight understatement. Mari *knew* she did. He had known it from the moment she'd set eyes on Jake, but then she was always matchmaking. Initially it had been a case of inviting her pretty female students around for private tutorials when she knew he would be home. Then, when his relationships with unsuitable men became too hard to ignore, it was pointing out guys that she thought would be *more* suitable. Usually quite boring and academic guys, even if they *weren't* all that hard on the eye.

"Good. I like her too," Jake said. "She has good taste in dogs."

"She would never be so rude as to compare you to a dog," Mari teased him. "Though I suspect you're going to be harder to train not to get yourself into trouble."

Jake laughed, then abruptly stopped with a little hiss.

"What do you mean? I'm housebroken and everything," he protested when he had recovered his breath.

Mari felt a pang of concern that his teasing had gone too far and reminded Jake of how sore his ribs were. He ran his fingers over the parts of Jake's upper body that were unbruised, wishing he could touch him more urgently. He tried to keep his tone light though as he agreed, "True, at least you don't piss on the carpet. Do you need more ice?"

"I need more you," Jake said. "Wanna try kissing it better?"

Mari wanted to kiss him all over but he didn't want to make Jake hurt any worse than he already did.

"Where to *start*?" he wondered aloud, his eyes roaming back over the cuts and bruises on that gorgeous body beside him.

"Well, he didn't kick me anywhere below the belt," Jake said, trying to look innocent.

"You are absolutely incorrigible, did anyone ever tell you that?" Mari sighed. "If I unfasten your pants, I must insist that you keep absolutely still. I really ought to get that rib strapped too," he added, though his fingers were toying with the buckle of Jake's belt.

"Sex releases all sorts of endorphins," Jake reminded him. "Way better than brandy."

"What kind of first aid lessons do they give you in the Detroit Police Force?" Mari laughed, shaking his head.

"Roll on your back, Chivis. I'll need to get your pants off before I put you to bed in any case."

Jake did as he was told. He tried to help Mari get his clothes off by lifting his hips but Mari could tell it ripped him apart to move even that much. He had to be crazy to be this hurt and simultaneously horny, but by the time Mari slid his underwear off, Jake was already half-hard.

He was also bruised along his left hip, in spite of his protests to the contrary. Mari swore again, in a husky voice. He wrapped his cool fingers around Jake's cock though, gently stroking him up and down and resting the other hand on his belly in an attempt to make him stop trying to roll his hips and thrust into the stroke.

"Ssshhh…stop wriggling, bad boy," he rebuked him.

Jake stilled under his touch and Mari could see he was making an effort to relax. His head was tilted down and those pretty amber eyes watched him intently. The cock in his hand thickened and twitched and Mari stroked him once, up and down, slowly.

"Mmmhhh…what an eager boy he is. He's got no respect for your health at all, has he, Chivis?" He bent his head, touching his lips to Jake's warm, silken stomach just a few scant millimeters north of his glistening cock head. The muscles beneath the skin spasmed of their own volition at his touch and he felt that velvet shaft in his hand kick and swell enthusiastically.

Jake lowered one hand to comb his fingers into Mari's hair, sliding them along his scalp in a gentle, encouraging massage.

"See? This is helping already. I can't feel anything except where your mouth and hands are touching."

"You know" — Mari chuckled softly against the warmth of his belly —"if you just wanted me to suck your dick, there were easier ways to get me here than this?"

Jake grinned. It had to hurt but he did it anyway.

"You do realize you just called yourself easy?"

Mari leaned back, propping himself on one elbow beside

Jake so that he didn't hurt him by lying full length against his injured body.

"How do you work that out, Mr. Smart Guy? I just said that you didn't have to play the 'pity' card, that's all. And you have a very sexy, suckable cock. But don't let that go to your *other* head, or anything. It doesn't make you Jesus, right?"

He winked at Jake playfully, relaxing now that he knew his delicious lover wasn't so badly damaged that he was beyond flirting.

"So, I'd really love to know, which card do I need to play to get you to do that right now?" Jake asked, his expression comically innocent, despite the devilish little grin.

Mari pretended to think about it.

"You could *ask* me nicely," he said with a small suggestive smile of his own. He stroked the tip of his index finger slowly up and down the underside of Jake's pert cock, admiring it while his suggestion sank in.

"That's all? I just have to ask nicely?" Jake said and when Mari just gave him a look he added, "Okay…will you, pretty please, wrap your lips around my boner, because that would feel really, really good right now, Ilmari? Please?"

"There, that didn't hurt too much, did it?" Mari said, delivering a light flick to the bobbing head of his partner's dick, ignoring the way Jake tried not to wince in response, and pushed himself up onto his knees again to bend over him. Normally he would have just rested his head on Jake's belly and swallowed him down but he didn't think that would be as comfortable for Jake as it was for him. Curling his fingers around that eager shaft again, he bowed his head and took the upper half in his mouth, bringing his lips together and drawing them slowly up toward the tip, still holding him at the root as he let Jake's glans slip out of his mouth, then nodding down and swallowing him again.

"Uuuuhh…" Jake exhaled, shivering under his touch. His fingers pushed back into Mari's hair, not forcing him down but just resting on his head, stroking his hair. "That looks as amazing as it feels." He bucked his hips as Mari inched down his length again.

Mari made an approving noise. He laid his hand flat against Jake's stomach though, urging him to stay as still as possible as he stroked his lips up and down the warm, rippled silk, enjoying the little rush of salty release that trickled across his tongue each time he came back up.

"You taste very good, Chivis," he observed. "This healthy lifestyle of yours has some benefits."

"Pineapple." Jake chuckled. He managed to still his hips at Mari's staying touch but his fingers curled a little tighter in his hair.

Mari sampled him thoughtfully, rolling back the silken cowl of his foreskin to caress the dome of his cock head with his tongue.

"Hmm…yes, I'm getting a little bit of that." He looked up at Jake and his pale blue eyes glittered with mischief.

"Fruit makes your cum taste sweeter. I've been trying to eat more of it lately." Jake winked at him, then moaned softly when Mari licked over his crown and took him in his mouth again. "Rrrrr…god! I love the way you do that," he purred as Mari squeezed and sucked him at the same time.

"Glad to hear it," Mari mused, with his mouth full. He adored giving head and even the ultra-critical Tomas hadn't had a bad word to say about his cock-sucking skills. Although maybe that had more to do with the fact that even he wasn't arrogant enough to criticize a man with his jaws around the shaft of his dick.

He experienced a moment or so of annoyance that Tomas was even able to gatecrash his thoughts when he was making out with another man. Then he pushed those memories aside and swallowed Jake deeper, nodding so low on him that his forelock brushed his lover's belly and he was almost gagging on the swollen crown of his lovely cock.

The muscles of Jake's stomach tightened, then jumped and fluttered, but otherwise he kept still, as instructed. Mari concentrated on those tiny, delicious physical responses and, as he sucked gently, Jake made soft sounds of happy acknowledgment that made his heart beat faster. Although he kept his body almost motionless, Jake still moved his fingers through Mari's hair, stroking and petting him there as his head bobbed. He was so attuned to Jake he could feel every little twitch and shiver. Every small, sexy sound he made seemed to pour into his ears like liquid heat.

He thought the pain of his injuries might keep Jake from being able to get off, or at least mean that it would take him a long time to come, but that didn't seem to be the case. Jake was stone-hard between his lips, the drops of bittersweet salt flowing regularly across his tongue as he edged closer and closer.

Mari moved his hand between Jake's legs, cupping the weight of his throbbing balls, caressing the firm orbs within the looser flesh of his sac and stroking his finger along the smooth, tight stretch of skin behind them. Jake's breathing deepened and quickened, the little mewls and whimpers he was making turning to growls and soft, husky moans. Jake's fingers tightened in Mari's hair, tugging a little harder, though he made no objection.

"Oh fuck, 'm gonna come, babe…" Jake murmured.

Mari came up off him almost all the way, just holding the head of his hard cock in his mouth as his fingers did the rest, stroking and teasing relentlessly up and down his pulsing shaft while his tongue lapped up any spillage. He lifted his gaze to Jake's earnest, frantic face again and struggled not to smile because he looked so cute, struggling to hold back as long as he could.

"Let go," he murmured around that delicious mouthful. "Just let it happen."

Jake could not keep still after that. His belly tightened up, revealing a gorgeous rippling six-pack and his thighs and buttocks flexed, pushing the throbbing head of his cock a little deeper. When he came, the spurt hit the roof of Mari's mouth and trickled down onto his swirling tongue.

"Ohh…ohhhh…yeesss!" Jake hissed.

Mari reached down with one hand, tugging his belt undone and popping the button on his fly as he absorbed the blast, still sucking and swallowing, feeling Jake writhe at the light pressure on his sensitive penis as he drew out the very last drops. He had been feeling needy when he'd lain down and with the salt-sweet taste of Jake's climax in his mouth, he was bone-hard and there was no disguising it. He let Jake's cock slip free of his lips, sank down carefully on the mattress beside him to ease his uncomfortable erection out of his work slacks and began to stroke it rhythmically. He turned his head as he did so, loving the way Jake's lips were parted, still gasping, his expression zoned out, his forehead and the bridge of his nose jeweled with perspiration.

"I love making you come," he whispered.

Jake smiled and he tried to chuckle but it came out all breathy, closer to a pleased whimper.

"You have no idea how happy that makes me." He craned his head toward Mari and kissed him, licked at his salty lips. Jake brought his hand to Mari's upper leg and stroked him there, then higher, curling his fingers around his inner thigh, his thumb caressing his balls.

"Mmhhh…you should be getting some rest," Mari crooned, wriggling his trousers and briefs down a little way. "I can take care of this."

He didn't try to stop Jake though. It felt too good, for one thing.

"I'm sure you can," Jake murmured, moving his lips to Mari's ear. "I like to have my hands on you though, to feel you getting off," he whispered over the ridges of Mari's ear, tracing the dips and curves with the tip of his tongue.

Mari shivered with something a little more than pure need. Jake knew instinctively how to touch him and the warmth of his hand, strong but gentle, felt so good that in truth he didn't want it to stop. But there was some sense of trepidation in him too, the idea that it was too much, too soon. That the novelty of this would wear off for one or both of them and they would be left trying to work around the uncomfortable reminder of what they had once shared. It was idiotic, he knew, to fear the failure of something that was barely more than a few hastily grasped moments of delicious lust but his heart grew tight and cold at the thought of just how this might end.

It was not as if his track record with other men stood as a shining beacon of encouragement. Right now, he thought, even his mother had more faith in his ability to keep Jake than he did.

Idiot! Keep him? He isn't even yours yet! his conscience chided him.

"Mmmmhhh…" he purred, pushing his doubts to one side for the moment. "I'm going to get off all right if you keep touching me like that."

Jake's lips were so close Mari could feel his smile where they touched his ear. He moved his hand between Mari's legs, caressing and gently fondling his balls for a few moments before he curled his fingers over them and tucked them up underneath, pressing firmly into his perineum. He did it only for a second, then eased off the pressure he was applying, only to do it again, and again. He didn't stray lower, but kept up that steady, firm push and release right there.

"Oh, fuck…" Mari breathed, rocked by the rush of tingling, trembling heat that touch stirred in the lower confines of his body. He kept on stroking the last couple of inches of his cock between his thumb and his first two fingers as Jake's hand conjured up the most intense sensations, teasing his ultraresponsive prostate from without. He'd only ever known one person who could do that to him so well and he was a physical therapist, not a boyfriend, sad to say. "What—mhhh—what the fuck are you doing to me?"

A theoretical question because he knew full well what was being done. Jake took his time, touching him with such care that he thought he would go crazy wanting more.

"I'm helping you get off," Jake murmured. He sucked

Mari's earlobe into his mouth. "Keep stroking...this is gonna feel so good when you come."

"You are a very bad man. I'm *so* glad you are, by the way. Ohhh...!" Mari sucked in a hard breath as the pressure of Jake's deft fingers between his thighs made his whole body tremble and he almost lost control of the erection in his hand. He closed his eyes, working himself faster, turning his head so that he could brush his lips across Jake's mouth. Jake responded with hungry fire, kissing him with renewed passion, even though it must have hurt.

"You are just so damn beautiful," Jake whispered into his mouth when their lips parted again. "So sexy. You make me want you, even when you already made me shoot like a geyser."

"Shhh...you'll make your face bleed again, Mr. Hot-Stuff," Mari purred, grinding on his fondling hand, his voice catching as Jake tormented him until he thought he wouldn't be able to stand much more. "That just feels so good. I am so close to—mmmhhh—so close!" he panted, his hand slowing on his cock as he tried to hold on to the swirling, tightening feeling in his abdomen and his balls just a little longer.

Jake nuzzled under Mari's chin, kissing and sucking his skin. He curled his fingers, pressing the knuckles of his second and third fingers into his hot spot and stroking his index finger back farther. He didn't try to push it into him, just circled the tip around the edge of his hole, teasing all the sensitive nerve endings there.

Mari shuddered, knowing what he was doing, where he was going, and his body tensed automatically. It felt so good but he was abruptly on edge, unable to stop the neediness that made his muscles tighten and his heart beat too quickly. He turned his face into the pillow, trying to hide the sudden gleam in his eyes and the constriction in his throat.

How could this always happen to him? What was wrong with him? He wanted Jake inside him so badly but the merest thought of it locked him down tighter than Wormwood Scrubs and he was left feeling desolate, even before he knew that he was not going to be able to come. Not like this.

His hands moved back to run over Jake's body, not pushing him away, just touching him and trying to focus on the contact with another warm, human body close to his own. To focus on anything but the desire to run away, to lock himself in the bathroom and bury his face in a towel so that he could cry in silence. Instead he kept his face muffled in the crisp linen and concentrated on stroking and caressing the man who could make him feel so good and yet so hopeless at the same time.

Jake stopped touching him there immediately. He moved his hand up, gently caressing over his tight balls and aching dick. The way his fingers feathered over the hard length of him was erotic but gentle.

"Mari…" Jake murmured his name. "Mari, don't turn away. Come back to me."

This was sort of an odd thing to say because he hadn't acted on the impulse to run away, but Jake must have felt him slam the metaphorical doors shut. His warm hand moved higher yet, his fingers spreading so his hand nearly covered Mari's belly, filling hard-clenched muscles with warmth. When Mari still didn't turn his head, Jake kissed his shoulder, drawing back a little himself.

"I would really, really love to get a hold of whoever hurt you so badly. Me and him, alone, for just five minutes."

Mari turned, startled by the vehemence in his voice, shaking his head a little. He dashed a hand against his cheek but thankfully the pillows had soaked up any telltale moisture and he twisted around in Jake's arms, missing his touch, wanting to be held and touched like that some more.

"No one hurt me. What does your brain get up to when I leave it alone?" He leaned in and kissed Jake on the nose, forcing a quivering smile. "I don't know! You are such a hero, but…really…no one's hurt me. I've been— I've been lucky. *So* lucky. And blessed. It's true, don't look at me like that. I swear it, Chivis. I'm just— I find it difficult to relax, that's all. I know you won't understand it. No one ever understands it. But I don't want you treating me like some kind of victim, I am *so* not that person. Do you understand?"

"Uh-huh. How could I understand? *You're* pretty sure I can't." Jake sighed gustily, disappointment in his eyes. "There are more ways to hurt a person than just physically, Mari. They might not have been the cause of your not being able to relax when someone touches you a certain way, but someone sure as hell made you feel like shit for the way your body reacts. So, tell me I'm wrong about that and I'll let it drop."

Mari tensed again, just for a moment, then pushed the anger away. He wasn't angry with Jake. He *would not* be angry with Jake. It wasn't his fault after all. It wasn't anyone's fault but his own.

"I can't blame anyone for that, Chivis. I wouldn't blame you for being annoyed and frustrated. You want to feel good, you want to have sex. You don't want to be saddled with some hopeless emotional cripple who can't..." He put a hand over his mouth, silencing himself for a moment before he lost his temper and swore and shouted and all the other things he had promised he would not do again. Not with Jake. Not his precious Jake.

"I'm sorry I let you think this could be something it can't be," he said quietly instead. "Do you want me to leave?"

"What is it that you 'let me' think, Mari? You haven't let me think anything. I know my own mind. And we *were* having sex, what do you think we've been doing? Is it not 'real sex' unless I get your ass? That makes no sense. So, I'll ask again. Tell me that no one has ever made you feel bad about what you can't do in bed, that no one ever put the idea in your head that you're a 'hopeless emotional cripple'."

Mari shook his head slowly. He wanted to kiss Jake, to silence him with his lips and tell him not to be so defensive.

He had not come here tonight meaning to make him angry.

"Clearly it's important, otherwise you would not be getting yourself so worked up about it," he pointed out, trying to be rational and calm. "And yes, you're right, it's not the first time I've felt bad about it and it won't be the last time. To be honest, I'm not really sure why I keep letting this happen to me."

He fought the slight tremor in his voice and held that solemn, unfathomable, amber gaze. Jake guarded his emotions well and sometimes it was hard to read in his face if he was angry, or bored, or just trying to wind him up.

"I just… I thought that maybe you would be kind to me," he said at last, trying to keep his tone neutral. "But maybe that's selfish of me. I should be the one being kind to you."

Jake stared at him so intently it was like his eyes were trying to burn a hole right through him. After several long moments he rolled onto his back again. Without a word, he swung his legs over the side of the bed and reached for the glass and brandy Mari had placed on the windowsill. He poured a couple fingers worth, drained it then poured another.

"Do you want some?" he asked.

Mari sat up slowly, pushing his tangled hair out of his eyes. He nodded. Right now, he thought, it would be very good to just get drunk. And he was not a heavy drinker either.

"Please." He was silent for a moment, then tried to lighten the mood. "I've driven you to drink then? That didn't take as long as I thought."

Jake handed him the glass, silent while Mari drank what he'd poured, then took it back and poured more and drank that one himself.

"If I were a cop, and you were a suspect, I'd wear you down until you cracked. I wouldn't let you get away with avoiding answering a straight question with a straight answer. But I'm not a cop, and you're not a suspect, and I don't want to fight with you. If you don't want to talk about something, just say so, okay? I'm not a jerk, Mari. I'm not gonna try and force it out of you. You don't have to figure out how to dance around an answer with words."

Mari beckoned for the glass when Jake poured another couple of fingers of the rich spirit so close in color to Jake's gorgeous eyes, and he knocked it back like a seasoned wino.

"I don't think you're a jerk, Jake Chivis," he said huskily, feeling it burn like molten lava down his throat, into his chest. "But you are nosy, yeah. What difference should it make to you what anyone has said to me in the past? You want to know about my last boyfriend, huh? Is that it? Why don't you just ask me then? *'Ilmarinen, tell me about the guy you used to sleep with? What did you do for him, huh? How did you get him off? Did you like it that the entire department knew he was a married man and he was stringing you along? Did the humiliation of it give you a hard-on?'* Well, yes…of course! What do you think? That just got my rocks off, big time, Chivis. And finding out that he considered my arse a challenge…well, I guess that was an honor, wasn't it? I mean, his wife wasn't letting him give it to her that way either, so I was in fucking good company!"

He held out the glass, trying not to let his hand shake, trying to keep the look in his eyes cold, untouched, even as his mind screamed at him, *What are you doing? What the fuck are you fucking doing? Shut. The. Fuck. Up.*

Jake said nothing. He poured a small measure into the glass for Mari and when Mari threw his head back and downed it, Jake tipped the bottle to his own mouth and took a healthy slug or two. Then he set it down and took the glass from Mari's trembling hand and placed that down gently too. He pulled Mari across the bed and into his lap with one strong arm, like he weighed nothing, like it caused him no pain to move that way when Mari was sure it must. Jake wrapped his arms around him and somehow managed to make them fit together without elbows and knees sticking out everywhere.

"I didn't ask you about your ex, because who the fuck

ever wants to hear about someone's ex? Also, I didn't know it was your last boyfriend that was such a bastard. And if you don't know why it matters to me what someone might have said or done to you in the past…well, I guess you'll just have to figure that one out."

Mari felt a shiver run through him as Jake scooped him into his arms like he was no more than a child. He wondered how it could be, that he could hate how easily Jake knew the buttons to push but still love the way that he pushed them. He bent his head, resting his forehead against Jake's, closing his eyes so that he didn't have to look into that knowing gaze.

"I bet you were a great cop, weren't you?" he muttered softly. "I bet no one ever got away from you without a confession. What the fuck does it matter? I suppose he wasn't really my boyfriend, even. It was just something I told myself to feel better about the fact that he only had to sweet talk me and I would get down on my knees and suck him off. There…so now you know. He didn't have to make me feel worthless, Jake. I was pretty much there already. If you're cute and you're nice to me, I'll blow you, gratis. I won't even embarrass you about it in front of your friends, if you don't want them to know."

"You are not worthless," Jake soothed, his words slurring ever so slightly. "And if you think you're a slut and feel bad about it, I'd say you just got a healthy libido, and fuck the haters! Also, I think I'm a little drunk so I'm sorry if anything I say doesn't make sense."

Mari lifted his head, surprised by this. He could feel the burn of the alcohol still in his belly and the raw, charred taste of it at the back of his throat, but he wasn't drunk. Booze tended to loosen his tongue though and Jake had been smart enough to figure that one out.

"You're either a cheap date, or you're still trying to make me feel better," he said suspiciously. "Maybe if your mouth doesn't know how to behave I should find something else for it to do. And yes, I have…well, let's say it's not an underactive libido. But then you already know that."

He stroked his fingers up through Jake's dark curls, gently massaging the back of his skull.

"Lie down with me, Chivis. You are not up to a drinking contest with me tonight."

"I told you, I don't drink," Jake said as he let Mari maneuver him back down on the bed, still facing him. "A beer or two at dinner once in a while, maybe, and I haven't eaten since breakfast, so I'm pretty sure that brandy just went straight into my bloodstream."

"Is that right? Well, let's hope that you forget all about this conversation in the morning then," Mari said, determined to remain cheerful for his man. He tugged up the blanket around them both and snuggled close, carefully working his arms and legs into positions that didn't make Jake any more uncomfortable than he was already. "You should get some rest, Detective. Let me watch out for the bad guys while you sleep off that booze."

He kissed Jake on the nose again, feeling his heart rate slowing down as they settled into each other's arms once more. Maybe he was crazy to think that Jake was actually starting to care about him, but he sure as hell wasn't going to embarrass himself by asking.

Not yet, anyway.

Just when Mari thought Jake had fallen asleep, Jake curled warm fingers around his left hand and brought it up to his lips to kiss the back.

"I'm sorry. I told you I wasn't any good at making guys happy," he murmured drowsily.

Mari returned the kiss, pressing his lips to the scraped knuckles and the warmth of Jake's fingers around his own.

"Well, I guess we make a good pair then, don't we? Get some rest, hero. Let's get you fit before we start to worry about *happy*."

He experienced a little pang of sadness at Jake's admission though, because that didn't seem right. He was such a gentleman, even when he was refusing to take no for an answer. Maybe, Mari thought ruefully, his heart was not the only one to have been broken.

Aren't we a pair? He sighed.

Chapter Twelve

Jake woke to a nasty headache and a body that felt like it had been hit by a bus. Twice! He hurt everywhere. Sleeping had only given the bruises some time to really set in. Maybe Mari was right. Maybe he shouldn't be so quick to try to lift Guylian out of the shit.

Mari was still asleep next to him and he indulged himself for a few moments, studying his peaceful face. He was so pretty, although he knew if he expressed that opinion out loud Mari would probably take his head off. He was though, pretty enough that he could have been a model probably, if he'd wanted to be. He had those high cheekbones and fine, sculpted features that Jake always saw on the faces of men in magazines wearing the latest designer labels. He had the body to carry off those clothes too, tall and slender but wide enough across the shoulders that he looked trim rather than lanky. While Jake slept, he had shed the rest of his clothes. His upper torso, where the blanket had slipped down to his waist, was nicely defined with a dusting of dark blond hair between his small, pale nipples. Probably he swam as well as ran, Jake thought, or worked out somewhere, because there was good muscle tone under the sleekness of his pale skin. He always dressed in a slightly looser fit than he really needed, though the clothing was so well cut that it never looked baggy, but it wasn't obvious when he was clothed that there was such a gorgeous body under there.

He had the softest lips Jake had ever kissed, two perfect cushions, so invitingly shaped, like a nocked longbow. He always felt like he was on the verge of pulling Mari close to suck face, no matter where they were or what they were doing. His eyes though, without any doubt, were his most striking feature. Vivid and intelligent, his gaze so sharp it was a wonder it didn't cut like a laser beam. Even when they were closed, Jake could imagine those crystal-sharp eyes watching him through the lids, all manner of mystery happening in their depths.

Shit. I'm totally in love with him.

That was a problem seeing as how, every time he made a move, Mari was trying to put obstacles in their way. He put so many emotional barriers around himself it was hard to say what he felt, if anything. Last night when Mari had apologized for leading him on, or whatever shit it was that he'd said, Jake had been sure he was about to get up and walk out. Then he'd get a phone call or worse, a text, telling him that it was better if they just stayed friends. It had cut him to the bone to hear Mari call himself worthless, and how could he think that being used and humiliated was something he deserved? Just because he liked sex didn't mean he should expect to be treated like garbage. How could he be so hot and so smart and not know that?

Maybe they could get around his body's fear-response to sex and maybe they couldn't, but Mari didn't seem willing to even try. Or at least, he didn't genuinely believe that Jake could be perfectly satisfied in bed without ever getting his ass. He'd already told Mari this though, and he might as well have been talking to a wall — he just refused to accept that it was true. If he thought Jake would simply give up on him though, he didn't know him well enough yet.

Even as he thought it, a snide whisper piped up in his head to remind him how much he'd already given up and walked away from. That was the end of his musing.

He carefully rolled over and even more gingerly got up, then hobbled across the living area to the bathroom in the half-light of early morning. Today was supposed to have been spent seeing the sights with Mari and having some fun. Instead he was going to make himself look as presentable as he could — which was a joke because the big bruise on his cheek wouldn't be mistaken for anything but a punch to the face—and try to see if he could find Phil Weston's real killer.

He finished using the toilet and washed his hands and face, pushing his wet fingers through his hair trying to tame it. He really, *really* needed a haircut. Maybe he should ask Mari to recommend a place. His hair always looked amazing.

He went to the kitchen and, as quietly as he could, set the coffee maker up to brew a pot. He was going to have to clean this place up and possibly think about replacing the coffee table, which was in pieces. The kitchen chair he had thrown was still whole but there was a crack in one leg and he didn't want to trust it. At least nothing else had been broken, apart from his ribs.

He dug a bottle of aspirin out of the cupboard and swallowed a few, leaving the bottle out on the counter in case Mari wanted some, which from the sound of things as he staggered through to the kitchen door, looking for the bathroom, still wearing the blanket like a sarong, he might well do. Pushing one hand through his tangled hair as the other gripped the coverlet at his waist, Mari blinked at the scene of chaos in the living room and muttered, "Wasn't a bad dream then. Shit!" He winced at Jake's battered features. "Does that feel as bad as it looks?"

Jake grimaced but shook his head.

"Nah, it's not too bad," he lied. Last night he'd been willing to let Mari baby him a little but in the gray light of morning, he figured he should toughen up some. "Coffee will be ready in a minute, if you want some."

"I think so, yeah." Mari waved a hand toward the bathroom. "Okay if I use the…"

"Go ahead." Jake nodded in the appropriate direction and Mari vanished into the littlest room in the already miniscule flat, where he ran the taps in an effort to drown out the noise of his coughing and retching, before stumbling back out again and flopping down on the sofa with his face in his hands.

"I fucking hate brandy," he muttered thickly. "Dunno why you drink the stuff."

Jake arched an eyebrow at that but didn't dispute it. He brought him some aspirin and a glass of water.

"Do you think you can keep this down? It might help. I was going to suggest breakfast, but maybe just some toast?"

"Huh? No." Mari shook his head without looking up but he did reach out one-handed for the aspirin and washed three or four of them down with a couple of slugs of ice cold water. "No food. Really bad idea. Slows your brain down. We have a killer to catch. Bad enough doing it with a hangover."

Instinct demanded that Jake put that idea out of Mari's head and tell him to wait at home while he went to interview the Marches at the site of Phil's last job, but two things stopped him. One was that he knew Mari would be pissed if he even suggested he stay out of it, and two, he needed Mari's help. He couldn't exactly wander around a stranger's house touching things. He was going to need a distraction.

"If you're not up to it today, we can wait," Jake said.

Mari swallowed down some more of the cold water. He set the tumbler on the floor between his feet and gripped his head in both hands as if he was worried that it might fall off.

"I'm not the one that looks like he went twelve rounds with a heavyweight champ," he said carefully. "Gimme a few minutes, I'll be fine. So long as we don't have to go far. Not sure I fancy a long ride in the country this morning, fresh air or not."

"I am not in the mood or the right frame of mind for a long trip or a rummage through a killer's house first thing this morning either," Jake said, although if he were doing this alone, he might have considered heading out sooner rather than later. "It's not far, only the other side of Hampstead Heath, but we're not exactly on a time schedule here—we can wait until this afternoon. How about we hold off until we both feel more human and then you can tell me where there's a good place to get my hair cut. Then we'll go find out if Phil's second to last job had anything to do with his death."

Mari looked up at him quizzically.

"Chivis, a man is dead and you're worried about your *hair*? I thought *I* was supposed to be the vain one! Pass me my fucking laptop, will you?"

A faint smile finally graced his lips though and it made him look more alive. Jake shrugged and picked up the backpack Mari had dropped by the end of the futon last night, handing it to him.

"It's not like we can change what happened. Rushing around is kinda pointless. Whoever killed him is still gonna be the one who killed him whether I take the time to get my hair cut or not," Jake said practically.

His partner uttered a little sigh, tapping at the keys distractedly to wake his precious machine from its slumber.

"Heaven forbid that you should look disheveled. If you're *that* worried about it, *I'll* cut your bloody hair for you."

He called up a sequence of files and began to scroll through them, looking for something. At last he just rested his fingertips against the screen and closed his eyes. The sequence kept scrolling, ticking through the lists of offender information that he'd summoned on Guylian's file until it reached the part that he had altered just a couple of days before.

"The gods of information technology help me," he exhaled. "I will probably regret this." Then, more firmly, he said, "Undo previous command."

Just those words. The screen flickered. A cool synthetic voice asked, *"Are you sure that you want to execute this command? This command cannot be undone."*

Mari did not open his eyes. "Yes. Undo, please."

The characters on the screen rejigged themselves in front of Jake's astonished eyes, returning their ex-offender's file to its previous status.

"Command executed. Do you wish to continue working with this file?" the voice of Mari's laptop asked.

"No...I'm done," Mari said. "Exit current files and log out. Thank you."

Like magic, the file closed and he pinched the bridge of his nose and sighed.

"I imagine that the Probation Service are going to have a hell of a job explaining this to Van, but it looks like they fucked up," he murmured. "Nothing on his file. Your conscience is salved, Chivis. Now, we just need to figure out which of Phil's conquests offed him and I can go back to bed."

Jake stared at him for a moment. Mari had explained to him what it was that he could do, but seeing it in the flesh was unnerving.

"That was...cool, what you just did with the laptop."

Mari glanced up at him again. "Weston never did tell you, did he? What it is that I do, I mean? Yes I'm a hacker, but the gift...it kind of goes beyond that. Doctor Dolittle could talk to the animals. I talk to the Internet. It's...an interesting sideline. What *they* make of me, I'm never entirely sure."

"You talk to your computer?" Jake said slowly.

"Voice recognition software, it's not rocket science, Chivis," Mari looked up at him with a weary smile. "I don't *have* to talk to it, but sometimes it helps me focus."

"What were you doing before, when you touched the screen?" he wanted to know.

Mari put the laptop aside for a moment, closing the lid. "It's hard to explain to a layman, but you're not, exactly...a layman, I mean. When *you* touch an object or a person, you act as an interface, right, accessing the residual contact memories in that locus?"

Jake nodded awkwardly. That wasn't exactly it, but close enough. "Kinda."

"Yeah...well, I'm kind of an interface for communications systems. They talk to me, if I can get on their channel. I need to get into one of their files to do it, the way you get into a stranger's head, but it can be a low security folder, their recycle bin, anything really — once I'm in there, I can go anywhere I like. So..." He exhaled when Jake was still looking at him bemusedly after that explanation. "We've eliminated Guylian from our inquiries. What next?"

Jake wanted to ask more questions but the look on Mari's face said he wasn't really in the mood for answering them. He pushed his thoughts back to the case.

"The scenario that Guylian laid out is as likely as any other. Professor Weston said his brother was seeing a married woman, Guylian confirmed that, and her name matches the one that the Millers told me was Phil's last job. All I need you to do is look in his datebook for their address. And, uh, maybe keep them distracted while I snoop around their house."

Mari picked up the laptop again and shut down the Probation Service site then ran a search for the phone records he'd pulled from Phil's mobile. He flopped back into the comfortable cushions of the sofa with the machine balanced on his blanketed knees.

"Distracted, how exactly? I'm not a performing seal, Chivis. What if they have a big house?"

"Don't worry, I know you can do this job no problem. All you have to do is keep them talking." Jake grinned as Mari's fingers went still again and he looked up at him. His companion was distracting enough sitting there half-bare, but Jake figured suggesting that would get him another impatient glare for his pains. "And I'll ask to use their bathroom."

"What do we tell them we're doing there? What if the police have already been round? What do I say if they get suspicious and start reaching for sharp objects?" Mari looked alarmed at the thought. That look said it had been bad enough knowing that Guylian had been around here, and he wasn't the actual killer.

"Don't worry, you've been watching too many cop dramas.

Innocent people act offended and get pissy sometimes when you put them under pressure, but the guilty ones are some of nicest, most helpful folks you'll come across. They want to make it seem like they are doing everything in their power to be cooperative so there's no reason to suspect them. We'll tell them that Phil's brother hired us, which is close enough to the truth, and that we have some questions as we're trying to get a picture of Phil's last few days before he died. I will be out of sight for five minutes, or less."

"Five *minutes*?" Mari looked appalled. "You want me to keep the smooth-talking, super-nice killer busy for *five whole minutes*? You do know that I was 'student least likely to convincingly improvise' in my drama class, don't you?"

"You can smooth-talk complete strangers, I've seen you do it," Jake told him, trying to sound reassuring. "You're a natural, you do it without thinking."

"I do plenty of thinking, trust me," Mari countered him warily. "I'm thinking they're going to see right through me in about thirty-four-point-oh-three-seven seconds."

"Okay," Jake said, blowing out a little breath. "If you don't think you can do it, I'll go in on my own. I can still get a look around, I might get a memory or two, I might get nothing. If I come up empty-handed we'll have to rethink our strategy."

Mari still looked less than happy. "Look, how about…we don't go in together? What if I can somehow lure them out and keep them outside, and then you can sneak in and have a look around? I could probably come up with something that would keep them busy on the drive for a while. I just… I don't think that I look like an investigator, Chivis. I don't think they're going to believe that for a minute. But I do sort of have an idea. I can bring their phone network down from the outside, then all we need to do is show up there with a toolbox and they will let us have access to just about any room that has a phone point in it. People might not like talking to the police, but if their phones are fucked, they will basically give you their keys and carte blanche to do whatever the fuck you want to their house so long as you can make their broadband work properly," he said rationally.

"Whoa, whoa, who said anything about pretending to be a cop? I might skirt around some ethics once in a while, but that'd get either one of us arrested, probably both. You're making this more complicated than it needs to be," Jake told him, then stopped as he got a look at the stubborn set to Mari's jaw and the closed look in his eyes and regretted shooting him down immediately.

"You were the one that suggested telling them that Tony hired us," he said coolly. "Cop, P.I., whatever…it would still be pretending."

They were both silent for a moment or two, then Jake relented.

"Okay. We'll do it your way." He would feel better not having to leave Mari on his own anyway, and it would probably mean a better poke around the house. Plus Mari could watch his back if he got a fix on anything important. He also kept it to himself that Mari might not think he looked like a cop but he sure as hell didn't look like a repairman. It was a chance they would have to take, but it was possible they could pull this off.

* * * *

Brendan March lived in a gated community on one of those exclusive roads off Highgate West Hill, in the leafy suburbs. His residence was a five-bedroom, mock-Tudor pile that even raised one of Mari's immaculate eyebrows. On the plus side, at least they could give him the excuse that they had to leave their van out on the main road. Even in well-worn jeans and a casual sweatshirt and borrowed cap, Jake didn't think Mari looked like a genuine telecom repairman, but since it had been Mari who hacked the household broadband system he supposed that he was not in a position to argue.

They had waited in the car until someone from the March household phoned in the fault, a call which Mari had also fielded. It had taken, almost as he had predicted, a little less than twenty-four minutes.

"We will send someone out to you as soon as possible," he promised smoothly.

They waited in Mari's mother's car for about twenty more minutes then decided enough was enough and made their way to the house where Phil Weston had carried out his last actual job of work.

"This is some serious financial clout, right here," Mari told Jake, a trifle unnecessarily, as they crunched their way up the gravel drive, trying to look inconspicuous. "If Phil was fucking the lady of the house, he must have thought he was invincible."

"Maybe," was Jake's only comment. He could easily imagine that Phil might have gotten off on the thrill of cuckolding a wealthy, powerful man. It wasn't just a one-time thing though, not if he'd told his brother about her. So was he just having fun getting his rocks off, or had deeper feelings come into play? The memory he'd got from Van suggested Phil was maybe ready to call it quits with her. Was that because he was growing bored with her, or maybe because he'd figured out that being a rich woman's boy toy wasn't as great as he might have first believed?

Whatever the case, it seemed like this affair might have cost Phil his life. Jake just hoped he could pick up a memory or two that made it crystal clear how and where Phil had died.

"Listen," Jake said urgently before they reached the door. "We'll check out the living room first, then see if we can go straight to the main bedroom. Those are the two most likely spots if I'm going to pick up anything."

Mari nodded and rang the bell. They heard the echoing chime somewhere deep within the house and a voice called out distantly, then just as he was about to try it again, they saw movement through the obscured glass panels in the doorframe and the locks clicked softly inside. The door swung inward and a lean, nervy-looking fellow peered out at them. His light brown hair was thinning at the temples and his eyes were the color of milky tea. They roamed over Jake speculatively then moved with a more inquiring frown to Mari, who was holding a clipboard and carrying his laptop bag over one shoulder. Mari flashed an ID card in a plastic wallet at him. It was his university work pass but it whipped before the startled man's eyes so quickly that this made no difference.

"Mr...March?" Mari consulted his clipboard. There was nothing on there but old printouts from his recycling file, though Brendan March didn't know that. "You called us about your broadband?" he prompted with a helpful smile.

"Oh... Yes." March nodded at once, his expression brightening automatically, just as Mari had predicted. "I don't know what happened, one minute I was checking my shares and the next I had a pop up box telling me that there was no connection. I tried rebooting the PC and the modem but it made no difference."

Mari nodded sagely. He and Jake knew this because they had been watching the fruitless attempts on his laptop out in the car.

"We've been getting calls about outages all over this part of town since last night. Don't worry, Mr. March, we'll get things running for you again. Can you show us where your upstairs phone points are, and then I'll take a look at the modem for you." Mari kept that effortlessly encouraging smile on his face. "How many users are in the property?"

"Uh...?" Their baffled client blinked at him for a moment, apparently wrong-footed by this question.

"Broadband users? Just yourself, or do you have a family? House this size, I expect you have kids on their PlayStations twenty-four-seven," Mari elaborated cheerfully.

"Uh...no... It's just me, usually. My wife runs a fashion design business, so she uses it too but she wasn't online this morning." Mr. March looked from Mari to Jake again. "Is

209

this…uh…going to take long?"

"Shouldn't take long at all," Jake said, smiling disarmingly.

Mr. March stepped back to let them into the spacious hallway, closing the door behind them, and led the pair to the broad, dog-leg staircase to their right. The carpet, which was a deep, pine-green color, swallowed all sound and smelled new. Mari was making nice with him, asking if he wanted them to take their boots off. Jake was tempted to tell him to just show Mari where his modem was and he would find the other phone points on his own but he hesitated. He knew Mari didn't want to be left alone with the man, and he could hardly blame him, as it was quite possible he had killed Phil Weston. Also, he figured, he could wait to see if he picked up any impressions first before trying diversionary tactics. They followed March up the wide staircase to an upstairs landing with an open railed balcony looking over the foyer below, and a long hallway with several closed doors leading off it on either side.

"We don't have a phone in every room, but I'm sure all the bedrooms have one," March said, opening the first door he came to which, given how tidy it looked, was probably a guest bedroom, and going around to the other side of the bed. He pointed to the phone jack in the wall. "Yes, right here."

Fortunately they had been smart enough to bring a compact toolbox and Mari had his laptop in his shoulder bag so they could look like they actually might be doing something. Mari made a note on his tablet and fished something out of his bag that looked like a hand-held scanner. He waved it vaguely over the phone point and tapped something else into the tablet.

"Okay, that's fine. You can point them all out to us and we'll get to work," he said, cheerfully.

They went through the upstairs bedrooms one by one and at last reached the master, at which point March informed them that was the last of them and Mari assured him again that they would have the problem fixed quickly. March took

Mari back down to his study on the ground floor, ostensibly to look at the modem, and the moment they were gone, Jake touched the lamp on the bedside table, ran his fingers lightly along the edge of a vase and moved across to a chair in the corner where he brushed his fingers over the arm.

Nothing. Just random flickerings of people coming and going. *A woman sitting in the chair and rolling on a stocking. A man's hands moving the chair into a spot by the window. The smell of perfume, light and floral.*

As he turned back toward the bed, a shade reluctantly, and ghosted his fingers across the foot rail, a tug on his consciousness brought him into a memory.

A woman with dark hair and flashing gray-green eyes screaming at him that he was useless... Then he was back in the room, alone again.

He hadn't gotten enough to know who she'd been yelling at, or why.

"Looks like Mrs. March has a bit of a temper," Jake murmured under his breath, moving on to a door that he'd initially presumed was a built-in closet but which actually led to an en-suite shower room. He got nothing in the bathroom except a flashback of another argument, this time about money, but again it wasn't much.

He wandered back out and poked his head out of the bedroom door to check the hallway but there was no sign of Mari or March. Returning to the bed, he steeled himself before touching it again. He wished he had more control over what he saw, so he could try to filter for specific memories, but it didn't work that way and for about two minutes he got a barrage of small scenes, some steamy, some emotional, some just the fog of semi-wakefulness. In short, nothing particularly useful.

With a sigh he came back into himself and texted Mari.

I'm not getting anything useful.
For a moment he considered trying the other rooms then his phone chirped at him.

Did you try the wardrobes?

That was a little riskier than just wandering around touching things but Jake had to try. The closet was built in, behind a glass-fronted sliding door that made the room seem bigger and brighter than it was. He opened the door and casually brushed his hand along the hanging garments. Cloth was strange. Sometimes it was as nonconductive as plastic when it came to holding on to psychic residue, and sometimes it could hold on to things that were decades old. Metal items were more reliable for memories but cloth was totally unpredictable. He was just about to give up when he lifted his head and saw Mari was looking at him curiously from the doorway. Jake shook his head at him.

"Nothing. I think we can go," he said.

Mari nodded and slid the wardrobe door softly shut, but then frowned at something he saw in the glass and turned around, pointing toward the bed.

"There's something sticking out from under there."

Jake wasn't sure he wanted to look but he lifted the edge of the bedskirt and saw the edge of a black leather belt. Or what he thought was a black leather belt. There was too much of it to be just a belt though. Jake swallowed. After the things he'd seen in Phil's apartment, he knew the man was into some kinky stuff. The leather straps and buckles looked like some kind of bondage gear and Jake was certain that he didn't want to touch it. He had to though. Reaching out hesitantly, he wrapped his fingers around the leather strap.

"Fuck! Fuck! Oh fuck!"

The words came out of his mouth in a panic as he stared in horror at the red and purple blotched face of Phil Weston, motionless and eyes wide, trussed up on the bed with black leather straps. A nylon cord was tied around his neck and it ran back in a hard line to his tied hands, so they were pulling his head back at a weird angle.

"Oh my god... Oh god, no..."

The voice that came from his throat was male, on the verge of tears. He gagged and struggled not to vomit, breathing hard and he looked at the clock – half past ten. There was light coming in the room so it must be ten in the morning. Blindly he clawed his way off the bed, stumbled away from the body and into the bathroom. Brendan March's pale, terrified face stared back at him from the mirror and he felt the burn of acid at the back of his throat right before he bent over the toilet... Then he was abruptly in the present again, falling back onto his ass and gasping.

Mari crouched over him, picking him up from the floor but he was not alone. Jake recognized the dark-haired woman from his flashbacks. She looked perplexed and still rather annoyed.

"What the hell do you think you're doing?"

"I suspect there may be an electrical fault," Mari improvised, with astonishing alacrity given his earlier assertion that he was not the quickest when it came to thinking on his feet. "Perhaps it might be an idea to turn off the power for a little while. Can you show me your fusebox? And maybe call an ambulance?"

"Who the hell *are* you?" she demanded, ignoring him. "Brendan! *Bren!* Who the hell are these men? What are they doing in my bedroom?"

Mr. March showed his sheepish face, peering around the door frame and looking worried. "It's fine, Helen. They came to sort out the connection fault. I told you. The broadband went down."

Mrs. March looked from Jake and Mari to her husband skeptically.

"Already? You only called them...what? Half an hour ago?"

"We were in the area," Jake said, recovering some of his equilibrium.

"You're not the only ones, we've looked at half the street," Mari assured her.

She narrowed her eyes and though she didn't voice her suspicions as to what they'd been looking at, it was plain enough from her expression that she didn't believe it was anything to do with their Internet connection. She kept looking at Mari curiously until he was forced to clear his throat.

"Um…I think we might need to come back with…um… different equipment," he said evasively. When she didn't look away, he carefully took a step back from her, offering Jake his arm in an attempt to get him up off the floor.

Jake managed to get up. "Yes, we found the issue, but we'll have to reset things from the depot. We should have this fixed for you within an hour, ma'am." He was already using his hand on Mari's elbow to push him toward the door. "Sorry for any inconvenience."

"Where's your ID?" Helen March wanted to know.

Mari put a hand to his chest then shrugged as if he had been expecting to find a pocket there. He looked at Jake enquiringly.

"I must have left it in the van, sorry. Have you got yours?"

"That one showed me his ID when I let them in," her husband said unhelpfully, pointing at Mari.

Jake groaned inwardly. This was exactly why he hadn't wanted to go with quite so elaborate a ruse. Too late now. Jake didn't even pretend to look for it.

"My colleague already showed you his identification. There are a dozen other stops we need to make, ma'am, we should be going. Have a nice day." His grip on Mari's elbow tightened and he practically propelled him out of the door past the startled Mr. March and down the stairs while Mrs. March shouted incoherently at her husband behind them to stop them, or call the police, or just stop being so 'effing useless'.

"Well…that was interesting. What did you see?" Mari asked him once they were outside and he was sure they were out of sight and earshot of the tempestuous couple.

"Phil Weston, tied up and strangled to death," Jake said. Maybe he shouldn't be so blunt but the memory was still with him like a slime on his skin that made him want to take a very hot shower. "Brendan March freaking out over

his body and running to the bathroom to puke. I saw my...
his face in the mirror."

Mari's eyes widened in disbelief. "It's true then. Guylian
didn't kill him. My days! What do we do now? How can we
tell the police about this?"

"I don't know. Even when I was still on the force, I had
to be careful how I handled things like this. People never
believe in clairvoyant memories. I can't say I blame them
either, how would anyone prove I wasn't lying? It has to be
backed with evidence, and I haven't got any. All I can do is
try to convince a detective that they need to look at Brendan
March as a suspect and hope they find something."

Mari mulled this over. "That weird little man? He *really*
killed him? He seemed like he might be scared of his own
shadow. Inconceivable!"

Jake shook his head grimly. "The thing is, what I saw...
I think it might have been an accident. They were in bed,
I... Uh, March was naked, and it looked like...like they had
been playing some kinda bondage game. There wasn't any
anger, he was freaking out, like he was upset."

"Curious, and we thought it was his wife that Phil was
screwing. He was screwing them both, literally. Even so,
Brendan didn't try to help Phil, or call the police. He's
responsible for that at least. How do we get him arrested?
What if we talk to Professor Weston again, ask him if he has a
number for the police officers that came to talk to him? They
weren't too bad, were they? Maybe Weston could explain
about the SEWN Program and we could tell them that we
were looking at Phil's Internet history for the professor.
Would they arrest us if he'd given his permission?"

"They couldn't arrest us even if he hadn't. It's not
illegal to look at a person's Internet history." Jake sighed,
overwhelmed by Mari's endless questions. "Maybe we'll
get lucky and someone will actually believe me for once. My
testimony isn't admissible in court but there is a precedent
for a certified psychometric analyst giving evidence to
police that has led to an actual arrest. The worse that can

happen is they don't believe me."

"If we don't tell them something, then he's going to get away with it," Mari pointed out needlessly. "And you'll have got beaten up for nothing, which would be a terrible waste."

He glanced apologetically at Jake, who still looked rather the worse for wear after his run-in with their initial suspect. Jake's bruises were soon to be relegated to second place in his concerns, however. As they were walking through the foot gate leading onto the main road and heading back toward the car, their debate was brought to a sudden halt by the arrival of a Met Police panda with its blue lights still flashing. It skidded to a halt just beyond them and two officers in combat vests jumped out and pointed Tasers at them.

"Put your hands in the air and move away from one another!" one of them shouted.

Mari actually looked over his shoulder to check that they hadn't walked into an unexpected ambush.

"He means us," Jake said, putting his hands up to shoulder height.

"What did we do?" Mari put his laptop case down on the bonnet of his mother's small, white Alfa Romeo and mirrored Jake's posture, edging away from him but not so far that he couldn't still talk. "When did it become an offense to walk down the street with a laptop?"

"I don't think that's what's bugging them. That bitch back at the house probably called them. It is my guess that we are about to be arrested," Jake said calmly.

"Ah...that's a new experience," Mari said with a little roll of his eyes. "Well, we did want to talk to the police, I suppose. Maybe we should be careful what we wish for."

"Don't tell them anything, just be polite and say you want to have your lawyer answer any questions," Jake advised, seeing as how they didn't have time to work out a story, and anything they said wasn't likely to be believed anyway. They were caught red-handed, so to speak. He would be lucky if he didn't get deported over this. So much for a new start.

The two armed officers separated them and by the time they had been pressed against different vehicles, cautioned and searched for nonexistent weapons, another car had arrived and they were both cuffed and whisked off separately to the local police station.

* * * *

Jake sat in an uncomfortable plastic chair in a gray-walled room deep within the Georgian block that was Kentish Town Police Station, with a uniformed officer sitting across from him holding a pad and pen. A plain-clothes detective inspector leaned against the wall to Jake's left. The duty solicitor, which was the equivalent of a public defender, as Jake understood it, sat in another chair on Jake's right.

Cop dramas got the whole hard-nosed interrogation scenes wrong for the main part. Most cops interviewing a suspect didn't lose their cool or bang on tables and use all kinds of psychological tricks to get answers, not unless they were working on a murder suspect, and even then that only rarely came into play as the majority of murders and rapes were often domestics and much easier to crack than the movies and TV made out. Kentish Town didn't even have a table, just a semicircular stand pushed up against the opposite wall to the one the DI was propping up, on which the black box recorder winked at them relentlessly.

Still, the slightly portly, older, uniformed officer, Sergeant Willcox, had pretty good game. He took his time asking questions, jotting things down on his pad, providing plenty of pauses so Jake would feel the need to fill them, and keeping things friendly so Jake would trust him.

"So you're a detective, Mr. Chivis?"

"Not currently employed as such, but yes," Jake said.

"And you have no idea why Mrs. March called the police to tell us that two men fitting the description of you and your friend had rifled through her house whilst claiming to be from Metro X Telecom?"

"It is possible she's trying to deflect attention from her husband. I'm not sure she knows that he killed Phil Weston though."

The two investigating officers exchanged a look. "Weston? The guy they pulled out of the Regent's Canal the other day? Why would you believe that, Mr. Chivis?"

"And what do you know about the investigation into Philip Weston's death?" asked the other, who been introduced as Detective Inspector Mark Hammond, speaking up for the first time.

* * * *

In the cell along the hallway, Mari was still flexing his wrists from where the cuffs had bitten into them on the car journey in. He had been searched, which wasn't nearly as much fun as he had expected, and told to hand over his keys, laptop, phone and wallet, and his watch, which had perplexed him. And now he was being quizzed by some middle-aged blonde bitch who obviously didn't like him much. His mother's elderly solicitor, Mr. Bramble, who had arrived a few minutes ago flushed and out of breath, was looking uncomfortable.

"You don't *have* to say anything, Doctor Gale," he pointed out.

"I *want* to say something. We *weren't* armed. We didn't do *anything* that was, strictly speaking, *illegal*," Mari protested. "I think that the police response was rather heavy handed under the circumstances. It's not as if we killed anyone. Which is more than I can say for Mr. March."

"Doctor Gale," the female officer interviewing him said. "Mr. March is considering pressing charges against you and your companion for obtaining access to his premises under false pretenses."

"Tell him to go ahead. My colleague, Tony Weston, is

mourning the death of his brother and his *late* brother *died* in that house. Why aren't you doing anything about *that*?" Mari asked, rather more determinedly.

"You have evidence supporting that allegation, Doctor Gale?" the hard-faced DS asked skeptically.

* * * *

"Fisher verses Mendoza made it clear that psychometry can be used to gather initial evidence even in cases of rape and murder," Jake said pacifically. "I know the law does not allow that evidence into testimony but it *can* be used as grounds for suspicion to further an investigation. I'd be willing to make any testimony or fill out any paperwork you need to go after March."

"Right. And how exactly does Doctor Gale fit into your 'unauthorized' investigation into Phil Weston's murder?"

"He doesn't. I asked him to drive me, that's all. He went into the house with me only because it's not exactly a good idea to enter a murder suspect's house alone."

"And what do you know about the problem with the March household's telephone and broadband connection?" the first officer wanted to know.

"No comment," Jake said atonally.

* * * *

"Is it *our* fault that they thought we were telecommunications engineers?" Mari asked innocently. "I mean…do we *look* like telephone engineers?"

"You didn't see fit to put them right?" the interrogating officer queried.

"They wanted their phone line fixed. I hate to disappoint people," Mari said with a little shrug. "And we fixed it. But we were more interested in finding out about Phil Weston's death."

"You are making a very serious allegation about these people, Doctor Gale," the female sergeant, whose name was

Jardine, reminded him. "Mrs. March wants you prosecuted for entering her home under…"

"False pretenses…yeah, yeah, I got that bit." Mari exhaled, shaking his head. "What I don't understand is why you consider that more important than investigating a man's murder? A man is dead and you're wasting time telling us off for trying to find out why. Here's a *why* for you… *Why* don't you go and ask March what happened to Philip Weston?"

* * * *

"I'd be happy to speak with your lead investigator on the Weston murder," Jake said.

"The Weston case belongs to Albany Street, Mr. Chivis. Nothing to do with us. You do realize you may have compromised their investigation, though?" Sergeant Willcox said wearily.

"Not if your people do their job. I'm willing to give a full report along with specifics on where to look for trace evidence. It's up to you to do the rest."

"Mr. Chivis, do you have a UK private investigator's license?" Willcox asked.

"No. As I said, I was not working in an official capacity. I didn't take depositions or make arrests or in any way present myself as an officer, I'm just a concerned friend. It has been established that evidence gathered through psychometry does not require prior authorization or a warrant to obtain, as it is mutable in nature. That means I can't control it. If I shake your hand and see that you're having an affair with your next door neighbor, that isn't my fault and is not considered an invasion of privacy."

The detective propping up the wall exchanged a look with his sergeant, who leaned back in the plastic chair, looking suddenly rather uncomfortable.

"You can seriously do that?" Willcox asked him.

Jake shrugged. "Like I said, it's not something I can

control." He held up one hand. "I touch things and sometimes I get a memory from someone else that touched that thing, and sometimes, most of the time, I get nothing. It seems to happen more, or the memory sticks better with certain types of objects, or if the memory is particularly emotional." Jake put his hand back on his thigh. "I saw Brendan March looking at Phil Weston's body in his bed and having a panic attack."

"So, you've said." The plain clothes officer spoke up then. Jake wasn't sure but he thought it was only the second thing the guy had said. He took out a dark blue biro from his shirt pocket and held it out to Jake. "Why don't you see if you get anything off that?"

Jake looked at the pen, then up at the cop, carefully trying to control his expression.

"You want to test me?"

"If you like."

Jake told himself to stop clenching his teeth and not to let his hands curl into fists. He hated it when people did this to him. Reluctantly though, he reached out and took the pen. It was plastic so he wasn't expecting to get much off it, if anything at all. At first he thought he was right, there was nothing to see then he ran his finger over the ballpoint tip and got a flicker of something.

"*Sign here.*" *The young, pale-skinned, red-haired man across from him was wearing a white name badge with a little symbol of a green house on it. He could make out part of the name.*

Then it was gone and he was back in the interview room with the two cops looking at him like he was some kind of scam artist getting ready to tell them their fortunes.

* * * *

"Look," Mari declared heatedly, "if you don't believe me, then go and talk to Phil Weston's brother. Professor Anthony John Weston – he works for the UCL at Malet Place and he's running SEWN, a project that tests paranormal or psychic abilities. My colleague and I are enrolled on his program. As part of his investigation he asked Jake and I to find out what had happened to his brother. We didn't know that Phil was dead then. All that the professor knew was that Phil had gone AWOL and it was a bit unusual. We figured we'd go to his place and poke about, get a feel for what he'd been up to and go back to the professor, who would tell us if we were warm or cold." He held his hands up in surrender.

Detective Sergeant Rosy Jardine looked quickly at her colleague again then back at Mari. "So you went to *his* *apartment*, do I understand you quite correctly?"

Mari felt his solicitor jab him in the elbow with his pen and he bit his lip, suddenly recalling what Jake had said to him.

"He gave us the key, it wasn't as if we were breaking and entering. He wanted us to take a look around. I thought it was part of the test, that Phil was in on it," he said at last. Beside him, the legal eagle groaned his name softly.

Jardine was staring at him as if he'd suddenly admitted to being an alien life form.

"Just *ask* Professor Weston," Mari said determinedly. "He was trying to establish what kind of information we were able to pick up using the...abilities that we have."

"So now you're telling me that you and Mr. Chivis are... psychics? Is that right?" Jardine pressed him lightly.

"Don't answer that question, Doctor Gale." That was his solicitor.

Mari looked at him irritably.

"Not exactly," he said at last. It wasn't an answer, after all.

"What would you say it was? Exactly?" Jardine wanted to know.

For a moment Mari was silent, turning over the question in his head. He wished he knew what Jake was saying in the other room.

"My colleague...he *sees* things," he said carefully.

"Visions? Those kinds of things?" Jardine leaned forward looking at him intently.

"No." Mari held his ground, meeting her eyes. They were very blue, darker than his own. Her hair was pale gold, smoothed back into a long braid at the back of her neck. He thought she looked like an older, crankier version of Disney's Queen Elsa. "He…he sees things that other people have seen before, as I understand it. He touches something they have touched and he sees what they saw at the time. He saw Phil Weston, dead, in the March house. He saw Brendan March panicking about killing him."

"Why were you in the March house in the first place, Doctor Gale?" Jardine wanted to know. Her expression was skeptical.

"Because…because they were possibly the last people to see Phil Weston alive," Mari told her seriously. "Because his brother wants to know what happened to him and we thought if we could get into the house, then we might find out. Look, just talk to Professor Weston. He will tell you that I'm speaking the truth. We didn't go there to steal anything or to harm anyone, we just wanted to know what happened."

* * * *

"You bought a house recently," Jake said thoughtfully. "*Maybe* recently, I'm not sure on the time frame but hey… disposable biro!" He twirled it around in his fingers. "Your realtor's name was Ron something. Ginger kid. Last name was S M…could be Smith or Smart, not sure."

The investigating officer, Willcox, looked at the DI again, the one who had given him the pen. The detective's eyes were wide. He opened his mouth to say something but the fellow just shook his head.

"Go on, Mr. Chivis. Do you see anything more?"

Jake handed the pen back carefully and reminded himself that he did not want to piss these people off by snapping at them.

"No. Sorry. If you want to know if your marriage is going to work out or what the winning lottery numbers are, you'll have to go to one of those new age shops. I don't see the future, only the past." He lifted his eyes to look at him. "Only people's memories."

"So…" Sergeant Willcox tapped his short, neat fingernails against the notepad in his lap rhythmically. "You went into the March household, completely on a whim, and you knew that a man was killed there. That still doesn't account for why you were in the house in the first place. Mr. and Mrs. March are very angry and upset about your presence there. Give me one good reason why they shouldn't prosecute you for trespass?"

Jake smiled but stopped short of outright laughing. "Well, for one thing, you'd have to prove my word against theirs, show evidence of forced entry or willful vandalism. It's not illegal to knock on someone's door and ask them questions. We were, after all, invited inside. Also, you seem like a good cop. You can tell I've been straight with you and there's no reason to hold me. I've laid out the whole case for you, all you need to do is make the slam dunk and arrest the bastard."

* * * *

"Doctor Gale," Jardine explained patiently, again. "You're an intelligent guy, I presume. You must know that, in order to charge Brendan March with murder, we need more evidence than 'my friend touched his bedpost and saw him strangle a man'. You understand *that* surely?"

"Well, go and find some evidence then," Mari told her, losing patience. "In the time we've been sitting here, they've probably scoured the place from top to bottom and done a runner, anyway, but isn't it *your* job to put together a case against them?"

"Doctor Gale, for a start, I am not responsible for the Philip

Weston murder investigation. It's not even the priority of this nick, so I'd appreciate you not taking that tone with me," she pointed out. "Secondly, I have a couple who are ready to see you serve time for invading their privacy, so I would be very careful what you say about them to anyone else."

"Ilmarinen," his solicitor added before Mari was able to finish drawing breath. "Please shut up. Let me deal with this."

"Tell them, then," Mari snapped, turning to face him, suddenly feeling cold inside. He wanted to know where Jake was, if he was all right. If this all went pear-shaped, he knew it would be his fault. "Tell them to go and *look*, please. Tell them to talk to the police that are dealing with Phil's case. I know it sounds crazy but it's true. We know where Phil was working. We know who he was seeing at the time of his death and we have very good reasons for believing that he was having an affair with Mrs. March and…and possibly Mr. March as well."

"What kind of reasons would those be, Doctor Gale?" asked Jardine, who had been listening to this outburst with narrowed eyes.

"If you'd checked his phone records you would *know* what reasons," Mari said, glaring back at her.

There was a pensive silence. The solicitor put his head in his hands. Inspector Jardine leaned forward, elbows on the table.

"How do *you* know about Philip Weston's phone records, Doctor Gale?"

Mari opened his mouth and closed it again. The LED clock on the table between them flicked over from 17:08 to 17:09.

"No comment," he said, feeling his heart beat too hard.

* * * *

The door into the interview cell opened at seventeen-eleven. A young, blond haired, white man in a crumpled blue suit entered and apologized for the interruption. The officer in charge identified him as DC Alan Murray and suspended the interview temporarily then went out with Murray into the hallway. Two minutes later, by the clock on the desk, he returned and sat down again.

"Interview with Mr. Jake Chivis resumed at seventeen-fourteen hours. Detective Inspector Mark Hammond and Sergeant George Willcox present. Mr. Chivis, can you tell me please how you obtained access to the telephone system at One-Forty-Five Makepeace Avenue?"

Jake had been waiting for them to get around to that. "I'm done answering questions. You can find out from my attorney anything else you need to know."

Detective Hammond looked at Willcox and sighed. "In that case, interview suspended at seventeen-sixteen hours. Mr. Chivis, you will be spending the night in the cells, I am afraid. Take him downstairs, Sergeant Willcox."

"Are you charging my client?" the duty solicitor wanted to know.

"Not yet," Hammond said flatly. "But his friend Doctor Gale has been officially detained on suspicion of illegally accessing telephone records. We can keep Mr. Chivis legally for another" — he glanced at his watch — "twenty-one hours and forty-eight minutes. Maybe a night in custody will help him to remember how he came to be illegally on private property and interfering with personal information."

"Or maybe you can go fuck yourself," Jake said mildly.

"You are not helping your case, Mr. Chivis," the DI told him, unfazed by his reaction. "I would suggest that you help the police over here with their inquiries, otherwise they may just decide to hand you over to the relevant authorities in your own country."

"I *am* trying to help you," Jake said, trying to force the false saccharine sweet out of his voice and not quite succeeding. "But you would rather chase your tails after a bogus trespassing charge than solve a murder case, so there isn't much more I can do for you."

"Are you denying that you and Doctor Ilmarinen Gale illegally obtained access to the property of Mr. and Mrs. Brendan March? Because *that's* what we're investigating here," Hammond said tersely. "Your situation is not looking encouraging. We need to speak to investigators over at Albany Street on the Philip Weston case and when we have done so we can review your situation, Mr. Chivis. But your friend Doctor Gale admitted hacking into a private telephone connection and he is potentially in a lot of trouble, so over the next few hours you'd better have a good think about whether you want to join him."

Jake sincerely hoped that was just a ploy to try to get him to talk and Mari hadn't actually admitted to anything.

"Chivis," his brief said more firmly, "I will speak to people at the university. I will contact Professor Weston and Doctor Gale's solicitor and we will get you out of here, but *please* don't say anything more until I come back."

* * * *

Along the corridor, Mari's solicitor was telling him something very similar but Mari was no longer listening to him. He had begun to panic when the blonde woman read him his rights again and told him he was going to be detained but now all he could think about was Jake. What had they done to him? Where was he? He wanted to be with Jake but he knew that they wouldn't let him in case they compared notes or whatever it was that criminal masterminds were supposed to do when they put their heads together.

"Let my mother know that I won't be home," he said distantly. "Please don't tell her that I've been arrested though, it'll kill her. I need to talk to her myself. Can I ring her? She's very ill." He looked imploringly at DS Jardine.

"You've had your phone call, Doctor Gale. I'm afraid not," she said, managing to sound sympathetic and totally unyielding at the same time, which was a neat trick. "But we can send an officer round to talk to her if you would like us to."

"I think I'd rather you didn't," Mari said, swallowing the sick feeling inside.

"I will speak to her, if you like," his solicitor said, in a kinder tone. He was a family friend and Mari knew he would break the news in a gentle fashion but it didn't make him feel any less treacherous. He nodded.

"Okay."

"Don't say anything to them until I come back, Ilmarinen." The brief looked at him hard.

"Okay."

"I will contact your professor. We are going to get you out of here."

"Fine. Yes." Mari wilted as a young policeman urged him to his feet and ushered him out into the corridor.

As they were making their way back through the station to the holding cells, a door opened further along the passageway and a pair of men in uniform came out with Jake between them. Mari felt his spirits lift a little bit, in spite of their grim situation.

"Jake! Are you all right?" he called impulsively.

"I'm fine, Mari, don't worry about me." Jake managed to answer before he was hauled back into the room and the door slammed shut.

Mari rounded on DS Jardine who was behind him on the corridor. "Please...let him go. He didn't have anything to do with the telephones, that was all my fault. Just let him go. He's not done anything wrong. He's a good man. He used to be a policeman, in America. He tried to tell me not to do it but I just wanted to find out what had happened to the professor's brother. I didn't realize it was such a big deal. Please, Sergeant, please don't charge him. They'll send him back... I don't think... I don't think..."

His solicitor gave him a little nudge with his elbow.

"What did I say?" he hissed.

Mari closed his mouth. He wanted to cry but he kept his

expression firmly emotionless.

"My client is a little overwrought," Mr. Bramble said. "Please excuse him. He's quite upset by the situation. Some time alone to compose his thoughts may assist us all."

He looked at Mari darkly. Mari shook his head but he did take to heart the advice about keeping his mouth shut this time.

Too late…all too late. You're never going to see him again, his conscience poked him.

Mari closed his eyes and let them propel him back along the corridor to the cells.

Chapter Thirteen

Spending a night in a chilly, basic, two-man holding cell with an incoherent crack addict for company and a local dealer in the cell next door kicking up a stink about his conditions for hours was bad. Not knowing whether Mari had been released or what was happening with him was worse.

Logically, Jake knew the police here were blowing smoke. Some rich bitch whined and the cops needed to react so it looked like they were earning their paychecks, but they had zero to hold either of them on. The phone stuff was a bit worrisome but Jake trusted that Mari knew what he was doing well enough that it couldn't be physically traced to him. Everything else they had done might be a little shady but hadn't crossed any legal lines. Even the threats of trespassing and illegal entry were bullshit.

After his worry about Mari, Jake's second concern was wondering if these jackasses had actually given his statement and information to the investigator on the Weston case. Had they even looked for trace evidence yet? Was it too late? Would they be able to crack March and get a confession?

They had Phil's body and there might be evidence on the harness under March's bed, if he hadn't destroyed it, or thrown it off a bridge. Would there be any evidence on Phil's body that would connect him to March, or had the river washed it all away? He was dying for answers and being stuck in a cell was driving him up a wall. He couldn't even imagine Mari being locked up. He knew that Mari would be pissed at him for thinking that way too, but he couldn't help it. Jake was big enough and looked mean enough with his bruises that no one was going to fuck with him, but Mari... Yes, he was tall, but there was something very fey and almost delicate-looking about him that was bound to mark him as a target even in a stupid jail holding cell.

All he could do was hope Mari's mom had either bailed him out or, if he was still stuck in a cell, that no one wanted to cause any trouble.

* * * *

Mari had actually been locked up on his own. Most of the remand cells at the borough stations were small units, singles or doubles at best, and Kentish Town was not the roughest London borough by a good way, so he had plenty of time to himself in which to think about his situation. He was given a blanket and they even brought food, though he was not very hungry and didn't pay it much heed. Before locking the door, they had taken his belt, his boots and even his socks, which he only thought about afterward when he realized with a little jolt that they imagined he might try to do away with himself.

"Idiots!" he muttered huskily, curling up with the blanket wrapped around his shoulders and his knees under his chin. "They could at least turn the bloody heating up!"

He was more distressed that they had taken his laptop and phone, although it had been kind of inevitable once he'd accepted that he wasn't about to walk out of the police station tonight. Jake was going to be furious with him, he thought with a little sigh. He had done precisely what his companion had told him not to, running off at the mouth until even his conscience refused to talk to him.

Why couldn't they see that someone was going to, quite literally, get away with murder if something wasn't done, and quickly? He'd always had faith in the police as a youngster, which was more than most kids at his college, many of whom came from tougher backgrounds. He was beginning to wonder if that faith had been misjudged.

Mama was going to be livid when she found out what he had done. But there was no turning back the clock, he would have to live with the consequences. Of course the consequences might actually mean prison.

That was a dark thought.

If he could spare Jake the jail time, he would do it, though, even if it was a case of falling on his own sword. If Jake was charged, he would never work as a cop again and Mari did not think he could carry the ruin of another man's career on his conscience. Certainly not if that man was Jake Chivis.

He tried not to think that just the other night they had been curled up safe and warm in each other's arms, on Jake's bed. He wished they could be together here, even if it was just to lie back to back and talk quietly to each other. After this fiasco though, he would be lucky if Jake ever spoke to him again.

It was a long time before his mind stopped running in circles around that thorny issue and he finally drifted off into dark, uncomfortable dreams.

* * * *

When the morning came, however, it was to the news that his solicitor, Mr. Bramble, had heroically negotiated police bail for him, on condition that he report at the station every other day and hand in his passport until the case against him either came to court or was dismissed. He was released just before noon.

"What happened to Jake?" he wanted to know.

"They let him go this morning, I think," the solicitor said, sounding weary—he had been up all night. "Professor Weston stood surety for both of you. He also backed up your story about the program and the work you were doing to trace his brother."

"You doubted me?" Mari fired him a dark look.

"Admit it, the story sounds dubious," the man said in a bland voice.

"I have never had so much as a dodgy parking ticket," Mari told him as they climbed into the taxi. "If I was up to no good, I'd have made up a better story than this, trust me. How's my mother?"

"She took the news well," Bramble said, nodding. "I called her as soon as they confirmed they were letting you out. She's expecting you."

"I need to stop at Jake's flat on the way," he said, combing anxious fingers through his hair.

"It might look better if you didn't," Mr. Bramble advised.

"That's tough!" Mari said, giving the driver Jake's address.

When they arrived at Jake's flat though, it was only to find it empty. At least Mari hoped it was empty and it wasn't that Jake just wouldn't answer the door. He couldn't even call to find out since his phone was dead. There was nothing he could do but go face his mother.

He was more than a little bit anxious as he stepped out of the cab, leaving his solicitor to go home too and get some well-earned sleep. Before he could turn the key in the door, it opened and Mama was face-to-face, looking solemn and rather disappointed too, he thought. She put her arms around him though, drawing him into the warmth of the house and closing the door before letting him go.

"Oh, Ilmari...what on earth have you been doing?"

"I'm sorry, Mama. I didn't think they would actually *arrest* us," he said in all sincerity. "But a man is dead, we couldn't just walk away like nothing had happened."

"I know," she said, a trace of pride mixed in with the resignation. "Your Mr. Chivis has been telling me all about it. Well some of it, anyway. I think he may be trying to protect your reputation."

Mari's eyes widened as he realized what she was saying. "He's here?"

Jake stepped into the hall from the kitchen doorway as if he'd been waiting there to give him a moment to say hello to his mother before interrupting. He looked so exhausted and gorgeous that Mari just wanted to hold him tight.

"I figured since you couldn't check on her yourself, I'd stop by," Jake explained.

Mari opened his mouth then closed it again, uncharacteristically lost for words. His heart swelled with a sudden rush of tenderness for the man standing before him.

"He's been very kind," Mama said, her voice noticeably warmer. "Come through, Ilmari. I just put some coffee on. I can't imagine the prison breakfast service is much to write home about."

He followed her but as he drew level with Jake in the doorway, he lifted a hand to place a brief, gentle touch on the man's face.

"*Thank you,*" he mouthed.

To Mari's surprise, Jake slid his arms around him and pulled him close. He didn't kiss him, but he did squeeze him tight, the way he had hoped, and pressed his face into Mari's hair and the side of his throat.

"I was worried about you," he murmured, "Are you okay?"

"You were worried about *me*?" Mari drew back for a second, looking at him in surprise. He was touched by the concern but also a bit bemused. "I'm fine, I promise. It was a shock, but my solicitor says that it can all be sorted out. Bramble Brothers have a very good reputation for that sort of thing. He said they didn't charge you. Weston must have laid it on thick."

"Even if he hadn't, I don't think they would have charged me. They had nothing really. I was more worried about you because…well, I figured you were good enough to cover your tracks, but I was still worried," he said that last in a hush so his voice wouldn't carry to Mama's ears. Mari bent his head at that, slightly ashamed.

"I was stupid, Jake. I thought if I told them it was my idea, they would let you go. I was worried they'd deport you if they thought you'd done anything wrong, but I seriously never imagined they'd actually charge me. UCL are going to sack my sorry arse when this gets out. The police had better come up with some proper evidence that Brendan March murdered Phil or I'm going to be cleaning toilets by the end of the year."

He forced a husky little laugh at that, shaking his head once or twice as he followed Jake back into the day room where Mama was already brewing coffee for them.

"I wouldn't worry too much about it unless they take it to court, which is unlikely. In the meantime I've talked to Professor Weston and he'd like to see us both regarding the case. It's possible with his clout that my statement can be used as grounds for probable cause to investigate the Marches."

"If they haven't already fled the country," Mari said darkly. "I couldn't stop thinking about it last night. What if they do? What if they know we're on to them and they just make a run for it?"

Jake shrugged. "That would be a pretty big red flag that he's guilty. Innocent people don't drop their whole lives and run for it unless they have a damn good reason to believe they're going to be caught."

Mari forced a smile. "You have a lot of faith in the rationality of humankind," he chuckled weakly. "I hope you're right. How soon can the professor see us?"

"I told him I'd call and let him know when you were out and ready. You have time to clean up and eat something first."

"Admittedly, it's been a while since I wanted to eat," he sighed. "Coffee smells good though. And a shower. It's good to be home." He smiled from one to the other of them as it hit him hard how much danger there was that he might lose all of this. "But yes, I think we need to talk to the professor as soon as we can. There is no way the police are going to believe that we got all the information we did without actually doing anything underhanded."

* * * *

When Jake entered Professor Weston's living room with Mari later that afternoon, they were not the first guests. They were introduced to Detective Inspector John Cordiline, from Albany Street CID, practically Mari's next door neighbor. Cordiline was maybe ten or fifteen years his senior, clean-shaven, tall and wiry, with short-cropped dark brown hair flecked at the temples with white, and blue-gray eyes the color of a stormy autumn sky. There was a little kink below the bridge of his nose, suggesting that it had once been broken. He was in charge of the investigation into Phil's death. The other visitor was DI Hammond from Kentish Town, whom Jake had already met under less convivial circumstances. Although current circumstances were not a whole lot better.

Mari was brief and cordial as he pressed the flesh with Cordiline. Jake greeted them stiffly and didn't offer to shake hands. That was okay because they didn't seem all that eager to let Jake touch them anyway.

"Professor Weston has been giving us some background to our ongoing investigations," Cordiline said, looking uncomfortable. "As I understand it, you have been carrying out unauthorized investigations of your own into his brother's disappearance."

"Not *entirely* unauthorized, Inspector Cordiline," Mari said. "Professor Weston gave us permission to look into Phil's affairs. He hoped that we could find out what had happened to him, bearing in mind that the *police* didn't seem to be all that interested in finding him at the time."

Jake felt his lips twitch at that observation but suppressed the urge to smile.

"I take it you have my statement on record," he added. "*Are* you going to question Brendan March?"

Cordiline glanced at Hammond, who looked embarrassed about something and his response enlightened them both.

"That's going to be slightly awkward. Mr. March flew

out to Curaçao on business this morning. His wife is still furious about the situation at the house yesterday," he said, avoiding Mari's accusing glare.

"Business. Right." Jake's half smile was just shy of smug. "So he's skipped the country and she's playing pissed off to create a distraction. You think she knows he did it and she's covering, or is she just being a bitch?"

"Maybe she simply doesn't like having her house invaded by have-a-go investigators," Hammond pointed out defensively.

"Did either of you go and talk to her about Phil?" Mari wanted to know.

DI Cordiline nodded. "Kentish Town sent people round yesterday on the premise of investigating the break-in. We're still examining the evidence they found."

"Have you recovered any trace evidence from the bo— uhh...from Phil?" Jake asked. "My statement should be good enough for you to get a warrant."

"SOCO have been giving him the works," Cordiline confirmed, then nodded to Professor Weston. "Apologies, sir, but it's procedure. They've done a full post-mortem examination, and we should have the results any time today. Since you're Philip's next of kin, you'll know as soon as I get the call."

Weston returned the nod in a more subdued fashion and smiled gravely. Jake suspected he was doped to the eyes— he was struggling to focus—but he couldn't blame him for that.

DI Cordiline's unblinking, storm-cloud stare roamed back over Jake, then returned to his notes. By his side, Mari folded his arms and shook his head with a little frown. Jake wanted to ask him what was wrong but suspected that he wouldn't get a straight answer.

"Have you asked March to return to the UK for questioning?" Jake enquired instead.

"We have his number but he isn't answering his calls." Hammond actually had the good grace to look embarrassed about that.

"But if you find his DNA on Phil's body, the Dutch can extradite him, yes?" Mari persisted. He had gone to sit with the professor, on the arm of his chair, one reassuring hand on his shoulder.

"They have to make a match first," Jake said. "And they can't do that if March isn't here to get a sample."

"They have access to his bathroom. His toothbrush? Hairbrush? Yes?" Mari looked a question at Cordiline who nodded admission, silent in the face of his quiet hostility.

"It's a murder investigation, Mari. They can use DNA found on an object to identify a missing person, but they will need a definitive sample from the suspect to make positive ID and have it admissible in court," Jake explained. "They need to have enough concrete evidence against him to charge him in order to get an extradition. It's a classic catch-22." He returned his attention to the two London detectives and sighed. "You let him slip through your fingers."

"They can use the existing samples to establish who he is and where he was when Phil died though, can't they?" Mari argued. "No wonder so many people get away with murder in this country. What if someone was to fly out to the Antilles and...I don't know...steal his dessert spoon or something?"

"Even to get his DNA off a toothbrush, they still need to convince a judge they have enough cause for a warrant, unless March is willing to give it to them to exclude himself as a suspect. I take it that he has declined to do so, seeing as how he's probably hiding in the Caymans right now." Jake exhaled, beginning to feel that Mari's frustration was contagious in some way.

"So that's it, is it?" Mari fired him a helpless look, as if Jake could somehow circumvent this problem. "We just shrug and say 'okay...we can wait and see if he ever comes back'."

"Ilmarinen, they're trying their best," Professor Weston

said, patting his knee.

Mari gave him a patient smile, like a mother with an over-optimistic child.

Jake was watching Hammond and he lifted one dark, straight, cynical eyebrow.

"*Have* you asked the judge for a warrant?"

"It's in hand," the detective said. "Like that's any of your business."

"Because we're *only* the ones that got arrested trying to make sure that he paid for his crime." Mari sounded more sarcastic now.

Cordiline sighed and ran a hand through his dark, gray-flecked hair. Jake gave Mari a quick, questioning look. Frustration was one thing, but he was being awfully snarky and kept shooting daggers at Cordiline with his eyes. When Mari subsided, Jake returned his attention to Cordiline. The local DI looked about as haggard and tired as Jake felt after his stay in the local lock up. He almost felt sorry for him.

"Contrary to what you seem to think, Dr. Gale, we do want the Met to solve this case and to see Phil Weston's murderer punished." Hammond looked up from his folded hands but turned to Jake again. "Is there *anything* else you can tell me, Mr. Chivis?"

That was about as polite as he had been about Jake's talent, so he didn't automatically tell Hammond to go read his statement again.

"I believe I covered everything that I saw in detail already," he said, shifting his eyes to Weston and back to let the detective know he wasn't about to get into the sordid details of how Phil died in front of his brother. "Neighbors might be able to corroborate what time the van was in the driveway or not. He had to have…" He stopped himself just short of saying 'dumped the body' and instead said, "Moved Phil's body sometime after ten a.m. on Saturday, probably that night, under cover of darkness. We think Phil probably used a workmate's Transit van to go to the house. Phil's contractor, Van Guylian, sent his assistant to pick it up on Sunday. Phil texted Guylian to say he was seeing someone that weekend and that they would run him home. We think that someone was maybe Helen March."

"That's the same Van Michael Guylian that we interviewed about Philip Weston's death the other day?" Cordiline queried, consulting his own set of notes.

Jake nodded his head.

"So you believe that the Transit was used to dispose of the evidence, then returned to the scene of the crime?" Cordiline was still making notes on his tablet and did not look up, but a frown creased his brow.

"Yes," Jake said, shaking his head at the residual memories he still had from the house.

"You know for sure that when you saw Philip Weston's body in the house, you were looking through Brendan March's eyes?" Cordiline looked up at him with a little frown. "Are you absolutely certain of that?"

Again Jake looked from Cordiline to Professor Weston, reminding him that the victim's bereaved brother was in the room. "I described in detail the memory I picked up, in the report I gave," Jake said. "Yes, I'm sure I was looking at Phil through Brendan March's eyes."

"But... Forgive me, Professor Weston" — the detective glanced apologetically at the man and Mari squeezed Tony's shoulder again for reassurance — "you didn't see him die? He was already dead when you saw him through the eyes of Mr. Brendan March?"

Jake paused a long moment then answered with as much care as he could, trying to spare Tony Weston the details of what he had seen.

"No, I didn't see him actually being murdered. I saw Brendan March's reaction after the fact. Phil was lying on the bed, and I could tell Brendan March was extremely distraught looking at him. I saw Brendan March's reflection in the bathroom mirror just after panicking over Phil's body. I wouldn't be surprised if his death was actually an accident."

Jake frowned as he related these details. There was something weird about Brendan March's memory but he couldn't quite put his finger on it. Cordiline tapped in something else and looked back through his notes. He looked perplexed too.

"You said in your statement that, on a previous occasion, you had touched the white Transit van belonging to Mr. Guylian and seen something from that contact which initially led you to think that Guylian had killed someone. Did anything about that memory give you reason to believe that it might have been March who was driving the van?" he asked carefully.

"No," Jake answered straight away, aware as Cordiline must have been that it was a leading question, but not an unimportant one. "When I see something, it's from inside the person's head, the person who saw it first, just like *they* would have seen it happen. It's not an outside view," he explained.

"Unless the person looks in a mirror, as Brendan March did in the bathroom, or is talking to someone that calls them by name, it's hard to determine whose memory I'm seeing. When I was in the van and turned my head to look in the back..." Jake stopped, his eyes moving to DI Hammond, who was scribbling furiously in his own paper notebook. "Sorry, that's just how I witnessed it. I wasn't actually, *physically* in the van, but I shared the driver's memory so..." He shrugged. "Anyway, in the van, the memory was of turning my head to look in the back and seeing a body wrapped in a blanket. I did not actually see Phil's face, only his hair. I did not see whose body I was in, only that the arms and hands on the steering wheel were male."

"You're sure of that?" Cordiline glanced up at him, his expression fascinated, then back down to his device where he made another note. "Were there distinguishing marks? Tattoos? Moles? Bitten nails?"

"You've left it a bit late to suddenly be interested in the details," Mari pointed out to him. He looked as angry as

Jake had ever seen him, but was managing to keep his tone icily polite.

Jake pinched the bridge of his nose and closed his eyes. He was running on no sleep and he was trying to remember things that his brain really didn't want him to remember. He wanted to explain that when he got these memories off things it was disorientating, that it was hard enough to figure out where he was and who he was and what he was seeing, much less make note of fine details, especially when they sometimes only lasted seconds. He couldn't tell Cordiline and Hammond all of that though, or they weren't going to trust anything he said.

"It was dark. There were oncoming headlights shining through the front windshield. He was wearing long sleeves. The hands on the steering wheel were big, bigger than most women's hands. No nail polish. I didn't see anything that you might call distinguishing."

Cordiline looked up at him again, his expression softening as he watched the struggle going on in Jake's weary face.

"Nothing at all?" he emphasized. "No jewelry? No *wedding ring*?"

"If I tell you that I saw one, I would be guessing," Jake said. "There might have been, there might not. I don't recall, and I'm not going to start plumping up what I actually saw to make it stick."

The DI exhaled a forceful sigh and shook his head.

"We have nothing to work with, then. I can't demand an extradition on the basis of something that you may or may not have seen and can't properly remember, Chivis."

"But the DNA..." Mari put in with considerable vehemence.

"Any DNA evidence would be purely circumstantial at this point. Phil Weston was in the house doing building work, so his DNA is going to be in the property." Cordiline scowled at Mari, apparently aware that he was being goaded. "Furthermore, there might well have been the opportunity for his body to become cross contaminated with Brendan March's DNA, if they used the same mug, for example."

"But if March killed him, then there could be *something* that the forensic examination might turn up. And he *was* upstairs, so March would have had to get him down again, and into the van. And out again. What are the chances of him doing that without leaving some trace on the carpets?"

"All possibilities that we might be able to work with, Doctor Gale." Cordiline nodded curtly. "*When* we have evidence. It's my job to extract as much potential information as possible about this case and if that means wringing out your *friend*'s brain until I have every last drop of his memory distilled into my case notes, I will do it. And you shouting at me is *not* going to help."

"Look." Jake sighed. "You have enough circumstantial evidence to pull March in for questioning at the least. You can corroborate with Guylian that he left his van parked at the March residence on the dates in question. He will also tell you that Phil talked about his affair with Helen March. That alone, without anything from me, is enough to throw suspicion on Brendan March. But from what I saw, I'd say Brendan was sleeping with him too, and this was some kind of rough play gone wrong." He cast an apologetic look at Professor Weston, who was just staring blankly from one face to the next as they spoke. "I've given you everything I can, Inspector."

"And I am grateful for your patience, Mr. Chivis," Cordiline responded, closing his tablet down with a little sigh. He rose to his feet and turned back to face Tony. "I will contact you if we have any developments, Professor Weston. Rest assured, in spite of Doctor Gale's opinions to the contrary, we are doing as much as we can to find and apprehend your brother's killer."

Mari glared at him but didn't have anything to add, for once, and Professor Weston also rose and shook the detectives' hands, thanking them for their time. As Cordiline and Hammond were on their way to the front door however, the Albany Street DI's mobile phone rang—it had a custom classic ringtone, which Jake recognized as it was a tone which the US police departments tended to use as well. Generally, film and TV themes or *Crazy in Love* by Beyoncé didn't go down well as ringtones if they went off when you were breaking bad news to a relative.

Cordiline stayed at the far end of the hallway, speaking in a hushed tone, then returned to the lounge as the call ended, his expression unreadable.

"Professor Weston, that was the coroner. He has confirmed for us that your brother, sadly, had been dead for several hours when his body went into the canal, most probably through asphyxiation as a result of some kind of ligature being placed around his neck. Which ties in with former detective Chivis' information. There were other marks on the body at the wrists and ankles and across his torso, indicative that he was restrained shortly before, or at the time of his death, although SOCO cannot find any signs of a protracted struggle. Toxicology reports, however, show that he had an excess of opiate derivative drugs in his system, a mixture of sleeping pills and antidepressants, which might well have left him incapable of resisting an attacker."

"And DNA?" Mari asked hopefully, having been patient thus far.

"Yes, Doctor Gale, there was foreign DNA upon his person—strands that were not his own. SOCO want to investigate the sources of these DNA strands and will be revisiting Philip Weston's last known locations prior to his disappearance."

Cordiline looked visibly relieved. Mari clenched his fist hard but, at a look from Jake, he at least did not punch the air. Professor Weston sat down hard in his chair again as if reality had finally begun to sink in.

Chapter Fourteen

Jake kissed Mari goodbye in the park after their run, a rather long and passionate kiss for so early in the morning, but for once he didn't care if anyone saw or objected. They arranged to meet up later, then his boyfriend's sexy buns went swaying off in the opposite direction, and Jake watched him go, saw him glance back once with a little smile that warmed his heart and made his dick hard. It had been two long weeks since they had been arrested and released and they had heard nothing from the police about the investigation in all that time. As frustrating as that was, it was not entirely unexpected. It really brought home to Jake how much he missed his badge, though. Technically, even if he had been a law enforcement officer here, he wouldn't have been automatically clued in on the case, but it was much more likely that he would have been kept in the loop, at least unofficially. That was why he was so surprised, when he trotted up the stairs to his flat, still sporting a semi under his loose running sweats, to see DI John Cordiline leaning against the landing wall, looking out of the window adjacent to his apartment door, down onto the street below.

"Inspector?"

"Morning, Mr. Chivis," the detective said formally, his eyes traveling briefly over his sweat-damp running gear before returning to his face, all professional seriousness. "Your neighbor let me in. Have you got time for a quick chat before you go to work?"

Jake lifted a curious eyebrow but otherwise kept his surprise and frustration in check. He'd been hoping for something a little more physical, in the shower, thinking about Mari's gorgeous ass before he had to go to work, but there was nothing quite like police procedure to dampen the ardor.

"Sure. You want some coffee?" he asked politely, sliding his key into the new lock on his new front door and letting Cordiline follow him inside.

"Wouldn't go amiss," the cop admitted, with a dry smile. "What the hell time do you get up in the morning? Most sane people are still in bed right now."

Jake dropped his keys on the new end table, a stylish chrome and glass replacement for the one that had been smashed, and got two ancient mugs out of the cabinet in his kitchenette. The coffee was already brewed. It was set on a timer so that it tended to be done just about the time he was getting back from his run. He set out a jug of milk on the counter top and a bag of sugar that was mostly untouched.

"I like to run before there are too many people out," he said, pouring a strong, dark roast brew into both mugs. "So, does that mean you were hoping to pull me out of bed?"

Cordiline accepted the cup with a quirk of his lips.

"I think the current situation is preferable. Nice brew, by the way. Actually I'm quite glad to find you in a state of… alertness. I wanted to talk to you about your impressions of the Weston case again. There's been a development."

Jake lifted both eyebrows as he looked at Cordiline over the edge of his mug. The detective hadn't spoken to him since the interview at Weston's house. Jake had figured he probably wouldn't find out anything until the press did.

"Yeah? What's happened?"

"Brendan March is flying back into Heathrow this morning," the DI said bluntly. "According to our contacts at Interpol in Willemstad, he handed himself in to them yesterday. And his wife has been in to talk to us. Her story was *very* interesting."

Jake set the cup down on the counter rather more heavily than intended. He wanted to ask why Cordiline was telling him this, when he probably shouldn't be, but he didn't want to take the chance that pointing this out would make him think twice about sharing details of the case.

"What did she have to say?" Jake asked.

"When we confronted her with phone records and texts that showed she was having an affair with Philip Weston, she admitted to it," Cordiline said and carefully took another sip of coffee. "She also accused her husband of killing Phil."

"Whoa...*really*?" Jake said, thinking fast. "That got you your extradition warrant, I take it."

"Yes," Cordiline said more slowly, and in such a way that it made Jake look at him hard.

"Yes...*and*?" he prompted.

"We have recovered evidence indicating that Brendan March also, possibly, had a sexual encounter with Weston. We don't know the particulars yet."

Jake nodded. "That fits with what I saw."

"We'll know more when we speak to him about it. According to Helen March, her husband confronted her about the affair and she argued with him about it then left the house. She came back, after spending the weekend away, and her husband confessed to her that he had killed her lover when Philip showed up on their doorstep. She says she stayed quiet, initially, so that she could try to keep her husband. But when confronted with the phone evidence and the fact that Brendan scarpered without her, she decided enough was enough and blew the whistle on him."

Jake mulled that over for a moment.

"Something doesn't fit. If Brendan March was having an affair with Phil too, he'd hardly confront her about her own infidelity. Has he lawyered up yet?"

"He works in international finance, Chivis. Go figure." Cordiline laughed bitterly. "I can't imagine that he's going to walk into our nick without a high-profile legal team in tow. We've got some serious evidence building against him, though. I thought that you and your…colleague, Dr. Gale, would be interested in knowing how things were proceeding."

Jake rested his hands on the counter and gave him an appraising look. He should probably correct him about that 'colleague' thing. Mari was more to him than that, and he suspected that the DI had guessed as much, but old habits were hard to shake and he didn't really want to lay out his personal life.

"Thanks," he said.

"We'll talk to Professor Weston before we interview March. We are fairly confident that we can get a quick conviction and I'm sure Doctor Gale will be delighted to hear that. It should make his own defense somewhat easier."

"What defense? I thought they'd dropped that, considering there's nothing you can charge him with."

"Kentish Town have decided not to prosecute but the decision ultimately will rest with Mrs. March." Cordiline exhaled. "We have advised her that there is no physical evidence that the doctor interfered in her private calls but she is still pushing for a civil prosecution. Possibly the case against her husband will occupy her mind to the extent that she can disregard such concerns. Actually, it was Dr. Gale's access to evidence that I was curious to talk to you about. We can't find any trace at all of hacking into Philip Weston's phone accounts, or into the Marches' household connection. So how did he get hold of so much information?"

Jake shrugged. "If you didn't find anything, that would probably be because he didn't hack them. Tony Weston gave him permission to poke around and see if he could find his brother. We had Phil's laptop with his brother's blessing. Nothing wrong with hunting around online for someone," he hedged. "And as far as Mrs. March and her supposed case, any judge in their right mind would slap her with a frivolous suit if she actually pushed it that far with zero to go on. Mari's got nothing to worry about because he didn't do anything wrong."

"You seem very protective of him," Cordiline said, draining his coffee mug and setting it down between them. "Interesting, given that you've barely known him more than, what...? A couple of months?"

"I'm not protective of him," Jake lied, with a prickle of anxiety at the idea that Cordiline had been checking up on them, even though he knew it was probably nothing more than straightforward procedure. "I just know bullshit when I see it. She's trying to throw shade on Mari to get the heat off her own back."

"You should warn him, in any case, that he doesn't do himself any favors by running off at the mouth," the detective informed him. He hesitated then added, "You can do better, Jake."

"I can do better than what?" Jake asked cluelessly.

"If it's...company you're after. A man like yourself, you could have your pick, you know." Cordiline rose to his feet as Jake straightened. He reached out with cautious fingers, barely touching them to Jake's cheek.

Jake looked at the hand and felt stupid. Was his gaydar so far off it no longer worked? Or was he just so wrapped up in Mari he was oblivious? Maybe Cordiline just played straight really well. All of a sudden, the dark looks that Mari had been shooting at the inspector the other day began to make sense.

"Uhh...that's... I'm not..." He stopped himself from stammering random words and just as he was trying to figure out how he should tell him that he was only interested in seeing Mari, Cordiline leaned in and kissed him. Jake brought his hand up at once and put it on his chest, taking a step back. "I love him. Mari, I mean. And I'm not the type to cheat, okay?"

For a moment, the DI just stood there, then he blinked his stormy eyes and shook his head.

"Love, is it? You don't mess around making up your mind, Jake Chivis. You're sure?"

"I'm very sure." Jake folded his arms across his chest.

Cordiline nodded. He looked disappointed for a moment, then it was gone and he was all business again.

"Okay. I'm done here. I'll see myself out, Chivis. Thanks for your help. And the coffee."

Jake just stood looking at his closed apartment door for several moments after the man had departed, while his brain reeled. He hadn't seen that coming at all and his next thought was, he would so *not* feel guilty about keeping this from Mari. It was much better off for everyone just to forget that kiss had ever happened. There wasn't even tongue involved. He would not feel bad, damn it.

* * * *

When Jake got to work, Mari was already parked at the empty desk in his office, laptop open in front of him. He glanced up with a distracted smile, reached to move glasses that he remembered at the last minute he wasn't wearing, then narrowed his crystal blue gaze.

"Are you all right, Chivis? You look…flustered."

Jake closed the door behind him and perched on the edge of the desk. He kept his voice low.

"I got some news this morning about Brendan March. They've arrested him and he's being transported back to London today."

Mari tapped his fingertips against the frame of his laptop.

"How on earth did you find that out? I've kept abreast of the news stories. There was nothing in the press this morning."

Jake rubbed the back of his neck with one hand and then made himself stop because he knew it was a nervous habit. And if he knew he was doing it, Mari would have noticed it too, he could bet his life on it.

"Cordiline stopped by to tell me about the break in the case. We need to keep it to ourselves, but I think he just wanted to let us know what was happening."

"That was…considerate of him." Mari raised an eyebrow and returned his attention to the screen. His fingers skated over the keys and he called up a new window, tapped in an inquiry, closed his eyes, touched the screen, nodded and laughed without humor.

"Interesting…oh yes…very interesting."

"What's interesting?" Jake asked, watching him.

Pale blue eyes opened slowly and for a moment Mari stared at the screen, lips parted, drawing a slow breath. He looked so hot that Jake felt himself get hard again in spite of their situation.

"She shopped him? That bitch wife of his shopped him to the police, after everything she did when we went to the house. The cheek of the cow!" He turned his head, looking up at Jake, his gaze suddenly very intense. "Why on earth would that policeman come round to tell you such a thing in person? One might imagine he's a little sweet on you." Mari gave him a playful wink.

Jake felt the flush rise all the way up his neck to his cheeks but there was no way to stop it, all he could do was hope Mari didn't notice. He cleared his throat and adjusted the pockets of his trousers.

"Well, her husband *did* kill her lover and then skipped out to another country. She probably figured she's got nothing to lose by turning him in now. And if she's an accessory after the fact, she might get some leniency if it looks like she's cooperating," he said, ignoring Mari's comment about why DI Cordiline would pay him a personal visit on purpose.

Mari stared at him for a moment and a little smile twitched his soft lips.

"He *is*, isn't he? He's sweet on you? My days! Not that I can blame him, I suppose. You *are* very handsome." His gaze softened, the smile growing warmer.

"He is not sweet on me," Jake said in a low, disgruntled tone, a discouraging scowl on his face. "And even if he was, I made it pretty clear I was seeing you."

Mari actually looked surprised. "Did you? My goodness, that was bold of you. How did he take that?" He uttered a husky laugh and shook his head again, still amused. His fingers brushed the keyboard but they did not tap hard enough to prompt a new command. A hint of color rose to his cheeks though and he gave another little huff of nervous laughter.

Jake understood him well enough by now to recognize that Mari was wrong-footed, even after all they had been through, knowing he had the confidence to tell someone else about their relationship.

How the hell he had ended up spilling that to Mari within two minutes of seeing him, after most definitely deciding to keep it to himself, Jake had no idea. He relaxed though as he realized Mari wasn't about to fly off the handle. At least, he didn't look like he was about to. Alex would have already flipped his lid and accused him of all kinds of things.

"I, uh, I don't know, really. He just left when I told him," he said.

"Hmm, he did, did he? Poor soul," Mari murmured, surprising him with his sympathy. "Definitely smitten then. Though he's far too old for you."

"He's not that old," Jake said, then wondered why he would even bother defending the inspector.

"Forty-five if he's a day. You're what, *thirty*?" Mari teased, because they had already established that Jake was anxious about his impending transition from his twenties to his thirties. A year and a half younger than him, Mari found it amusing to poke lighthearted fun at this irrational fear.

"Twenty-nine," Jake said in defiance.

Mari just chuckled. His hands were moving deftly over the keys again. He closed his eyes once more and as his fingers stilled, he seemed to sink into a trance. The screen in front of him was no guide, merely a blur of numbers and characters, scrolling at random like a scene from *The Matrix*, as he traveled deeper into the web of information that they contained. Jake had only watched him do this once before and he was both startled and intrigued that Mari was confident enough to use his gift in public and in front of him. He wanted to ask what Mari saw but was afraid of breaking his concentration at some vital moment and doing more harm than good.

When he surfaced at last, Mari drew a shaky breath and nodded.

"Interpol are hard to crack," he murmured, his tone respectful. "But whatever they promised March, it made up his mind for him that it was in his best interests to come home. I wonder if he knows that his wife has dropped him in the proverbial. Because according to his statement back on Curaçao, he's not too sure what happened the night Phil Weston died. Whatever it was, he seems to have convinced himself that he was responsible though." Mari looked up at Jake as if he might have all the answers.

Jake just stared at him.

"Are you fucking crazy? You just broke into Interpol?" he queried at last, under his breath.

Mari bestowed a sweet smile on him.

"Chivis! You know I don't do that kind of thing. I just asked their computers a few friendly questions, that's all. Not exactly breaking and entering and, as the Met have already admitted to me, nothing they can *prove* in any case. I think perhaps I frighten them a little. Can you imagine that?"

"Mari, just because they haven't caught you yet doesn't mean they can't. You have to be careful, okay." Just the thought of Mari being given some ridiculous sentence for any sort of tampering was enough to make Jake's chest feel tight. Interpol were the real deal, they could lock him up and throw the key away if he scared them too much.

"I'm careful, Chivis," Mari huffed, indignant now. His tone was irritable even though he was whispering too. "But what's the point in me being able to do this if I can't use it to help anyone? Phones and computer systems are talking to one another all the time, I just...sit down next to them and…eavesdrop, if you like. It's nothing more than most government agencies are doing, all the damned time!"

"I don't care about what anyone else is doing, damn it. I don't want to see you get in any trouble. It's not worth it."

For a moment Mari bristled and looked hurt, then he turned back to the laptop and slammed it shut, pushing himself to his feet and tucking the slimline machine under his arm.

"My fault," he exhaled with a dramatic sigh. "There I was thinking that you were actually excited about the possibility that we could do something practical with the Program, but if you're *not* interested, I get it. I suppose the boys in blue will get their man without our help, sooner or later. Heaven forbid that we might actually do anything useful or *dangerous*."

Mari nudged past him without meeting his eyes and headed for the door.

Something hot flashed through Jake, and this time it wasn't lust. He grabbed Mari's elbow as he reached for the knob and spun him around, pinning him up against the door. Those glacial eyes sparkled back at him, shocked and just a little bit angry and…something else that he couldn't read.

"You are infuriating. Do you know that?" Jake rumbled. "Don't you understand? If you're caught you could go to prison. We very narrowly avoided being hauled in front of a judge for that stunt at the March house as it was, and *you* still might not be totally in the clear. And *yes*, I'd rather March go free and get away with murder than lose you, okay."

The impossible blue of Mari's eyes burned hot for a moment as he was forcibly detained, then the ardency of Jake's words sank in and he began to shake his head.

"Well, that's where we differ, I guess, Chivis. You know… you're a very decent man in a lot of respects and I really…I *do* like you a lot, but there is a man lying on a mortuary slab a few miles away from here who can't even get a decent burial until someone finds out why he had to die. And if you genuinely don't care about that, then I think maybe we're coming from very different places, Jake." He looked down for a moment, then raised his eyes again, looking uncomfortable. "Please, take your hands off me. Now."

"Don't you dare pull that shit with me, Mari," Jake snapped, losing his cool. He had dared for a little while this morning to believe that this beautiful, impossible man felt the same way that he felt about him, but Mari seemed determined not to admit it. Maybe, just maybe, Jake thought with some bitterness, he had got it wrong. Perhaps he should have pulled Cordiline into the shower and just fucked him raw after all. For certain he wouldn't feel as frustrated and irritable as he did right now. "We did everything we *could* to point the cops in the right direction and they have the bastard in custody. It's not like I don't care that a man is dead, I just care about you staying out of jail *more*."

Mari looked daggers at the knuckles of Jake's fingers where they gripped his upper arms. His unblinking stare moved back to Jake's face, filled with determination.

"I have no intention of going to jail, Chivis. But something isn't adding up for me. I wish I could be a fly on the wall at that police interview when they get March back here. I keep on thinking about the night we went to Phil's apartment. There's something…something important and I can't work out what it is. I thought you would understand, Jake, that's all."

Jake loosened his grip on Mari's arms but instead of letting him go he slid them up to his shoulders, then further up to cup his face in his hands. Mari still seemed mad at him but Jake kissed him anyway, because if Mari Gale was about to stomp out of his office and his life and never speak to him again, he at least wanted a goodbye kiss to remember him by.

Mari made a small, muffled sound as Jake pressed up against his mouth, his protest all but silenced by Jake's hungry lips. He didn't resist but he clung to his laptop with one hand, using it as a defensive barrier as the other pushed up against Jake's chest. His hand felt warm through the crisp cotton of Jake's shirt. After a long, wordless moment Mari tilted his head and closed his eyes, returning the kiss with passionate intensity instead of trying to push Jake away.

Jake pressed closer, thighs then hips bumping against Mari's. He slid his fingers back into his hair and deepened the merging of their lips, pushing his tongue between his teeth and tasting his sweet, warm mouth. When Mari made a soft, yielding sound in his throat, Jake curled his hips, rubbing his crotch along Mari's, their cocks pressing against one another through the layers of their clothes. He didn't want to argue, he just wanted to strip Mari completely and lick him all over.

When their lips parted and Mari managed to draw a ragged breath, he exhaled a rush of words as if they had never stopped speaking, as if he'd just been cut off mid-flow.

"Jake…I swear that you get me riled like this on purpose because it gets you hot to watch me lose control."

"You get me hot anyway, but yeah, it does turn me on when you get worked up," Jake murmured and kissed him again. He dropped one hand down to Mari's hip and caressed him there, squeezed his ass then pushed his hand between them so he could cup Mari's balls through his trousers, fondling and rubbing him deftly.

"I really want to suck you off," he whispered, kissing Mari's mouth and his jaw and nibbling on his earlobe. "And I want you to blow me too."

Mari shuddered. The swelling in the crotch of his immaculate, tailored suit pants told Jake that he was having a hard time keeping up the ice-queen act.

"Is…is…" He swallowed hard. "Is that really wise, Chivis? Anyone could walk right in on us…" He drew in a sharp breath as Jake pressed his palm more firmly on his shaft and stroked him over his trousers. *"Omigosh! Mmmhhh...* You are such a bad man!"* he mewed huskily. "At least let me put the bloody machine down before I drop it!"

Jake unzipped Mari's pants and snaked his fingers into the opening, outlining Mari's cock with his fingers as if he hadn't heard him. When Mari's breath hitched in his throat, Jake sank down to his knees and took the laptop from his shaking hand, setting it on the edge of the desk beside him before he popped the button on his pants and skimmed them down Mari's lean thighs to his knees. He pushed his shirt up out of the way and fastened his mouth on Mari's stomach just above his bellybutton, kissing and sucking and nipping the skin there before licking a path downward. He dragged those tiny, pale blue briefs down to join his pants around his knees and he nuzzled into Mari's crotch, breathing in the clean, warm, heady scent of him right at the base of his rapidly thickening cock. Jake gave him a stroke or two, loving the feel of that long, curved shaft growing even harder in his hand.

Looking up at Mari, he licked a swipe over the crown of his glans, back and forth, his gentle, questing tongue probing the slit. Mari turned his head to one side, shoving his index finger lengthways between his teeth and biting down to silence the urgent whine that clearly wanted to break free, unable to watch as Jake tormented him with tenderness. He was panting and trembling though, his body saying more than any words what he wanted. In a husky voice he swore in what Jake presumed to be Finnish and snaked the fingers of his free hand through Jake's hair, tugging as he bucked against the warmth of his lips on the sensitive length of his erection.

Jake wrapped his fingers around the base and took his time rubbing the glossy head over his lips, sliding back and forth for a few moments, teasing Mari with licks and kisses before he opened up and took him into the warm, wet confines of his mouth. He swallowed him down halfway before drawing back and doing it again, and again. He made a ring with his thumb and forefinger and circled it tight around the base, taking him down deeper and jacking him off at the same time.

Mari cursed under his breath again, chewing on his knuckle as he squirmed and writhed under Jake's seductive ministrations. He swore, this time in English so that his lover could understand him.

"You are a demon, Chivis. *Uuhhh*... Fuck you! I wanna be so angry with you—*mmmhhhhhh*... Bastard!"

Jake moaned around the throbbing shaft sliding in and out of his mouth. His eyes fluttered shut as heat rushed down to his groin, making him ache with need. He had always felt weird about dirty talk. He just felt dumb when he tried it and kind of dirty when Alex had whispered such things in his ear, but when Mari cursed and moaned and said words like that, it was just so damn hot. He unzipped his pants with his free hand and got out his own cock, stroking it in time with the pull of his lips on Mari's beautiful dick. Sucking harder on him, his head bobbed faster in an unconscious echo of the first time they had made out, in Phil Weston's hallway, wordless and frantic for each other.

Mari had him now, moving in an urgent rhythm with him, his hips thrusting in time with the nod of Jake's head and the sliding motion of his lips. He uttered a small, strangled crooning sound as he was overcome by the speed and pure demand of Jake's mouth.

"Oh...my...fuck!" he exhaled in a dazed tone, then Jake brought him up to the edge and he quickened and thickened on his tongue, coming in five hard, fast bursts of longing, before his lean frame sagged against the office wall and he turned his face toward the door again, wary and conscious of how public this was.

Jake swallowed the load of semen Mari jetted and sucked more gently, slowing the pace of his mouth even as his hand sped up on his own cock. Within moments he was coming, spurting a creamy white arc that landed on the floor between Mari's spread feet. Only then did he finally let Mari's wilting penis slip from his mouth and grinned up at him, dazed and delighted by the buzz of his long-postponed orgasm.

Those luminous, blue topaz eyes were looking down at him again with a mixture of mischief and disbelief.

"You are fucking crazy, Chivis," Mari whispered, hoarse and breathless still. "How can I stay righteously angry with you when you are so deranged? Get up here, you mad, gorgeous, unpredictable idiot."

Jake obliged, rising until he was toe to toe with Mari again and he kissed him, with more tenderness this time.

"You're as unpredictable as I am," he argued, kissing him harder, while Mari hitched his underwear and pants back up. "You don't care about the things I worry you'll get pissed over, and then you get pissed about things that shouldn't make you angry. I don't want to fight with you, Ilmari," he murmured, caressing his cheek with his fingers.

"You have a nerve telling me what I ought to get angry about," Mari said, but there was fondness in his gaze this time. "Fasten your damned pants before we get caught and sacked, you mentalist."

He tangled his fingers in Jake's hair again, towing him in for a rougher kiss as his partner in crime reluctantly obliged. As their lips parted, Mari whispered, "I promise I will not go to jail, Chivis. But I won't stop until we know that Phil's killer has been properly punished for what he did, either."

His expression was very serious and somehow sad as well. Jake rested his forehead on Mari's and stared into his eyes for what felt like minutes but was really only seconds.

"Okay," he conceded at last. "But don't get mad at me for worrying about you, Ilmarinen. I can't help it."

Mari's lips framed an odd, reluctant smile.

"I don't think I've ever been with a man who worried about me before," he said. "It feels rather peculiar."

Jake brushed another kiss over his lips, and he almost let the *L* word slip out but held back. He told himself it wasn't fear of rejection so much as him not wanting Mari to think he was only using it as leverage. Not that his tough cookie would be fooled by that, he laughed at himself. It just wasn't the right time.

Yeah, that was the reason.

With reluctance Jake pulled away from him and sighed. "Okay. Phil Weston. The pathologists found DNA evidence on Phil as well. Not Helen March's, but from Brendan March."

Mari picked up his laptop and flipped it open, shutting down the Interpol feed while Jake collected his thoughts. He closed the lid again and hugged the small, warm device comfortingly to his chest.

"You know," Mari said in a thoughtful tone, "the van was in the wrong place at the right time, unfortunately for Guylian, but handily enough for March. You remember when we went to the house, in the hallway, everything smelled new. They'd just had the carpets replaced. What if that was the job Phil was doing? The van was there to take the old carpet away. You remember you told me that Phil texted Guylian asking him to pick up the van. What if he didn't? What if March had his phone? And after killing him, he panicked and dragged Phil out, wrapped him in an offcut, which is why you couldn't see his face in the flashback, and put him in the van. He dumped him in the canal later, brought back the van, used Phil's mobile to text Guylian and thought he'd got away with it?" He paced around the desk mulling this over. "Where was Mrs. March while this was happening, I wonder?"

Jake's eyes flicked down to the laptop in Mari's hands. Cordiline had mentioned that Helen walked out on her husband after they argued about her lover, but he hadn't said where she went.

"I could ask Cordiline," he said, thinking that might be better than Mari risking himself more by sneaking around in police files.

"Yes." Mari uttered a sarcastic laugh. "And he could tell you that it's none of your business, especially since you're not planning on sucking *his* cock any time soon."

He put the laptop down on the table and flipped the lid again with a questioning glance in Jake's direction. Jake sighed but there was no point in asking him not to snoop. It would just cause another argument, then Mari would leave and go do it anyway. He didn't say, one way or the other, what he thought, he just left it at that single sigh.

"Oh, Chivis, what am I going to do with you?" Mari leaned across the desk to plant a placatory kiss on his lips, smiling coyly. "You taste good, Jake."

He sat down and logged himself in with his customary speed, retrieving his access flash drive and plugging in, long fingers flicking across the keys as if on autopilot as his keen eyes scanned the screen. Jake watched his little frown of concentration, the now familiar way he tapped his short, neat fingernails restlessly against the side of the casing between bursts of frenetic touch typing. It became almost a question and answer game as he entered another code then another, waiting, watching, asking again then the brief, fierce smile of triumph as he was into the files that he wanted. His hand pressed flat to the screen and he closed his eyes and rode the ether, face perfectly serene as his extra senses became one with the long streams of code he was intercepting. Jake got lost in just watching him, both fascinated and anxious, his gaze fixed on the stillness and perfection of his lover's face.

The office door opened with a bang and Jake jumped violently. He saw Mari flinch but keep his hand on the screen as Nolan stared at them both.

"What the fuck are you doing, Marilyn? Your boss is looking for you and he is not a happy camper," he said, leaning forward to wave a hand at Mari.

"Have you ever heard of knocking, you rude fuck?" Jake snapped at him.

Nolan looked at him like this was the funniest thing he'd ever heard.

"Why? You were hoping for a private moment with

the princess, huh? You'll have a long wait from what I've heard." He turned his head to scrutinize Mari again. "What the fuck are you playing at, Miss Marilyn? You superglued to that thing, or something?"

Mari didn't open his eyes but in a voice that sounded like it was partially stuck to his tongue he murmured, "Fuck off, Nolan. Go tell Karden I'll be ten minutes. I'm busy."

"You are *dead* if I tell him that, Mary May," he spluttered. "No kidding, you need to get your arse up those stairs to Eight like *ten minutes ago*. He is practically epileptic right now, sunshine."

Mari moved his hand from the screen and slammed the laptop shut. He kept his eyes shut for a few seconds more, breathing harder.

"Are you looking at porn?" Nolan wanted to know. "Hot damn, the Ice Queen's looking at porn! Who'd have guessed?"

He was grinning now, like the idiot he was. Jake itched to punch him. He really, really wanted to. It was riskier to just grab and deck him when he wasn't physically putting a hand on Mari. He did stand up though and move toward him threateningly.

"Shut your stupid, fucking pie-hole, asswipe. Get the fuck outta here before I show you the door."

Nolan opened his mouth but Mari beat him to the punch. Quite literally. He turned to face the bigger man impassively enough but his flying left hook put Damien Nolan on the floor of the security team's little paneled office, clutching at his jaw.

"One day, Damien, that stupid mouth of yours is probably going to get you killed," he said, in a very quiet voice. "Not today, fortunately for you." Mari hesitated, tilting his head sideways to survey his supine victim. "I'd say you need to put some *ice* on that," he added with a theatrical twirl of his fingers. "Shame, I don't have any on me."

He grabbed his laptop in one hand and Jake's elbow in the other and headed for the door at a fast walk. Damien's swearing muted the moment it slammed behind them.

Jake let Mari drag him down the hall to the elevators and got in when the doors opened. For a wonder the thing was empty. He waited until the doors slid shut again.

"You're pretty hot when you're throwing punches," he said. "You should have decked that fucker a long time ago."

"I wasn't about to get sacked a long time ago," Mari told him, flexing his fingers with a little scowl. "I enjoyed that though. Bastard! I was *that* fucking close! I should have sealed his mouth shut permanently. Helen March told the cops that she was at her mother's the night Phil was murdered. Her mother, unsurprisingly, backs this story up."

"You're not about to be sacked," Jake said. "*Are you?*"

Mari looked at him almost pityingly. "I wish I had your optimism, Chivis. I just punched the shit out of a colleague. If I wasn't already on a verbal warning, then I'd be more than halfway out the door."

Jake snorted. "That pussy isn't going to tell anyone you punched him, Mari. If he does, then it will come out *why* you punched him and I don't think he'll come out of that smelling like a rose, given all the sexual harassment he dumps on you."

"I am not about to run to Karden whining about Nolan and his pathetic excuse for harassment." Mari laughed bitterly as the doors slid open on Seven and he stalked out through them with his laptop still clutched to his chest and headed for the stairs that led up to the top floor. "I can handle him. My boss, however, expects an important project for MI6 completed this morning and I am going to tell him now why it isn't. And in all probability he is going to demote my backside right back down to data input. I don't even have a particularly valid excuse, Jake."

He stopped at the foot of the stairs and leaned against the wall with a sigh. Soulful blue eyes flickered sidelong to meet Jake's devastated stare. "It's been good to work with you, Chivis. Albeit briefly."

Jake grabbed him before he disappeared up the stairs, this time more gently, and he planted a kiss on his lips before he could think better of it. That was all the comfort he could offer though before Mari had to go face the music on his own.

* * * *

The tongue lashing, when it came, was not as lengthy or as vicious as Mari had dreaded. Karden was a fellow academic after all, and though he had a reputation for his temper, it was oddly restrained today. He did not dress Mari down in public, nor did he have him forcibly escorted to the front door of the building and ordered never to return. His remonstrations were delivered in his private office, in a tone of withering disappointment which made Mari grit his teeth. He hated to disappoint and for all that Karden liked to cast his verbal inferences about his employee's lack of commitment round the office, he had plainly not expected Mari's reaction to be a complete withdrawal of labor. They were a Team, Karden emphasized. He needed Team Players.

There was definite stress on the capital letters.

Mari winced silently. He did not need to be told that he did not play well with others — he already knew that.

Worse was the feigned sympathy for his situation, his mother's health, the trouble with the police, his ongoing involvement with the Six Elements Program. He recognized a guilt trip when he heard one and closed his ears. Yes, he was an embarrassment to his sponsors, to Professor Willmott — his mentor and friend at Albany who had written him a glowing testimonial when he applied for the position — and to poor, grieving Professor Weston who had been so keen to have him here, albeit for his own nefarious reasons. Mari accepted that in despondent silence.

Then Karden took him by surprise, as he was so good at doing. Mari was just gearing up his brain and schooling his sharp tongue to apologize with suitable contrition — for wasting his time, for letting down his colleagues, for being born — ready to go back to his cubicle and clear his desk, but Professor Emmanuel Karden merely handed him a weighty, A5, cream-colored parchment envelope and said to him, "I think you need some time to make up your mind what it is that you want from an academic position, Doctor Gale. In the meantime, I would like you to take this and go home. Have a good long think about what is being offered and come back and talk to me when you have made a decision."

He moved to open his notice of dismissal but Karden put a hand on his. "Not here. You have a great deal to offer, Ilmarinen. Read the letter and think about it in private. You know full well what you are and are not permitted to say to others but I will remind you that you signed the Official Secrets Act when you joined us. That restriction still stands. Now go home, Doctor Gale. Let me clear up the mess you have left me."

He waved his hand impatiently when Mari just stared at him.

"But…?"

"You have a problem, Doctor Gale?"

"Did you just sack me or not?" Mari wanted to know, feeling suddenly uncertain.

"It's all in the letter, Ilmarinen. Take a few weeks off, consider what it says, come back and see me when you've made up your mind." The bone-thin, elderly Doctor of Mechanical Sciences smiled like a vampire at him across his chaotic desk. "Good day to you, Doctor Gale."

In the elevator on the way down, clutching his laptop and the mysterious envelope to his chest, he chewed on the insides of his mouth in silence, kicking himself for not saying more in his own defense. Had Karden expected him to fight for his job? Was that the reason for his look of lingering disapproval as he'd shaken Mari's hand at the door to his private office? Yes, of course he knew how much prestige was attached to working on the Eighth floor.

Of course he knew, but still he had managed to blow it. Or had he?

Karden had asked him to come back. That didn't make too much sense to him.

As he stepped out through the glass doors into the little side road that accessed the faculty, feeling the weak sunlight on his face, he breathed in a long, deep, shaky sigh of relief and regret.

What in the world was he going to tell Mama?

Mari didn't go straight home. He went to the Reading Rooms at the British Library instead and found a quiet nook in which to open the letter. He read it three times, his incredulity ramping up a notch with each reading. Then he opened his laptop and logged into the public Wi-Fi system and rebooted the police files he had been trying to look at earlier. This was dangerous, he knew. If the Met caught him poking about, they could identify him from his public login details, but he was past caring.

No one else seemed to care why Phil Weston had died but Mari was determined that he would find out. Phil might have been a cocky little shit who liked to play the field but still, no one deserved to end their days throttled and discarded in the canal like an unwanted mongrel puppy.

His phone vibrated discreetly in his shirt pocket as he was closing the lid on his machine. Mari scanned the message display with a halfhearted sigh, then sent a brief text back, arranging to meet Jake at the Istanbul Café near the tube station but not answering the question about how his morning had gone. There was too much to convey in one simple SMS for a start. In spite of the walk from Euston Road, he was there first and commandeered a seat outside, it being a little too early for the regular post-office drinks crowd yet. He ordered a large mug of strong Turkish coffee which came in a huge, bowl-shaped vessel that he cupped his hands around, drawing some warmth and comfort from just holding it.

Jake showed up a few minutes later carrying a bouquet

of fresh flowers, which he handed to Mari as he dropped a kiss onto his forehead then sat next him.

"What's this? I feel like Tara Lipinski," he declared, dipping his face into the fragrant bundle to breathe in the scent of the perfect white lilies, then setting them on the table in front of him with a sigh.

"I take it that didn't go well," Jake said in sympathy.

"*Perhaps in hindsight Doctor Gale is not suited to the routine and discipline of an academic role*," Mari quoted from the letter, then wiggled his eyebrows like a theatrical villain.

"I need something stronger than coffee. Ask me what else I was doing this morning?"

Jake asked him. Mari opened his laptop and showed him the documentary notes he had been working on since completing his initial surf of Phil and his contacts, right up to his search of the Metropolitan Police database today, at the British Library.

"We know who Brendan March is," he said, pointing to the part of the telephone transcript highlighted in yellow. He pointed to one highlighted in pale blue. "Amber le Bon is…I'll let you guess, shall I? You get three goes."

Jake frowned down at the screen.

"Helen March? She used a fake name to contact Phil? Why would she do that? Unless…" Jake looked at the dates that were on the screen next to the caller IDs and saw that 'Amber' had shown up before Helen. "She met him first as Amber, then decided to hire him for something other than sex, using her real name."

"Mm-hm, now look at this." Mari tapped a key and another screen popped up. This one showed a map with markers on it, and a timer widget at the bottom that ran through numbers while the little lights moved around.

Jake frowned at him expectantly.

"What am I looking at?"

Mari smiled coolly. He had been waiting for that question.

"This is a GPS map and timeline of the night Phil died. These two dots"—Mari pointed at the screen where the

March house was located and a pair of markers flashed red and blue—"are signals from Brendan March and Phil Weston's phones. These two"—Mari pointed to another set of dots in different shades of green, one dark one light—"both belong to Helen March. The number of one of those phones is listed in Phil's contacts as Helen, and the other is listed as Amber. I'm guessing that she uses one as her personal and business phone and the other strictly for hooking up with men she meets online."

Jake glanced at him sharply but Mari ignored the look and tapped the screen.

"Observe."

Jake looked at the dots and watched what Mari wanted him to see. The map played like a time-lapse video and showed both GPS signals from Helen's two phones moving on Friday morning several miles north and stopping for a few hours, then one of them, the dark green marker, moved back to the March residence that afternoon. The little light blinked there constantly as the timer scrolled from four p.m. until one a.m. on Saturday morning before it moved again, going back north.

"Holy shit!" Jake murmured. "She was there, at the house, when Phil died. This doesn't make sense though." Jake sat back and tried to come up with a scenario. "I know what I saw. I saw Brendan March standing over Phil's body. She wasn't in the room with them."

Mari sipped the last dregs of his coffee and set his mug down with a shake of his head and a little sigh.

"Do you think we ought to show your Inspector Cordiline this?"

Jake shook his head. "I don't know. It definitely would, at the very least, make her an accessory if she knew Brendan killed him and said nothing. Showing Cordiline this might get you in trouble though."

"Maybe. I'm willing to risk getting into trouble to see justice done," Mari said, bracing himself for Jake's disapproval.

Jake didn't immediately try to shoot him down though. Instead he reached over and put his hand over Mari's.

"How about this. Let's see what they pull out of Brendan March when they get him back here and if they don't figure it out, then we'll go to them with this info. It won't hurt to wait a day or two. If he confesses and she still wants to press charges, you have it as leverage against her in any case."

Mari wasn't sure if he liked that idea but Jake was being reasonable so he thought he should at least try to meet him halfway. And he was still pondering just how to tell the man he was slowly beginning to fall in love with about the rest of his employer's proposals in that astonishing three page letter. But that could wait. It could definitely wait.

"All right," he agreed, and was rewarded with one of those patented Jake Chivis smiles that made his knees go weak and his stomach flutter. The fellow was positively dangerous.

"Do you think you could stay over at mine tonight?" Jake asked with an optimistic smile.

Mari pretended to think about it.

"I believe that could be arranged."

Chapter Fifteen

They were making their way past the bar beneath his apartment, Mari's warm presence leaning into his right side in a way that was most certainly not unpleasant, when he saw two people—a man and a woman—standing directly outside the security door that hid the stairs up to his little flat. He thought nothing of it until they got closer—the street was full of shops, bars and cafés and at this time in the evening it was rarely empty.

"This is a terrible idea," protested the man, who was wearing an expensive suit but with none of the elegance such a garment probably demanded.

Until he met Mari, such a contrast would never have occurred to him, Jake thought distractedly.

"Just shut up and do your job," the woman snapped at him.

She was much more sharply turned out, her hair and makeup perfect. Jake came to a halt and put his hand on Mari's left arm to stop him too as he recognized Helen March. This could in no way end well for them.

"Shit!" Jake muttered under his breath.

"What's that bitch doing here?" Mari hissed, clenching his teeth. He practically bristled through the light fabric of his immaculate suit like a territorial alley cat. Then he was pulling free, striding toward the two of them with a look like thunder on his face, his ire in no way compromised by the huge bunch of lilies and white chrysanthemums still nestled into the crook of his right arm.

"Mari..." Jake called urgently, trying to stop him. The couple waiting at his door turned at the sound of his voice.

The guy was thin and waxen with a look on his face that said he'd rather be anywhere but here. Mrs. March lifted her chin and pressed her lips together, eyes flashing with anger like Jake had seen in the memories he'd picked up from her house when she'd been arguing with her husband. She immediately prodded the man next to her with a scarlet, manicured fingernail.

"There they are. Give them the papers."

The young man looked as if he would rather not have to do anything of the sort but he pulled himself up to his full height—which was still a good few inches shy of the intended recipient—when Mari came to a halt directly in front of them. In an act of chivalry he positioned himself between the irate computer scientist and his client.

"What the blazing fuck do *you* want?" Mari demanded, ignoring the man and glaring past him at Mrs. March. "If we're not allowed to come within a half mile of you and your pathetic husband, then I'm sure that works both ways. Fuck off, now!"

Helen March looked far too smug and not the least bit intimidated as she smirked at Mari. "Don't worry, we aren't staying long. Just long enough to serve these papers." She gave a little toss of her head back toward the building behind her. "And to mark where you live. Although this place is barely fit for habitation. It should be shut down and condemned really. I'm sure some of my friends on the council planning committee would agree."

"*I* don't live here, for your information. And I doubt you have any *friends*," Mari informed her. "Even your husband isn't too keen on you, from what we've heard and seen so far."

Jake had come up while Mari and Helen were bitching at each other and he held his hand out toward the man he assumed was Helen March's solicitor. The man looked like a deer caught in the headlights, frozen to the spot and holding a sheaf of papers in front of his chest like a shield. He just stared at Jake's hand until Jake curled his fingers in a 'give it here' motion, then he remembered he was *supposed* to be handing them over and nearly slammed the sheaf of documents into Jake's grasp.

"Is that supposed to be a threat?" Jake asked Helen in a calmer voice, as he unfolded the papers.

"Just an observation, Mr. Chivis," she said, her tone cold. "I suppose I shouldn't have expected better from the type of people who make a living breaking into the homes of their betters."

Mari made a rude noise in the back of his throat and just shook his head. His blue eyes were chips of ice, fixed without blinking on Helen March's face.

Jake ignored her attempts at insult as he looked over the document in his hand. He had expected to see some sort of court order for him to stay away, or even something saying he was being sued on some ridiculous trumped up charge, but this took him by complete surprise and he looked up again, speechless for a moment. Slowly he shook his head.

"This... is this even legal? This can't be serious." Jake looked at the lawyer then back at Helen March. "This 'contract' as you so helpfully call it is what we call a 'bribe' where I'm from. Staying silent in return for dropping charges...charges that won't stick anyway and you know it."

"Oh, I can make them stick," she promised with some malevolence. "I can have you on a one-way trip back to whatever one-horse town in the States you rode in from, just by talking to the right person. And as for you" — she turned to glare up at Mari, who didn't flinch from her stare — "prison will just be the start of it."

"You're a fantasist, *Amber*," Mari said in a cooler voice that was less aggressive but somehow more unsettling than his anger. "Your husband invited us in. He asked us to look around and we fixed your phone. Are you going to charge us with upgrading your utilities? We could easily *bill* you for that. We aren't going anywhere. *You*, on the other hand —"

"I think you should go home, Mrs. March," Jake interrupted evenly before things could escalate. "I'll have an attorney of my own look over your 'offer', as well as the detective investigating Philp Weston's death...you remember Phil, don't you? The guy you and your husband were fucking? The one he *killed* in your bedroom? Maybe you should concern yourself with that."

"You slanderous bastard!" She raised her hand as if she would strike him but Mari caught her wrist before she brought it back down toward Jake's cheek. "If you repeat a word of that anywhere, this deal is off and I'll send you both down. Let go of me, you filthy faggot! I have a witness that you laid hands on me."

Mari shoved her away in disgust and wiped his hand on his suit pants.

"We have witnesses that you attempted to assault Jake," he said, nodding toward the bar where several patrons were peering out, curious to see what was kicking off outside. "Try it, bitch."

If Jake had been the betting type he would have laid money that she'd choose this point to storm off in a huff, cursing and threatening legal retaliation as she went. He would have lost that bet too. She just looked too much like money and good breeding to act out in a physical way. Instead of stomping off however, she twisted the strap of her pocketbook around her wrist and started swinging like an old lady chasing bums off her plot. Both he and Mari were forced back and her lawyer took cover too. She landed a whack on the back of Mari's shoulder, then caught Jake on the arm, which made the latch on her purse open. It spewed its contents on the pavement all around them and the denizens of the bar uttered a ragged cheers at this unexpected entertainment. Helen March howled in rage at them, as if it were their fault that she'd started swinging the bag around to begin with.

Finally her lawyer, seeing the potential legal ramifications of the situation, grabbed her around the waist, almost hauling her off her feet and holding her back until she stopped screaming and struggling. Jake and Mari stood their ground bare inches apart, equal looks of disbelief on their faces. Meanwhile, most of the patrons of the bar were grinning, applauding and laughing, as they watched the free show outside.

Quick as a flash, the attorney grabbed up the spilled contents of Helen's purse and shoved the items back inside, taking her by the arm and steering her in the opposite direction.

"Good day, gentlemen. I suggest you sign the agreement as quickly as possible."

He nodded at them, looking ridiculous, his hair sticking up and glasses askew on his flushed face. When he and his client were halfway down the street and out of earshot, Jake looked at Mari.

"Did that really just happen?"

His companion, who had hesitated a moment, stooped to pick something up before following him to the door. When he reached Jake's side he uncurled his fingers from around a small, purple plastic capsule with fake gold trim—an upmarket version of the kind of contraption used to store pills. He flipped the cap back with his thumb and tipped out some of the contents, murmuring as he examined the little blue tablets, "Well, she's on benzodiazepine for something. Maybe she ought to consider upping her dose."

Jake frowned as Mari closed the pill bottle back up and handed it to him. He took it without thinking. He rarely got impressions off plastic, but as soon as his fingers touched the bottle the street disappeared and he was standing in the Marches' living room again.

His hands were long fingered, well-manicured, uncapping the pill bottle and dumping several of the innocuous blue tablets out into his palm before tipping them into a bottle of liquor. They put the cap back on the bottle and swirled it around, lifting it up several times and making sure the capsules dissolved. He set the bottle back on the table next to the two glasses there, then heard voices and quickly ran toward the door. Pressing his back up against the wall, Jake could feel the way his heart was pounding – too fast and hard. A peek back in the lounge showed him Brendan March and Phil Weston entering from the other side of the room, laughing together. Brendan pulled Phil to him and kissed him and rage flared in his heart. Brendan made two failed attempts at pulling away before finally succeeding and pouring them both some of the whiskey.

Jake sagged back against the wall in the entryway of his apartment building, next to the mailboxes. Mari was practically holding him up, his face fraught with worry, the flowers tucked under one arm.

"I'm okay… I'm okay…" Jake gasped out. "Mari… Mari, she drugged them. Oh fuck, we need to call Cordiline."

Those concerned blue eyes widened in astonishment but Mari knew better than to ask stupid questions about how he knew that. He was fishing his phone out of his messenger bag as he murmured, "Of course…the police said that there was some kind of narcotic in Phil's system, we just figured he was a casual user but if someone else… Oh my word, Chivis. We've got them! We've *got* them!"

"We've got *her*," Jake corrected. "Now we know why the GPS on her phone shows she was back at the house when Phil was murdered. She went back to drug them, and waited for them to pass out before she killed Phil. It explains how when I saw Brendan's memory in the bedroom he was so freaked out, and why in the memory I got from the Transit he was practically sobbing. He really thought he'd killed Phil accidentally."

"And she let him believe it. The conniving cow!" Mari said with some relish, hitting dial on his device with a purposeful jab of his finger. "Oh, I'm going to enjoy this."

Mari handed Jake his phone and when Cordiline picked up Jake told him, "John, it's Jake Chivis. I have some info for you."

Chapter Sixteen

An hour later, Jake was seated at a table tucked in the back of a noisy pub on the corner of Islip Street, looking across at Cordiline and telling him everything, without actually telling him how he knew. He told him what Cordiline would find if he looked up the records for the GPS system on Helen March's two phones, and about his run in with her and the subsequent vision he'd gotten after touching the pill bottle.

"You do know, don't you, that you and your 'friend' Dr. Gale could get into serious trouble fucking around with people's phone records," Cordiline told him placidly, sipping his beer.

Jake looked at him over the top of his own pint glass. They both knew that Cordiline wouldn't be sitting here drinking beer with him if he meant to haul anyone in on charges.

"I'm just telling you where to look. You can find this information out for yourself. Actually, it's a pretty sweet deal. You get tips from your 'psychic' friends that will solve your case for you, and you get all the credit for your keen investigative skills and no one needs to know any different."

Cordiline snorted amusement.

"Fine, I'll look into it." He leaned forward and looked intently at Jake. "But I'm warning you, Chivis, stay out of this now. Don't go poking around anymore. Is that clear?"

"Crystal clear," Jake said, tipping his glass toward him in a little salute and taking a drink.

* * * *

Helen March was arrested and charged with Philip Weston's murder later that day. The TV news headlines reported telephone records did not match her story that she was visiting her mother the night Phil died. Cordiline filled Jake in on the finer details across the table at the back of the same Kentish Town gastropub about a week afterward. Traces of metabolized benzodiazepine showed up in Phil's toxicology scan, which Helen March happened to have a prescription for. A search of the wardrobes at her house turned up the murder weapon, in a collection of other bondage equipment. Minute traces of Phil's DNA were found in the setting of her wedding ring. Her skin cells were also found on the black nylon bondage cord used to strangle Phil.

They still did not have a full confession from her and she kept changing her story, but Cordiline put the last pieces in place for Jake and Mari, who had invited himself along in spite of Jake's reservations about taking him to the meeting. His lover was strangely quiet though, as if preoccupied with something else for much of the time.

"Helen began her affair with Phil several months ago," Cordiline confirmed. "She paid for hookups in fancy hotels all over London. Then she hired him to do a remodeling job on the house that she and her husband were planning to put on the market. Soon after the work commenced, she began to suspect that Brendan was also cheating. Since she wanted a divorce, she figured she might as well stack the deck in her favor by collecting some evidence of his infidelity."

Mari raised one curious eyebrow and sipped his wine. Cordiline grinned humorlessly, taking a long slurp from the pint of lager in front of him before he continued. "She told Brendan she was going away for the weekend, guessing that he would take the opportunity of an empty house to bring his floozy home, then returned to catch him in the act. She heard her husband and his lover in the bedroom and recognized Phil's voice right away. It was then that she came up with the idea to kill her cheating toy boy and frame her husband for his murder. Instead of barging into the bedroom like a normal madwoman and taking incriminating pictures, she quietly went back downstairs and dumped half a bottle of sleeping pills and some of her benzodiazepine prescription into the open bottle of scotch they had been drinking, and then she waited."

"Clever," Jake observed. His lover shrugged one shoulder and turned the stem of his glass between his fingers, eyes still watching the detective inspector.

"Phil and Brendan must have figured they had all weekend, so they came downstairs after a while, drank the rest of the wine, and went back up to the bedroom to play with Brendan's new bondage equipment. Kinky boys!" Cordiline winked at Jake, and Mari shook his head once or twice, giving him the evil eye until he resumed his account. It didn't wipe the smirk off his face though. "All Helen had to do was wait for her husband to pass out, which he did first, being a heavier drinker and less well built than their mutual boyfriend. When she was sure he was out cold and Phil was too groggy to put up a fight, she slipped in and put the cord around Phil's neck and wrists, leaving him to strangle himself. Then she calmly left the house and went back to her mother's like nothing had happened. She hadn't counted on Brendan being cool-headed enough to try and cover it up though."

"So, what did he do about the van?" asked Mari, who knew full well but just wanted to see how clever the opposition was.

"As far as we can ascertain," Cordiline said thoughtfully, "one of Weston's contractors texted Phil asking when he could bring it back and Brendan March must have still had possession of Phil's phone, presumably before he got rid of the body. He seems to have used it to send a text back telling the contractor that it had been left at Makepeace Avenue while Weston looked into another job, and telling him he could pick it up later that day. Brendan ditched the body as soon as he could, wrapped in a roll of carpet, as far as we can tell—there were fibers from it all over the body. Then he cleaned out the van and left it out front with the keys in. The contractor came round to collect it later the same day and, bam! Body and evidence out of the way before the missus got home from her mother's. He must have thought he'd got away with it too, until the body turned up and you guys started asking questions."

"Are the charges against Brendan going to be dropped?" Jake asked.

"The murder charges, yes. He'll still be charged as an accessory after the fact for dumping the body. A good attorney will probably get him a slap on the wrist though, considering the circumstances," Cordiline said in a tone that indicated his disapproval.

"Seems unfair, really," Mari agreed, for once, sipping his white wine with a contemplative look on his face. "He didn't have a thought for Phil or his family, just for protecting his own arse. Slimy bastard!"

Cordiline shrugged. "People will do just about anything when they're panicked. I'm not saying he'll get off entirely, but he certainly won't see as much prison time as his missus."

"So we didn't do an entirely bad job then?" Mari managed not to smirk.

Cordiline gave him a sharp look.

"I would suggest you two keep your noses clean from now on," he sighed, silently acknowledging that this was unlikely to happen. "Or at least get your UK P.I. license."

"Ooh, now that *would* be a career change." Mari chuckled.

"I didn't exactly mean *you*," Cordiline said with a shake of his head. "I doubt you're quite discreet enough to be a sleuth, Dr. Gale."

Mari flipped him the bird and Jake took a long drink of his beer and found something else interesting to look at. On the one hand he wanted to defend Mari, but on the other he wasn't sure if Mari would appreciate it.

When neither one of them said anything else, Jake finally murmured, "I'll think about it."

"I suppose the rest of it will be on the news sooner or later," Cordiline told them grimly. "So watch that space, I guess. And, uh, thank you, I suppose. If it hadn't been for you, she'd have got away with it scot-free. At least Weston can bury his brother with some closure now."

Jake tried not to look as surprised as he felt but he had a feeling it showed anyway.

"That's what we were aiming for."

Mari nodded his head emphatically, but for once he kept his silence, turning the stem of his wineglass slowly back and forth in his long fingers. If this was a result for him, it was a hollow triumph.

* * * *

They walked back to Jake's flat afterward arm in arm. Mari's warmth, leaning against his shoulder, was not unpleasant, in Jake's opinion. Nor was the way that he felt so comfortable showing his obvious affection, which was another surprise for Jake. If someone had asked him when he'd first come to London if he'd have been at ease walking out with another man, he would have laughed in their face.

At the front door, outside the bar downstairs, which was just beginning to warm up for the evening with people coming and going, Mari turned to look at him, a fond smile on his face.

"This feels kind of like déjà vu. Well…what now?"

"I seem to recall, the other day before we came back here, you said something about a reward," Jake said with a grin.

"I may have implied something of that sort," Mari conceded, winking at him. "Does that mean you're inviting me up, Chivis?"

Jake slid his other arm around him and pulled him close for a kiss.

"Inviting you up, inviting you to stay, whatever you'd

like," he murmured against Mari's plush lips.

A whistle came from the vicinity of the bar and some catcalls and laughter, but Jake couldn't care less. His attention was only for Mari, who wrapped himself around him rather more intimately, fingers tangling in Jake's curls as he pulled Jake's mouth harder onto his own, returning the kiss with interest.

"Mmhhh...you know what I'd like?" he whispered huskily.

"I think I'm getting some idea." Jake chuckled.

"You'd better take me upstairs then, because I want you in considerably less clothing, Chivis," his partner growled in a suggestive tone.

"I think that's an excellent idea, Dr. Gale." Jake grinned at him, and before Mari could pull free he dropped his hands lower, tucking them under the backs of his thighs and lifting Mari's long legs up around his waist. He carried him three steps like that and pressed him up against the wall, next to the door of his building, much to the delight of their whooping audience. Jake was not a bit bothered by the whistles and carrying on, if anything he was more than a little turned on by it, and he kissed Mari harder.

Just as unperturbed by the cheers and applause from the bar, Mari allowed his lips to be ravaged and gave as good as he got in that department, writhing up against Jake as he was pinned to the wall. When Jake allowed him to come up for air, he panted, "If I'd known how hot an audience got you I'd have made you bend right over and take it in the park last time."

"Don't tempt me like that or we'll never get a decent run in again," Jake told him, only half-serious. He kissed Mari's neck and ground against him until it seemed like a good idea to get him upstairs before one of the barflies decided he wanted to try for a threesome. He somehow got the door open without dropping either Mari or his keys but had to put him down to get up the stairs as fast as he could. He couldn't deny Mari's observation though. That bit of exhibitionism *had* got him fired up, something he never would have guessed.

Mari couldn't keep his hands off him as they stumbled up the stairs and while Jake was juggling the key to his apartment door, Mari's arms were around him, pulling his jacket and shirt undone and sliding down the ridges of his chest and belly to tug at his belt. His lips were still roaming over Jake's neck and tugging at the curve of his ear. Then the door swung open and they tumbled inside. Jake shoved it shut behind them with a bang and Mari slammed him against it, popping the button of his jeans and rolling down the zipper to get his hand into Jake's pants.

Jake sucked in a breath and groaned as Mari's fingers skated along his cock. Barely in the door and halfway undressed. He could get used to this!

Mari's long fingers curled around his shaft and Jake rolled his hips, pushing into his touch while their lips meshed. Mari's tongue circled his teeth and withdrew then that soft mouth was under his jaw kissing his throat as he retrieved his hand to shuck off his coat and wriggle out of his light sweater. His palm flat to Jake's heaving belly, he slid it back down, all the way into his crotch and began to stroke him harder. With white teeth he worried Jake's hard, dark nipples and let the tip of his tongue worm around them wetly, one at a time, sending sparks down to his groin as Jake thrusted in the cage of his smoothly stroking fingers.

Jake pushed his fingers into Mari's hair, loving the soft, silky feel of it gliding between each digit. He tried not to squirm but couldn't help it. Ever since Mari had figured out how sensitive his nipples were, he was relentless in tormenting them, not that Jake was about to complain. It was almost too much though, and his cock throbbed in Mari's hand, a drop of wetness spreading over the tip.

"Ohhhh, fuck that feels good..." Jake exhaled, his voice shaking.

"It does." Mari's breath spilled warmth over the slick of saliva on his chest and he kissed his way back up to Jake's bobbing Adam's apple and from there to his mouth again as his thumb stroked the slippery pre-cum over the smooth, hot dome of his hard cock. "It feels so big and thick and ready to come," he panted into Jake's mouth.

Then he was sliding back down again, braced against Jake's strong legs, slipping further until he was on his knees and pulling Jake's jeans and jersey shorts to midthigh. Needing no instruction, he got to work with lips and tongue on the dark, hooded glans in the palm of his hand. Jake watched him lick and kiss a slow, teasing route down to his balls and nuzzle the delicate skin of his sac, inhaling his scent then taking each orb in his mouth, one at a time, sucking it down and letting it pop out before lavishing attention on its twin.

Jake looked down and wasn't sure which was better, the way it felt or the way it looked to have Mari's lips around his balls, his heavy cock laying on his cheek. That beautiful face and those lush lips seemed unreal, and the things his mouth did to him were amazing. He was about to suggest they try to make it into the bedroom when Mari stroked him again, gripping him tight and his thoughts scattered on the light breeze from the open window.

Eyes the color of shallow summer seas looked up at him and Mari whispered, "You have such a gorgeous body, Jake Chivis. My eyes want to eat you up. I can't get enough of seeing you naked and hard like this. Makes me want to do all kinds of bad things to you."

He pulled Jake's throbbing cock head against his lips, practically glossing them with his pre-cum before they parted around his dick and swallowed it about halfway down.

Jake's head tipped back and he hissed in a breath almost like he was in pain. He could feel the muscles in his thighs give a tiny shiver and goosebumps spread down his back, all from the heat and wetness of Mari's mouth around him. He tried not to thrust but couldn't help pushing it in a little deeper.

"Sshhit, that feels— Uuhhh!" Jake groaned, one hand

moving to rest on Mari's head as he sucked him hard.

Mari kept one hand around the base of his cock, rhythmically massaging his balls as he nodded lower. With the other he reached down for his zip and got his own pants undone, then pushed down the front of the small, blue mesh bikini briefs beneath so that he could stroke himself in time with the nods of his blond head, freeing his slim, toned body from the confines of his clothing inch by inch. The way he reverently handled and sucked Jake's cock was almost like an act of worship, but there was nothing pious about the look in his glittering eyes as he peered up through his tangled forelock at Jake, a little smile pulling his lips tighter around Jake's thrusting length.

Jake held it together for a minute or two but he knew he was going to blow his load if Mari kept on like that, it was just too damn good. Panting raggedly, he glanced down again, his fingers trembling where they touched Mari's hair.

"Babe, I love the way you're doing that, but if you keep it up, I'm gonna come. You want it, or you wanna go to the bedroom?"

Mari drew his lips back up to the tip of Jake's dick and planted a little kiss on the head of it. Running his fingers through his hair, he pushed it back from his face and whispered, "Yes. Both."

"Well, okay then." Jake uttered a weak chuckle. He wiggled his hips back and forth, making his cock slip from side to side along the crease of his lips. "It is seriously not going to take much," he whispered.

Mari opened his mouth and took him in again, not deep, but running his gentle lips over his cock, letting Jake dictate the pace this time. He never looked away, keeping his eyes on Jake's face the whole time, letting him see that he was ready and willing whenever Jake was. His hand was a warm, reassuring presence on Jake's exposed thigh, resting high in the hollow of his groin as he kept up that slow, smooth nodding motion, sucking and swallowing him almost constantly. The flow of salty fluids into his mouth increased its frequency in response to his touch.

Jake's breathing deepened and his balls tightened. He was teetering on edge already. That look on Mari's face, somehow tender and hot at the same time, coupled with the way he touched him, firm but almost teasing, was enough to put him into orbit. He rocked his hips, sliding the head of his cock on Mari's tongue and butting the thick, smooth crown against the roof of his mouth and suddenly he was right there with hardly any warning. He spurted once between Mari's open jaw and his gorgeous lover closed his lips around his cock head. Jake wrapped the fingers of both hands around the back of Mari's skull, holding him still while his hips stuttered back and forth with each new spasm.

Mari contained him, keeping absolute control as he sucked and gulped faster and harder, his tongue caressing the pulsing mass of excited flesh between his lips. When Jake sagged against the door behind him at last, panting hard, Mari released his glistening penis and smiled up at him like an angel.

"You are never disappointing, Chivis," he purred. "That was very impressive."

Jake chuckled again, barely able to stand upright. He bent and kissed Mari, taking his time and sweeping his tongue between those talented lips.

"I wanna get you naked, in bed, now," he insisted.

"What a glorious idea," Mari purred, allowing himself to be hauled to his feet, and out of his loose slacks and underclothes, as Jake put him over one shoulder and carried him like a hard-won prize into the bedroom. Mari traced the striking design on his naked back as they stumbled those few short steps.

"My own horny caveman!" He chuckled.

Jake slung him down on the bed, making him bounce on the mattress, and grinned as he finished stripping off their clothes before sliding on top of him. He mouthed the side of Mari's throat and licked up to the corner of his jaw then kissed him, deep and hot. His body was still tingling all over from the earth-shaking orgasm but Mari had him so turned on he was far from finished, his half-hard dick already perking up for more where he pressed it into the crease of Mari's hip.

"So, my naughty little firehose, what am I going to do to you now?" His sexy bedmate grinned at him, jewel-bright eyes sparkling with mischief. His fingers slid down Jake's naked back to the curve of his ass and squeezed hard there.

Jake kissed along his cheek and his lips and bucked his hips when Mari gripped him. He could feel the hot, hard length of Mari's cock pressing between their exposed bellies and he was ready to give him just about anything he desired.

"I'm all yours, babe, any way you want me," he promised, sliding his hands over Mari's ribs and hips while they kissed and rubbed against each other.

Mari looked at him oddly, he thought.

"You mean that?" he asked, though his hands did not cease in their thorough manipulation of his buttocks. "You mean…just from a 'being in bed with me', kind of angle, right?" He shut his mouth when Jake frowned at him. "Ignore me. My mother always says that I overanalyze things. She's probably right."

Jake leaned up a little on his elbows, hovering a couple of inches from Mari's face so he could look at him, watching his eyes, his expression. He should admit how he felt, but a tiny niggle of doubt held him back. It was too soon, and if Mari didn't feel the same way he might start avoiding him, and Jake didn't think he could take that right now.

"I can do a lot of things, but ignoring you isn't one of them," he settled for, and brushed a tender kiss across Mari's lips.

"That's good." Mari pretended to think for a moment, his palms warming the chill of the unheated flat from Jake's backside. "Because I'm hoping that you still have some of those rubbers under your pillow."

Jake did, and he got one and tore the little square open, then rolled it onto Mari's straining erection as his companion watched him with a smile of approval.

"Very good," Mari murmured, when the mission was accomplished to his liking. "Now do you still have a bottle of lube under the bed, I wonder? Or do I have to eat you until you cry for mercy?"

"You really want me to grab the lube after saying something like that?" Jake chuckled. He did though, reaching over and putting it within easy reach. He had moved up a bit to grab it and now he straddled Mari's hips, curling down to kiss him. He reached down between them so he could wrap his hand around both their cocks, stroking them together a few times.

"Come up here, hold the top rail," Mari said in that voice that, had his doctorate been in medicine, would have had prospective patients bent over the examining table in double quick time. As Jake moved to obey him, Mari scooted down between his legs and proceeded to make him cry for mercy anyway.

Mari's mouth had to be blessed, or magic. There was no other explanation for the things he could do to him. He had Jake trembling and panting with absolute desperation at one point, his breath quick and hot between his spread thighs, his slippery tongue wriggling over the most incredibly sensitive regions of his lower body. When Jake was ready to just beg to be fucked, he tumbled to one side, rolling on to his back and Mari was on him, pushing between his legs and kissing him ravenously in what seemed like all one movement. Jake hooked his knees around Mari's thighs and skated his hands up and down the sleek, hard muscles in his back and ass.

Practiced fingers flipped the cap of the little bottle and in seconds he was slick and wet and ready, inside and out, with those slim digits doing things to his prostate that made him whine like a puppy. Then they were slipping out of him and Mari's sheathed cock was taking their place, pressing up against him and pushing into him, smooth as silk. His face was perfectly still, eyes downcast but not by any means despondent, watching his erection make its slippery way into Jake's body. When he was safely sheathed to at least half his length, his eyes closed and he uttered a shuddering sigh of pleasure, his hips moving in a slow, lazy rhythm designed to inch him gently deeper with each roll.

Jake met his rhythm, lifting up in small bucks of his hips each time Mari pushed forward until he was buried as deep as he could go.

Porn always made it seem like pulling almost all the way out and slamming it back home was the best way to fuck, but there was a lot to be said for shorter, deeper thrusts like Mari was doing to him. Jake's eyes just about rolled back in his head it felt so good. He didn't look away completely though, he wanted to drink Mari in with his eyes, and to watch him watching the way their bodies were joined together. He lifted a hand to brush his fingers over Mari's cheek and pushed his fingers into his hair, gripping there, not too tight but enough to hold on.

"You are amazing," Jake whispered.

"You too." Mari's voice was little more than a breath. He eased up so that he was astride Jake's hips, one hand on the underside of his left thigh, pushing back gently but firmly, the other reaching out beyond his shoulder, gripping the pillows for support as he began to drive and grind harder, still moving slowly but with more purpose. "I hardly... dared to hope...that you'd let me do this to you again. Ohhhh, Jake...it feels so good."

Jake lifted his knees higher, crossing his legs behind Mari's back. He still had one hand pushed into Mari's hair and with the other he caressed his arm. His cock lay on his stomach, so hard he ached. Every stab Mari drove into him sent a spike of lust down his quivering shaft until there was a puddle of clear drool glossing his stomach.

"Ilmari...oh fuck, fuck, Mari that is sooo fucking hot!" Jake gasped out as his thrusts came even harder and faster.

Jake hardly ever came without a helping hand on his cock but he did then, his dick lurching and shooting another creamy blast over his chest and belly.

Mari's blue eyes were darker, the heart of them wide with lust as he lifted his gaze to Jake's face, a ghost of a smile on his parted lips as he continued to thrust through the powerful muscle contractions of his partner's second climax. When he came it was as silently as before, just a hitch in his breathing and for a few moments his pale, silky lashes shuttered the incandescence of his eyes. Then he was sinking down onto Jake's body, between his thighs, kissing him again, long and slow and passionate, like he could go on this way all night.

"Can I stay here tonight?" he whispered hoarsely at last in Jake's ear, pulling out of him with care and discarding the scrap of latex over the side of the mattress.

Jake wrapped his arms around him, letting his hands move up and down in slow strokes on Mari's back.

"Stay. Yes. Please. I'll make you breakfast in the morning," he promised, holding him closer.

Mari managed a chuckle. "You don't have to do that. But I want to sleep beside you tonight. I need to hold someone, and to be held. Please."

Jake kissed his hair, his fingers combing through the silky blond locks gently, soothingly. With his other hand he pulled the edge of the duvet over them, creating a snug cocoon and settled his arms around Mari like a protective cage of muscle and flesh. Warm and comfortable, Jake cuddled up beside him.

"Is there anything wrong?" Jake wanted to know, letting his lips brush Mari's ear tenderly. His body was singing and it felt so good to hold him like this, but Mari had been very quiet since they'd finally discovered the evidence of Helen March's wrongdoing, as if he was distracted by something.

"No. Not wrong, exactly," his lover conceded in a lazy purr, wriggling against him beneath the covers.

"Something is bugging you. Is it to do with me? Us?"

Half of Jake didn't want the answer, if it was, but Mari just shook his head.

"No. I like you. I like *us*," he confirmed.

"So what's the problem?"

For a few moments Mari was silent, just reaching back to run a caressing hand over his stomach and hip. Jake eased one leg between Mari's knees and hooked the other one over his thigh, pulling him close and kissing his neck tenderly. He was considering whether to ask again when Mari whispered, "I don't want to keep secrets from you."

"I'm glad," Jake murmured in his ear. "That's a good thing, Ilmari."

"I'm going to have to though, and...the idea of it scares me a bit." Mari half turned in his arms to kiss his mouth hungrily and for a short while Jake accepted the balm of his kisses. When they broke apart he heaved a sigh.

"Why is everything so complicated around you?"

"Just the way I am, I suppose." Mari offered a weak smile.

"Why do you have to keep secrets from me, then?" Jake stroked a finger through his sleek blond hair, twisting a strand of it around and around.

"The other day, when I spoke to Karden," Mari told him, seeming to reach a decision within himself, "I gave you the impression that he'd sacked me. That wasn't entirely the truth."

"Oh?" Jake raised an eyebrow, peering over Mari's shoulder at his serious face. "So we'll still be working together?"

"No." Mari shook his head again. "He's made a request for me to be transferred to another department. A government department."

"Good money?" Jake asked, though his heart sank a little at the idea that he wouldn't be seeing his gorgeous Mari every day.

"Very good."

"In London still, though?" A rush of panic went through him at the sudden thought that Mari would be sent away.

He wasn't sure if he could handle that so soon after giving himself heart and soul to this man.

"Mostly, yes." Mari reached up to stroke his cheek. "I'll still see you, Chivis. If you want me to."

"Of course I want you to." Jake pulled him into a fierce hug and a little huff of air was forced out of Mari's lungs by the gesture, though he didn't object.

"My fierce warrior," he whispered huskily.

"Whatever you want, Ilmari. I'll be whatever you want me to be. Can you tell me what the job is?" he asked, still feeling somewhat afraid. Mari seemed so listless about the whole business, like some of the light went out of him when he thought of it.

"No. Not details anyway. Jake, it's…Karden's giving me to MI6. And I can't say anything more than that." Mari turned his head again, looking up at him, his eyes pale and luminous and very beautiful.

"Nothing at all?" Jake kissed his nose. "Is it dangerous?"

"I don't know. Maybe."

He saw Mari bite his lip and leaned in to kiss him there.

"You'll probably enjoy it then," he teased.

Mari laughed weakly and reached up to tousle his hair. "Idiot!"

"I'm right though." Jake pulled him close again and felt him relax in his arms. "Don't worry. I'll be here for you, whatever happens. If you can't talk about work we'll find other stuff to do."

"That sounds good. Other stuff. I like the idea of that." Mari twisted about completely in his arms and kissed him harder, a hint of relief in his eyes this time. "You're sure you want to stick with me? I know how you hate me doing anything dangerous."

"I'm not going anywhere. Sleep, Ilmari." Jake kissed him again. "Sleep well, and when you wake up I'll still be here."

With a little smile still on his lips, Mari eventually did just that, curled against him with the fingers of one hand resting on Jake's broad chest and the others caressing his scalp behind his ear, trailing through his hair. When Mari's long, lean body finally stilled, and his heart rate began to slow, Jake realized with a start that it was the first time that he had ever properly relaxed with him. On the previous occasions that they had shared a bed there had always been an element of tension between them, even after the exertion of good sex. He held his precious Mari tighter, breathing in the warmth of his beautiful body, and knew without a moment of doubt that whatever was coming their way, he wasn't planning to let go any time soon.

As New York explodes with dangerous creatures, their passion goes nuclear.

AURA

QUINN'S GAMBIT

BELLORA QUINN
ANGEL MARTINEZ

Quinn's Gambit

Excerpt

Chapter One

Surely just a kiss, an embrace… These things can only be beneficial. Valerian let his hands slide down the lovely human boy's back. He leaned in to press his lips against those full, lush ones offered up to him so willingly…

Perhaps it was the human scent or the way the boy ground against him a bit too eagerly. None of it was right or familiar, all of the foreign human-ness grating on his nerves. He pulled away and turned to face the window, arms crossed over his chest.

"I'm sorry. This isn't working."

"You telling me this was a waste of my time? You drag me all the way up here for nothing? Time's money, big boy."

Val ground his back teeth together, fighting his temper. "I neither break nor bend my promises. Your money is there, on the bureau. You may take it and leave me."

"Hey." The sharp voice calmed to something more soothing. A gentle hand caressed his arm. "I didn't mean it like that. Just gotta be careful, you know? We don't have to do anything. I have clients that just wanna talk or cuddle. I have one who just wants someone to hold him while he cries."

Is that what I'll soon be reduced to? Paying someone to comfort me? "I spoke harshly. I apologize. But I have... It was a mistake. Please. I occupied your time. The money is yours. I simply need to be alone now."

"Okay. I get it. But you change your mind, you call me, yeah?" The boy shoved the roll of cash into the pocket of his threadbare jeans. "Give me a chance to see if those yummy pointed elf ears are as sensitive as they say."

With a grin and a wink, he swaggered out of the room. A moment later, the door to the apartment clicked shut. Val leaned his forehead against the cool glass, gazing down at the late evening traffic ten floors below. He could open the window. Lean out. Tumble to the waiting pavement.

Val heaved a weary sigh. A human would die, but with his bone structure, he was likely to survive—in a good deal of pain, but still alive. Living alone had begun to wear on him, nothing more. Perhaps he should have a roommate. It wasn't the same as having a *senrist* of young males waiting for him, but at least it would be someone with whom to converse. Gods, but he missed them. He had tried to describe the *senrist* to his human work partner once. The closest parallel he could pull up had been a harem, but it didn't begin to convey the love and devotion he had once been so privileged to have.

There were days he felt better, days when he thought, perhaps, he could adjust. Then something like this would happen to remind him that this was not his world. He would never belong here. The city bustled below him, sunlit streets and people hurrying about their days. Life—all around him life—while every day he died a bit more inside.

* * * *

Quinn sat on the sunny park bench watching ducks paddle around in the pond a few feet away. He had been sitting enjoying the warm weather and waiting for just over an hour when a young mother walked by with a toddler clutching her hand. An older boy tagged along beside them. Both kids had ice cream cones, the little girl with most of hers on her hands and face and down the front of her shirt, but she was still adorable in springy, golden pigtails.

Quinn watched as the family made their way down the path toward the footbridge that crossed the duck pond. They seemed completely unaware of the dark shape moving under the water, tracking their progress. Just before they reached the bridge, the dark shape resolved, lurching up out of the water. A tangle of weed, muck and pond scum streamed down a huge face twisted into a monstrous grimace, and the creature gave a low, menacing growl.

"Shit!" Quinn muttered and shot off the bench. This was not supposed to happen.

The mother and children screamed, their ice cream cones flying as they raced away from the bridge in the other direction. Quinn knew they were headed directly toward a cul-de-sac that ended in high shrubs, a fence and nowhere to run.

The monster lumbered out of the pond, growling, gnashing its pointed teeth, arms outstretched as it went after the terrified family. Quinn was faster, though, and raced down the path, darting between the monster and its intended prey. The woman had just figured out she had run right into a dead end and was trapped. She clutched the crying kids and they huddled together, terrified.

"Don't worry. I'll protect you!" Quinn yelled, boldly turning toward the reeking beast. He raised his staff, muttering an indecipherable incantation. The end of the staff began to glow brightly and he pointed it at the pond monster. "Begone! Leave these people alone, foul beast!"

The creature hesitated, then took a few more menacing steps.

"I said, begone!" Quinn shouted, brandishing the staff. "I warn you...if I release the fireball from my staff, you will not survive it, fell creature!" *Begone... Fell creature... God, I feel so cheesy saying stuff like that.*

The swamp monster came to a shambling halt. Groaning, it lifted its gray-green, seaweed-draped arm to shield itself from the light that glowed bright from the end of the staff. With a cry that sounded as if it were afraid and in pain, it started to back away. Quinn followed, keeping the staff thrust forward, driving the creature back. At last it fled, shuffling back to the pond and sinking into the murky water.

Quinn breathed a sigh of relief and let the energy drain out of the spell. The glow at the end of the staff winked out. He turned back to the shaken family.

"It's okay. It's gone now. It won't bother you again," he said in his most confident and soothing voice.

"Oh, God, thank you! Thank you so much! I don't know what we would have done if you hadn't been here." Tears of relief shimmered in the woman's eyes now that it looked like she and her children were safe.

"You don't look like a wizard," the boy said, looking up at Quinn with huge round eyes. "You look like my brother, Robbie. He's in high school and thinks he's too good to play games anymore."

Quinn managed a smile. "I'm a little older than that. Every wizard was young once, though. Good thing I was here today or that troll would have had you guys for lunch."

"You'd think those people from AURA would make sure beasts like that were locked up! I don't know how I can repay you," the mother gushed, already reaching into her pocketbook.

Quinn held his hand up, "No, no, I couldn't. It's no more than anyone would have done. It's quite all right," he said humbly.

"I insist, please. At least let me buy you lunch." She pressed the bills into his hand.

Quinn hesitated and finally closed his hand around the money. Bowing his head graciously, he made the cash disappear, this time with sleight of hand rather than real magic.

"Let me escort you past the pond so I know you've made it safely out of the park. Then I'll go back and see if I can hold the monster until AURA gets here," Quinn said.

He led the grateful family away, over the bridge and back toward the street, making sure they were in a more populous area before he took his leave. On his way back to the pond, he stopped at a hot dog cart and bought four footlongs with some of the money the woman had given him.

The pond's surface was smooth as glass when he returned, no sign of the monster or people anywhere. He waited, listening. He walked up the path about twenty yards, checking for any pedestrians, then walked back. "All right, coast is clear," he said to empty air.

The 'monster', who wasn't a troll at all but a boggle, rose up out of the depths, face split in a gruesome smile.

Quinn put a hand on his hip and looked at him sternly. "I thought we agreed you'd wait until I gave you the signal?"

"Aw, c'mon, Quinten. That was the most fun I've had in ages!" the boggle said.

"I said no marks with kids, Groof! They'll probably have nightmares for months!"

"Oh, listen to you, Mr. Moral High Ground." Groof snorted, which sent a spray of pond water from his nostrils. "What about that octogenarian you signaled on last week? He could have had a heart attack. Besides, the old ones don't run nearly as fast." He laughed, a wet sound, as if mud was stuck in his throat.

Quinn sighed. "Next time, *wait for the signal*, Groof. Here..." He tossed the hot dogs one at a time, still wrapped in paper, into Groof's open maw, saving the last for himself. He tried not to grimace as the boggle chewed open-mouthed and his black tongue licked not just his lips but also his chin, cheeks and nostrils after swallowing each one. Groof was cool as far as boggles went and he was a pretty good partner, but his eating habits made Quinn a little queasy.

"Mmm… Extra mustard and onions, just like I wanted. You are a good friend, Quinten," Groof rumbled with a happy chortle.

"Yeah, yeah… All right. See you tomorrow." Quinn sent him an airy wave over his shoulder as he hefted his backpack and started in on his own hot dog on his way out of the park.